RUE

Rue

AMY Q. BARKER

www.amyqbarker.com

ISBN: 978-1-7353581-0-9
Library of Congress Control Number: 2020913298

Printed in the United States of America

For Bobbi

PART I

❧ Chapter I ❧

RUE WAS SINGING "Tea for Two" in her best Doris Day voice when she heard a couple flirting at the bar. Sometimes at this time of night, when the lounge was starting to wind down, she would separate herself into two halves – one half singing and playing mechanically, a robot programmed to run the regular night-shift protocol, and the other half detecting, sniffing out, listening to the moody, listless, replete surroundings to seek a target – an anchor of interest or curiosity on which to focus and attach.

On this night, a typical Friday in February, Rue's voice sang, "Picture you upon my knee, just tea for two and two for tea, just me for you and you for me, alone..." as her mind went to the couple.

"Oh, come on! There is no way! I was at that same concert! Are you sure? Red Rocks? July 2017? How is that possible? Wow!" A second later, the woman's voice went down an octave as she said with a coy challenge, "Wait a minute. Wait one minute. You're just teasing me, aren't you? You big fat liar, you! I mean, otherwise it would be a crazy coincidence, wouldn't it? I'm going to need some proof. What was the weather like? The best song that night?"

The man laughed and said, "How can you doubt me? I'm hurt. You don't trust me?" He took his time with the next sentence, "Okay, here goes, let me think. It was pretty warm, like maybe eighty degrees. I remember because I wore one of those Mexican poncho things, and I was roasting and finally took it off. As far as best songs, I guess I would say 'Ain't No Man'." He waited and then asked, "Now do you believe me?"

She pondered alluringly. "Hmmmm, maybe. I might need more convincing. Let's see...where were you seated? Heck, we may have been right next to each other and not even known it!"

"Possibly. I was up on the right side, if you're facing the stage, kind of far back. Where were you?"

"Front left. Oh well, there goes that theory," she said sadly.

"Hey, wait," he said suddenly, "who was the opener?"

"The opener?" she asked, wondering where he was headed.

"It was a three-night stint, remember?"

"Oh yeah! Good point. Chatham County Line."

"Ah, well, there you go – it would have been impossible anyway. I went Sunday night. It was Shovels & Rope."

"Of course," she said, resolved. Then they sat in silence for a minute. Finally, with an upswing to her voice, she wondered, "Aren't you going to ask me what my favorite song was?"

He let out a little laugh and replied, "Yeah, sure…?"

Rue strained to hear the answer. "What about 'I and Love and You'?"

The man purred in response, "One of their best. Hey, we should request it." Then softly, "Do you think she knows it?"

Rue sat up straight, refocused on the final lyrics of "Tea for Two," and waited. As she finished, the man was at the piano asking, "Excuse me, do you know 'I and Love and You' by the Avett Brothers?"

Rue smiled and answered, "I think so. I'll give it a try."

"Thanks," he said with relief and a flurry of cash retrieved from his wallet and dropped into her fishbowl.

Rue began, her two halves becoming one again. The couple was quiet and listening attentively. Rue did her best to do the song justice and was rewarded with a round of applause. She smiled and nodded appreciatively.

Afterward, she launched into "Que Sera Sera" followed by a Frank Sinatra number and several other old standards until the couple left and the lounge settled into its nightly state of mystical loneliness, otherwise known as closing time. Rue stood up from the piano, carefully lowering the cover over the keys, and walked to the bar with her fishbowl in hand.

"Not a bad night," she said to Bob, the bartender.

"Nope, not at all. Let's see…looks like um, eighty-three, no eighty-eight bucks. Let me give you some twenties, hang on…" He went to the register and brought her back the cash, which she placed in her purse.

"Great, thanks," she said. "You do alright?"

"Yep, pretty good for February. You want a tea?"

Rue nodded and he went away. Rue thought about the couple, probably off kissing somewhere, maybe exchanging more coincidences from their past, looking for common ground. She wondered absently what that must feel like – to be on the verge of something new, the precipice before you fall, the edge of a cliff – trying with all your might to put your best foot forward. And then she thought of the duplicity of people. Was it natural, an innate instinct, to put on that mask when you meet someone new? The facade: say the right things, listen politely, be interesting and interested. Then what happens later when you reveal your true self – the one with all its selfishness, inner demons, foibles, flaws?

Rue scoffed, as if she knew! She hadn't met a new person in years. Not to mention, as far as duplicity went, wasn't she the worst kind of hypocrite? She sat at her piano night after night, putting herself out there for all to stare at, singing her heart out in the spotlight, a force of nature to be applauded or criticized or ignored. You name it, she could take it; she wore her suit of armor when she played. But that was because she never let them in, never brought them any closer to herself, never let them see or get to know the real Rue. Sure, she was a good little soldier – always on time, polite, professional, reliable – but underneath, especially on nights like tonight, she wished for something more. Something wild and new, something bigger and better than her current state of isolation, containment, order, and routine. She wished for some new hope.

Bob interrupted her thoughts. "You okay?"

Rue snapped out of it and replied, "Um, yeah, sure, sorry."

"Here you go," he said, placing her tea in front of her.

"Thanks." She took a sip and said thoughtfully, "That couple, they were cute, eh?"

He answered, "Uh-huh, see it every night, young love…"

Rue nodded and tried to break a smile.

Bob went about his business, rinsing some glasses and wiping down the bar. Rue drank her tea quietly, listening to the busboy's clatter as he cleared the tables and swept the floors. When she finished her tea, she hollered down the bar to Bob, "Okay, I'm heading out. Have a good night."

"You too," he replied. "See you tomorrow."

Rue pulled her cane out of her purse, unfolded it, and tap-tapped her way down the steps of the lounge and out the exit door into the lonely night.

❧ Chapter II ❧

One week later, Rue was interrupted from her typing by an elderly woman's voice. "Miss? Miss?"

"Yes, hello, sorry, may I help you?" Rue asked quickly.

"Yes, thank you, I was wondering, could you direct me to Mr. Barthol— Heavens to Betsy! Why, you're blind!" the woman exclaimed.

Rue chuckled. It happened this way sometimes. "Yes, ma'am, I am. You have an appointment with Mr. Bartholomew? Is that right?"

"Um…er…yes…Mr. Bartholomew," she stuttered.

"Your name?"

"Mrs. Ritchie."

"Okay, great, I'll let him know you're here. Third door on the left."

"Great, thank you."

Rue nodded, smiled, and said, "You're welcome. Have a nice day."

"Uh-huh," the woman replied, still processing.

With a swift press of a button and a tap of her wireless earpiece, Rue said confidently, "Mr. Bartholomew? Yes, Mrs. Ritchie is here to see you. Very good, thank you, bye."

Several minutes later, Rue popped open her watch and felt the time. Five ten. Good. She shut down her laptop, stowed it away, grabbed her things, unfolded her cane, and walked out onto the busy street. It was Friday. It had been a long slog of a week. She was glad it was over. Those extra reports and transcripts for Mr. Shortino had nearly done her in, and the worst part was having to smell his extra douse of cologne every day in such close proximity. Did he not know the meaning of moderation?

The Muni bus pulled up, and as she got on, the driver said, "Hello, Miss Rue. How are you today? There's a spot three seats back on the right."

"Great, thanks, Dale," Rue said with a smile. Sometimes she lucked out with the seat directly behind him, but it was rush hour and she would have to hike back past a few pole-standers. She sighed as she maneuvered and settled herself into the slightly sticky third seat for the sixteen-minute ride home. She stowed her cane in her purse and smiled. It was Friday, and she had the whole weekend ahead of her. Plus, an extra bonus – her friend from the office, Vy, was coming to see her at the lounge later that night. Apparently her mother was in town, so Vy was leaving her daughter, Kaylen, home with Grandma and was coming out for a drink with her boyfriend, Anthony.

Several minutes later, Rue was startled when she heard a woman get on the bus and yell, "Get up!" Rue hugged her purse to herself. She heard the woman coming closer and thought, is she talking to me? In answer to her unspoken words, Rue felt a hard pinch on her arm and the woman's hot breath in her face. "You! Yes, you! You're supposed to vacate your seat! Can't you read the sign? Up!" Rue jumped up with a jolt, clutching her purse with one hand and reaching in a wide arc with the other, finally connecting with a metal pole. She grabbed onto it for dear life. Before she had steadied herself, she heard the woman plop down in the vacated seat and mumble, "'Bout time, disrespectful, entitled, oblivious, on a day like today, too, crowded and hot…"

Dale noticed and hollered back, "Lizzie, what do you think you're doing? Get outta that seat!"

She simply yelled back, "I will not."

Rue blinked and said to Dale, "It's okay." Why bother at this point? The next stop was hers anyway.

When the bus started to slow, she unfolded her cane, using it to weave toward the front. As she perched above the stairs waiting for the bus to stop, Dale said, "Sorry about that, Miss Rue. You have a nice weekend." She shrugged her shoulders and thanked him. At the stop, just as the doors were closing behind her, she heard Dale say to Lizzie, "Why'd you have to be so rude? Can't you see she's blind?"

Lizzie paused and then replied defiantly, "Shut your piehole."

Like a turned-up dimmer switch, Rue found herself slowly grinning and then laughing out loud. She walked on, her head held high, her cane click-clicking along the sidewalk. It was, after all, just another day on the Muni.

Two blocks away, Rue put a key in the side entrance of her apartment building, opening the door to the loud din of children's voices. One small voice came up to her and said, "Hi, Rue, you have a nice week?"

"Hi, Chen, yes I did, thank you for asking. How was your week?"

"Oh fine, fine. We had a field trip to Muir Woods today. It was so cool. Those trees are huge!"

"Yes…"

"You been?"

"Well, no…"

"You gotta go! It's amazing. Did you know those trees are two thousand years old?"

"No, I didn't. Wow, that's old."

"Yes, but not as old as China."

"No? How old is China?"

"Teacher told me four thousand years. Well, he said some say five thousand, but anyway, it's like super old."

"Super," Rue agreed with a smile. "And how old are you, Chen?"

"Ten and a half."

"Oh yes, the half is very important."

"Uh-huh. How old are you?"

"Thirty-two and a third."

"Wow, that's old!"

Rue laughed out loud. "Yes, it is."

"Well, I better get going. Talk to you later."

"Bye, Chen."

Rue walked up the three flights of stairs to her apartment, tripping over a toy on the second-floor landing. When she opened her door, she called out, "Hank, Hankie-boy, where are you? Come to Momma."

Nothing. She tried again. Still nothing. No bell, not even a patter of paws, that surly beast. She hung her purse and cane up and went to the bathroom. She felt her watch. Good – she had at least forty-five minutes before she had to leave. She fixed herself a cup of tea, laid down on the couch, turned on the TV, and listened to the Kardashians. Almost as soon as she began to relax, there was Hank, purring and pushing his forehead into her hand.

Rue laughed. "Oh, so now I'm your friend, eh? Don't you know I'm the one who feeds you? You ought to be more grateful." Rue rubbed his chin and belly. He rolled around like a furry rag doll. Silly boy. Alright, he was forgiven. A few minutes later, Hank jumped down, and Rue adjusted her head on the pillow, sighed, and fell fast asleep.

❧ CHAPTER III ❧

LIKE CLOCKWORK, forty-five minutes later Rue woke up, changed her clothes, and headed out the door. As she plodded up the hill to the lounge (the Big 4 at the Scarlet Huntington), she wondered what time Vy and Anthony would show up. Rue had dressed with particular care, knowing Vy would notice every single detail of her outfit. Many years ago, Vy and Rue had come up with an arrangement: Rue provided Vy with cash every few months, and Vy bought Rue's clothes and arranged her closet. Periodically Vy would appear at Rue's door and say, "I'm here to snazz you up!" Then they would spend hours organizing each hanger with the right top, bottom, accessories, and shoes. Vy recorded an audio clip for each outfit with a corresponding bar code so Rue could get dressed independently every morning by scanning the bar code from an app on her phone.

That evening, Rue had tentatively considered "Oowweee, girl, this number will set the men on fire! Black silk blouse, racy tap pants in blush, and black ballet slippers. Don't forget the chandelier earrings," only to reject it for "Honey, this is called 'legs for days.' Black pencil skirt, black hose, black peep toe wedges, tight rose-print top. A long line down the side, and don't forget the long silver hoops." Perfect. Or perfectly ridiculous. She was never quite sure. She put in her hoop earrings and headed out the door.

Rue's cane hit a dent in the sidewalk, and as she tapped around it, she wondered when they were going to finish the construction work. A large portion of the sidewalk had been torn up for over a year, and they never seemed to make any progress. It had caused her to stumble more than a few times. She sighed. Oh, the joys of blindly getting around in a big city. A few minutes later, she was at the entrance to the hotel, and she smiled when she heard, "Good evening, sassy lassy. Don't you look smashing tonight." Hayes gently took her elbow and led her to the lounge. The perfect doorman, Hayes might also have been the perfect man. Kind, thoughtful, sweet. And he called her "sassy lassy" for some reason. Rue smiled every time she heard it.

"Well, you're in a good mood tonight, aren't you?"

"Yes, I am." Rue laughed. "I think something's in the air, don't you?"

"Yes, I do – no doubt about it."

"Who's here so far?"

"Just Bob and Holly and a couple of gentlemen up at the bar. You just missed a little incident, though."

"Sounds intriguing."

"I'll let Bob tell you. Hey, Rue?"

"Yes?"

"Is Billie on the docket tonight?"

"Oh, I think so. She would fit the mood."

"Yes, ma'am, she certainly would."

"Any request in particular?"

"No, no, you pick. You know I love them all. I'll be listening."

"Will do. Thanks, Hayes." He placed her carefully beside a barstool and she sat down, saying hi to Bob and handing him her purse to stow behind the bar.

Holly, the hostess, came up and greeted Rue, telling her they had sixty-two reservations. "Good," Rue said, "Busy but not too busy." Rue detected the smell of disinfectant and something else underneath, a bitter acidy stench. She frowned. Bob had walked away to talk to some customers at the end of the bar, but when he came back he poured Rue a ginger ale and said, "Man, you missed it. These five women came down from the spa, totally drunk. They're in their robes and those disposable slippers, you know, and they sit at the bar and I can't refill their glasses quickly enough. I ask them what they're celebrating and they say a bachelorette party, which makes sense because one of them is wearing some sort of crown or tiara thing on her head. So they're whooping it up for about an hour when I notice the bride-to-be is swaying in her seat and, without any warning, promptly pukes all over the floor!"

Rue shuddered. "Well, that explains the smell."

"Yeah, what a mess. I sent them back upstairs to the spa, told them not to come back. Jacob got the mop and scoured everything down. I'm just glad it happened when it did. Imagine during the dinner rush…"

"Right. That would have been much worse," Rue agreed.

As Rue sipped her ginger ale, the lounge slowly started to fill up. It was the witching hour. Rue sat in a trance and listened. She loved the sounds of people talking and laughing, chairs being pulled out by handsome gentlemen, and the clinking of plates, glasses, and silverware. It reminded her of her childhood when her parents would throw lavish dinner parties. She would sit on the stairs behind the banister and listen to the bangle bracelets, martini glasses, and friendly banter. The guests always sounded so engaging, as if every word out of their mouths was a quote from a book. The food smelled divine, and they never failed to praise her mom about its execution. Sometimes one of the guests would come over and talk to Rue, which was exciting and frightening at the same time. She had been painfully shy back then, fearful and guarded. She usually managed a timid hello, yes, or uh-huh and a small smile. Later, she would slip upstairs to her bedroom and fall asleep to the enchanting sounds of music and laughter from below.

Whisked back to the present, Rue sensed that the wood-paneled room was full, so she took a deep breath, laid aside her drink, headed carefully to the piano, lifted the lid, and sat on the bench. She had her usual trepidation at the start, tinkling gingerly on the keys and wondering where to begin. She heard several people shift in their chairs to face her. This was the point when she felt herself most exposed, on the precipice of a mountain ledge, naked and raw. She forcefully blocked their expectations out of her mind, said good evening into the microphone, and plunged lightly into "Beyond the Sea." It was a warm, sleepy song, and she drifted languidly into the lyrics and melody with a casual lilt. To keep the momentum going, following the song's conclusion and the obligatory polite applause, she went directly into "I'll Be Seeing You" and then "Chances Are."

On nights like tonight, she always felt like a hot-air balloon being ignited with a starter fire and gradually lifting her higher and higher into the welcoming air. She heard the crowd warming up with her, their accolades louder, their fingers tapping, their voices singing along. It was a spectacular feeling to be one with a crowd of strangers. Rue could never get over the sheer invitation and wonder of it – the music's power, the transportation into another world, the gathering up of people's inner beings into a common circle of understanding. Whoosh! Up, up, and away.

Sometime later, Rue was still smiling and transfixed when a man came up to request a song, and then a woman, and then several others. She went right into each song, confident and calm, wondering if her fishbowl would be full tonight. At some point, Rue heard a group of raucous, drunken women come in and rudely ask Holly about their table. Holly replied that it would be a few minutes. Rue wondered if they were the bachelorettes from earlier. No sooner did she have that flash when one of them came up to her, cutting her off midsong, asking her to play "Jessie's Girl" for the bride. Rue obligingly began, only to be interrupted again a few minutes later by another slurred voice requesting "Ice Ice Baby." Rue kept her face as placid as a piece of glass but inwardly cringed. This was the bane of Rue's employ, being asked to play mindless drivel for the drunken clientele. Not that she didn't like that song – it had a certain catchy phrasing – but still, was it the right song to listen to while partaking of filet mignon and asparagus hollandaise? Rue said quickly and quietly, "Sorry, don't play it."

"What?" the girl harangued. "Why not?"

Rue sat mutely, waiting, shrugging her shoulders, then went back into the rest of "Jessie's Girl." People were sometimes so adamant about their requests. Especially drunk people. Rue had never quite figured out a way to refuse them without evoking their ire. At the end of the song, Rue took her break.

Poor Holly, Rue thought as she heard the girls inquiring again about their table. Rue went into the restroom and came back out to find them still challenging. She went up to the bar, where Bob said with a low, gravelly laugh, "Stellar crowd tonight, eh?"

"Ha! Yeah, they're baaaaack. Lucky us."

"If they puke again this time, I'm going to make them clean it up."

Rue smiled and said, "Ain't nothing like a bridezilla and her brood of velociraptors."

"Who let them out of their cages anyway?"

She grinned. He brought her a hot tea, and she sipped slowly. He chatted with her a few minutes and then went to wait on some others. As he walked away, she smelled the familiar scent of spilled beer and dish soap wafting up from behind the bar. The smells of her adopted home, she thought with a chuckle. To think a bar was her *home*?! Well, not a home exactly, but a place she felt safe. These smells, these sounds, these people – they had been with her all these years. A family of sorts.

Rue finished her break and, back at the piano, she heard the blotto buffoons finally get seated, mercifully in the rear of the lounge. Then Vy and Anthony showed up. Rue knew they were there when she finished "Witchcraft" and heard Vy's clapping and "Nice!"

When Vy came over to the piano, she told Rue she was putting a twenty in the fishbowl and wanted "Piano Man."

"Very funny," scolded Rue.

Vy said, "Okay, okay. What about 'Push It'? Ha. Just kidding. I know, I know. 'Gold Digger'? 'Lose Yourself'? 'It Takes Two'? Sorry, ignore me. Anyway, Anthony's so excited to get a date night, he's been holding my hand and whispering sweet nothings in my ear, like when we first met." I smiled. "How's it going? You look great, by the way. I remember buying that pencil skirt. I *knew* it would look perfect on you."

Rue laughed. That was Vy, so amiable and kind. Rue remembered the first time they met over ten years ago when Vy asked her if she was French, to which Rue replied, "Um, no." Vy simply laughed out loud and said, "Then why do you have a French name?" Without waiting for an answer, she continued, "Or is it English? Who knows? You're probably like me – your parents come up with some name that makes no sense. You see, I grew up in Los Angeles, and I have this crazy British-sounding name, Violet Francine Scott. Who names their child that? And here you have this name that sounds like a street in Paris. Heck, it probably *is* a street in Paris! Oh well, what can you do? Make lemonade, right? Anyway, unique-named folk must stick together. By the way, you can call me Vy, like pie with a V."

Rue remembered shaking her hand and feeling awkward and shy. It was rare that someone introduced themselves to Rue. Over the years, Rue had learned that most people were trying so hard not to offend her or say or do something inappropriate or impolitic or simply stupid that they tended to avoid her altogether. She recognized this and had grown used to it. Furthermore, during her day job as the receptionist at a law firm downtown, she had become skilled at putting people at ease as best she could, smiling and filling in the gaps or gaffes in their speech. But then she met Vy, who approached her without hesitation or confusion or fear. From that first meeting, she had always treated Rue like anyone else. On top of that, because Vy was so talkative and extroverted, she fit well with Rue's quiet, calm, listening nature. Vy's job as one of the head lawyers at the firm required many intense hours with her colleagues upstairs, but she always took time out of her day to chat with Rue, and soon they started going to lunch and spending time together outside of work.

Back at the piano, Rue felt Vy's kiss on her cheek and said sincerely, "Thanks for coming. It's nice having you here. Where'd you two eat?"

"Vito's. Anthony was craving pizza. Oh my god, it was so good. They have the best salads there too. Anyway, I called Momma as we headed over here, and she said Kaylen's already in bed, so that means we're free and clear for the rest of the evening – woot, woot!"

"Awesome," said Rue. "So, do you want a song? A *real* song?"

"Ah, yeah, you didn't think that twenty was for nothin', did you? You know what I want – the usual – a little Billie."

"Okay, good. Hayes wanted her too. Perfect. I'm on it, even though I can't do her justice."

"Sweetheart, who could?"

"Right!" Rue agreed and launched into "What a Little Moonlight Can Do."

At the end, Rue quickly began another number, but after that she felt Hayes's hand on her shoulder as he said, "She does it for me every time. My heart is full. Thank you." Rue smiled and squeezed his hand.

As she began the next song, "Summertime," Hayes drifted away, and she heard Vy and Anthony talking and kissing at the bar. Somewhere between the first and second verse, Rue felt an uncharacteristic shot of envy. Over Vy and Anthony? No. Surely not…but then…there it was. Incongruous and potent. What was it like to have someone talk to you and touch you that way – with delight, and with a sense of belonging and adoration? Was it comforting? Exciting? Relaxing? Or was it annoying? Confusing? Chafing?

Rue played an instrumental next, letting herself think. What was it? She had never known. Would she ever know? Here she was at the ripe old age of thirty-two (which Chen thought was old!), and she had never been in love. Was she *defective*? Is that why love had never come her way? She knew she was blind, shy, awkward, and reserved. She had trouble opening herself up to people. She took a long time to trust people. She had a border wall up around her heart – built with cement and reinforced steel. But was that all it took to be alone? Forever?

Vy had tried to set Rue up with a few random men over the years. Rue had been nervous and quiet. She felt her blindness on those dates like a flashing neon sign around her neck: "Blind. Banal. Bumbling." Rue realized it would take a certain kind of man to see beyond her "handi-capabilities" and beyond her fortressed heart. Vy's candidates – strong, debonair Don Juans – weren't the type. Maybe it just wasn't meant to be. Rue began a new song, singing and playing, still thinking about the sad trajectory of her nonexistent love life. Just then she heard and smelled two men walk in and pass in front of the piano as she played. She noticed one had an English accent. The other's voice was American, deep and playful. Sensing their eyes on her, she noticed that they paused, and like a fool wondering ridiculously and without reason if they had read her thoughts, her fingers stumbled and her voice went off pitch. She felt herself blush, and trying to pick up the pieces of the song, she fumbled on. She heard the American chuckle – low and throaty – a light acknowledgment, not malicious, just curious and charming, and maybe a little charmed.

She felt her mind and pulse racing. Who was he? Why did he stop and laugh at her that way? And why was it having such an instant kinetic reaction within her? It was as if his presence and that laugh sent a firebolt into Rue's chest. She couldn't explain it. She'd never had an immediate response to a stranger like that before. She tilted her head toward Vy with an unintended look of desperation on her face. She knew Vy had witnessed the whole thing. Rue quickly finished the song and took a deep breath. Now what? Her fingers were trembling. It was the most unexpected bit of trickery – her betraying hands!

Rue stopped playing, listening intently to Bob talking to the Brit, getting his drink order and asking him where he was from. Vy came over to the piano and sat next to Rue on the bench.

Rue put her hand over the microphone and whispered quickly, "Who are they?"

"I don't know, sweetie – I've never seen them before in my life."

"What are they doing?"

"Well, the Indian dude—"

"Indian?"

"Yes, I mean, I *think* he's Indian – he looks Indian, but he has a different accent…like something else…not Indian…"

"English," Rue confirmed. One of her many random talents, she could detect the origin of nearly any accent.

"Yeah, probably, maybe, heck, I don't know…anyway, he's talking to Bob. But the other one – the tall, handsome one – he's turned totally around and looking directly at *you* right now, my friend."

"What?! No." Rue grabbed her cheeks, feeling the heat rise there.

"Oh, yes he is. And he is rather yummy."

Wondering if he heard that, Rue put one hand back over the microphone and asked, "He is? What does he look like?"

"A tall white dude. Broad shoulders, nice smile."

Rue felt the hair on the back of her neck stand up. "Oh my god, Vy, what do I do? He's hot? And he's looking at me? Why? *Why?*!"

"I think you know why. And he has the biggest shit-eating grin on his face. He knows we're talking about him. Cocky. Cute, though. Very cute. Dark eyes, dark hair, really nice eyebrows. And he must be six two, six three. As tall as Anthony, I would say. And the way he's looking at you – my, my, my, I believe that man is undressing you with his eyes!"

"No!" Rue nearly shouted, feeling her skin tingle. She lowered her voice and asked again, "What do I do?"

"Oh wait, he's ordering his drink from Bob now. Do you want me to go talk to him? Or have Anthony talk to him?"

"No! I mean, maybe he's never seen a blind person before. Maybe that's it..."

Vy grunted at that. "Honey, he ain't staring at your eyes. That look is universal. Believe me."

"I *don't* believe you. It can't be. This...this doesn't happen to me. Ever."

"Well, there's a first time for everything. But really, you need to calm down. Start another song. I'll get the scoop. Do your thing. Don't worry – I got ya, girl."

Vy tried to stand up, but Rue kept a firm hold on her hand, at which point Vy had to pry it off, telling Rue to simmer down. Rue let go, steadying herself, and began another instrumental, deciding not to sing – unsure of her wavering voice. When Rue finished, someone walked up to the piano. Rue thought, please don't let it be the handsome stranger, *please*. It wasn't. Phew. It was someone requesting "A Fine Romance," which Rue began immediately, forcing herself to block out everything else. Afterward, Rue went into several other songs, and right at the point when she was starting to feel somewhat normal again, she heard (with horror) the handsome stranger say smoothly, confidently, "Hi there." God, that voice! He was *right* there! Then she felt a warmth, like something melting and cascading down her core.

"Hi," Rue responded in a whisper.

"Can I request a song?"

Rue noticed again the unique deep, humorous note in his voice. And he smelled good – like a man who knew his own business.

Rue said quickly, too quickly, "Yep, sure, uh-huh."

She heard him place one hand loosely, possessively, on top of the piano, tapping his fingers and coming closer to her. Her heart skipped a beat.

Rue had a thought – what if he requested "Toxic" or "Radioactive" or some other such nonsense?

"Do you know 'Let My Love Open the Door' by Pete Townshend?" he asked.

Oh, thank the Lord, he's not a total tool. But then Rue had a flash – the double meaning of the song! She blushed; her voice stuck in her throat.

"What?" he asked, concerned by Rue's hesitation. "Don't know it?"

"Oh no, no, I mean, I know it. I just, well, I...I...I, okay, I can play it," Rue replied lamely, attempting to focus on her words, feeling like a complete idiot.

"Great, thanks," he said. Then as she began to touch the keys, he said, "I'm putting something special in your bowl, okay?"

"What?" She hadn't heard him.

"Check your bowl, okay?" he said, louder.

"Oh, okay," Rue said and plowed into the song, wondering what on earth he put in her fishbowl. She heard him walk away but sensed that he watched her every note from his barstool. She heard him say to his friend, "Spectacular."

It was a palpable thing – this attention – it was so unfamiliar to Rue. It was disconcerting. She wondered again, Why? At least he picked a great song. As she sang the lyrics, they revealed a whole new meaning she had never comprehended before. At the end, she heard his applause and a long, low whistle. Rue took a slow, deep breath and sat still, smiling. Wondering, marveling, confused, she began "They Can't Take That Away From Me" and kept going, song after song, until she heard, an hour or so later, the stranger saying goodbye to Bob and then to her, in a purr, "Don't forget the fishbowl."

Rue nodded, trying to look unemotionally pleasant while feeling like a stuffed pig on a spit with an apple in her mouth. They were gone and she could breathe again. She stopped playing after a few minutes as the lounge cleared out. When she got to the bar, Vy squeezed her shoulder and went back to grab the fishbowl.

Rue hollered at her, "No, leave it!"

"I will not!" Vy said with a delighted laugh.

"Come on," Rue said, indulgently, still not believing. "Please."

"Oh my god, it's a hundred-dollar bill!" Vy screamed, completely ignoring Rue's protests.

"Really?" Rue's eyebrows raised. "Well, that's a first..."

"Wait, there's something more...Rue, he wrote on it! It says, 'You have put a song in my heart.' Oh, he *didn't*! That is *too much*!" said Vy, stopping to giggle with Anthony and Bob. "Then it says, 'Call me. Josh Quinn' and his number."

Rue grabbed her cheeks and shook her head. All she could say was, "No, no, no..."

Anthony inserted, "Yes, yes, yes..."

"But...but I don't even know him," Rue pressed emphatically.

"Like that matters," Vy said. "I knew something big was going to happen tonight – I could feel it in the air. And seriously, it was written all over his face. You should call him right now! Give me your phone."

"Vy!" Rue cried.

Bob laughed, apparently investigating the hundred-dollar bill himself, and said, "I have to admit, nice line." He asked Rue, "So, what are you going to do?"

Rue ignored them all and asked for her purse, which Bob handed over just as Vy grabbed her phone from the side pocket, unlocked it (Rue was just then regretting the fact that Vy knew her password), and was busy typing and saying, "Entering 'Hot Guy' into contacts" and responding to Bob with, "Don't you mean *who* is she gonna do? Let me dial him right now..."

"Vy! No!" Rue screamed, and Vy just laughed and told her to calm down – she wasn't going to call. Rue asked Bob timidly, "You were talking with him a bit. What did he say? What was he like?"

"He seemed nice. He didn't say a ton. His friend is from London. The Brit talked more than the other one. They're roommates, both live nearby, both work for some type of tech company. Your man Josh was more interested in talking about you, actually. Wanted to know your name, where you were from, how long you'd played here, if you were married or had a boyfriend."

Rue put her hand over her mouth, "No, he didn't! Really? What did you say?"

"I said you were a complete psychopath and that you were only here on a work-release program."

Rue laughed through her hand. "Haha. Very funny. What did you *really* tell him?"

"The truth," said Bob, tweaking Rue's nose with his finger. "That you've been playing here for years, that you're single and ready to mingle...and that you're the cutest, sweetest, kindest person I have ever known."

"Oh!" Rue said, shrinking under the rare compliments and what it must have implied to the stranger.

Vy said, "Call him" and handed Rue the phone.

"No, no way. Not tonight. I'll think about it, but for now I'm heading out." Bob gave Rue twenties to replace the small bills in the fishbowl. She tucked them in her purse and walked out with Vy and Anthony, effectively ending the conversation. As they parted at the corner, Vy gave Rue a hug and said in her ear, "What do you have to lose?"

Rue, her eyes as big as saucers, didn't say a word.

❧ Chapter IV ❧

Rue had trouble sleeping that night. She got up several times to check the lights. Whenever she was anxious, she walked around her apartment making sure the light switches were turned off. Of course, the lights didn't mean a thing to her, but from a security standpoint, living alone, she had gotten into the habit of turning them on during the day and off at night. Maybe it seemed completely irrational and paranoid, but it made her feel safer – letting all the nonexistent would-be intruders know she was at home and guarding her fort.

But this night, Hank wasn't happy with her; after she had tossed and turned, gotten up and come back to bed several times, he ran away in resentful disdain. No matter how hard Rue tried to think of something else, her mind kept going back to the stranger and the hundred-dollar bill. Should she call him? She had definitely felt some type of spark, but still…there were so many what ifs – what if he was married, divorced, gay, stupid, mean, unemployed, a cheater, a smoker, a gambler, a pervert, what if, what if, WHAT IF?

And what if she *didn't* call him? The margin of error was so much smaller for not calling than for calling. Didn't it make a lot more sense to let it go? She liked her life how it was. Granted, it wasn't very exciting. She had her set routine, her income, her tips, her one friend, her books, her Kardashians. She had Hank and a nice apartment in Chinatown – well, "nice" was a stretch. Regardless, she was gainfully employed and fairly well situated. She had her little activities on the weekends. She had the city. She didn't need anything else, did she? She wasn't bothered by anyone, and they weren't bothered by her. Sure, she was lonely. She often wished she had someone with whom to go to dinner or a movie, to talk, to read, to walk, to be with. But Rue had accepted long ago that wasn't in the cards for her.

Status quo. Smart. Safe. Good. Done.

Rue gave up on sleep at five forty-five, had her coffee, and listened to the news for a while. When that got boring, she turned off the TV and started a new book – the latest to arrive in the mail from the Library of Congress: *Big Rock Candy Mountain* by Wallace Stegner. She read for two hours until her fingers were tired, finally throwing it down on the table and saying out loud, "God, that book is depressing." That was it. Feeling antsy and restless, she got ready and left. She needed to get out of her apartment and out of her head.

She decided to ride the Muni to the end of the line, to Lands End. Along the way, she thought she heard three other passengers sounding as sleepy and ungrateful for the morning as she was. It was rainy, a slight drizzle spattering wet drops against the windows, and Rue wondered if she should have brought an umbrella. As the bus came to a stop, she pulled the hood of her windbreaker up around her head, descended the stairs, and asked the driver which way to the main road.

As she walked along the sidewalk, hearing the seagulls calling off in the distance and tasting the salty sea air, she smiled. Aaahhh, okay, this is better. The rain wasn't too strong and didn't bother her at all – it had a fresh, wormy smell and pelted her covered head lightly. Someone walked by and Rue giggled with shock as a dog pushed its wet nose into her free hand. "Why, hello, doggie, top of the morning to you," Rue said lightly. The owner apologized, but Rue didn't mind – she petted its head and stroked the velvet of its ears. After a moment they were off, and Rue headed on her way, turning the corner when her cane hit the truncated domes on the sidewalk.

The main road was rather wide and had no crosswalk audible beeping signal, so she had to pause to listen for cars. At times like this, she felt a slight flutter of taking-her-life-in-her-hands, but then she thought, for goodness' sake, if a driver was going to hit anyone, surely they wouldn't hit a blind woman with a cane, would they? Gulp. She made it across safely and stopped to sit on the concrete wall for a few minutes. Taking a deep breath of the cool, humid air, she listened to the ocean's waves crash against the surf, feeling peaceful and calm. She wondered absently how landlocked folks survived life without this. Did they just live in a world of dust and dirt? What sounds, smells, and tastes did they encounter? Manure, mulch, grass, goats, crows, cows? Sure, she was in a big city, which should feel like the opposite of the country, but because it was surrounded by water, it felt freer and more open than a city would normally feel. Of course, she knew about exhaust fumes, bustling people, car horns, closing doors and windows, bakery smells followed inevitably by stale beer, sewage, and vomit. And she knew about the random screams, yells, howls, and shrieks of people and their pets. Rue had taught herself not to startle, but still, sometimes she went weak in the knees. Why were people so loud? Why was this world so *loud*?

But during quiet moments like this, she thought it didn't matter anyway; she was at the edge of the earth, the ocean's swell lulling her senses with its peaceful salty-sweet ballad. After a while, Rue stood up with a sigh, stretched, and hiked up the sidewalk to the Cliff House. She wondered if Roy, her favorite waiter, was working this morning. She was out of breath when she opened the door. Feeling her watch, she knew they had just opened a few minutes earlier, and she heard the hostess on the other side of the floor. Rue heard Roy too – he was talking to someone, but when he noticed Rue he came right over and seated her, saying, "Good morning, sunshine."

She took off her coat and retrieved her wireless earpiece and phone from her purse, setting them down beside her. Roy placed a menu in her hand and then a split second later retrieved it and said, "Whoops. Sorry, force of habit." She laughed. Wasn't the first time. She felt along the pane of the window beside her chair and then along the square framed pictures hanging there.

"Well, who are my fellow compatriots today?" she asked.

"Tyrone Power and Sonja Henie."

"Oh good. Zorro!"

"Yes, and an Olympian. You should be quite secure."

"Indeed. She had such a great accent. Weren't they together in real life?"

"Yes, I think so. But alas, I think he was a philanderer. Although, I always suspected, or rather hoped…," his voice dropping down conspiratorially with a chuckle, "well, I always hoped he, you know, went *both* ways."

Rue laughed. "Oh! Maybe…who knows? Not unheard of."

"No doubt, but they had to stay deep, deep in the closet back then. So sad. Anyway, okay, missy, let me grab your coffee. Be right back."

When Roy came back, he said, "I saw a pod of dolphins out there by the rocks a minute ago."

"Really?!" Rue exclaimed in delight. "How many?"

"Maybe five or six. Those little ones – small, dark dorsal fins with bodies the size of terriers."

"Wow, I wonder what they're doing out there in the rain."

He laughed and said, "Well, I don't think they particularly mind the rain. I guess they're feeding, as usual. There are also about fifty cormorants on the rocks, preening and puffing themselves up like bodybuilders. Rather funny, conceited fellows."

"Yes, and they don't make a sound. What good is a bird that doesn't speak?"

"Good point. They look like black polka dots scattered across the landscape. Hey, speaking of dots and spots, give me those glasses, my dear – you're a mess."

"I am? Okay, I guess I didn't notice."

"No?" They both laughed, feeling witty with their little conspiratorial blind joke. "Yes, they're completely covered."

He wiped off her glasses, chatting away the whole time. When he handed the stylish horn-rims back, he said, "Here. By the way, these are adorbs. Where'd you get them?"

"The eye doctor's," she said with a grin.

"Very funny," not giving an inch.

She laughed and replied, "Naw. My friend Vy picked them up. She said I needed to, quote, up my game."

"Well, you certainly have."

She took them from him but opted to leave them on the table so as to not get them dirty again. Roy took her order and said he'd be right back. He was off, and with a strange wash of feeling she realized that even though she didn't really know Roy, she appreciated him. He always took the time to talk to her and make her feel safe. And more importantly, he had a skill – he knew how to make his vocabulary descriptive so that Rue could imagine the things of the sighted world. Rue had learned over the years that this was a skill not many possessed. Most people talked in colors or flat, nameless words that held no meaning for her. Once, many years ago, when Rue first started going to the Cliff House for breakfast, Roy took the time to read her the entire menu – including the history of the restaurant, cover to cover – adding his own embellishments along the way. "The Johnson omelet (like a crab and an avocado met in a bar and had a threesome with the sour cream), Joe's Special Scramble (very filling, better plan to walk it off later), Shakshuka (somewhat Middle Eastern)…"

She smiled and touched the windowsill again, thinking about the dolphins. As a child, she'd had a tactile children's book with a slot for a dolphin that felt like a combination of stretched plastic and leather. She still had finger memory of that dolphin. She always wondered if that was what a dolphin felt like in real life. She sighed, thinking about it. Oh well, not something she would ever know. She picked up her phone, put her earpiece in, and began listening to a book. Roy brought over a basket of popovers, and she spread butter and jam onto one, biting luxuriously into the sweet, savory goodness.

After a while, Roy came by with her food and asked what she was listening to.

"A book. *Riders of the Purple Sage*."

"Hmmpf. Never heard of it. Some type of Western?"

"Yep. I had started something else earlier this morning, but it was making my fingers hurt, not to mention my head – it was interesting, but depressing. I decided to switch it up – something more upbeat."

"Nice. I was on a Western movie kick for a while – all that lawlessness, shoot-outs, muscled men in chaps…what's not to like? I switched gears a few months ago, though – been watching these crazy comic-strip superhero movies now. They're all the rage."

"Oh yeah, not my thing."

"I'm still debating if they're *my* thing. I must admit, I get lost in the middle most of the time."

"I hear ya." Roy left again to attend to other customers.

Rue escaped into her book, thinking how Zane Grey's landscapes were spectacularly described – what words! She had been reading Westerns on and off for several months, starting with Louis L'Amour's *How the West Was Won*, then Willa Cather's *My Antonia* and Owen Wister's *The Virginian*. She was still on the fence about paper (braille) books versus audio. They each had their own pluses and minuses. The weight of the braille books was a hindrance for traveling around town, so she usually read those at home, but when she stuck to audio only, she found herself being spoiled and letting her braille get rusty. Regardless, she was glad she had both because she loved that feeling of escaping into a new world, time, and place. Transporting herself away…it was the same otherness feeling she got from singing. As she thought of this, biting into a piece of bacon, she smiled to herself in pure gratitude; she really was lucky – she had everything she needed in this world, didn't she?

Suddenly, interrupting her reverie, a deep, humorous voice asked, "What's so funny?"

She choked on her bacon. As if someone had shot a syringe of adrenaline into her heart, a warmth stole through her – it was *that* voice – the hundred-dollar bill man! It was Josh Quinn! Here at the Cliff House! How could that be? Was she hallucinating? She took her earpiece out with a shaky hand.

"Hello," he said lightly, hovering over her. She smelled him and blushed.

"Hello," she managed to say.

"Using my tip for breakfast?" he asked with a light laugh.

She shrugged and said, "Something like that…"

"Oh, my manners," he said, seeming to catch himself. "This is Dennis Tharpe, a client of mine…Dennis, this is…" Josh said with a significant pause. Oh god, now I have to give him my name. That rogue!

She complied reluctantly, "Rue…Cavendish…nice to meet you." She held out her hand, and the client took it loosely as Rue set her lips together.

"Rue. Wonderful. Funny seeing you here," Josh said with a smile in his voice.

"Yes, it's quite a coincidence," Rue admitted, somewhat suspiciously.

He asked casually, "Do you come here often?"

"Once in a while…," she replied vaguely, thinking, get to your table! She smelled the hostess's perfume and sensed she was standing aside curiously, watching this transaction with interest, waiting patiently to escort them the rest of the way.

Josh asked, "It's a great place, isn't it? I was just telling Dennis what spectacular popovers they have. Not to mention the view."

"Um, yes, the popovers…the view, I…," Rue stammered, willing her heart to stop pounding and thinking, how am I going to comment on the view?!

The hostess cut in with impatience (*thank you!*) and said, "Sir?"

"Oh yes, sorry, of course," replied Josh, speaking to Rue instead of the hostess. It was then that he touched Rue's shoulder lightly and said, "Sorry. Goodbye for now, Rue." She could feel his hand through her shirt, warm and strong, and it sent a shiver down her spine. Seemingly as an afterthought, while walking away, he said, "Call me, okay?"

Rue didn't reply. She sank down in her seat in utter embarrassment, a fluttery mess. What just happened?!

A moment later, Roy came up and asked curiously, incredulously, "And *who* was *that*?"

Rue laughed self-consciously and sputtered, "I'm not sure…some guy…I don't know…he gave me his number last night…it's crazy…what are the chances? I met him for the first time last night…and now he's *here*, this morning?"

"Wow, crazy," Roy confirmed.

"I'm not even sure what to think. The whole thing is so…so bizarre!"

"You know what I think?"

"What?"

Roy answered assuredly, "Maybe the forces of nature brought you two together. Who knows? Stranger things have happened. By the way, he is one tall, dark drink of bourbon."

Rue giggled, trying not to think about her burning cheeks.

Roy laughed a little with her and then asked, "Anyway, you want more coffee?"

Rue came back to reality and replied, "No, no, just the check. I'm going to get out of here."

"Uh-huh, I bet you are. Run away, my dear – scurry, scurry," Roy chortled knowingly, slipping away and back again with her bill.

After she paid, Rue quickly gathered her things and stood up to leave. It was the first time in a long time she felt self-conscious about her cane. Usually it was second nature, but at this moment it felt like navigating a minefield with an iron poker. What if she ran into someone? What if she tripped and fell? What if she knocked a glass over? She went slow as a sloth and thankfully got out the door in one piece, stepping outside and taking a long, deep breath of the sea air. She felt her heart beating hard in her chest as she zipped up her windbreaker and headed down the hill, wondering if *he* could see her out the window.

Safely away, she felt as though butterflies were floating around inside her abdomen. So, *this* was what people talked about! This tingly, weak-in-the-knees, sparkly feeling. She had never known it before. God, she wished she had a mother to talk to. She needed advice. Thinking about her mother always made her sad, so once she was far enough away from any prying eyes, she sat down on the cement wall above the beach and let the tears well up in her eyes. Insufferable tears! She hated to cry. It brought her right back to those childhood agonies and frustrations, those fearful years of instability after her parents died when she'd been a boat adrift at sea with no sail. Letting her memories take over, she sunk her face down into the collar of her jacket and wept.

Many minutes went by. She sat contemplating and calming herself for a while. She tried to focus on the sounds of the beach. She heard a group of people playing volleyball, a dog barking, the waves crashing against the surf – wonderful, reassuring waves. Then slowly, forcefully, she shut the door to her sadness and wiped her eyes. After all, these tears today, they were simply a result of being rattled. Nothing catastrophic had happened – a man talked to a woman. So what? What was the big deal? It happened every day! Nothing could be more typical, blasé, common, run-of-the-mill, right? Rue's eyes got big and round as she thought, but not with me! Not *to* me!

Finally, she got up, crossed the road, and hiked the short trail leading to her favorite spot – the bench beside the Dutch stone windmill in Golden Gate Park. The robins were chirping, and the grass was slightly damp under her feet. She laid her purse on the bench, found a flower on the ground, and plucked it. A tulip. She sat down and fingered her watch. It was ten twenty, so she had over an hour to work. She pulled three things out of her purse: a sheet of precut four-by-four-inch white card stock, a slightly larger piece of cardboard, and a small, thin art knife. Sitting down and laying the purse on her lap, she used it as a flat surface, placing the sheet of paper on top of the cardboard. In her other hand, she rubbed each petal of the tulip like a piece of fabric. They were dewy, silky, and soft. She felt along the stem and then reached down into the center of the flower, pinching the pistil and getting pollen on her fingers. She paused and committed each touch to memory. Then she spent the next hour cutting the paper into an image of the flower with a tight, distinct stencil. First, she did one image of the flower, straight up and down, and then another slightly bent, then two more at other angles, each on its own piece of card stock. At some point, a woman stopped on her way to another bench and said, "Those are lovely." Rue smiled and thanked her.

Coming out her trance, Rue took a deep breath. The air was like the steam that wafts up from a clambake. As she often did at this spot, she paused and opened up her senses to absorb the atmosphere. She smelled flowers and freshly mown grass. Her fingers grazed each of the stencil sheets, admiring their precision. Her tongue tasted the salt in the air. She heard people in the garden talking softly. She felt their presence as something tactile, real, palpable – they were *here* – and yet, she didn't know what they looked like, how they lived, their names, their hopes, their fears, their dreams. She didn't know anything – but she *felt* them. Sometimes she wondered if she was formed as a vessel simply to observe the human interactions, transactions, and operations of this world and not to partake in them. She had always been a solitary creature, thriving on her independence and self-reliance, but she must acknowledge that she was on the periphery of life, inside a bubble with a tight seal. At times, she wished to escape into something more, but the bubble was so safe, quiet, and secure.

Rue remembered back to a time, several years ago, when she was sitting under the Victory Statue in Union Square, much the same as today, sitting still and drinking in her surroundings. Out of the blue, she heard a man in the middle of the square belt out "I Left My Heart in San Francisco" at the top of his lungs. The loitering crowd stopped in their tracks to listen. Rue laughed out loud – what bravado! His voice was deep and powerful – spectacular! Now that was a man putting himself out there! Was this what Rue had to do – take a leap, jump off a cliff, walk out onto a scary, dangling limb? She had always been so *safe* with her life choices. Stuck in a pattern of static routine. Even now as she ran her fingers along the four cut stencils, she was still focused on *four*. She smiled wryly. The Fabulous Four: Mom, Dad, Daniel, Rue. In her childhood, they had done everything together – her parents, her brother, and her. It was stupid, really. She was *one* now. Not four. Her parents were gone. Daniel had his own life. Rue was just Rue. Was she simply stuck?

Speaking of Daniel, Rue snapped back to reality, feeling her watch, and realized she was going to be late.

❦ CHAPTER V ❧

As soon as Rue's feet and cane hit the sidewalk, her phone rang, telling her it was Vy. Of course. She would be curious to know if Rue had called Josh.

"Good morning, Vy."

"What happened?" asked Vy breathlessly.

"Nothing! What did you think?" replied Rue, laughing and exasperated.

"Well, I don't know...I thought you'd maybe take this opportunity to grasp life by the balls and maybe grasp something else by the balls too." Rue grunted and laughed. Vy added, "I'm sure he stayed up half the night waiting for your call. You shouldn't leave a man hanging like that."

Rue replied, "As a matter of fact, he sounded well-rested and very refreshed this morning." Rue paused, thinking (based on her gasp) that Vy's head was exploding. "I, on the other hand, slept horribly."

An exclamation or two later and Vy said, "Wait, what?! What do you mean, 'this morning'?"

"I was at the Cliff House, listening to a book, eating breakfast, and minding my own business when out of the blue, somehow, he was standing right next to me. He was there with a client."

"Whoa, how is that possible? It's like kismet or cosmic or karma or...or... something! So, what did he say? Did he talk to you? Did he sit with you? Tell me everything!"

"No, no, nothing like that. We only spoke for a minute. He introduced me to the client, I think partially as a ploy to get my name, and then he put his hand on my shoulder and said goodbye and told me to call him."

"I think Bob told him your name last night."

"Oh yeah, well, maybe he was just being polite. Or wanted to hear it from me. Heck, I don't know...the whole thing is so strange, and it kind of threw me for a loop."

"I bet." Vy empathized. She asked, "How did he look?"

"Vy!" I shouted into the phone with a laugh.

Vy groaned and said, "Sorry…I forget sometimes…how did he…smell? Taste?"

"Very funny. He smelled nice. Like a man should smell, I guess, not that I know…"

"All women know how a man should smell."

"Beer and chips?" Rue asked with amusement.

"Pizza and body odor."

"Taco Bell and whiskey?" Rue continued until they were both giggling and gave up. She heard some loud noises in the background. "Hey, aren't you at the museum today? What are you doing calling me?"

"Yeah, yeah, I'm here. Kaylen's bouncing around with my mom right now. I gotta get going, but I had to hear if anything went down. So, what happens next?"

"I'm still thinking about it. I'm headed to Daniel and Cathy's right now, and I have to work tonight, so nothing immediate."

"All right, all right…but don't wait too long; fine-looking, rich, hot men don't grow on trees, you know. Call him!"

"Okay, okay. Later gator. Have fun at the museum."

"Right-e-o, later, buh-bye."

Rue finished the last block with a smile on her face, putting her phone back in her purse and feeling her watch, noting that she arrived at her brother's house at noon on the dot despite her worries about being late. Just as Rue was folding and stashing her cane, Daniel's wife, Cathy, greeted her at the door and said, "Hi. Here. Take Jordan. Raquel's having a meltdown." She hastily handed the baby over to Rue and took off up the stairs toward the sound of a screaming child. Rue gave a kiss to Little Miss Jordan, saying, "Hello, sweet cheeks. How are you today?" Rue fancied that this one looked like her. That's what people told her anyway. When they saw Rue and Jordan together, they said they had the same dark hair and periwinkle eyes. Rue's mom's eyes. Jordan laid her head down on Rue's shoulder, and Rue placed her cheek softly on the baby's forehead. Awww. Rue walked up the stairs to the kitchen and said hi to her brother, Daniel, as he explained that he was prepping food for lunch.

"Hey, sis. How's it going? You okay with deli sandwiches? It's about all we have in the house. Haven't had a chance to go grocery shopping – been out on the boat since Wednesday."

"Yeah, that's fine. I'm not super hungry anyway. How was the sailing? Weather been good?" Rue asked. Jordan clapped her hands.

Daniel tweaked Jordan's nose and said, "It's a little more complicated now that this one is weaned because, well, she eats enough food for three grown men, I swear. Don't you?" Jordan giggled obligingly.

Rue asked, "How did she do?"

"Good. She got sick a few times when we hit some big swells. Just spit up. I think she's still getting her sea legs."

"Jordan," Rue asked, squeezing her, "are you going to be a sailor?"

"Ah, ya," Jordan replied.

Cathy came in holding Raquel, who was still whining and sniffing. Raquel said with a small whimper, "Hi, Aun' Wue."

"Hi, sweetie, are you okay? What's the matter? You having a bad day?"

"I okay."

"Good."

Cathy took both girls into the other room to play and came back into the kitchen. Rue asked, "Was this the longest trip they've had so far?"

Cathy answered, "Yep, three days. Raquel couldn't get over the wind in her hair and the speed. She kept telling Daniel, 'Faster, faster, Daddy!' It was too cute. It got a little chilly at night, so we had to keep them bundled up in the berth, but other than that it was perfect. You would not believe the stars at night – so many more than we see here. Totally filled the sky! Next time, why don't you come with us?"

"Sure, I'd love to. I don't know about three days…it would be hard to get away that long with my work schedule…"

"What?" Daniel cut in sharply. "Are you still at that lounge?"

"Yes," replied Rue defensively, "Of course I'm still at the lounge." Then trying to redirect, she asked Cathy, "How is Raquel doing with her reading?"

Daniel stopped Cathy from responding and continued, "Why, Rue? Why? I mean, if you need money, I'll give you some. You don't need to do that… that ridiculous job."

"It's not ridiculous, Daniel, and it's not about the money," Rue countered, feeling the heat rise in her. Not this argument again.

"Then what is it?"

"I don't know…the money helps, but also…I really like it there. I like the people, and I enjoy singing. And why do you care anyway?" Rue's voice rose as she fought to control it.

"Why do I care? Why do I care? Because it's base and seedy and stupid. There's no need to pander to all those drunken idiots. Up in front of everyone like that…"

Rue's face turned red. She'd heard it all before from Daniel – he still treated her like a baby. He acted as though he was trying to protect her, but in her mind he was just trying to control her. He still remembered every snub and sneer from their childhood, and he thought her working as a lounge singer was just another platform for the world's cruel taunts and treatment. He didn't know that the audience liked her, applauded her, sang with her, tipped her. He didn't know how much it fulfilled her, released her, gave her confidence and purpose. She tried to explain in exasperation. "But…but, it's not what you think…"

Daniel said angrily, "I know it's not what Mom and Dad would have wanted."

That was it. Rue shot back, "Hey, leave them out of it! Not that it matters, but I'm sure Mom and Dad would have wanted me to make my own way, and that's exactly what I'm doing! I'm not doing anything illegal or illicit; I'm simply making a living using the skills I have. There is nothing wrong with that. I love to sing, and it is not 'seedy,' it's…it's Nob Hill, for goodness' sake! If only you would come and see for yourself…!"

"Um," interrupted Cathy, "not to change the subject, well, yes to change the subject," she laughed grimly and continued, "speaking of your mom and dad, Daniel found something the other day. Did he tell you?"

"No, what?" asked Rue, immediately forgetting the argument. "What did you find?"

Cathy answered, "Oh, it's not much, honestly – don't get too excited. It's Great Aunt Louise's jewelry box. Daniel found it in some trunk in the basement. When we opened it, we thought it might contain lost treasures or something, but mostly it's filled with old photos and cheap jewelry. Nothing special."

"Oh," Rue said, disappointed.

"Do you want it?" Daniel asked.

"Sure, I suppose."

"It's all yours. Let's eat."

Daniel brought the food into the living room, and Cathy led Rue in, sitting her down on the chair. They chatted and played with the kids for the next couple of hours. Rue's mind was distracted thinking about Daniel's criticism and, somewhere in the back of her mind, about Josh Quinn.

At four o'clock, Daniel drove her home, saying with conciliatory calm, "Listen, if you need anything, let me know, okay?"

"Okay. You know I'm fine, Daniel, I really am. You don't need to worry about me."

"Uh-huh, okay, whatever you say," he reflected with sarcasm. She sensed him peering up at her grimy Chinatown apartment building and not believing a word she said. Rue got out of the car, thanked him, and waved goodbye as she entered the building. Trudging up the stairs, she acknowledged that what bothered Daniel more than anything wasn't his worry for her but rather the fact that she refused to accept any help from him. She was fiercely independent, and in his misguided protective big brother role, he resented her refusal. He wanted (in some approximation) to fill the role their parents had left vacant. When Daniel thought she was being foolish, headstrong, and ungrateful, Rue thought she was being scrappy, strong, and smart. Rue sometimes wondered if they would ever see eye to eye.

Rue opened her apartment door, set down the jewelry box along with her purse and cane, and scooped up Hank, his collar bell dinging at her feet. He was mewing and uncharacteristically needy. As her mind drifted back to the Josh situation, she sat with Hank for a while on the couch, scratching and petting him, and said with a sigh, "Well, Hank, I've been propositioned. Can you believe it? What should I do? Meow once for yes and twice for no." He was silent – defiant and squirmy, the traitor. She set him down and he ran off, done with her interrogation. Then she took her phone out of her purse, found Hot Guy under her contacts, and sat and pondered. Vy's mantra was repeating in her mind: What do you have to lose? Her brain went something like this: Um, everything, um, nothing, um, hard to say. Wavering. Like a blade of grass in the wind. What to do? Alright, Rue, be strong. Time to dive into the deep end. Don't hit your head on the bottom! She took a few deep breaths and dialed. Her heart was in her throat. She hoped he wouldn't answer.

Of course, he picked up on the second ring. "Hello?"

"Um…yes…hello. Josh?"

"Yep, one and the same. Who's this?"

"It's Rue, from last night…and from this—"

"This morning!" he finished her sentence. "Yes! Hi. I'm so glad you called! Ha! This is great! Can you believe this morning? Running into each other like that?! Totally wild!"

Whoa, she hadn't expected his enthusiasm. Like a raging bull! She stuttered, "Um…er…yes, very coincidental."

"Or as I like to say, fate," he replied with a small laugh. "So, what's going on?"

"Uh, not much, just thought I'd call to, um, to—" Rue mumbled, stumbled, muddled through, feeling like a complete idiot. With horror, she realized she was so not familiar with the ways of conversation with the opposite sex. What does one say? How does one begin?

Fortunately (or unfortunately, as still remained to be seen), Josh seemed to be a pro. He cut in calmly, "Hey, hi. Thanks for calling. Great to hear from you. How are you doing? Did you have a nice afternoon?"

Rue chuckled, thinking, okay woman, just talk. He's a human and you're a human. Remain calm. This is not the signing of the Declaration of Independence. "Yes, I did, thanks for asking. I went to the park and then to my brother's house."

"Golden Gate?"

"Yes, I, um (would he care?), I sat by the windmill for a while."

"Huh," he said with a small laugh, "no kidding. And visited with your brother?"

"Yep, he lives nearby the park. I hung out with my nieces."

"Awesome! I have a bunch of nieces and nephews myself. They're a lot of fun, aren't they?"

"Yes, they are." Rue thought, he seemed nice, and he liked kids. Hmmm.

"And what else did you do?"

"Oh, miscellaneous. What about you?"

"I had some follow-ups with clients, so I ran around and did that, then came back to my place."

"Do you always work on the weekends? I mean, what exactly do you do?"

"I'm a sales rep for a tech company, TorkOps. So, yeah, sometimes I work on the weekends. This week was busy because there was a tech conference in town, and we had a booth there, so I've been chasing down potential clients – strike while the iron's hot, you know?"

"Right," Rue said, as if she had any clue.

There was a slight pause and then Josh asked, "Are you home right now?"

"Yes," Rue answered slowly.

"I wonder…do you want to meet for coffee or something quick? I'd love to see you again."

"I don't know…I have to work tonight…," she waffled, scared out of her mind.

"What time? I mean, I can come get you or meet you somewhere. Or would you prefer I come to the lounge tonight?"

Rue panicked. No, no, no, NO. She didn't want him in her space again. It threw her off. Too disconcerting. She didn't want that distraction while she was playing and trying to concentrate. She replied quickly, "Uh, no, no, that's not necessary, I don't think that will work."

"Oh, okay," Josh said with slight hesitation. "No problem. Then when, where? I think it would be fun to talk in person."

"You do? Why?" she blurted out. Then, to try to dial it back, she said, "You don't even know me."

"True, true, but I want to *get* to know you. I know it's, well, it's kind of crazy! I can't explain it myself, but from the moment I saw you in that bar last night, I wanted to meet you and talk to you and find out more about you. Sorry, well, sorry, not sorry." He laughed and Rue laughed too. He was so eager! "Can we meet. Right now?"

Rue paused and he urged further, "Come on. It's just coffee. I can be anywhere in fifteen minutes, give or take. I have a car. I'll pick you up. Or we can meet. Whatever's easiest. I assume you're local…?"

"Chinatown." She figured that was vague enough.

"Okay, great, great, let me see…what about Brioche? Do you know where that is?"

"Yes."

"Okay, do you want me to pick you up?"

"No!" Rue nearly shouted, realizing her tone was harsher than she meant it to be, but he didn't seem put off.

"Okay, sure, no problem. I'll just meet you there in, say, fifteen minutes?"

"Um…what about thirty instead?" It would take her ten minutes to walk there, and she needed to change clothes. And take a large quantity of Xanax.

"Sure." His voice dropped down an octave as he said, "Rue…Rue…great name, by the way. See you soon. Can't wait."

"Bye," Rue replied, her heart pounding as she hung up.

Oh my god, oh my god, oh my god!

She heard Hank off in a corner and cried, "Oh Hank, what have I done?!"

So much for her usual quiet time resting before work. So much for exploring Great Aunt Louise's jewelry box. She quickly went to her closet and listened to Vy's description of ten different outfits – which one to choose?! Finally, she heard this one: "Not too sexy, not too sweet. Like a cocktail in the rain. Slightly flared-out, medium length black skirt with light blue V-neck blouse paired with black hose and black flats. Your eyes look amazing in this one! Don't forget the silver hoop earrings – you know, the larger the hoop, the closer to God!" Rue shook her head as she dressed, wondering what on earth that meant. Vy!

Rue touched up her makeup and tweaked her hair. She cleaned off her glasses and placed them back on her face, armed for battle. Then she grabbed her purse and jacket and headed out the door. Hank's bell called from across the room as she threw him kisses goodbye.

Rue was trying her best not to overthink things or get nervous. Instead she decided to walk as fast as she could without tripping or getting out of breath in order to get there before him. She wanted to arrive and sit down with plenty of time to gain her composure, and she didn't want to worry about him staring at her the whole length of the street outside the café before she had even entered. Of course, her plans were foiled. There he was, right at the door to greet her. She said hello weakly, and he offered to bring her something to drink as he helped her to the table. When he was up at the counter getting her tea, she thought to herself, give me strength. She felt as though her heart was going to explode and her cheeks were on fire.

When he sat down across from her, he said encouragingly, "Take your coat off and stay awhile."

Rue smiled, caught. She sighed and detangled herself from her purse, coat, and cane.

"You are so beautiful," he said matter-of-factly.

"Thank you," Rue said, even redder, and she thought, and you are hot, according to Vy and Roy anyway.

He asked, "Do you normally wear glasses? I don't remember you having them on before…"

Rue took her glasses off. So much for her armor. "Only sometimes…"

"Ah, that's better. Why the glasses? I mean, how do they work?"

Rue chuckled at that. Wow, he didn't beat around the bush, did he? She replied, "No, they don't offer any vision correction, if that's what you mean. I'm completely blind, have been since birth. But I like the feel of the rhinestones here." She showed him the corners of the horn-rims that were bedazzled with three tiny rhinestones on each side.

"So, you never wore the dark, tinted kind?"

"Well, yes, I used to. It was sort of an indicator, like a traffic signal, you know, hello people, I'm blind, watch out. Haha. But I recently switched to these. Now I like to keep people guessing."

He laughed and she grinned, thinking *he gets my sense of humor – that's a relief*. With a kinetic spark, she felt his hand touch hers as he reached for the glasses. Involuntarily, she pulled away.

After a second, he put the glasses back in her hand and said, "Do you mind me asking questions?"

Rue shrugged and replied, "Well, since you've already started…"

He admitted, "I guess I have, haven't I? First let me say thank-you for coming. I was hoping…that we could get to know each other. Isn't it crazy that we've seen each other three times in the past twenty-four hours? What are the chances?"

"Yeah, pretty strange," Rue said, warming her hands on her tea. Being polite, she asked, "Do you live around here?"

"Yep, up on Nob Hill. The guy I was with at the bar last night, he's my roommate, Harsha. Or as he says, my 'flatmate.' We rent a place over on Pine. It's so funny – we've never been to your lounge before. It's so close, but then again, I guess we thought since it's in a hotel and all…I don't know… anyway, it must have been fate. Because we finally went, and there you were." He stopped and she felt his gaze upon her. He had used that word again: *fate*. Is that what this was? She smiled obligingly. She opened her mouth to ask another question, but he jumped in first. "So, where do you live? Where are you from? Did you grow up around here? What's your family like? How did you learn to play piano and sing like that? What do you like to do? What's your favorite thing in the world? Worst fear? I want to know everything." *Wow, machine gunfire!* She wasn't sure if she should get out of range or just allow herself to be shot. Probably the most anyone had asked her about herself in years, and certainly the most in one long string.

Waiting to make sure he was done, Rue paused and then stumbled, "Ah… um…okay…," she decided to keep it simple. "I live in Chinatown—"

He said quickly, "Oh yeah, I knew that. You already told me that. I can't believe you live in Chinatown. I don't know anyone who lives in Chinatown! Well, of course, there are thousands of people who live in Chinatown, but I guess I thought they were all Chinese. Sorry, I'm nervous. I didn't mean to cut you off. You make me nervous." She heard his abashed voice and shook her head, incredulous. *He* was nervous!

Then before she could take a breath to process and begin again, he kept going, "And almost no one makes me nervous, I swear. It's the wildest thing! I can't figure it out. I mean, I feel like a thirteen-year-old boy again. My hands are shaking. Look!" When he was quiet for ten seconds, she realized he must be holding up his hand. She shrugged, and he woke up and cried, "OH! Sorry, I'm an idiot!"

Rue smiled – it wasn't the first time someone had tried to "show" her something. He said, "Well, you'll have to trust me – my hands really *are* shaking." He laughed self-consciously. "I'm sorry," he pleaded. "I'll stop interrupting, I swear. I promise. Please ignore me. Continue."

"Okay," Rue said with a small, indulgent smile, waiting. Was he done? Yes? Okay, good. She said slowly, "I grew up around here, well, out near the Presidio. But I've lived downtown since I was seventeen. I have one brother, the one I already mentioned. I learned to play the piano and sing as a child. Let's see, favorite thing and worst fear, hmmm, you'll have to give me time to think on those two…," she stopped, then asked, "What about you?"

"Oh me? Not much to tell," began Josh, but stopped. "Wait. Did you go to music school or something? How do you know all of those songs anyway? I watched you last night – you don't use your phone or anything. How do you do that?"

"I don't know exactly," replied Rue, thinking a moment about the mystery of her musical abilities. "I took piano lessons when I was little. But ever since I can remember, when I hear a song, even just once on the radio or in a store or on my phone, somehow, I'm not sure how, I just immediately know it. I guess it's kind of like how you might remember what you wore to work yesterday or what you had for breakfast this morning…"

"Well, that's impossible," said Josh with a laugh. "I have no idea what I had for breakfast this morning. I was too…distracted."

Rue laughed, realizing he was talking about the Cliff House.

Then he challenged, "But, what about those older songs? Some of those songs you played were from, like, fifty years ago, weren't they? How on earth do you know them? You wouldn't have heard them on the radio."

"Oh, those, well, yeah, that's sort of a long story. I don't want to bore you…" she hedged.

"I've got all night. You go right ahead. I'll be a good boy and try to stay quiet."

She smiled. "Well…okay…um, when I first moved downtown, I worked at a nursing home, and they had a piano in the common area. The residents there, they loved it when I played for them, and they would request these old standards, so I'd look up the songs on my phone and play whatever they wanted. And also, after I quit the nursing home, I would sometimes spend my Saturday mornings at the park, where these two old guys led bird hikes. For whatever reason," Rue chuckled thinking about it, "they loved to sing as they walked."

"Wait. What?" He laughed with her.

Rue said, "I know, weird, right? So, yeah, they'd play this sort of game, you know, like 'Guess the Song.' One would hum the tune, and the other had to figure out which song it was. One said, 'I'm going to throw you a softball,' meaning an easy song, or 'a hardball,' meaning a difficult one. Come to think of it, I'm not exactly sure about the baseball reference, but anyway, once the other got it right, they had to sing the song all the way through. Most were songs I'd never heard before – wartime jingles and classics." Rue paused, thinking she was talking too much. When Josh didn't say a word, she continued, "It was kind of funny because sometimes they would stop midsong and whisper, 'Shhh, off to the right in that bush, there's a spotted towhee.' Everyone would stop and get quiet, likely to steady their binoculars. I would simply listen, hanging onto one of their arms. Anyway, by virtue of those bird hikes, I memorized most of the old standards, not to mention most of the bird species native to the Bay Area."

"Wow," said Josh. "Amazing. You still do those hikes?"

"Not much anymore, unfortunately," Rue said, shrugging. "I went once last fall, but only one of the old guys was there. I think they're both getting rather frail and infirm. It was kind of sad to have one without the other. I tried to play the game with the one, but he didn't seem to want to participate, so I gave up."

She sat and waited, sipping her tea. Finally, he asked, "How old are you?"

She nearly spit out her tea. But she replied unflinchingly, "Thirty-two."

"Ha, okay, good. I was beginning to worry," he said.

"Hey!" Rue cried and he laughed. He was teasing her.

He said, "Well, with the nursing home and the birds and the old guys and all…"

She shrugged and countered lightly, "And what about you?"

"Twenty-eight," he said. Then, without a moment's hesitation, he reached over and grabbed Rue's hand and challenged, "What do you think about dating a younger man?"

There it was again – the shock – electric and sudden. She sat stunned and on fire. His hand was so warm and soft and manly – somewhere between an elephant's hide and a sheep's. He gripped her like he never wanted to let her go. She was speechless, so he waited a few minutes and finally pressed gently, "Well? Don't leave me hanging."

Rue slowly got her voice back and began, "Um, I don't know…I mean, I need to know a few things first."

"Sure, anything, I'm an open book." He leaned back, releasing her hand.

She felt herself breathe again. She stated, "The basics."

With no hesitation, he said, "Fire away."

"Are you married?"

He laughed. "No."

"Dating?"

"Yes, clearly."

Rue laughed. Duh.

"Serious?"

"About you? Yes," he replied definitively, and she stopped to smile.

"Ever been married?" she continued.

"Nope, but I was engaged once. Didn't work out."

"Why?"

"Heck…I don't know…we were too young, I suppose, weren't right for each other. We were high school sweethearts, but I had bigger plans for my life. She wanted to settle down, pop out a few kids, raise a family on a farm. That wasn't for me. I wanted college, work, travel, friends, life, you know? She was a great gal and all, but that just wasn't for me. Man, if she could see me now! Living in the big city, with my big boy pants and my big boy job. Aren't you glad it didn't work out with her?"

Rue replied honestly, "I don't know."

"You don't know? What don't you know?" He grabbed her hand again. Her breath caught in her throat.

"I don't know because…," Rue continued cautiously, struggling to concentrate, "I think even if you do have a 'big boy' life, as you say…you're still just a boy, aren't you?"

"Yeah, that's probably true," answered Josh unabashedly, with a chuckle. "If you mean that I like to have fun, go out, drink, socialize, you know, *date*."

He squeezed her hand and challenged, "Anything wrong with that?"

Her guard went back up as she stiffened in her chair, releasing her hand from his, but before she could respond, he countered quickly, his voice warming, "Hey, don't get me wrong, I'm not out dating a different woman every night or anything." He laughed, but Rue didn't. "I mean, I work hard, so I like to play hard. That's all."

At first Rue wasn't sure how to interpret this cryptic statement. Warning bells were going off in her head. She said abruptly, "I have to go." When she stood up, grabbing her purse and coat, he touched her arm.

"Wait," he said, contrition in his voice. "Don't go. I'm sorry. I've said something stupid. I'm a fool. Please...please don't go."

"Josh," said Rue decidedly, "listen, you seem like a nice enough guy, but I really need to get going, and...," she paused and then said slowly, "if I'm being honest, it seems like we're different kinds of people. I don't think I'd fit into your...crowd."

"What? Come on, sure you would!" Josh said with entreaty and then with a groan. "Wow, I don't think I've ever struck out so quickly before." He let out a small, self-conscious laugh.

"Hey, no harm, no foul, right?" said Rue, as she shrugged away from him in order unfold her cane.

"Wait, listen," said Josh, "will you sit down for one more minute? Please? Will you?"

"I really do have to get to work," said Rue, but something in the tone of his voice made her pause. She sat down slowly, her body half off the chair.

Rue sensed his mind racing through the plethora of canned enticements that usually brought women back into the fold. And she could also sense his mind hitting a roadblock. He cleared his throat a few times. Rue found herself reluctantly empathizing with him – she imagined his good looks usually got him ninety percent of the way with women and his charm the other ten. How was he to succeed with his cards flipped, the ninety inconsequential and the ten mired in confusion? Rue had to admit she was just as disconcerted as he. She was unfamiliar with the ways of love and dating. She only knew to be blunt and honest and not to temper those impressions with flattery or false edicts. And yet, she liked him – there was something physical and forward about his manner that drew her in – against her better judgment – she was easy to warm to his voice and touch. On the one hand, she wanted him to win her back. But on the other, a voice in the back of her mind was saying,

He's a player, Rue – a *player*. She was torn.

He began again, softer, less self-assured, "Um, well, okay, I think…I think you might have the wrong impression of me." Rue raised a speculative eyebrow. He ignored that and continued tentatively, "But listen, I'm leaving for a business trip tomorrow and I'd like to call you. On the phone, just talk… nothing more. What do you think? You don't have to ever see me again, but maybe we could be phone buddies or pen pals or something?" He laughed. He was creative, she'd give him that.

"I don't think you'd be able to decipher my braille," Rue said dryly.

"Oh yeah," he chuckled. "I forgot about that. Well…hmmm…let's see… typewriter? Morse code? Flag-waving? Carrier pigeon? Smoke signals?"

Rue tried to hold down the corners of her mouth. He was, after all, putting up a fight. She said, "I suppose a phone call would be…harmless."

"No, not that!" he protested.

She laughed. "Well, neutral anyway. Yes, you may call."

"Yes?" Sheer joy.

"Yes." Careful. She stood up again, getting ready to leave.

He jumped up. "Let me walk you out. My car's right out front. Can I drive you to the lounge?"

"No, no, that's fine. I'm fine."

He took her hand and wrapped it around his elbow, leading her out the door and stopping beside what she presumed was his car. Rue felt his height and size against her, her fingers pressed on his bicep.

He must have noticed the discrepancy in their stature too because he said with emphasis, "You're tiny."

She shrugged and smiled.

He said, "Okay, I'll call you. Is there a better time – morning, evening, when?"

"Well, I work during the week, so night is best. Except for Friday and Saturday, obviously."

"Okay, wait, you work another job? Not just the lounge?"

"I have a job downtown."

"Wow, a worker bee! Well, I can't wait to hear more about that and also more about your geriatric activities. Are you headed off to catch the blue-plate special or the five o'clock news?"

"Hey!" she cried, punching his arm.

They both laughed, facing each other. For a second, she sensed (frightening!) that he wanted to kiss her, but she quickly turned to go, taking her cane out and saying, "Okay, well, thanks, talk to you later..."

Before she had a chance to think, he pulled her back, melting her frame into his chest. He said gruffly into her hair, "No. Thank you. I'll call. I promise. Give me a chance. Okay?" It was only an instant, a lightning blip, and he released her. Every synapse on fire, she nodded mutely, unsteadily, and walked away.

❧ Chapter VI ☙

As Rue walked, she tried to unsnarl the cobwebs that had formed in her brain from that hug. It had been so warm and safe in that space with him, just like a cocoon. She felt herself in real danger. How was she to resist? Should she?

She thought back on her limited (well, truly minuscule, basically nonexistent) dating life. Sure, she had met other guys before – the lawyers at the office who'd asked her out, the men at the lounge catcalling her, the random guy at a restaurant or café or museum, Vy's attempt at setups. But she had thwarted their advances, maybe not consciously, maybe not because she wanted to put them off, maybe simply because she was afraid. Wasn't it better – safer in her compact, neat, autonomous little world of routine and order? She had always known, even as a child, that she wasn't like other girls. She wasn't boy crazy in school, didn't feel the need to flirt or dress provocatively or say witty things. Yes, of course, she wanted to look good and she wanted to be attractive, but being blind, she wasn't coerced by the physical, outward appearance of people, and she didn't feel the need to pander to the visual in that way. When she thought about sex, it was about the other senses being fired – the smell, the voice, the touch of a man. And about kindness – was he sensitive, thoughtful, selfless? In reality, up until now, these thoughts were kept tightly sealed inside of her – she had had almost no real-life experience to test them or to execute their powers. They were vague and blurry in her brain, tucked in the dark recesses, rarely tapped.

And here was a tall, strong man who put his body around her, sending a thousand thunderbolts into her core. It was so foreign! And so spectacular! She'd never felt this way before, and it scared her to death.

Just then her phone rang. Hot guy! OMG, she needed to update her contacts.

She picked up.

"Hello?"

"Hi, just wanted to make sure I had the right number."

"We did talk earlier, remember? What, too many Rues in your contact list?"

"Funny. No, I wasn't sure if I'd have to dial you up later on your analog line."

Rue chuckled, "Haha. Very funny. Hasn't that joke run its course by now?"

"Yes, yes, it has. Hey, though, seriously, I wondered, I feel like maybe I've messed things up."

"Um…no…no…what do you mean?" Rue stumbled, rather loosely denying it. He was still struggling to find his way, wasn't he?

Instead of answering, he said, "By the way, you smell so good. I cannot believe you smell even better than you look." The charm offensive. Of course. Standard protocol.

She said, "Thanks."

"So, what time can I call you tonight?" asked Josh.

"Tonight? I was thinking more like next week sometime…," replied Rue, slight tension in her voice.

"Well, what I'd really like is to come see you play tonight—"

Rue cut him off. "No, please don't…I mean, I appreciate it and all, it's just that…it would make me uncomfortable." What happened to just talking on the phone? He was a child. She changed the tone of her voice slightly, thinking apparently he needed kid gloves, literally and figuratively, she continued, "What I mean is, I only get one break and the rest of the time I'm playing, so it isn't the right environment for…socializing. In fact, I need to get going now…"

"Sure, sorry. If I must wait…it won't be easy, but I'll shoot for tomorrow then," he said.

She smiled and said, "You'll be alright. Okay, tomorrow then. Bye now."

"Okay, bye," he replied and hung up.

She turned the corner, breathing hard, crossed the street next to the Fairmont Hotel, and grabbed Hayes's elbow at the entrance. He began to ask her about her day when her phone dinged. She let out an annoyed expletive – was he texting her now? Then she apologized to Hayes – no, not you, Hayes, sorry. She waited until she was settled into a barstool to pull out her phone. She sighed – it was only Vy asking, "Did you call him?"

Rue texted back, "Yes, I called him, and I met him!"

"YOU DID? OMG, WHOA! 411. STAT. EVERYTHING. NOW." Really, Vy.

"Calm down. Stop all-capping me – my screen reader's going haywire. It was just coffee. Nothing more."

"Can I call you? Too hard to do this over text."

"No, Vy, I'm at the lounge. I'll call you tomorrow. Okay?"

"Whump-whump. NO, not okay. But okay."

"How was the museum? Did Kaylen have fun?"

"Yes. She and Momma dragged me ALL over that place. My feet still hurt. But enough about that – tell me more about Mr. Hundred Bucks."

"Too much to type. I will say he's talkative and funny, but he's a complete player, you know the type, a man on a mission. That's all I've got. I'll call you tomorrow."

Before Rue could turn her phone off, Vy texted back, "A man-whore? That's perfect! That's exactly what you need."

"Goodbye, Vy." Rue shook her head.

The restaurant filled up quickly that night. Of course, it seemed that despite herself, every song she played had some sexual innuendo or overtone. It was as if she had been given a shot of "Love Potion Number Nine," and as she laughed to herself, she sang the song of the same name. Some small fissure had formed in her being – a new tingle that stemmed from that hug – so unfamiliar and yet so homey, like a new blanket hot out of the dryer. When she tried to shake the feeling, she found herself getting lost in it, letting it wash over her – feeling his strong arms around her, her face breathing into his wide chest, his voice in her hair. It had been so long since anyone had touched her that way, if ever.

Finally, sometime after midnight, Rue went home exhausted. She noticed she had missed three calls from Vy, who apparently presumed there was more of a scoop to tell. She would call tomorrow and disappoint her. Rue walked up the stairs to her apartment, quickly took off her clothes, and fell into bed where Hank had already curled in a tight ball on her spare pillow. She made sure her phone was in airplane mode and dropped into a deep slumber.

Rue got up Sunday morning and made herself breakfast. She was still in a strange dream state, thinking about Josh and thinking about what it would be like to fall off a tightrope wire with no net. As she pondered, she turned her phone back on, heard it ding, and then heard her coffee mug tap against

Great Aunt Louise's jewelry box, which was still sitting on the kitchen table. She got up and opened it. She toyed with several flowered broaches that were resting on top and felt along a set of fake pearls, the enamel chipping off the beads. Underneath the costume jewelry was some sort of postcard and several brochures or programs. Then she lifted a shelf to reveal several rows of small velvet-covered slots. These were filled with clip-on earrings, coins, pins, buttons – miscellaneous "crap," as Daniel would say. But in one slot, there was a ring wrapped in a piece of silk – had Daniel and Cathy missed this? Rue knew this ring. It had been her mother's. Rue sat down and placed the ring on her middle finger, feeling the neat row of diamonds encased in a filigreed setting. It was a square art deco design with tiny rectangles etched on the band. Rue remembered playing with it as a child when it was on her mother's finger. Rue felt a wave of memory flow through her – Oh, Mom! Where are you now when I need you? A small sob escaped from Rue's mouth. Just then her phone rang, causing her to scream.

"Call from Josh Quinn" drummed out of the phone. She was thankful she had used her break last night to update his name in her contacts.

Rue wiped her eyes, cleared her throat, and answered, "Hello."

"Hello! Good morning. Or is it afternoon? Anyway, how are you? Did you get my text?" Josh sounded fresh as a daisy. There was a lot of noise in the background, though, and he was out of breath.

"No, sorry, I just got up. I haven't listened to my phone yet. Where are you?"

"At the airport. I'm walking to my gate right now. Sorry, I know it's loud. I'm catching the one fifteen to Chicago. Wait, you just got up?"

"Yep, Sundays are my day to sleep in."

"Nice. So, hey, I feel so bad about yesterday. I'm such an ass. I have no social graces, and I talk too much. Will you forgive me? I swear, as soon as I'm back from this trip, I'll make it up to you. Okay?"

"Sure," said Rue, thinking well, he's persistent, I'll give him that.

"Good. So how was last night? Any more hundreds?"

"Of course, that happens every night."

"Hey now! Who's trying to get in on my gig?"

"Don't worry, the others requested nursery rhymes."

"Phew!" he laughed. "Child's play."

"Uh-huh. It was a good night, good tips, the usual crowd," replied Rue. Then she redirected with, "Why are you flying to Chicago?"

"Oh, I guess I haven't told you that yet, have I?" He laughed breathlessly. Rue could tell he was walking fast – she felt her watch and it said twelve forty. "I…I…uh, sold a big package to this company a while ago, but the sale finally went through last week, so I'm headed out there with my team – the engineers, designers, and coders – to build out the requirements. I'm only there to grease the skids a little before they get started."

"Wow, sounds interesting. So, that client yesterday at the Cliff House, Dennis? Was that his name? You sold him some software?"

"What?" There was an announcement overhead. Then he said, "Hey, sorry, I have to go. I'm at my gate and we're boarding."

Rue said, "Okay," but he broke off for a second to talk to someone.

He asked, "We'll talk tonight?"

Rue wasn't sure – was he talking to her? He repeated, "Hey, Rue, can I call you tonight?"

"Oh, sorry, yes, that's fine."

Then the phone disconnected. Hmm, okay. Seemed strange that he bothered to call in the first place if he knew he could only talk for a few rushed minutes. Oh well, maybe as a sale rep, this was his MO – multitasker extraordinaire. Whatever. She shrugged and got up from the table, putting the ring and the rest of the contents back into the jewelry box. She fed and played with Hank for a few minutes. Then she got ready (realizing half the day was gone!) and walked to the market.

Willie, the owner's son, helped Rue walk around the store and fill her basket. This was a ritual. Rue guessed Willie was around twelve years old (although when he first started helping her, he could barely talk in full sentences, so they were old friends by now). He would make suggestions along the way. "Miss Rue, the cantaloupes are perfectly ripe today. What about a loaf of sourdough? Fresh from the bakery this morning. You need any flowers? Dad just filled the bucket outside with gladiolas. What about cereal? We have this new homemade granola that's really yummy. My favorite has almonds and chocolate pieces in it." He was sweet. Rue hated to say no to him on anything, but then she could only carry so much – it was a two-block walk back to her place and hard to do with a handful of groceries in one hand and the cane in the other. And she always bought her fruit from the landlady, Mrs. Wai Hing (Chen's mom), because it was easier to carry up from the ground floor than from two blocks away. So, Rue only purchased the necessities from Willie and headed home.

Back in her apartment, she heard Hank swiping at her spider plant, so she scolded him, thinking he was probably ruining her babies. She unloaded her groceries and called Vy. She told her everything about Josh.

Vy's only commentary on the whole thing was, "He's out of town now?! That stinks. How are you going to get to know him?"

Rue replied, "Virtually."

Vy laughed and said, "Yes, how very sanitary."

After Rue hung up, she started the streaming music on her speaker system (set to "shuffle") and began preparations for her homemade tomato sauce. She was getting hungry, and this was one her favorites. She pulled out her tactile measuring cups and spoons, her pots and pans, cutting board with food chute, tomato slicer, talking thermometer, splatter shield, and liquid level indicator, and spent the next half hour prepping the ingredients. Finally her big pot was full, so she set it to simmer on the stove and reached for her raised number timer, setting it to ding at ninety minutes.

She rinsed her hands, dried them off, and sat down at her drafting table to work on her stencils. First, she stretched a piece of canvas onto an eight-inch by eight-inch pre-cut board and stapled it to the wooden frame so it was flat and taut in front. Then she felt the braille on her acrylic paint tubes and squirted out a few colors onto her palette board. Pulling one tulip stencil from her purse and using masking tape, she adhered it to the canvas. She dabbed her paintbrush onto the right side of the palette where the bright yellow was and then painted thickly with precision over the petals so that the color pushed through the open slots onto the canvas. Using each color to complete the other components of the flower, she finally set the canvas aside to dry. Then she spent the next half hour working on an earlier canvas, feeling along the ridges of three pink zinnias in order to layer on the fourth and final one, creating a bouquet.

Rue got up occasionally to stir the sauce, sometimes dancing to the music, sometimes lifting a completed canvas from the stacks on the floor to touch the crusty parts, sometimes petting Hank, who sat contentedly on the couch licking his fur. Some were flowers, some were animals, some were insects. She laughed to herself because, more than likely, some were truly heinous blobs of horror. How would she know? She simply liked the way they felt and her sense of accomplishment when they were done.

When the timer when off, she put a pot of water onto the stove and sunk her sensor in to let her know when it was boiling. She proceeded to rinse off her paintbrushes in the sink. Her phone rang, causing Hank to jump off the couch and knock something over. She'd have to investigate that later. Josh! She felt her watch – five forty-five. Had he just landed?

"Hello," said Rue.

"Hi there. I made it to the windy city. Just got checked into the hotel."

"Great, glad you made it safely."

"Yep, it's almost eight here."

"Oh, of course, the time change."

"Uh-huh."

Silence. Awkward.

Finally, he asked, "How are you?"

"Oh, fine."

"What have you been doing all day?"

"Um, not much..." She didn't think he'd want to hear about her boring Sunday.

The line was quiet again.

He said with a laugh, "Well, okay then."

Rue waited and then asked politely, "So, have you been to Chicago before?"

"Sure, tons of times. Good pizza. You been?"

"Nope, never."

Silence again. God, this was going to be a short and painful call. She scrambled for something to say. She asked slowly, "You going to dinner with your, um, team tonight?"

"Naw, I just ordered room service. I told them to go without me." Then he said, "Listen, I want to be...polite...you know, because normally I tend to... dominate the conversation, but do you mind if I just...jump in?"

She smiled. Ah-ha! Okay, now things were starting to make sense. She said readily, "Yes, please."

"Okay, let's start from the beginning. You're from San Francisco – where did you say again – out near the Presidio? Wasn't that some type of military base? Is your dad in the military?"

"Oh, um, no...I, uh, I mean, no, my dad wasn't in the military, and we didn't live at the Presidio – just a house nearby. Presidio Terrace. And actually, the Presidio was mostly a park back then – well, and George Lucas."

"Oh yeah! That's right. I almost forgot – I need to take that San Francisco bus tour again."

She laughed. "Yes."

"So, Presidio Terrace – kind of an upscale area, isn't it?"

"I suppose. We only lived there until I was ten."

"Where did you go after that?"

"Boarding school."

"Wow, pleated skirts?"

She smiled. "Uh-huh."

"Okay, let's see…when's your birthday?"

"October eighth."

"And your favorite time of year?"

"Fall."

"Ah-ha! I knew it!" he exclaimed.

She had to ask, "How did you know?"

"Wait, I have a theory. What time of day were you born – morning, afternoon, or evening?"

"Oh, I'm not sure, I think maybe evening. Why?"

"And what is your favorite time of day?"

"Yes, I see…evening, I suppose."

"There it is! I've been conducting a poll. My theory is that everyone's favorite time of year is the season they were born in, and their favorite time of day is when they were born. Makes sense, right? Like, it was the moment you hit the ground running, so of course your body is wired toward it, like a magnetic pull or something."

She smiled. He was so giddy. She said, "Now you have to tell me yours."

"August second, eight twenty-five a.m., so summer and morning, of course."

"Of course," she said with a chuckle. "Where were you born?"

"Arizona. I'm a transplant. Couldn't you tell? I moved to San Francisco, let's see, about seven years ago."

"For work?"

"Yep, I was recruited by TorkOps right out of college. I grew up in Flagstaff and went to the University of Arizona, in Tucson. My senior year, they sent someone out to interview computer science majors because they were so hard-up for coders back then, you know, Java and all that, so I moved here. Eventually I worked my way up the chain and ended up in sales. It's been quite a ride."

"I bet. Sounds interesting…," she said, thinking, I have no idea what he's talking about.

"Yep, it's not bad…I enjoy it. What about you? You have that singing gig at the Big 4, but didn't you mention another job downtown?"

"Yep, the Big 4 is sort of a side job. I work full-time at a law firm as—"

Before she could say any more, he interrupted incredulously, "Are you a lawyer? No way, that's amazing! I knew you were smart as a whip the moment I met you. Wow, a lawyer…that's impressive!"

Rue sighed. "No, I'm not a lawyer," she corrected. "I said I work at a law firm. I'm a receptionist."

"Oh," he laughed apologetically. "Sorry, I guess I should shut my trap. Can you tell I'm a salesman? Yippity-yap. No excuse, I realize, I'm sorry."

"It's okay. Sorry to disappoint you."

"What? No. You didn't. You're a receptionist. Cool. Isn't that kind of… difficult…I mean, sorry to ask this, but…isn't that difficult…being blind?"

"Sometimes," she admitted, "but I'm used to it, I can hear people when they come in. Or in some cases, haha, I smell them before I hear them."

"Whoa, that must be fun! I'll have to watch what cologne I wear around you."

She wondered if he was flirting. She remembered the hug and couldn't imagine anyone smelling better. She said, "None at all is perfectly acceptable. I'm rather hypersensitive when it comes to smells, actually."

His voice dropped an octave, "Uh-hmmm, good to know." Oh, the relish in his voice! Had he read her thoughts? A pause, then he said smoothly, "Tell me about your job."

"Well, when I first moved downtown, I was working at that nursing home I mentioned as an aide, but it didn't pay very well, so I started applying for other jobs, and it was kind of crazy because I sent out four hundred fifty resumes before I got the job at the law firm."

"Four hundred fifty!"

"Give or take. Not that I was overly qualified for much, but still, for all the working world thinking it's 'inclusive' or 'diverse' or whatever the new catch-phrase is, it certainly doesn't know what to do with a blind person."

"Wow, that really sucks. So, how did you get the job?"

"I made one change. I took the words 'I am blind' off my resume, and boom! Got several callbacks right away."

He laughed. "God! Really?"

"Really," she said flatly. "I had two or three phone screenings, then was asked to come in for several live interviews, so of course at that point, I let them know. It was still crazy because two of those interviews were kind of awful – not because I was nervous, but because they were! They didn't know how to see past my blindness. Once I let on that I was blind, I think some of them were just trying to fill some type of quota. It was so disappointing."

"So, what was different about the law firm?"

"In a word, Janie. She's my boss and she's great. She did the interview, she didn't care that I was blind – I mean, she cared, but she didn't treat my blindness as separate and distinct from me. She just wanted to make sure I was a good fit for the job. She hired me on the spot. And that was…let's see…over ten years ago now."

Rue paused, hearing Josh breathing on the phone. This was the most she'd revealed about herself (to a relative stranger) in her life. After several moments of silence, she said quietly, "Josh?"

"Yes, hi, I'm here. I'm thinking – wow, you're quite extraordinary, aren't you?"

Had she been bragging? She said, "What? No, not at all. I'm suppose I'm just like everyone else."

"I don't know about that…I'm beginning to feel unworthy. You're so strong and persistent and independent!" He waited a minute for that to sink in, and then he said with a laugh in his voice – right out of *Wayne's World*, "I'm not worthy, I'm not worthy."

"Ha! Come on," she shrugged and laughed. She found herself smiling. He was quite nice, she reflected, and then she asked, "I take it you have to talk a lot for your job?"

"Well, yeah, that, and I also grew up in a house full of people, so talking comes naturally to me. I had to insert myself into every conversation, every situation, just to get a word in edgewise."

Her water sensor was going off. She said, "Would you mind hanging on a second? I need to tend to something in the kitchen."

"Sure."

She put the pasta in the boiling water and stirred in some kosher salt, lowering the burner to medium. She gave the sauce a stir and tasted it. Coming along nicely. Back on the phone and not skipping a beat, she asked, "Big family?"

Lowering his voice, "No, I grew up in a brothel." When she laughed, he said, lower, "Let's schedule your tutorial."

"Um," she replied enigmatically, with a tingle down her spine. How to respond to that? She remained mute.

He continued, back in his normal voice, "Yeah, back in Flagstaff, I was the youngest of seven. And my grandmother also lived with us. We had a small four-bed, one-bath ranch. Kind of crowded."

"Wow. Ten of you in one house! I can't even imagine. What did your parents do?"

"Mostly smacked us around a lot," he said flatly.

Rue laughed.

"Well, no, not exactly. They did discipline us a lot, but we certainly deserved it. Especially me. I was a bit of a live wire. Out of control like ninety percent of the time. It didn't help that we were poor. I mean, we had enough to eat and all, but we didn't have any of the extras, you know? And since I was the baby, I got all the hand-me-downs. I don't remember ever having a new pair of shoes or a new coat. And this was back during the Air Jordan days – so humiliating, wearing hand-me-down Kmart sneaks – you have no idea! Are you crying yet? Yeah, I was the brunt of many jokes. Wah-wah-wah."

"Aww," Rue said sympathetically, with a twinge of sarcasm.

"What? You don't believe me?" he countered with false hurt.

"Oh, I don't know…," Rue said, remembering back to some tortured moments from her own childhood. She didn't think what he was alluding to was quite the same.

"Well, okay, so I wasn't bullied exactly, but I was made fun of – mostly by my brothers and my buddies. Those pussies! Never fear, though, I make them pay for it now – every time I go home and see them. They didn't realize the short, scrawny pipsqueak from elementary school was going to grow up to be six foot three and strong as an ox."

Yes, you are, she thought, remembering the hug. She breathed.

Misinterpreting that, he said thoughtfully, "I suppose you had some rough times growing up…?"

She snapped back to reality and confirmed, "Yeah, well, you know how kids can be…"

"Yes. Cruel. That must have been awful."

"It made for some interesting times at the playground," she said with a bitter laugh. Then she changed the subject, "So, what did your parents do – for a living?"

He said, "Oh! Is that what you meant before? Haha. What they do, yes, they both still work. Dad's a mechanic, and Mom's a schoolteacher. He was all about discipline, and she was all about education. It was a good combo. You know, all seven of us have college degrees, which is kind of amazing considering our lack of money. We had to figure out how to get scholarships and financial aid and all that."

"Hmm," she said, impressed, "that's great."

He groaned with a laugh, "Yes, you would think so, but then I also had to know how to fix a car, stock grocery shelves, wait tables, work an assembly line, oh and let's not forget, stand on the street dressed as a foot-long hotdog holding a sign that says, 'Largest Wieners in Town.' Right. That too."

She laughed, imagining him. "Wow, did you at least get free hotdogs?"

"Sure, all I could eat, which is why I can't stand the sight of a hotdog now."

"I bet. And your family, they still live in Arizona?"

"Yep, every one. In fact, my oldest brother just moved back in with my parents and brought his two boys with him. Of course, Mom and Dad weren't too happy about his divorce, but they love having the grandkids. The rest of my siblings live a few miles away."

"Wow, you must be the black sheep?" Rue asked with a chuckle.

"Pretty much. They think I lost my mind when I moved out here. And that I travel so much for my job...they can't even begin to understand..."

"You do? Do you get sick of it?"

"Sometimes. I'm probably on the road ten to fourteen days a month. Last week's conference at the Moscone Center was nice because I slept in my own bed every night. My flatmate, Harsha, he works for TorkOps too, but he doesn't have to travel as much – he gets the place to himself most of the time. It's a great deal for him."

Josh paused for a minute. While he had been talking, Rue had set the phone down on the counter in the kitchen in order to drain the pasta in the sink with her colander.

He asked, "What are you doing?"

"Actually," confessed Rue, speaking louder for him to hear on the speakerphone, "I'm about to sit down to dinner. I don't mean to be rude, but can we talk later or tomorrow?"

"Of course," said Josh quickly, but with a note of regret in his voice. "But I feel bad – I was going to grill you about your life, and all I've learned so far is that you like fall and that you grew up near George Lucas's studios. Maybe I should call you back in an hour?"

Rue thought about that for a minute…she didn't mind talking to him – he did have a nice voice, and she was finding his life story kind of interesting (so different from hers). And she was still pondering that comment about the brothel tutorial. But it was Sunday night, and after dinner she wanted to finish painting one more tulip before going to bed. While these thoughts were rolling through her head, she heard a noise at his end, someone knocking loudly.

He said, "Hey, someone's at my door, probably room service. Hang on." Rue wanted to say goodbye, but he didn't give her the chance, dropping the phone. The voices in the background were muffled, but she heard him talking in a way that didn't sound like room service. Rue couldn't detect any of the words, but the tone was oddly angry.

Suddenly she heard him pick up the phone and say with a quick whisper, "I'll call you tomorrow, okay?" Click.

Rue touched her phone, thinking, oh I see, now it's tomorrow, is it? What was that was all about? She felt her watch – it was nine twenty-five there. Who was at his door at that time of night if not room service? Did she care enough to speculate? After a second, she thought to herself with a twinge of terror, yes, I do care! She took a deep breath as she plated her meal on a TV tray and thought, heck, why am I invested? There's no reason to care so much, and *certainly* no reason to be paranoid. Maybe the room service order was wrong.

Still contemplating, Rue ate her meal while listening to an episode of *Southern Charm* and to Hank's bell jingle as he pawed his food around in his dish. After cleaning up the kitchen, she went back to her drafting table to work on the tulip and then got ready for bed. Later, when Hank jumped up in bed with her and she hadn't yet fallen asleep, she asked him, "Hank, what do you make of it?" He mewed indecipherably and tiptoed away toward her feet. Mysterious cad – a lot of help he was!

Sometime later, as her body and mind finally relaxed, an involuntary sense of heat and longing began to course through her body, triggered by the thought of Josh's voice and deep encircling arms, her face pressed into his warm, strong chest.

Chapter VII

RUE GOT UP AT HER USUAL TIME and got ready for work. Mondays always seemed to come too soon. She was still groggy – it hadn't been the best night of sleep. She wasn't sure what to make of Josh. He seemed so different from her – outgoing, bold, extroverted, but then he was also attractive, sweet, and funny. And that voice, that smell! But there was also that mysterious knock on his hotel room door. In a flash, she wondered if he was thinking of her at this very moment when she was thinking of him, and she felt a chill run up her spine as she sensed the answer was yes.

She went to the kitchen, made coffee, and put a few pieces of bread in the toaster. She opened a can of cat food into Hank's dish and filled his bowl with water as he rubbed against her leg. She peeled an orange and munched on it and wondered how busy it would be at work this week. A short while later, riding on the Muni, Rue was jostled by a gruff, smelly homeless man, but she didn't mind. Her thoughts still lingered on Josh.

Later at the office, she logged in and said good morning to the steady stream of attorneys, paralegals, and office workers marching in the door. She checked in several visitors and responded to a few emails. When Mayumi Saito came in, she stopped and talked to Rue for a while. Mayumi was one of the attorneys in the law firm, and she occasionally went to lunch with Rue and Vy. Rue liked Mayumi's soft, quiet demeanor and the fact that she always took time out of her busy day to chat with Rue – not just as the receptionist, nor as the blind woman downstairs, but as a human being. Once, many years ago, Vy had told Rue that Mayumi was one of the best attorneys in the firm.

Rue had asked, "Better than you?"

"Well, I didn't say that," Vy said with a chuckle, "but still, excellent."

"Don't you have to be sort of ruthless to be a good attorney?"

Vy responded, "Yes, that's what Mayumi is!"

"No!" Rue reacted – she didn't believe it – kind, sweet, shy Mayumi?

"Oh yes, it's true. Mayumi's a total shark in the courtroom – you should see her in action. She doesn't give an inch. She will take you *down*. And the amount of research she does – woowee – she buries them with evidence. But that's how she gets them, you know, with her thoroughness. And I think she also throws them off with that soft voice – all timid and reserved, lulls them into a false sense of security – then wham! She slays them. Totally fierce!"

Wow, who knew? You really couldn't judge a book by its cover. As if Rue didn't know that! The other reason Rue liked Mayumi is that she gave Rue work to do. Not sit-here-and-greet-people-work either. Research. Rue was a fast and near-perfect typist, so Mayumi gave Rue transcription work – typing up recordings and notes. But Rue sometimes noticed things while she was typing – inconsistencies in people's stories, dirty dealings, clues, evidence – and pointed them out to Mayumi. After that, Mayumi started loading her up with other assignments. It was interesting, and it certainly made the day go faster. Janie, Rue's boss, she said she didn't mind as long as Rue could keep up with her regular responsibilities.

On this Monday, Mayumi approached Rue, said good morning, and gave her a new assignment. This one sounded juicy. Mayumi sent her a link to a site with several audio files. The conversations recorded on the files were between several different people – interrelated people from the same case. Rue was supposed to flag anything that sounded like a bribe. Mayumi told her it wouldn't be as blatant as "I'll give you this for that" – it would be subtler and more conniving. After the morning rush was over, Rue put in her earpiece and began listening. At first, it was rather boring – just people talking about their daily lives. Rue kept trying to read between the lines, but still…nothing. And some of the files had background noise. She was straining to listen when Vy came in and tapped her on the shoulder, nearly scaring her half to death.

"Ooops, sorry about that. How ya doin'? Working for Mayumi?" Vy asked.

"Yep."

"Nice. So hey," cried Vy, dropping her voice. "I am so proud of you, missy! You went on an official date and everything!"

"Oh please, it wasn't a date – it was just coffee," corrected Rue. "And technically, I only had tea."

"Splitting hairs, splitting hairs," said Vy with a sweep in her voice. "Did he call last night? How long did you talk?"

"Yes, he called, we talked, oh…I don't know…maybe twenty minutes, maybe thirty."

"That's it? Come on, I thought you would talk all night. Didn't you have anything in common? I need details."

Rue said, "Actually, he talked most of the time. He's from Arizona. Has a big family. Works for some place called TorkOps…doing sales or something…I didn't quite understand. But he called me when I was getting dinner ready, so we didn't stay on long. Anyway, he has a nice voice."

"Yes, and a nice bootie."

"Vy!"

"Oh come on, don't tell me you didn't think about that all weekend."

Rue shook her head, grinning, not admitting anything. Instead, Rue asked, "Did you have a nice weekend?"

"Yes, yes, fine," Vy answered with annoyance.

"That good, eh?"

"Mm-hm," Vy grunted. "Mom and Anthony were in rare form. That's all I'll say about that."

Rue said, "So, hey, let's talk more at lunch, okay? I'm trying to get through these recordings, and I haven't made much headway."

"Sure, noon then. Be ready to spill."

"Nothing more to spill, but I can make up some stuff if you like."

"Please do. Make it good. You have, let's see, two hours to spin a tale."

"Will do."

"Later."

"Later gator."

Rue smiled and went back to her research. After a while, the audio files got interesting – in fact, she felt herself blushing – this batch of conversations was personal. Rue wasn't sure how they could possibly have anything to do with corruption or bribery, but she kept her antennae up anyway.

For example, one exchange, between a man and a woman:

"What time you want me up tonight?"

"No earlier than eight – I have practice until seven thirty."

"Perfect. I'll be there. What's on tap?"

"Your choice, baby."

"In that case, the barstool."

"That's where we'll start then. Any particular prep requests?"

"The leopard skin number. And make sure you're clean down there."

"You got it. I'll set the video up in the living room."

"No, on the table."

"Okay. I brought the Jameson and those nuts you like. You bring the dope."

"Yes. Send me a tit pic right now to hold me over."

"You got it. Hang on." Twenty-five seconds elapsed. "How's that?"

"Oh, yeah baby, good one. I'm grabbing my hard dick right now for you."

Rue stopped that recording, feeling her face hot, and instead listened to several others – between several men. Finally, she had a hit:

"How many pallets are they bringing?"

"Two-fifty last time I checked."

"Down to Ojai?"

"Yep, Delaney Street. I got Larry waiting there."

"I'll send my guys in too. What time exactly?"

"Three thirty."

"What's the cut?"

"Twenty percent, but that's assuming Norris follows through. He's been known to welch in the end."

"Well, that's not going to happen this time."

"Okay, if you say so. That's at seven eighteen per, right?"

"Seven eighteen? I thought we agreed to seven twenty."

"I don't know, Miller was confused."

"Why does that not surprise me? Miller's a fucking idiot."

Snort. "Yeah, anyway, I'm not sure what was agreed to."

"Great, now I gotta go there myself to straighten it out. Bunch of fucking incompetent ingrates."

"I mean, I don't know…that's what Miller said."

"Yeah, okay, I got it. I better get going then."

"Okay, bye."

Click.

Rue told Mayumi about the conversation and several other suspicious calls, and Mayumi said, "Jackpot!"

Rue asked, "So, that's what you were looking for?"

"Well, I'll have to verify, but that could definitely be something. You know, I've had three others in my office listen to those recordings already, and they didn't find anything." She leaned over the desk and whispered, "Except for a lot of smutty stuff."

Rue blushed a little and said, "Oh yes, I heard that part too."

"Sorry. You never know what you're going to find..."

"Right," Rue agreed, smiling and trying to get her cheeks to calm down.

"So, do you have time for more this afternoon?"

"Sure."

"Okay, if you go back to the root folder on the site, go into 'Hepper' and there are about twenty more. Different case. Looking for the same stuff, though."

"Okay."

"By the way, I'm going to lunch with you and Vy. She invited me. Do you mind?"

"No, of course not, that would be great. And here she is." Rue heard Vy's shoes and purse coming toward them.

Mayumi laughed and said, "How do you do that?"

Rue shrugged her shoulders and tapped her free ear.

Vy came around Rue's reception desk and grabbed her arm, and they stepped outside. Rue breathed in the dry, clear air. It was a nice February day – not too hot, not too cold. So, essentially like every other day in San Francisco. They headed to the bakery down the street. Vy chatted about her weekend, leaving Rue and Mayumi to listen in contented silence. At least Vy wasn't going to accost Rue right out of the gate about Josh. But when they sat down at a table with their sandwiches in hand, Rue was about to take her first bite when Vy abruptly said to Mayumi, "Rue had a date this weekend."

Rue choked.

"You did?" Mayumi said with curiosity and a little shock.

Rue corrected, "It wasn't a date, but yes, it was something...he gave me a hug at the end."

"Hold up," Vy cried. "He hugged you?! You didn't tell me that! How was it?"

"Warm," Rue answered dryly.

"Warm? That's it?"

"Well, I told you before, he smelled good. And the top of my head only came to his chin, so he's quite tall."

"Yes, he is that."

"When will you meet him again?" asked Mayumi quietly, seizing the moment to speak while Vy was occupied with her food.

"I don't know. He's in Chicago right now for a work trip. We talked on the phone last night. I'm not sure when he'll be back. He said he'd call tonight. We'll see..."

Vy jumped in, "Oh, he'll be wanting to see you as soon as he gets back. I'd bet on it!"

Rue and Mayumi laughed. "No one is asking you to bet on anything," Rue said serenely. Then she asked them both timidly, "I wonder…is there a way to sort of…look into…a person? I mean check on background…to figure out if they're who they say they are? He says he's not married and has worked for this big company for a long time and all that, but how do I really know what he's saying is true? Maybe I'm being paranoid, but I wish there was a way I could *know*, not just assume, he's a good guy. Okay, so I'll admit it," Rue continued with chagrin, "I'm a complete novice when it comes to this dating thing, so I don't know how it works, but do girls nowadays just trust a guy when they meet him in a bar? Do they believe every word he says right off the bat?"

Vy grunted as if Rue was being ridiculous, but Mayumi said thoughtfully, "You know, when we're researching a client or a witness, we check out social media, you know, Google, Facebook, Twitter, and all that, but we also use these sites that look into someone's background to see if they have a criminal record, where they've lived before, and their previous jobs. Some of the sites you have to pay for, but there are quite a few that are free. I could send you the links…"

"Yes, that would be great!" replied Rue eagerly and gratefully.

Vy said flatly, "All I would want to know is when is the next date."

Rue simply smiled. Vy went on to chat more about her weekend until they were safely back in the office, at which point Mayumi said over her shoulder on the way to the elevator, "I'll send you those sites, okay?"

Rue called back, "Yes, thank you!"

The rest of the day progressed quickly. Rue was occupied by the audio files, trying to skim past the irrelevant (but interesting!) conversations to see if she could find anything else that looked like corruption or some vein thereof. Finally, it was time to head home. Waiting at the Muni stop, she heard a text from Josh. It read, "Sorry about last night. I'll call tonight."

Rue wrote back with a thumbs-up emoji.

When she got home, she played for a few minutes with Hank, then opened her laptop. She had typed the list of sites Mayumi recommended into her phone. As she began her search, she was thankful that "Joshua Quinn" wasn't a super common name, although there certainly were enough…it still took her screen reader forever to find the right Josh Quinn. Finally, she hit on him and thought, at least he has a profile and it matches up with what he told her, so he wasn't a complete fabricator.

Compiling the information as she read, she was able to confirm that he was single, from Arizona, and worked for TorkOps. Check, check, check. Then she learned he was super active on social media – could he have any more accounts? Jeesh. How did this man get anything done? Also, apparently, he played volleyball – that explained the broad shoulders – and he went out on the town (a lot!). He commented on everything – sports, beer, food, music, politics, work, travel, women, life, everything. An open book! Not much of a wallflower, this one. Wow, so different from Rue!

He had 3,255 friends on Facebook!

She texted Vy, "How many FB friends do you have?"

"Um, hold on. 485. Why?"

"Josh has 3,255!"

"Holy shitballs! That's a lot. That boy is hooked up!"

"Yes, he is."

"How many do you have?"

"27."

"Wow."

"I know."

"Hey, opposites attract, right?"

"Yes, like the sun and the moon."

"Don't be cute. AND don't be chicken."

"Easy for you to say."

"Bauck-bauck."

"Not. KK, later."

"Later."

Rue sighed and put her phone and laptop down. Seriously, was there really a reason to ride the anxiety train about this? She didn't even know where the train was going. Or if there really was a train. And if there was a train, why couldn't she just ride it for a while – come what may? Life was short! It was time to live it, wasn't it? Sure, that was what she was already doing in her perfectly manageable bubble. But maybe it was time to pop the bubble and see what happened. Maybe…

PART II

Chapter VIII

Monday flew by, and now that it was five o'clock, Josh wasn't sure what to do about tonight. He thought about telling Alyssa he was tired or sick. He wasn't sure what he would tell his team. Who was he kidding? Alyssa and the team would never buy it if he bailed. They had seen him schmoozing the clients all day. He had been on fire – laughing, joking, kicking back. God, he loved his job! It didn't hurt that he had bought the client's whole IT department free VIP tickets to the opening of the latest *Star Wars* movie. Nothing techno geeks liked better than free *Star Wars*. They were like putty in his hands. The boss even mentioned buying five hundred more licenses of TorkOps's software this quarter. Would that get him to his quota? He would need to figure that up…

Back to the topic at hand, Quinn. Come on. Okay, let's think about this… it was only three o'clock in Cali, so he had a good four hours, maybe five, before he had to make his call to Rue. That should be plenty of time to dine and dash and make an excuse to Alyssa. The key was to get back to the hotel by ten. Maybe he could convince the team to eat in the hotel restaurant. Naw, that wouldn't do – Dwayne always wanted Chicago pizza when they were in town. And he always insisted on that place in Rogers Park. Fucking hell – that was halfway across town. They'd have to Uber. Then the obligatory drinks at that dive bar across the street. How was he going to get out of it? Hmmm…

Maybe the brother excuse. That seemed plausible, didn't it? When the team assembled in the hotel lobby a little while later, Josh put on his best sympathy face and said, "Hey, I can't stay out too late, my brother's calling me tonight – going through a nasty divorce…" Alyssa looked at him funny but didn't say anything. The rest of the team said that was fine. It was, after all, a Monday night. Trying to keep his wits about him, Josh drank only two beers at dinner. They wasted twenty minutes while Dwayne posted an Insta-gram of his attempt to shove an entire slice of deep-dish pizza into his mouth. Not to be outdone, Josh posted his own rendition. Both required retakes. A little while later, at the bar, Josh ordered a round of shots. Oh well, one more wouldn't hurt. Or two or three.

At some point during the evening, Alyssa texted him, "What time?"

Not responding, he began a conversation with Sagar about the integration testing schedule. After a few minutes, Josh glanced down at those two words, trying to think what to do. He saw Alyssa's annoyed, impatient look as she walked up to their conversation, pretending to listen. She was so goddamn controlling. Chickenshit that he was, he ignored her on the Uber ride back to the hotel and waited until he was safely in his room. He was hoping his healthy buzz would give him courage. Then he texted Alyssa, "Not tonight. Bro's calling in a few minutes."

She wrote back, "Yeah right. I'm on my way."

Fuck, he thought, she won't take no for an answer!

Just then, she knocked. He sighed and went to the door to let her in.

She came in quickly, closing the door behind her, and wrapped her arms around his neck, pulling his mouth down to hers. He pulled up, but she wouldn't let go.

She said, "Isn't this better than talking to your stupid brother?"

Josh forced a grim smile while extricating himself from her grip. Her shrewd eyes looked into his and then, like a snake in the grass, she struck – yanked his phone off the bed and barricaded herself in the bathroom. The click of the lock was like a death knell. That fucking bitch.

She yelled through the door, cool as a cucumber, "So what's your brother's name again?"

Of course, she has the passcode to his phone, the devious wench. "Rob," replied Josh flatly, thinking, shit, when was the last time I talked to Rob? Two, three weeks ago?

"Open up, Alyssa. Come on, open the door." His voice was strong, but calm, trying to reason with her.

No reply.

"Alyssa, please, come on, you're wasting your time."

Still no reply.

"Come on, sweetheart," he said, thinking it couldn't hurt to butter her up. "Maybe we can fit something in before Rob calls – get that hot ass out here.

You always say we don't have enough time together, and here we are, perfectly alone together, and you're wasting it in the bathroom. Come on!"

Nothing.

"Alyssa! You're starting to kill my buzz," pathetic, shrill.

Crickets.

"Alyssa!" desperate, out of options.

She yelled through the door, "What's Rob's number?"

"I don't know – what the fuck, Alyssa, do you think I have everybody's number memorized?" replied Josh. Methinks I doth protest too much?

"Where does he live?" she hollered calmly.

"Arizona."

"Wife's name?"

"Well, they're divorced now, but Sheila."

"What? You told us they were *going through* a divorce."

"Going through, done – what does it matter? Would you get out here!"

"Don't lie, you shithead," said Alyssa, this time with a low growl.

"What? What are you talking about? I'm not lying. I just want my fucking phone back!" Josh was about to go through the roof now. What was this – the Inquisition?!

A full minute went by in silence. Finally, Alyssa calmly unlocked the door and stepped out, her face a block of ice, handing Josh the phone. She said, "Then why does your brother have a San Francisco area code?"

Josh snatched the phone from her, thinking thank god he hadn't plugged Rue's name into his contacts yet. He said blackly, "What are you talking about? Besides, it's none of your business. Get out. I want to be alone tonight."

"Sure. Sure thing. Whatever you say, Joshie-boy. Go call 'Rob.' Sure, go fuck 'Rob,' for all I care." She grabbed his crotch forcefully as she said the word *Rob*, causing him to curse and swipe her hand away. He grabbed her elbow in a pinch and led her out the door. He growled, "Put your dick away, Alyssa, and get back to your room!" She smiled sickeningly back at him as he closed the door in her face. She laughed on the other side, unfazed. All he could think was, that's what I get for diddling with a hot, impulsive, eager little psychopath. Fuck, fuck, fuck. He would have to smooth it over later. Oh well, whatever – he knew the art of the sale – this was just a hazardous target, like fireworks. He would have to tamper with the fuse later.

Whatever. Women. Without another thought for the crazy one, he called the calm one. Miss Rue. Such a sweet, little name for a sweet, little beauty.

"Hello," Rue answered, sending a spark through the phone into Josh's heart. Such a contrast to the harsh, piercing siren who had just left.

"Hiiii," said Josh, drawing it out with warmth as he lay down on the bed. "What'cha doin'?"

"Not much. Just got off the computer, putting something together for dinner. What are you doing?"

"Lying in bed, thinking of you. Wish you were here."

She laughed and said, "What? Did everyone else turn you down?"

If she only knew, Josh thought. "No, what? Come on. It's you I can't get off my mind. I want to know more, more, more. Sorry about last night. I got pulled away… anyway, tonight, we can talk all night if you like."

"Well, maybe not all night, but sure, let's talk for a while." Rue's voice was open, but also slightly taut, as if she was proceeding with caution.

"Okay. Good. So, let the interrogation begin," said Josh. "What are you eating?"

"A salad. What did you eat?"

"Pizza."

"Oh right – Chicago. Was it good?"

"Yep, yummy. What were you doing on the computer?"

"Oh, just looking up a few things," she answered mysteriously.

"I see…porn?"

She laughed, not skipping a beat, and said, "Yes, blind porn, it's quite descriptive. Of course, it's actually two three-hundred-pound eighty-five-year-olds reading cue cards from separate basements in Tallahassee. But it really gets my juices going."

He laughed out loud. She was funny! "Aren't you a card. Okay, not to change the subject, but where do you work? I mean, which law firm?"

"Dwight, Chitwire, and Goldberg."

"Where is that exactly?"

"Off Market."

"Hmmm. And wait, how long did you say you've worked there?"

"Oh, let's see…ten years."

Josh blew a puff of air out of his mouth and said with a whistle, "No kidding? That's a long time! Did you start there as a kindergartener?"

"Aren't you sweet. Yes, my first assignment was to clean the finger-painting wing."

He smiled at that. "How long have you been at the Big 4 then?"

"Um…I honestly don't remember. Maybe seven or eight years. When I started there, it was still called the Huntington…"

"Wow, you must be very loyal! Ten years at one place and eight at the other."

"I suppose. It's not easy for me to…try new things…so when I do, I usually stick with them."

"That's what I'm betting on," said Josh, his voice an octave lower.

Rue didn't respond to that, but instead said, "Well, you too, right? Didn't you tell me seven years at TorkOps?"

"Yep, seven years…hey! Wait one second…I didn't tell you that. At least I don't think I did…"

"OH!" her voice cracked, "sorry, I thought you had…"

He laughed out loud and said, "Ah-hah! That's what you were doing on the computer! Looking me up! You little detective, you." He was getting somewhere now, wasn't he…

She laughed and admitted, "You caught me. Well, I wanted to make sure I wasn't talking to a serial killer. Can you blame me?"

"Naw…I did the same thing. But what I found out about you was even scarier."

"What? Come on. You're teasing me."

"No, I'm not!" he said with false disdain. Hook, line, and sinker with this one. "I found out you're basically an unknown quantity. Very little to be found. Now, how can I be sure I'm safe with you?"

She replied sarcastically, "I think there's a level of assurance over the phone, isn't there?"

"Hmm, I suppose. Although that hug the other day…way too…what's the word? Too tight!"

He felt her warming up and smiled to himself.

She laughed and said, "Poor baby."

"Uh-huh, I've got my guard up, that's for sure."

She grunted with a chuckle and changed the subject, "So, I take it you like it at TorkOps?"

"Sure, I mean, some days are better than others. Depends on if I meet my quota or not. This year has been great so far."

"Well, that's good. Tell me more about your team. Do they all report to you?"

"No, I don't have any direct reports, thank god. Most of the people I work with, my quote 'team,' they report to the IT director, but I travel with them to make sure the sale is successful."

"And who do you report to?"

"A district sales manager. He lives in Sacramento, so I only see him once a quarter. It's a pretty good arrangement."

"Sounds like it," Rue paused, and then, "so are there a lot of women on that IT team you travel with?"

Josh had a strange flash – does she know about Alyssa? Shit! Wait, how could that be possible? No way! He was being paranoid. Stupid.

He answered with a light ring in his voice, "Jealous, my dear?"

"No, just curious…," she said.

"Well, you've got nothing to worry about. I'm talking on the phone to you right now, aren't I? Giving you my undivided attention. And besides, there's only one girl on the team and she has three chins, a wooden leg, and a snaggletooth. You'd like her. Super nice."

Rue laughed. "She sounds lovely."

"So, hey listen, if you want to meet the team, I'll bring them by the lounge this weekend."

"Oh, that's okay. Bob doesn't like it when too many people talk to me during my set."

"Who is this Bob person? Does he have a wooden leg? If not, I'm gonna give him one!" he exclaimed with false bravado.

"Calm down there, sparky," Rue said with a laugh. "Bob's the bartender, remember? He's sort of my boss at the lounge."

"Oh yeah, I remember him now. Smart man. Bob's great. Bob's the dude. I better get on his good side – he's the one with the drinks! Are you sure you don't want me to bring the team in? I promise I'll pummel them into giving you massive tips. What do you think?"

"Just what I need, a bunch of drunken fools heckling me. I'll pass."

Josh scoffed, "Drunken fools? I'm insulted. We would never…! Well, maybe we would…"

"Uh-huh."

"I get it, though, I make you nervous, don't I? Is that it?"

She laughed and replied, "There's a difference between being nervous and being uncomfortable."

"Is there? Hurts so good…?" Josh said, chuckling.

"Not like that."

"No…not like that…maybe something else," he said, his voice husky. Then suddenly, "If I can't come by the lounge, when can I see you? I need to see you."

Her voice had dropped too – he liked it – soft, receptive. She replied, "Um, when do you get back?"

"My flight's scheduled for Wednesday night, barring any weather issues – you know, this is Chicago in February, so who knows…but let's see, can I take you to dinner Thursday night?"

"Sure," she answered, still soft.

"Good," he said simply, warmly.

There was a moment of stillness on the line. It was the strangest sense with this Rue woman – like nothing he had ever felt before. She wasn't a sledgehammer like most of the women he dated. She was quiet, thoughtful, reticent, shy. But she also seemed funny and adorable and sweet. Did he know how to handle that? He was a bit of a sledgehammer himself. But then again, had he ever been turned down before? Naw, of course not. Should be a snap, right?

He waited for the moment to sink in, then said, "Okay, it's a date."

"Okay," she whispered.

"Hey, Rue?" he asked quietly.

"Yes, Josh?"

"I can't wait."

She paused and didn't say anything. Then, "Me either."

"Okay, I'll talk to you soon."

"Okay."

"Bye."

"Bye."

Chapter IX

It was Monday night, and Alyssa Greer was devising a plan. She had just walked back from Josh's room, the fucker. Did he think she was an idiot?! She had memorized the unmarked number on his phone, sneering at the suggestion that it was somehow related to his brother Rob. Such a joke. As if she didn't know it was a girl. As if he could just tell a bold-faced lie to her like that. She would call the number, but not tonight. She would wait until tomorrow, and in the meantime she would watch Josh's behavior. She wouldn't even acknowledge anything was wrong. Let him sweat it out a little. Let him guess what she was up to. Let him work it out in that pea-sized brain of his. She wasn't his toy – he had to earn his reward. She went to bed working out every possible scenario in her head.

Tuesday morning, Alyssa was all smiles, bright as sunshine. She even wore her little yellow dress – the one she knew Josh liked. It was the dead of winter in Chicago, but she didn't care – she wore a thick coat over the thin material. And it worked – he raised an eyebrow when he saw her and growled a foul comment into her ear. There it was – Josh's real brain – the one in his pants – coming to take the reins. Well, at least that hadn't changed. God, so easy. And he really thought she was over that little tête-à-tête in his room last night. Typical salesman – hadn't even put in the effort and assumed he was winning. Mirror, mirror, on the wall, who's the most conceited of them all?

It was busy that day at the client's office. Embedded in their space, interacting directly with the team, Alyssa and the guys coded and tested in rounds, looping back each glitch until it worked out. It was like banging their heads against the wall until finally the pulpy middle spilled out in a glorious display of gray matter. They barely had time for lunch – wolfed down subs, crumbs falling into their keyboards.

Several times throughout the day, Alyssa took "a bathroom break" and called "Rob," making sure to obscure her own number, thinking she would simply hang up if anyone answered. But it went to voicemail, and someone named Rue said to leave a message. Rue? What kind of name was that? The voice sounded weak, small, childish. Alyssa was pleased – why worry about a little voice like that? Total cakewalk.

The team was at the office until nine, and they decided to bail on dinner. Everyone agreed to be on their own. As soon as Alyssa got back to her room, she called Kevin with the obligatory husband check-in, pretending to sound sincere – she was good at that. She was tired, it had been a busy day (that much was true), she was going to order room service and pass out (that much was subject to interpretation). Had he had a nice day? Oh yes, a new project, great, where was that? Near Stark – right in town then? Uh-huh, interesting. Um, no, no particular plans for the weekend. Why? Oh, well, we'd have to see – might be busy, might have to spend some time at the office – wouldn't know until she was back in town. Flight gets in tomorrow night. Uh-huh. Okay. Yep. Later. Bye.

Hubby call: check. Okay, now Alyssa walked down the hall and knocked softly on Josh's door. He opened it right away and she slipped in.

He stood in front of her and said, "Have you calmed your hormones?"

"What?" she asked, biting her tongue and biding her time. "I'm not sure what you mean. I'm fine. Did you order us anything?"

He scoffed at her, "No. I ordered myself a burger."

Of course he did, the selfish prick. "Fucking hell, Josh. You know our routine. Order me a salad."

He sat down on the bed and grabbed the remote, saying absently, "How was I to know you were over your hissy fit? Whatever…you order it. I'm tired."

"Fine," Alyssa answered, restrained. She called and placed the order.

She lay down beside him, and they both stared at the TV – a standoff of sorts. Finally she said, "What's your deal?"

He looked at her disinterestedly and said, "What?"

"What?! What?!" she repeated, ticked off. "You know, we only have a small window of time together, and you're sitting here watching fucking TV. Do you think I have nothing better to do with my time?"

He looked at her and said, "I'm getting a little sick of your attitude, that's all."

"My attitude? Really?" she cried. "Listen, I can't imagine why you're pissed at me. You're the one fucking other women."

"First of all, I told you last night I was just trying to talk to my brother. Second, no matter what I do, it is none of your *goddamn* business, and third, Alyssa, you seem to forget you're fucking *married*, remember? Looks who's calling the kettle black, you hypocrite. I don't need *you* to tell me what I can and cannot do. Clear?"

Alyssa sat in frustrated silence. This was the argument they always came back to – he just loved to throw her marriage up in her face. He knew how unhappy she was – and yet he worked that guilt bullshit on her to justify his own bad behavior. Fucker.

Finally, after a few minutes, she unclenched her jaw, sighed and rolled over on top of him, saying, "Let's not fight."

He watched her, still pouting, as she sat up on her knees above him. She waited a moment, pushing her crotch into his. Then she slowly pulled her dress over her head, letting it drop to the floor. She took her thick blond hair out of its clip, and it cascaded down her back in a wave. His eyes softened as he regarded her thickly. She cupped her breasts in her bra, pinching the nipples, and he reached up to caress one, but she grabbed his hand, guiding it lower instead, helping it under her panties. His face became slack, his eyes closed, and he groaned, feeling his way into the warm, wet space there. She kissed him, pushing her tongue into his mouth, and he promptly flipped her on her back, his one hand raising up inside her while the other pressed roughly into her bra. She lay back, fully prone and prostrate.

Sometime later, they were just finishing up, still breathing hard, when room service arrived. Alyssa snuck away to the bathroom, and Josh went to the door in his boxers. They ate their dinner side by side in bed, watching basketball, feeling sated and easy again. She wondered if she should bring up the Rue woman with the little voice. She thought about it for a few minutes but decided, why rock the boat? Whoever she was, he certainly wasn't thinking about her now. And she was probably just another passing fad for him. She knew there had been others – flashes in the pan, not worth a second thought. Who gave a shit what he did on his own time? Didn't mean a thing. She was with him now. And she would be with him going forward.

When the game ended, Josh immediately rolled over and fell asleep. Alyssa stayed up thinking. She remembered back to the time when Josh came into her life. It was right after her first affair ended – the earlier one had been with a financial analyst she'd met in a bar. He had been married too and, after a few months, had decided to work it out with his wife. Alyssa had enjoyed it while it lasted but wasn't too broken up when they called it quits.

When Alyssa started working for TorkOps, she had been assigned to a different team from Josh's. But the company was growing fast, and after a year they reorganized, placing Alyssa as a software engineer on Josh's team. Right from the beginning, she targeted Josh like a heat-seeking missile. He was hot as hell, tall, dark, and a kick-ass salesman. He would be a perfect boy-toy, especially on their long, boring-as-fuck work trips. What could be better?

In the beginning, she bided her time – gallivanting around, torturing him – wearing her tightest tops and shortest skirts. Leaning over his keyboard, her breasts an inch from his face, so he could smell her. "Accidentally" walking her ass into his hand when they were leaving the building one night and then laughing together about it. She even got invited to that football party over at Josh and Harsha's place – she was the only girl. She was in her element. She knew more about sports than half the guys there. As the night wore on, the drinks flowed, the best team was winning, and Alyssa ended up in Josh's lap. Oh, it was only a split second – a trip over his coffee table and whoops, spilling backward across his knee. But he took his time with his palms helping her up. There was no denying the lusty look in his eyes. And in hers.

He was plenty hot and bothered by the time he made his first move a week later. It was on their third out-of-town trip, this one to Minneapolis. A night out dining and drinking with clients and there he was, knocking on her hotel room door. She saw his eager smile through the peephole and opened the door wide. Without a word – it was like an explosion – he grabbed her up in his arms, suctioned his lips to hers, and slammed her down on the bed, tearing her clothes off. She didn't resist – she relished it. It was over in a flash, and they lay side by side, laughing at each other, disheveled and sweating.

Now, all these months later, they were still banging like rabbits. But unlike her other affair, she wanted Josh. Not just these dalliances – although they were spectacular in and of themselves – but she wanted more. She wanted all of Josh. The whole package. She didn't want him to be with anyone else. She didn't want him to think of anyone else. She wanted to be the first thing he thought of when he woke up and the last thing he thought of before bed. And she wasn't going to take less. It was all or nothing. In her mind, life had screwed up the time line and trajectory for both them. By some cruel turn of fate, she had ended up with her namby-pamby, boring-ass husband, Kevin, and Josh had ended up with this crazy, freewheeling bachelor life. Clearly, they should have been with each other all along. They were each other's exact equal and were meant to merge. So what that it hadn't happened that way so far? Sure, they should have been living in a big ol' house by now, with a white picket fence and a couple of brats running around. Sure, they should have been the envy of all her friends and family. Instead, she was biding her time – she would have her do-over, her mulligan. She would have her Rembrandt, and it wouldn't be a forgery – it would be the real deal. None of this phony bullshit she was living today. She would have her masterpiece – it was only a matter of time. She only had to be patient, be smart, be persistent, be the conqueror.

Yeah sure, her parents would be disappointed in her – her failure to make her marriage work – and they would be angry over Alyssa's recklessness and all that money spent on the wedding. What would the neighbors say? What would her sisters say? Divorced after only a few years – scandalous! But Alyssa didn't care. It was a piece of paper – it could be torn up as easily as it was signed. Like a work project, she would plan it out, work through the steps in the right order, and make sure all the *i*'s were dotted and the *t*'s crossed. Boom, done. Easy-peasy. So what if there was collateral damage? She couldn't help that, and that wasn't her concern right now. The concern was to get the prize.

Of course, poor, hapless Kevin was clueless. As was Josh. She was working the plan – she needed Kevin to stay in the dark, and she needed Josh to fall in love. She could tell Josh was on the cusp. They were in a wonderful routine right now – the sex was great; so were the secrets they shared, the intimate moments, the lusty stares and prods in hidden places. She knew he wanted more – why wouldn't he? She was sensational! He'd even given up his little traipses with the tramps – the past several months, they had dwindled down to nothing. She monitored him closely, and up until this latest skank, Rue, he was free and clear. In fact, lately in his fervor he had even gotten sloppy, calling Alyssa at home, whispering to her at work, shooting her looks in front of the team that could only be interpreted as partly pornographic. Dumbass. She had scolded him – not that he listened – he was threatening to ruin it all. He said only Harsha knew and no one else, said they were fine – she was just being paranoid. She wasn't sure about that – certainly some of the guys at work suspected – they weren't blind – but luckily, they didn't go blab if they did know. Alyssa knew them; stagnant and stuck in the missionary position at home with their wives, they were probably envious, living vicariously through Josh. And Josh just scoffed – he didn't care if they knew! Let them watch and be jealous, the sad fuckers. She tried to reason with him – they could both lose their jobs, not to mention Kevin could find out. Josh's response was, who cares about the job – they could both go somewhere else in a heartbeat. And as for Kevin, who gave a shit – wasn't she miserable anyway?

Yes, that was true. Well, not miserable – just bored stiff. What had she been thinking, marrying her steady, stable, standard (cookie-cutter) college boyfriend and moving out here with him? Away from family, away from friends, away from fun. At the time, it seemed like the right thing to do – land that wedding before anyone else did. Oh yes, her sisters had been so jealous! But now, looking back, what had been her big hurry? Now she was stuck, and she had so much more life to live, so many more things to experience. How could she do that with a ball and chain around her neck? The only thing keeping her fresh and happy these days was this affair. At least with Josh, she knew life would never be boring. She was holding her cards close to her vest. Kevin didn't suspect a thing – she made sure of that – even with Josh's recklessness. She always deleted everything from her phone involving Josh straight afterward. She was thorough about all the logistical things, but right now she was still working on slotting the chess pieces into place – waiting for the final checkmate.

Lying next to Josh, looking at his chiseled jaw, rugged chest, and the dark feathered hair that fell over his forehead, Alyssa thought god, he is a good-looking man! That was somewhat of a hindrance. No matter where he went, he garnered attention, as did she. But he seemed unable to ignore it. Such a man-whore – needy, restless, relishing the stares and praises, wanting all eyes on him. Was this Rue skank another fawn to lay down at his feet? If only he wasn't so indulgent. Never a thought to set aside the compliments, to walk away. Just the smallest inch, and he took a mile. No self-control! At least with the other whores, Alyssa knew Josh was just passing the time – feeding an urge, winning a conquest. But she had a strange feeling about this new one, this Rue. She had detected, if only for an instant, something new in his eyes and in his defensiveness. Something that pissed Alyssa off. She noticed it the other day when he was talking on the phone in the airport and then again when she came to his room the night before. What was it? The slightest glowing heat in his eyes. A certain warmth. He was having to work to win her. Usually, it came so easily for him. Maybe this one was playing hard to get.

She knew that drove him crazy. Who was this Rue, after all? Certainly with that little name and that little voice, there could be no threat, right? Alyssa fell asleep with that comforting thought in her head.

✣ Chapter X ✣

Kevin Warren was standing in the apartment Tuesday evening, looking at a black-and-white photo of a banyan tree. Look at that thing! How did something so huge and foreboding stand so delicate and inscrutable? Why did the roots grow up instead of down? Why so many roots? Why were the roots outside the soil instead of safely ensconced in it? For goodness' sake, how did the colossal thing stay stuck in the ground? It was as if it had grown its own training wheels. Why? For what purpose? To withstand treacherous typhoons and hurricanes? The heat, the sun, the insects? It must be what – seventy-five or a hundred years old, maybe more. But those roots, roots, roots!

He remembered back to the day (many years ago, a lifetime ago) when he took the photo walking through Marie Selby Gardens in Sarasota, Florida. He had been on a spring break trip with his parents. They'd let him go off on his own for a few hours, supposedly to take some shots for his photography class, but really he just wanted to get away. He wasn't much of a beach person, and he had been in the car with them and his brother for nearly sixteen hours, so he was antsy. They let him go, and he was rewarded with a beautiful, dry spring day spent wandering through the greenhouses filled with orchids (his camera lens steaming up – too humid in there to get a good photo). Then onto the butterfly garden out front – what was that orange one? He'd had to look it up on his phone – an orange fritillary. Then a yellow tiger swallowtail and a monarch. The camera had no problems with steam outside in the yard – spectacular colors in those flighted friends.

Eventually, he made it past the mangroves (snapped a stellar shot of a little green heron standing stock-still) and stepped out onto the open courtyard overlooking the bay. He sat down on a bench, and that's when he noticed the monoliths there – the trees – right out of Stonehenge or Easter Island or Lord of the Rings. Massive goliaths, roots and branches the size of a dinosaur's leg, trunks the size of a car. He first trained his camera's eye on the Moreton Bay fig tree, impressive in its own right. He could hear the flutter of the leaves against each other and see birds ducking in and out of the canopy. He smiled, loving the refracted light shooting down in white streamers between the tree's branches as if God was beaming down his answers from the heavens.

Then he stopped. He spotted the banyan tree. Now this was something! Abandoning the fig tree, he got up and walked around the banyan, feeling the roots – hard and smooth, like the steely legs of a muscled horse. Although, the legs of this tree were many and varied, as small as a worm in spots and as large as a couch in others. Kevin trained his lens directly up at the tree's canopy, around it, and then down the length of a long root that stretched from a hefty limb down and crossways across another and into the ground. What stories lay in that maze? Were the roots of this family tree as intricate and layered as a human's? Had explorers sailed up to these shores and found this tree here? Or had one of those explorers planted it as a sapling transported here from distant lands? Where had its original seed come from? What had the natives thought about the upside-down tree? Was it considered a castaway, cast-aside, a sideshow, a freak?

Staring at the photo now, a million miles away in his tiny apartment in San Francisco, Kevin thought, maybe I'm the freak. He was beginning to think his wife thought so. He chuckled mirthlessly – he certainly didn't have his roots planted in solid ground now, did he? He was like the banyan – a tangled mass of bundled, confused roots with no center, no direction, his soul flailing and landing nowhere in particular. Nothing to hold onto. And yet, he had always been so calm, so steady, so secure, like the great oaks of his youth in Evansville, Indiana. He'd always had such solid roots with his family, dating back generations – good Midwestern stock, his mom had always said. Folk who worked the farms, went to county fairs, helped their neighbors, never missed a Sunday service, took part in village parades, waved at strangers as they drove by on the country roads. Folk who married, settled down, had children, formed their own roots. What had happened to Kevin? Where were his roots now?

He was frustrated and unsure how to proceed. It seemed petty to spy on Alyssa – to even suspect her of anything untoward seemed ugly and wrong – but he was at his wit's end. Her phone calls to him on those nights when she was away were short, blunt, and entirely too staged to be innocent. Like the one he had just hung up on. Could she have gotten him off the phone any quicker? He was like a fly being swatted away. Shoo! Go. Get. Leave. Go back to your own corner and stop taking up my time and space – you are a nuisance. And yet, he was her husband. Should marriage feel this way? He went to bed in a depression…something had to give, but what?

On Wednesday night, she came home from her trip, and they were like ships passing in the night. With barely a hello (and certainly no kiss), she promptly said she was tired and went to bed. Alright, that was it. He had to take action. What other way was there? He couldn't let it slip away, like melting ice cream on a dirty sidewalk. They had built this life together, and yeah, maybe it wasn't perfect, but still, he wasn't going to let it go. At least not without a fight. He couldn't. It was all he had. She was all he had. And he loved her. Despite her flaws, despite her selfishness, despite *herself*. He waited until she was asleep and slipped her phone away from her hand, brought it into the kitchen, typed in what he guessed was the password (and it was), and scanned through it.

He noticed right away that she had called a certain San Francisco number several times but hadn't plugged the contact information into her phone. Then he saw several calls with members of her team. Kevin saw the calls to him. Then he went into her texts. Back and forth with her sisters, her mom, her dad, her friends. Photos sent, jokes, gossip, recipes, news, questions, answers – you name it – her texts were frequent and far-ranging. And there were the texts back and forth with her team members: Matt, Dwayne, Sagar, Harsha, Bridgett, Amit, Pankaj, Tonya, Eric. He started to read the texts. They all seemed rather innocuous – usually about technical things, but sometimes about social things – where they were going for dinner, favorite cocktails, TV shows, and so on. Rarely about anything personal. Kevin couldn't figure out why they texted so often when she sat right next to these guys.

Then he noted with a strange queasiness that none of the phone calls or texts were exchanged with Josh Quinn. It was odd because she talked about Josh quite frequently – how she really liked his style of leading and what a great salesman he was. When she first started working with him, she seemed to worship him, which drove Kevin a little crazy. He was happy that she liked her job and all, but did she need to talk about this dude all the time? As of late, though, the chatter had died down. In fact, the only time she brought up his name lately was when Josh told her team that they had been nominated for a quality award at TorkOps. She felt certain they would win and was excited because the prize entailed an extra bonus in their paychecks.

Kevin had met Josh at a handful of outings – the company picnic, the holiday pitch-in, the after-work gatherings (during the few-and-far-between times Alyssa had invited Kevin – she told him once that he "cramped her style"). Josh seemed like a good-looking, arrogant, crowd-pleasing cocky son of a bitch, but then what did Kevin care – he didn't have to work with him, and as long as Alyssa got along with him, what did it matter what Kevin thought? But now, in retrospect, should Kevin have noticed more in particular? A flirt, a look, a gesture? Anything telling between Josh and Alyssa? Hmmm, maybe…Kevin couldn't figure out why there were absolutely no phone calls or texts between the two of them, and yet so many between Alyssa and everyone else. Maybe he wasn't on this trip. Although, yes, he was on the group texts about dinner, so…but still, that was it. The rest of the texts to her teammates were one-off, and yet there were none directly with Josh.

He saw that her last Instagram post (from earlier in the day) displayed a photo of her hands and stated that she had found an "awesome new nail salon in Chicago" that gave her "power-punch-pink gels." Her Facebook had a photo from Monday night, the usual selfie with her whole team in the background – a pizza joint. Josh was in the corner of the photo, holding up a beer. Her browser history just showed searches for "best nail salons in Chicago" and "best quick blowouts in Chicago." Nothing unusual there. But there was also this strange search: "Rue in San Francisco," which brought up all kinds of people's Facebook pages, random soup cafés, and a mystical shop down in the Tenderloin. He couldn't figure that one out. Maybe trying out a new boutique or restaurant when she got back? He shrugged.

Kevin began to think he was just being paranoid. The lack of interaction over her phone with Josh was probably nothing. But then he had a thought – what if the phone calls to the unknown San Francisco number were to Josh? Maybe Josh had a burner phone. He looked at the kitchen clock – it was ten fifteen. Not too late. Maybe he would just call the number and see! Kevin picked up his own phone from the couch, came back to the table, and typed the unknown number from Alyssa's phone into his. As he dialed, his heart began to thump. What was he doing? What was he going to say? Hi Josh, this is Kevin Warren, are you having an affair with my wife, Alyssa? Sure. Right.

His hand was quivering over the hang-up button as the line rang, his palms sweating. Then unexpectedly, disconcertedly, incongruously, a female voice answered, "Hello?"

Kevin let out a gasp of air and laughed out loud as he said, "Hi, oops! Sorry…wrong number" and hung up.

He sat staring at his phone, breathing hard. Who was that? Was Alyssa having an affair with a woman? And did that woman have a voice like an angel?

❧ Chapter XI ❧

When Rue woke up Thursday morning, she felt a new jittery excitement in her heart. She was going to see Josh tonight! Was she nervous? Excited? Scared? All of the above? Yes, she thought, definitely, all of the above and then some. She shooed Hank off the bed and jumped in the shower. She had to get through the whole day first, so she needed to calm down. She let the hot water burn into the space between her shoulder blades, wondering what it would be like to have someone touch that space. Outside of that hug with Josh, it had been so long since she had felt anyone's hands on her body. She shut her eyes tight, turning and letting the water hit her forehead, cheeks, lips. Then she pulled away with a small scream — her mind had unexpectedly raced back to an image from her past. She tried unsuccessfully to block the memory while it pushed its way forward with unwelcome force.

It was the memory of a boy — Ronald Strom, aka Bonny Ronny Strom. In boarding school, all the girls thought he was soooo cute. Sure, Rue overheard their chatter — isn't Ronny amazing, did you see Ronny last weekend, what was Ronny wearing, isn't Ronny so clever, isn't Ronny so cute, where is Ronny, who's dating Ronny, Ronny-this, Ronny-that, Ronny-everything. And he knew it. Self-assured, entitled, cocky. He began to pursue Rue halfway through junior year. He was a senior at the all-boys academy next door to Rue's all-girls sister school. Most weekends, one or the other of the schools hosted coed mixers and other activities. During one of those events, Rue realized with shocked flattery that she was Ronny's next target.

At first, she dodged him…well, as best she could with her cane — which, under the right circumstances, could be used as a weapon. She had never been pursued by a boy before and didn't know any other way to react. But what Ronny lacked in subtlety and couth, he made up for in determination and sheer will. Finally, after a few months, worn down by his persistence,

Rue let him kiss her in the cleaning closet next to the science lab. She didn't find it too bad – he used a lot of tongue, and his breath smelled like ham sandwiches, but otherwise it was acceptable. After that, he found new places where they could "make out" and "touch each other." He kept telling Rue that he had a condom and he knew how to use it, so they were all set to "do it" whenever she was ready. Ronny went swiftly from light kisses in dark places to stuffing Rue's hand down his pants in broad daylight outside on the quad. She was beginning to feel pressure to get the deed done just to curb his brazenness.

Rue didn't have any feelings for Ronny, and he certainly didn't have any detectable "feelings," period. But she thought in her logical mind that at least he would know what to do and maybe that meant it wouldn't hurt so much. Right? Dumb, young, naïve Rue. They met down at the boathouse at midnight on a Wednesday night. It was cold, but Rue hid a blanket in her jacket. Ronny was there waiting for her. He took the blanket from her, laid it down in the bottom of a rowboat, and then helped her get in. She heard him take off his pants and underwear, and he motioned for her to do the same. She laid down flat, feeling him hover over her. She remembered she was uncomfortable, her back pressed hard against the boat's aluminum seam. He spread her legs apart, placing her feet on each side of the boat's hull. She gritted her chattering teeth in the cold and in anxious anticipation. She heard him put the condom on. He didn't even kiss or talk to her. It was maddening. Finally, he lifted her sweater and put his hand on one of her breasts and squeezed. Then he manipulated her body to push himself into her. It took him a while to get it in and then, like a whip he was cracking, he reeled and slammed down in five, detached, succinct slashes. It was over in an instant, leaving Rue bloody and raw, wondering if she was supposed to get up now. After a few moments, listening to the boat creak underneath his hasty, clinical movements, he grabbed her by the wrist and stood her up next to him. She used the towel to wipe herself and got dressed self-consciously as he handed her clothes to her. As they walked out of the boathouse, he kissed her briefly in a disconnected, perfunctory action and said "Thanks, bye." They never spoke again.

She remembered wondering back then, was this what all the fuss was about? She felt like a defective piece of clothing that had ended up on the discarded clearance rack. How horrible. Were people sadists? Why would anyone do *that* more than once? All the romantic movies, novels, plays, artwork, lives changed irretrievably, irrevocably, inexorably – for this?! Rue didn't get it. She would rather have a root canal. How was a baby ever conceived in this world? How did women not run out of their houses screaming every night? It was barbaric!

Back in her shower Thursday morning, her mind returned with a rush to the present – was this what sex with Josh would feel like? It was no wonder Rue had never had sex since Ronny. After that, she had decided that life without a man was just fine. She didn't need a man to make her happy or to define who she was. She set up her life the way she wanted it. She had her work, her small group of friends and family, her art, her activities, her apartment, and Hank. She had quiet, peace, anonymity, routine – she didn't need anything more.

So why go out with Josh at all? Rue began to weigh the risk versus the reward. If she played it right, the risk was relatively low. She wasn't going to get attached to Josh – there was no threat of that. For goodness' sake, she'd dated other guys over the years – well, maybe only a few and then only sporadically, but still, she hadn't fallen for them. They had amounted to nothing. Josh would be the same, wouldn't he? Sure, he set her heart aflutter, but that was just because this was new and different. It wasn't because she felt anything in particular for him. She would go on a few dates with him and maybe let him kiss her. What harm could come from that? And she might even get a few free meals out of it! She couldn't remember the last time she'd been out for dinner. If all went well – within a short period of time – she would have killed a few pleasant hours with this guy and then gone happily back to her perfectly ordered, humdrum life.

At nine fifteen that morning, Josh texted her, "Morning, beautiful. We still on for tonight?"

"Morning. Yes."

"Time and place? Your choice."

"Really? You sure?"

"YES."

"Ok, Osso at 6:15."

"Perfect. I'll make a reservation. Pick you up?"

"No, I'll meet you there."

"You sure? It's no bother."

"Yep, I'm sure."

"Ok. Can't wait."

"Ok."

She took a deep breath. No backing out now. She figured Osso was good because it was only a block away from the Scarlet Huntington, so if things went south, she would have an easy getaway. Not that she feared Josh – she could tell he was just a happy, excitable, harmless puppy dog. But he also seemed somewhat arrogant and self-absorbed, and she wasn't sure of her own tolerance for that – she might need an exit plan.

Later at the office, Rue was sitting at her receptionist desk, trying not to dwell on the impending doom of dinner, when she heard Vy's signature heels walking in and showed her the text.

Vy cried, "Breaking the boy's bank on the first date? You've got some nerve!"

"Well, I figured, I may as well get a decent meal out of it!" Rue countered logically, laughing.

"Good thinking," Vy said, impressed. She added, "So, six fifteen. Rather early. I hope he doesn't think you wanted to leave time for extracurricular activities."

"What? NO. Really?" Rue frowned.

"Probably. Is that what you intended?"

"Vy! Please! I was thinking more like, hey, I want to be home by eight."

"Of course you were. Alright. Calm down. I'm just kidding. No, it's fine, don't get all worked up about it. If you like, just set him straight up front – say you have an early meeting tomorrow and need to leave by seven forty-five or something. No fuss, no muss."

"Yeah, okay, good, I will," Rue said, mollified. "Hey, Vy, I have something else to ask you." Rue lowered her voice, and Vy had to lean over the desk to hear her. "Okay, so you're going to think I'm being paranoid, but I had three missed calls yesterday from a blocked phone and one wrong number last night at like ten thirty. You don't think they're somehow…related to this Josh thing, do you?" Rue blushed, thinking the words sounded ridiculous now that she was saying them out loud.

Vy paused for a moment and then scoffed, "Nah. Come on. I get robocalls like that all the time. Your phone's probably been added to some list. Did they try to sell you a car warranty?"

"No, I mean, I don't know. I only answered the wrong number, and whoever it was hung up quick."

"Well, there you go. It's nothing. Hey, I'd better get upstairs. I can't do lunch today. I have to be in court by ten. Have fun on your date tonight. I'll come by first thing tomorrow to find out how it went. Text me tonight if you need me."

"Okay, sounds good. Talk to you later." Rue listened wistfully to Vy's purse clanging away down the hall, thinking to herself, she wished she could go on a date with Vy instead. It would be so much easier. No pressure to talk about herself, no pressure to talk at all. No pressure to look good, to worry about being kissed or stared at like a foreign object in a museum. No pressure to engage in witty repartee. She chuckled ruefully, no worries on that front actually – Josh probably didn't even know what "witty repartee" was.

Mercifully, the rest of the day went by quickly and absentmindedly; she was absorbed in listening to a new audio file. In the afternoon, Mayumi came down to check on her progress. She filled her in on the sections that were the most suspect and then told her shyly about her date. Mayumi revealed to Rue, even more shyly, that she had never been on a date in her entire life! Rue had always wondered about Mayumi's personal life, but she had been reticent to ask. Vy always dictated the tone and tenor of their lunchtime conversations, so needless to say, Mayumi knew very little about Rue and Rue knew very little about Mayumi. It made Rue feel ashamed – why hadn't she inquired? What kind of a friend was she? In the absence of Vy, Rue decided to ask now. Mayumi proceeded to whisper to her that she had met her husband when she was thirteen years old and had married at sixteen. He was a friend of the family. Wow, wasn't that scary, was all Rue could think to ask. Mayumi laughed and said yes it was, at the time, but now they were the quintessential "old married couple." Mayumi went on to explain that for whatever reason, they didn't seem to be able to have children. Mayumi wanted to see a doctor about it, but her husband was against medical interference in such matters. So instead, Mayumi said she worked a lot, and usually her husband worked a lot, and someday she hoped by some miracle to get pregnant.

Rue said, "Wow, I didn't know...I'm sorry, Mayumi...I can't imagine not being able to..."

"Have you ever been?" Mayumi asked, a little too eagerly.

"Me? God, no!" Rue said reflexively, incredulously. "That would entail me having a conversation with a...man!"

Mayumi laughed and said, "Well...something must have shifted. You have this date tonight, right?"

"Yes, I suppose...heaven help me! I'm still debating..."

"Who knows? You might have a great time. My advice: be open to anything and be yourself."

"People always say that! Is that really true, though? Shouldn't you be on your best behavior instead? Essentially, lie?" Rue laughed, thinking back to that couple in the lounge the week before. "How else do you make sure you'll get a second date?"

"You're so cynical! Rue, I can't imagine 'your best behavior,' as you call it, is any better than your average, everyday typical Rue behavior. I wouldn't change a thing."

Rue smiled and sighed. "Well, thanks for that…just be Rue, okay, seems reasonable, I can do that. I guess if worst comes to worst and there isn't a second date, then I'll be right back where I started."

"Exactly. And you might actually enjoy the first date and the second date and…"

"Sure." I laughed. "I'll give it my best shot. One date at a time, please."

When Rue got home, she ditched her glasses, listened to Vy's descriptions in the closet for a while, and finally selected (with some hesitation) "I call this one 'Little Lord Fauntleroy.' Black velvet jacket fitted oh-so-snug around that tiny waist, tight slightly see-through pink tank shell underneath, and the black flare skirt. Pair with black hose and black wedges. No jewelry needed – let this one speak for itself, Rue-dee-patootie!"

She finished dressing, wrapped her purse around her chest, tweaked Hank under his chin, locked up, and headed down the stairs and up the hill to Osso. Thankfully, the weather was good – chilly but no rain and no mist. She could feel the setting sun on her face, and she smiled to herself. Look at me, going on a new adventure! As her cane clanked against the truncated domes of the sidewalk, she paused, listening for the crossing signal, thinking hundreds, maybe thousands, of people were going on a first date tonight, maybe even here in this big, spectacular city, just like her. If they could do it, she could do it! This wasn't revolutionary! This wasn't rocket science! Man meets woman. Woman meets man. It was natural. Like gravity. Like inertia. Like a duck to water. Except this duck had only been in the water once a long time ago, and the duck had felt like a butterfly being crushed by an elephant. Hmmmm…

She hoped she had counted her steps properly. It was difficult when she was nervous or distracted. She was hot from her hike and, standing outside the entrance to the restaurant, hearing the valets chatting nearby, she took a moment to breathe. She felt her watch – it was six twenty-two. Fashion-ably late, isn't that what they said? As she made her way to the entrance and fumbled for the door handle, she immediately heard someone come up to her, take her elbow, and kiss her on the cheek. She jumped as if she'd been slapped, but he only laughed in his low, throaty way, saying right next to her face, "Hi, beautiful."

"Hi," Rue responded, feeling foolish that she had been so startled. What had she thought would happen? She should have been fashionably early. Next time.

"You look great," Josh said quietly, still hovering over her.

"Thanks. You look great too."

He laughed. "You little liar."

She smiled up at him and said, "But I'm right, aren't I?"

He laughed. "I'm sure as hell not going to deny it!"

She still felt the spot on her cheek where he had kissed her – it was like a warm ember. She laughed and said, "So, shall we...?"

"Yes. Let's. This way," he said and led her in.

When they were seated, Rue stopped to listen to the chefs in their starched coats scurrying back and forth in the kitchen area, which seemed to be quite close to their table. She smelled a tray of food go by and suddenly realized she hadn't eaten lunch. She was starving.

Rue sensed Josh studying her. He asked, "Have you been here before?"

"Yes, but not since I was a child. Funny – it still smells the same."

"Really? This place was around back then?"

"Sure, we used to go to dinner here at least once a month. My parents had friends who lived upstairs."

"Wow, old-world San Francisco, eh?"

Rue shrugged. "I suppose. I don't remember their names...the Dyers? Dryers? Something like that. They were nice. They had two boys. My brother loved to come here just to have some friends to play with besides me."

"I'm still so amazed to meet someone who grew up here. You're the first person I've met from here. Must have been such a great city to grow up in."

"It had its ups and downs," Rue replied with a wry grin.

"Ah-ha! Funny." he laughed. Then, "So, anything in particular you're craving? I see you haven't even picked up your menu."

She gave him the "duh" smile, and he laughed self-consciously. "Sorry, I'm an idiot. Forgive me. I'm nervous. Should I...read it to you?"

"Naw, you're fine. I reviewed it online."

"Oh! You can do that?"

"Yep. Well, not every restaurant has a menu that my screen reader can decipher, but this one does. I know what I want. What are you gonna have?"

"Alrighty then! Let me see…first of all, what do you drink?"

"Um, water and, I don't know, maybe some wine?"

"Great!" he asked and added, "Fool's courage."

"Do we need that?" Her palms were getting sweaty at the mention of it. Then thinking he was probably right, she added, "Okay. I guess it couldn't hurt. I like dry red."

He said, "Perfect. Me too. I'll order a cab." The waiter came over, took the wine order, and went to retrieve the bottle. They sat in awkward silence for a moment. Rue wished she could read his expression. Was he studying her? What was he thinking? Was he reading his phone? Was he looking around the room? Was he reading the menu? She finally broke the ice and asked, "How was your trip?"

Before he could reply, someone came to fill their water glasses, and Rue took a drink, trying not to spill on herself or to put the glass down in the wrong spot. Josh waited and finally, not answering her question, said, "God, it's good to see you. I've missed you this week. What have you been doing with yourself?"

"Well," gulped Rue. He missed her? He definitely hadn't been studying the menu then. "Not much – just working."

"Oh, me too," said Josh, stopping for a moment as the waiter returned with the wine, allowing Rue to sample it before he filled their glasses. It felt good, the tannins hitting the back of her mouth and sliding down her throat like a warm elixir.

She heard him hold up his glass. He said, "To new beginnings."

"To new beginnings," cheered Rue in return as he clinked her glass.

He went on, "Yum, great wine. Can't beat living in California, can you? Ha! Anyway, so, what were we talking about…?" He paused for less than half a second and continued, "Oh yeah, work. Mostly this week I was getting the team set up with a new client – installing and testing – that type of thing. It was busy. Glad to be back, though, and I don't have another trip until next week. What do you think of that?"

He was like an ever-spinning toy top. She had to laugh. She answered, "I think…if you think that's great, then…well…I think it's great too! So… um…what do you do when you don't have to travel?"

"Well, hopefully take you out every night, if you'll let me," said Josh, flashing a smile that she could feel through her blindness.

She laughed. "Maybe…let's just focus on tonight first, okay?"

"Oh, all right. If you insist. Patience is a virtue, I suppose. Although I always did hate that expression. Okay, so in answer to your question, I either go into the office or I drive around visiting local clients. Anyway, tomorrow I have a bunch of follow-up calls to make – potential sales left over from that conference last week."

The waiter came by to take their order. They both ordered the steak, and Josh asked to start with Osso's signature skillet bread. As the waiter drifted away, Rue heard Josh's phone buzzing and wondered if he was struggling to break free of its tether. She sipped her wine and waited.

Finally, he said, "Sorry about that. Let me turn this stupid thing off. Okay, great. Squashed. Back." He asked, "So, I know we talked on the phone the other night, but would it be okay if I asked more questions?"

She laughed. God, what was he going to ask that he hadn't already asked? "No, that's fine. Well…I can always plead the fifth."

"Okay, good. What's your favorite color?"

"Josh!" she exclaimed with a grin.

"Just kidding. Sorry. What – you don't like blind humor?"

"Sure, right up my alley. Continue."

"Okay, what's it like being blind?"

"Yikes!" she snorted. "That's what we're starting with? Hard to summarize in a couple of sentences. I mean, I don't know…it's all I've ever known my whole life. For the most part, I manage my daily routine just like anyone else: go to work, go home, go to sleep, get up, repeat. I have to navigate the world differently from everyone else, like when I count steps on the way to the office, but over time these things have become second nature." She contemplated for a few seconds before continuing, "Of course, there are days when it can be awful."

"Hmmm, that doesn't sound good. How so?"

"Well, the other day I fell in the middle of the street, in front of what I presumed were hundreds of people, so that kind of sucked."

"Whoa. Were you okay?"

"Scraped up my knee pretty badly," she admitted and then added ruefully, "and bruised my ego."

"Holy crap! Did anyone help?"

"Some jerk laughed and kept going. But yes, thankfully, a few seconds later some nice woman helped me, moved me to the side, and stopped the bleeding with some tissues from her purse."

Apparently not hearing the latter part of the story, Josh cried, "Dickhead!"

"Yeah…it happens," Rue shrugged, thinking, god, if he only knew how awful people could really be. She had learned over the years that certain insecure people liked to prey on those who were weak – making fun of anyone who is different in order to make themselves feel bigger and better. She'd always tried to let it roll off her back, but some of those barbs and lances stuck with her. Once in a while, they got her down, but then she remembered a mantra that her mom used to tell her (with absolute conviction!): "Rue, God doesn't make mistakes." As a child and even now, whenever Rue was having a bad time or being bullied, she thought back to those words and felt a sense of relief from the negativity, knowing she had a right to be who she was, exactly as she was, and no one was going to make her feel otherwise. She'd also learned that there was always a port in a storm – like the woman who had helped her on the street when she fell. Ultimately, the world was made up of mostly good people, and Rue felt the good would always win out over the bad.

As she sighed thinking about all this, Josh said sincerely, "I'm sorry." Then his voice dropped to a low gravel as he continued, "Hey, I'm going to make you a promise: when you're with me, I'll never let go and I'll never let anyone hurt you or be mean to you."

She smiled with a sort of "aww" to her face. Was he for real? It seemed so. Chivalrous. She liked that. The waiter brought the bread, and Josh cut a piece and put it on her plate. She nibbled on it – it was savory and delicious – and felt a lightness wash over her, thinking how nice it was to be on a bona fide dinner date with a handsome man!

After a minute, he switched gears, asking, "Hey, speaking of your favorite color, haha, do you even know what colors are?"

She had to think about that one for a second – not about the concept, but how to explain it to a sighted person. She said, "No, not really. For the most part, they have no meaning to me. Like, if you say, that's a red ball or a green bowl, that would mean nothing to me. But from a conceptual standpoint, I understand that colors are a way to identify something for a sighted person. Sometimes, if a color is associated with some other sense, I can also use it as an identifier. I may take a taste or smell and tie that to a color association in a certain context. For instance, the wine," she held up her glass, "it's red, right? Well, I don't know what red is, but I know that the taste of this wine is distinctly classified in my mind as tasting red, which is different from white wine or a Coke or a glass of milk. The difference is that you might be thinking of the wine as separate and distinct in your mind based solely on the color or the way it looks, whereas I would only ever think of it based on the way it tastes or possibly the way it smells. But it would still be deciphered in my mind much the same as you would decipher it, just with different elements and criteria. Or I guess you could say fewer criteria. The same would be true for the sky or the grass or the night. I know these are described as blue or green or black, but in my mind they are open or crunchy or cold or some other nonvisual descriptor or classification that helps me identify them based on the circumstances of the moment. See what I mean?"

"Yes, I see!" he replied. "I see!"

She laughed. Silly boy! "Yes, you see, you goober. And I don't. So, now you know."

The salads arrived, and Josh kept the dating game going. "Okay, next question. What's your favorite food?"

"This is what you ask? I feel like I'm on a Gymboree playdate."

"Hey! Get the easy ones out of the way, right?"

Rue shook her head. Couldn't argue with that. "I like steak a lot. Obviously," Rue said, waving her hand toward the kitchen's beefy-smelling air. "I love pasta too. But, actually, one of my favorite things in the whole world… now don't laugh at me…is capers. Aren't they just tiny, salty bits of heaven? I really love them on chicken or fish…yum…with artichokes and tomatoes. So good."

"Capers, eh? Whoa. Wait a minute, officer, I'm dealing with a rogue foodie…she likes…no, officer, she *loves*…capers. We may need to bring her in…"

She laughed. "Okay, buster. If you're so special, what's your favorite food?"

"I like it all, honestly. Certainly, I'm with you, steak and pasta are great. But sometimes I just want a big burger. Or pizza. Or fried fish. Or a tenderloin. I guess I pretty much want it all."

"Well, that's good. You're not picky."

"Not with food," he corrected, his voice doing that thing again, and Rue blushed.

He unexpectedly reached over and grabbed her hand. She jumped. He forgot she couldn't see his actions. He apologized and said soothingly, "Speaking of color, I like it when your cheeks turn red like that…"

She mutely turned a deeper shade, and finally, with a catch in her voice, redirected, "Next?"

"Question…oh, okay, let's see…height? Weight? Salary? Pregnant? Virgin? Ever been arrested? Done drugs? Past demons?"

"Hey, is this a job interview?" she countered with a grin, not skipping a beat.

"Yes. Essentially. I'm waiting…"

She smiled but didn't say a word, so he laughed and moved on, "Okay, what about tattoos?"

"Hmmm, what do you mean, do I have any or what do I think of them?" clarified Rue.

"Both."

"I don't have any and don't want any. Not my thing. What would be the point? For all I know, I would ask the tattoo artist for a flower and he'd give me a smiling turd instead."

He chuckled. "True, I never thought of that…"

"So, I take it you have one?"

"Yeah," Josh admitted. "Just one."

"Where?"

"My chest."

"What is it?"

"It's a volleyball," he admitted, somewhat abashedly. Then, "Not my finest moment."

"Why? You play, right?" she asked, even though she already knew from her online search.

"Yep, as much as I can. It's just that my whole team in college went together to get the same tattoo at the same time – a very drunken night – and by the time the tattoo artist did mine, I think his hand was tired. Mine looks like a bad mole or a piece of dirty lint. Not sexy *at all*."

She grinned and said, "Poor baby. Well, you'll never have to worry about that with me." Then Rue had a momentary snap where she realized what her sentence implied.

He laughed and said, "What? About the tattoo or about being sexy?"

She didn't say a word for a few moments, and she knew he was reading her mind. Her betraying cheeks again! Finally, with a hint of amused confidence in his voice, he said, "Tell me more about your family. Did you ride the trolley with them?"

She laughed. "Do you mean the cable cars? Haha, no we left that to the tourists. We had our own ways of getting around."

"Yeah?"

"Well, both of my parents had their own cars, as I recall, but then our nannies also like to drive us around in the Mercedes. Sometimes they took us to the park and let us walk around the polo fields or dip our toes in the lake. Daniel sometimes rowed me around in a boat. It was fun."

"Wait," interjected Josh, "you had nannies? As in, more than one? What was that like?"

"Yes, when we were little. My dad had a job where he traveled a lot, so sometimes my mom went with him and left us at home with the nannies. We had a daytime nanny and a stay-over nanny." Rue put her head down, thinking of those long-since-gone happy days, like a short bright blip in time. A blip that was cut short in an instant.

Luckily, Josh didn't seem to notice her introspection and said, "Wow, I can't even imagine! My mom, she was so hands-on, she would never have allowed a nanny, not that we could afford one anyway. She would get up early every day – take care of the older kids and make sure they were helping the younger ones get off to school. Then she'd head out the door herself, usually by six thirty. We wouldn't see her again until dinnertime, but she'd always have one of my sisters stick something in the oven for us – a casserole or lasagna or whatever...I don't know how she did it. She helped us with homework, came to our games, made sure we were all fed and clothed. Amazing! And she was always so calm and patient with us – never yelled or cursed – and believe me, we certainly deserved worse at times. The funny thing is, the way we knew we were in real trouble was when she said she was disappointed in us. That was the absolute worst – you never wanted to hear that.

"And Dad, well, he worked a ton of hours at the garage, so we didn't see him a whole lot either, but he was great when he was home – showed us boys how to fix cars and play sports." He paused for a second, then said significantly, "Taught us how to talk to girls. You know, how to treat girls respectfully, but also how to get a girl. He would say, 'Girls are just like boys, but with boobs.' That always made us laugh. Then he'd say, 'You just talk to them like you'd talk to your friends. But be realistic – no girl's going to want to hear about your big game or your fast car – she wants you to ask about her – be a better listener than a talker. Be nice, pay attention to her, and above all, be a gentleman.'"

Rue chuckled at this, thinking of Josh with his sweet-talking ways. He said, "What? You're thinking I learned a lot from my dad, aren't you?"

She said, "Uh-huh, something like that." Then she asked, "So, have your parents ever been out to visit you?"

"Heck no...come to the big city and deal with the crowds and traffic? No way. They're still thinking, why would I move away from home, where everyone and everything I could ever want already existed?" he said dryly. "I've had to explain to them over the years that if I wanted to be successful in my field, I needed to move to California or New York. There aren't any opportunities like that back in Flagstaff. My mom, I think she understands, but she worries about me a lot. When I come home, she always hugs me a little too long. And she says I'm too thin now – she tries to feed me and fatten me up when I'm home."

"That's kind of nice, actually," said Rue.

"Yeah, I suppose. Sometimes she babies me, and I hate that. I guess that's because I'm the youngest."

Just then the steaks arrived, and they began eating. Rue couldn't remember the last time she'd had steak. She chewed slowly, savoring the flavor. When she sipped her wine, she began to feel a soft buzz in her head. She listened to Josh talk about the food and various other topics, and she imagined he was the most handsome man she had ever met. His voice was smooth and warm, like butter. She wanted more than anything to touch his chest, shoulders, arms. To rub her fingers along his collarbones and down the sides of his arms and then over to the center of his abdomen. She imagined his body being like a sculpture in a museum, one that she could make a study of – feel the smooth, marbled skin, the strong muscles. She could put her hands on the back of his jawbones and pull his mouth toward hers...if only he would place his soft, luscious lips on hers...

"Hello – Earth to Rue, come in Rue," he suddenly teased. Oh god, how had she been looking?

"Et-um," Rue cleared her throat. "Sorry...what were we talking about?"

"Family," he answered as he reached across the table and picked up her fingers, which had been resting at the base of her wine glass. "Yeah, my sister Angela – she's a schoolteacher like my mom – she was just telling me how difficult it is to memorize kids' names nowadays. They're all these new, modern names with strange spellings. She was saying how she has three Carsons in her class right now – two are boys and one's a girl, but they're all spelled differently, one with a *K* and one with *s-y-n* instead of *s-o-n*. Can you imagine? I couldn't do it. I mean, I have trouble keeping track of the coders at work…we have two Ashishs right now – one goes by Ash and the other by Ashish, but sometimes I forget and get them mixed up…I know, I know… this is really bad of me, but I swear, I can't help it. Then there are these three ladies on the marketing team who all look alike to me…"

As Josh rattled on, Rue listened to him and found herself grinning and ruminating on the feeling of his hand in hers. So soft and yet so strong…like the leather of a horse's saddle.

After several moments, he released her hand to continue eating and changed the subject. "So, how did you end up in Chinatown? You don't have any roommates?"

"No, I used to – I had an apartment a long time ago with three other girls, but I hated it. After a couple of years, a woman from work who was getting married told me that her apartment in Chinatown was opening up, so I moved in when she moved out and took over her lease. It's not very big, but it's enough for me and Hank," Rue said with a slight giggle. She took a drink of wine, laughing. God, she was starting to get tipsy!

Josh said with mock aggression, "Oh, and who is this Hank guy? Boyfriend? Rival? I can take him! Where's he at?!"

"Leave Hank alone!" Rue didn't like the thought of any harm coming to Hank. She furrowed her brow at Josh.

"Okay, okay, whoa," reassured Josh, laughing at her angry face, which seemed to have the opposite effect of Rue's intended purpose. "Simmer down. I would never dare harm your precious…boy? Dog? Fish? Iguana?"

She answered, "Cat. Hankie Hank. He's my buddy. We do everything together. Well, not everything…he's an indoor cat, so we can only do indoor things together. We eat together, play marbles together, cook together, watch TV together, sleep together…he's my buddy…I love him." Rue stumbled through the passionate diatribe, feeling an overwhelming love for Hank that she hadn't realized before. She wondered absently what Hank was doing right now. Probably asleep on the couch. She smiled.

Josh chuckled and said, "He sounds like a very faithful chap. I like him already. But let me ask you this: have you never thought about getting a dog? I don't mean to be rude, but don't they have trained dogs for blind people?"

"Oh, Seeing Eye dogs? Yes, of course. Unfortunately, I'm allergic, which I found out after my parents tried to match me with one when I was a kid. At first, we seemed to be fine together, and during the training period I really bonded with the dog – her name was Penguin. Yes, Penguin! Haha. Don't ask me why – she had that name when I got her. For the first few weeks, I went to this training facility and worked with her out in the yard. But then when we brought her home to do more one-on-one training in our house, I turned into a complete mess; my eyes all itchy, swollen, and red, and my nose all stuffed up. It was awful. We had to give her back. I felt so bad for Penguin and for the breeders and the trainers; they were so nice and had such high hopes. I mean, I did too. Oh well. Now I live with Hank, who's not much help around the house, but still, he keeps me company.

"Well, here's to Hank," Josh said, apparently holding up his glass. She got the message and held up hers.

"To Hank!" she echoed, their glasses clinking. After a moment, she asked suspiciously, "Are you laughing at me?"

"Definitely not," he replied with a new hoarse quality to his voice that made a strange liquid warmth spread through her chest. "I think you are utterly fascinating. It's odd...I never know what's going to pop out of that mouth of yours. That...*perfect* mouth of yours."

Rue blushed. So many compliments! This was definitely new territory for her!

The waiter came to fill their glasses. They talked for another hour or so about their lives, and Rue was feeling warm and safe and full. It was a strange new feeling – one she wanted to bask in, absorb, inhale, like the fine wine they were just about to finish. Sometime later, after a quiet moment, Josh called the waiter over. He wanted dessert, so they chatted about the options and settled on cheesecake. Just as they were sharing one last bite, Josh asked the waiter for the bill and then asked Rue, "Where to next?"

She was thinking she didn't want the night to end, so she said (quite boldly, she thought!), "Hmm, I'm open to anything...what do you think?"

"All right then! I'm sure I can think of something," he answered happily. He paid the bill, helped her with her things, and led her out the door with his hand on her elbow.

When they got outside, Rue instinctively started to get her cane out, but Josh stopped her, putting his arm around her shoulder lightly and saying, "Hey, I've got you. No worries, I'll drive." She heard him hand the ticket to the valet. Then he added with a laugh, "Besides, friends don't let friends walk drunk."

"Hey!" she protested, "I'm not drunk." But in her mind, Rue began to question herself. Was she drunk? She certainly felt buzzed and less reticent, as if her normal inhibitions had disappeared. Then she thought, what the heck? When was the last time I let loose? When was the last time I had a good time? When was the last time I had a meal like that? With a man like this? Um, let's see…never! Why not see where this leads?

Rue was thirty-two years old, for goodness' sake! Wasn't it about time to try something new, to let herself be free and unencumbered, to experience some of life's joys and many-splendored wonders, including…maybe…dare she think it…SEX?! She gulped and smiled. But she was getting ahead of herself. Josh broke into her thoughts with, "Where to?"

"Oh!" she exclaimed, a little loudly, causing him to laugh. Pushing away all of her shocking thoughts, she came back into her body and wondered, what did people actually do on dates? Did they go to a bar for drinks? A "nightcap"? What was a nightcap, anyway? Sounded like something an old Englishwoman wore on her head. Did they go to a movie? Get coffee? Hang out with friends?

Josh, patiently waiting, finally asked breezily, "Wanna come over to my place?"

Without wanting to give any of her jumbled thoughts away, she answered just as casually, "Sure."

As they waited for the valet to bring the car, Rue found his arm around her shoulder so reassuring and strong that she leaned her body up against him as he squeezed her and kissed the top of her head. With that innocent kiss, she felt the warmth and happiness of having made a decision – rather un-expectedly and suddenly and, oddly enough, without any reservations: that she would see where this was headed, whatever *this* was, with this handsome man holding her and wanting her, and with her heart open and yearning. She would take a risk, take a leap, take a chance, come what may!

A few minutes later, quiet and calm against him, Rue remembered that conversation with Chen the other day – about the huge trees at Muir Woods – and she thought, this is what it must feel like to stand next to one of those Goliaths. Tiny, dwarfed, shaded. Rue pulled back a little and murmured perplexedly up into Josh's face, "Are you a redwood?"

He laughed out loud and hugged her closer. Without skipping a beat, he said, "Yes, yes, as a matter of fact, I *am* a redwood."

Had she said that out loud? She laughed too, holding her hand to her mouth. She liked the fact that he seemed to always be in a jovial mood. She heard his car drive up and heard him tip the driver. Then he helped Rue into the passenger seat (which incidentally felt as comfy as a baby's carriage) and went around to the driver's side. Just like that, they were off! Rue couldn't help but smile with giddy anticipation. Come what may, Rue – come what may!

Chapter XII

During the ride to his place, she began to question herself – just a little – was she being a fool? He was, after all, almost a stranger to her, but interrupting her thoughts, he said, "Well, aren't you looking rather stern. What on earth are you thinking about?"

She smiled self-consciously and said, "Oh, nothing. I guess I was hoping you weren't a rapist or sadist or any other type of 'ist.'"

He laughed out loud, right in the face of her irrational fears, and said, "Nope, sorry to disappoint…I'm quite safe. I hope you're not worried, really – you shouldn't be. Harsha will be there. And I promise to be a complete gentleman. Remember, my dad taught me well."

She murmured, "Okay," and leaned back in her chair with a sigh. She breathed easier. She was being ridiculous, and this was an adventure. She needed to stop thinking so much and to start *feeling* instead.

He pulled into something that sounded like a parking garage and came around to help her out of the car. She was still wobbly and fuzzy from the wine. He held her safely in the crook of his arm and led her to the elevators. When they got off at his floor, she found the hallway piercingly quiet. This must be one of those new modern high-rises. Lots of insulation and steel. Her apartment was mostly wood and plaster; it reverberated sounds from every direction and made for some interesting and fearful nights. Sometimes she woke up in a fright to the sound of an unusual creak or whine. Then she would sit up in bed, trying to remain stark still until the noises disappeared, finally calling to Hank and allowing him to nestle up to her face and relieve her fears. Then she would get up and walk around the apartment, checking the door lock and the lights.

But right here, right now, with Josh's arm around her, she felt about as safe as a book on a bookshelf. Quite the opposite feeling of those sleepless nights!

Josh opened the door to his apartment and led her in. Her first impression was that it smelled clean – as if it had never been cooked in. Harsha, sitting toward the middle of the room, apparently watching something on television – scuffed sneaks and grunting players – must be basketball – said hello.

"Harsha, this is Rue," said Josh.

"Cheers," said Harsha, getting up and taking her hand from her side in a shake. He seemed to be shorter than Josh. Maybe a maple instead of a redwood.

"Hi, nice to meet you," she said with a smile.

Josh took Rue's coat and purse, placing them near the door and leaving her swaying like a reed in the wind for a moment by the entrance.

Harsha asked bluntly, "Hey, so aren't you the blind girl from the Scarlet Huntington?"

"Yep, that would be me," replied Rue with a grin.

"Wait, so you're telling me," said Harsha with joking shock in his voice, "that hundred-dollar bill actually worked with this bloke?"

Josh fiddled with something in the kitchen and then came to her side, placing a glass of wine in her hand, and exclaimed to Harsha, "Hell yeah, it did!"

"Will wonders never cease," said Harsha, impressed.

Rue shrugged and said, "I guess not."

Josh sat her down cautiously in a chair, hovering over her.

"What have you two been up to tonight?" asked Harsha casually, as if he already knew the answer.

Josh said, "Went to dinner."

Harsha asked, "Nice. Where?"

"Osso," she said.

"How was it?"

"Really good," Rue answered. "We had steak."

"I've never been, but that sounds tasty," said Harsha.

After a moment, Rue asked Harsha, "I like your accent. Where are you from?"

"London. Well, originally I'm from Ceylon, which you Yanks call Sri Lanka, but I've lived most of my life in London."

"When did you move to San Francisco?"

"Hmmm…let's see…about four years ago, I suppose."

"Do you like it?" Rue asked.

"Yes, I like it. Good job, good night life, good friends – excluding this guy, of course. And the American women are lovely as well. I think I'll stay."

Josh said, "Glad to hear it. I need your rent check every month." Harsha grunted.

Rue asked Harsha, "What are you watching?"

"Some college hoops."

Josh added, "Duke! Come on man, they're the worst!"

Harsha thought that was hysterical and contested, "Why, dude? Because they're so good? No doubt they'll make it to the Final Four this year. It's a guarantee."

"Please. Oh, they'll be at the tournament, that's a given, but I'm hoping they're gone in the first round."

Harsha directed his comment to Rue (as if she could add to the conversion, which of course, she couldn't), "This guy! Always rooting for the underdog. Pitiful! His bracket is for shit every year."

"That's not true!" Josh countered. "I made nearly three hundred dollars just two years ago. Remember?"

"Bullocks!" Harsha exclaimed and then conceded, "I forgot about that. A fluke!"

Josh laughed and said, "No, that's called skill, my friend, and an innate sense of intuition about the best of the best."

"Whatever," Harsha ended.

Josh asked Rue, "You like sports?"

Rue, out of her element completely, answered definitively, "Sorry, no."

Josh responded, "Eh. No biggie. It's just something we do."

Rue asked Harsha, "How do you understand American sports so well?"

"When in Rome, I guess. Don't get me wrong, I still watch my fair share of cricket and football. I really only like basketball. I find American football boring as hell, and I would rather die than waste an afternoon watching golf or baseball."

"Oh yeah," Josh inserted, "I took him to a Giants game a couple of years ago. He said the beer was flat, the players were sissies, and the game was, wait, what did you call it?"

"I believe I referred to it as odious and nonsensical. Like I said, a waste of time."

"And that shows how little he knows," Josh scoffed.

Rue just smiled as they sat silently for the next few minutes with the sound of the game in the background. Then Josh said to Rue, "Come on, I'll show you the rest of the place." He took Rue's hand and led her down the hall. Josh pointed out the bathroom and Harsha's room, then led her into his room, closing the door behind them. She laughed nervously as he sat her down on the side of the bed.

She said, "So, this is Shangri-La? What does it look like?"

He sat down next to her and said, "Okay, let's see. It's basically boring. I have a bed with a black headboard and a plain gray bedspread and one black night-stand with a speaker on it. One window overlooking a building. I have a closet filled with my boring clothes and two dressers – one short and one tall – both black. You'd be surprised to hear that I'm quite neat – no clothes on the floor, no papers lying around, no girls' panties hanging off the headboard – at least not yet." At this, he leaned over and kissed her on the mouth. She was in the middle of laughing at his silly joke when she felt her lips sinking into his. His mouth was somehow soft and strong at the same time. She leaned into the kiss with a yearning she hadn't expected. Her nerves began to dissipate. It had been so long – she couldn't remember the last time she had been kissed – but it was just like riding a bike, wasn't it? And this kiss felt wonderful.

When he pulled away, Rue said, "That was nice."

He chuckled and agreed, giving her another touch of his lips on hers.

Then Rue asked, "Why would I be surprised?"

"About what?" he asked, thinking she was still talking about the kiss.

She laughed and answered, "That you're neat."

"I guess just being a guy and all, I figure most women assume we're slobs."

"I don't assume anything," Rue admitted openly. "I'd be a fool to."

"Oh? Why is that?"

"Because…," Rue began tentatively, "because I'm…well, I'm rather… unfamiliar with the ways of men, I suppose."

"Ah, hmmm, I see," he said softly and thoughtfully. He took her hand and went on, "Then we'll have to take this slowly and carefully, won't we?"

"Yes," she answered meaningfully. Her chest heaved in relief and with a newfound longing.

He began by adjusting something nearby, and she heard Ed Sheeran play-ing on the speaker. Then he drew her up into a standing position, facing him. He kissed her lightly and took her wineglass from her hand, setting it down somewhere.

"Come," he said, pulling her into a hug. "How does this feel?" he asked with a smile in his voice as he stroked the back of her hair.

"Amazing," Rue replied, sinking into his chest. He smelled so good, the same as he had that day outside the café. She had her arms around his back and felt the muscles there.

He put his hands on her shoulders, moving her away from him slightly, and tipped her chin up with his knuckle, bringing her lips to his again. As he kissed her, she felt the impact of his lips not only in the direct contact but also in the pit of her stomach. It was as if she was split in two – thinking about both the action itself and its effect on other parts of her body. It was a slow simmer – safe, spacious, disarming.

He pulled away, breathless, and asked in a deep whisper, "Are you okay?"

Rue thought for a moment and stuttered, "I don't know...I'm...I'm...a little scared."

"Do you want me to stop?" he asked.

"No," Rue responded, feeling the pit in her stomach melt away into a lava flow through her veins.

"Good," he said, placing her gently onto the bed.

His lips were on hers again in an instant, and they were locked in an embrace, tipped back against the pillow. The lava flow sent its warm liquid down into her groin. The sensation was such a shock that she broke the seal of their lips and gasped. It was like nothing she had ever felt before. Josh's reaction was like a pistol – he lifted her on top of him, his lips clamped onto hers, his hands roving over her back, her chest, her face, devouring her. She was open – with no control over her person – she simply yielded to him, pliable, palpable, putty – all the while feeling every touch of his hands. Everything went so swiftly, like a rocket ship taking off. He was pulling her blouse over her head, deftly unsnapping her bra, his mouth engulfing a breast while she cradled his head in her hands. With a groan, he wrapped his arms around her, rolling her onto her back. Then his mouth was back on hers, directed with purpose and velocity. Her entire body was on fire.

Rue felt herself in a trance. As he removed the rest of their clothes, he cooed to her, making sure she was okay as she assented in a soft, humming murmur. She couldn't help herself. Every single touch of him was boiling through her skin and into the fibers of her being. She was quivering all over, echoes emanating from her throat. Josh's hands and mouth swept the traces of her body like a thundering summer storm. She was gripping his back and shoulders, feeling every muscle and tendon as it wrapped around her. He was seeking every new place like a famished animal. At some point, he separated from her to get something close by, and she felt as if he had exposed her to the frozen tundra.

She cried out, "Josh?"

His hand was on her waist in an instant and he answered reassuringly, "Yes, I'm here. Are you okay?"

"Yes," was her simple rejoinder, her mind and body still fluid and yielding, awaiting his next move.

Then he was there again, all encompassing, his hands arranging her thighs apart as she wrapped them around his hips. He used his fingers to feel inside her, slowly placing himself in the warm liquid channel as she moaned under the weight of the sensation. He was slow and methodical in the beginning, like a wave lapping against the sand. His mouth was still on hers, ever hunting, ever exploring. Then, as the breakers rolled into the heat, it was suddenly like a tsunami – a force, an inertia, an inevitability – slamming against the tide, breaking them both wide open, resplendent, explosive. In a rush, it was there, and they were both lost to it – like a dark, wild, black void – and finally, fatefully, fully, it was gone, like a whimper in the night.

They lay breathless and spent, together for a while, and finally, agonizingly, released. He was off and away as she curled herself into a ball on the bed, tender and tiny. When he came back, he enfolded her small, round form into his arms and held her there, not speaking, taking a blanket and placing it over the top of them. She felt such safety, she found herself dozing off for a time, and when she awoke, she heard his breathing coming in a low, even rhythm. She put her hand lightly on the side of his throat and felt the steady, comforting beat under the gruff, manly stubble. This was a man's throat. A man who had touched her. A man who had been beside her and inside her. A man here, under her fingertips, a man in form and in being. She was in awe of the foreignness of him and the intimacy of him. He was within and without. He was man.

Time passed without intention or meaning, and she stayed – solid, ample, complete – within his enveloping arms. At some point, he awoke and began to find her again, his mouth in her hair and on her neck. She lay under his spell, feeling the waves of passion form all over again like a flower in bloom. This time, he moved inside her in a way to draw her out. At the valley and then again at the peak, his undulations would cease, leaving her to press into the movement from her hips, thrusting against his waiting consent. When she was done and fully sated, she sank back but suddenly realized he was holding himself for her, his jaw tight under her hand. She whispered acquiescence and, with a loud moan, his body became a rigid clenched fist as he finished and then, like a weightless, wasted rag doll, collapsed softly on top of her.

They were both breathing hard, their hearts pounding against each other, as he rolled off to the side of her. Some amount of time went by. He waited and then kissed her and said, "Come with me." He carefully led her to the bathroom, stepping in for a moment to attend to himself and then telling her where everything was. Then he went back to the bed, closing the bathroom door behind him.

She should have savored that moment. She should have sat there letting it sink in. She should have basked in the glory of what had just happened. But instead, the moment he stepped out of the bathroom, the full force of reality hit her like a ton of bricks. She began to cry uncontrollably. What had she done? What had they done? It was a marvel! But was it wrong? She hardly knew him! What must he think of her? What did she think of herself? Was she just like all of the other girls who came to him? How many others were there? Were they easy, vapid, unscrupulous? Was she? She felt cracked open like an egg, with no power to stop her insides from pouring out.

She was in the bathroom so long, he came back and knocked on the door. He stepped in. She was still sitting on the toilet, crying.

He said quietly, a little startled, "Hey, what's wrong?"

Rue sniffled and didn't answer, crouching over her exposed body.

"Come back to bed – let's talk. Okay?"

Rue nodded as he slipped away again. She blew her nose and cleaned herself up. She grabbed a towel to wrap around herself and stumbled back to the side of the bed.

He said, "So, what's going on? Come on, get under the blankets with me."

Rue stood there, stunned and stunted. She croaked out, "I should go. Where are my clothes?"

He said, somewhat hurt, "Hey, don't be like that…come on, stay, it's still early…please, I want to talk to you. Tell me what's wrong."

She sat down on the edge of the bed, and he placed his hand on her knee. He said kindly, coaxingly, "Lie here with me, will you? Come." She gave in, her body once again under his power. It was like a magnet. She lay beside him, his arms around her, the towel falling off to the side. They faced each other, and she felt his breath on her cheek as he talked.

"Tell me what you're thinking."

She sighed, not knowing how to begin or how to formulate a sentence from her jumbled, rambling thoughts. "I…I…feel…like…*a lamb*."

"A lamb?" he asked with surprise. "What? Why?"

"Yes, a lamb…with you…like you've led me to a new place, and I've followed, not knowing where I was going…and now that I'm here…I'm frightened. Like a lamb. I'm not sure…what to do…"

He touched her cheek and kissed her. She smiled as he pulled her to him. It was so much easier to bask in the man – so much easier than to think. She relaxed and waited.

After a while, he said, "A lamb, eh? Hmmm, not sure I understand. What seems to be the problem?" He chuckled softly and added, "Call me crazy, but I usually don't find someone crying…afterward…"

Rue responded quietly, thoughtfully, "Yes…see…that's the thing…the 'usually' – that's what I'm afraid of. There's no 'usually' with me…don't you see…but there is with you. I would imagine, there's probably been a lot of 'usually,' hasn't there?"

He must think her naïve and inexperienced. And of course, she was. He waited a minute before speaking. Then he said, "Okay, you caught me. I'm not a virgin. I've lived a life before this. Rue, I'm twenty-eight years old! But hey, I'm here right now, aren't I? With you! And I don't care what's happened in your past. Well, I *care*, but what I mean is that none of that matters anymore, does it? My past. Your past. Let's focus on this. You and I, together, right here, right now. Yes?"

Rue nodded, blushing. How could she not blush? It was the most amazing, disarming, satisfying, scary, heart-wrenching night of her life. And now she was having difficulty processing it – so many conflicting thoughts. She lay there, feeling his presence so close, and answered resolvedly, "Okay."

"Okay, good," he said, bringing her back into his embrace. They lay like that for a long while, and finally he asked, "Do you want to stay?"

She was shocked back into reality with a jolt. Her memory that this was Thursday night and she had to work tomorrow – both jobs – came back to her with a rush. "No, I'd better go," she said with a croak in her voice. Oh, to stay here forever, in the warm safety of his arms! And then the sudden feeling that her carefully crafted world of routine and order had been shattered into a million pieces. She didn't know how or where to begin to pick up those pieces in the deep, dark, disturbed recesses of her brain. Rue's mind began to race. What time was it? How would she get home? Walk? Muni? Uber? Cab? It was so late! And she didn't even know where she was! She tried to feel her watch but couldn't quite reach the end of her arm.

He broke into her thoughts, "Are you sure? Okay, no worries, I'll drive you home." He gave her a brisk peck on the cheek and jumped up, handing her clothes to her.

She dressed, still discombobulated in body and spirit. She wondered absently if she should let him see where she lived. Did it harm anything? Yes, maybe it harmed those shattered pieces...one more break...oh well, she didn't have a choice at this point. She tried to comfort herself with the thought that he would probably never contact her again and that this was all part of his "usual" repertoire. Post-coitus drive home. But then her next thought was shocked sadness. Would he really never contact her again?

He led her to the car in silence. He asked for her address, and as she gave it, the car began to move. Rue stayed mute, facing and holding tightly to the inside of the passenger door.

"Rue?" he asked cautiously after a few minutes.

She jerked her head to him and answered, "Mmm-hm?"

"When can I see you again?"

"You...you...," she stumbled, "You...want to see me again?"

He laughed – oh, that carefree, devil-may-care laugh! "Yes, I want to see you again, you minx. Did you think I'd let you get away after...well, after *that*?"

Rue blushed. He thought it was amazing too! Rue had a revelation – maybe...could it be? He wanted something from her. More than just sex! It had been so long since anyone had wanted *anything* from her. Sex or otherwise. Would it really be, could it be...otherwise? Maybe it was sex *and* otherwise!

She turned to him, hesitant, tremulous. "Okay," was her response.

"Okay? Just 'okay'? Then when? I need dates and times or else I won't get a wink of sleep tonight." He grasped her hand and she found herself grinning from ear to ear.

Chapter XIII

Josh woke up the next morning with a smile on his face. He felt as if last night was a mirage – a happy, new, hope-filled space where he could pause for a while. Rue was a revelation – not like other girls, and not even because she was blind – it was because she was so reserved, so thoughtful, so sweet, and yet in bed…god! She was like a newly budded flower in spring opening up to the sun! Her crying in the bathroom afterward was unexpected and vulnerable. He couldn't make heads or tails of it, but he knew he wanted more, of that he was sure. He jumped in the shower, savoring the thought of her.

He had to admit, the blind thing was slightly awkward. Not in the sense that he wanted her any less but rather because he was uncertain how to act. It's not as if he usually used a filter – for his words or his actions. Also, outside of being the gentleman that he had been raised to be, he rarely gave a second thought to what a woman was thinking or feeling. Not really, anyway – just enough to make sure he wasn't going to be fooled or dumped. He had always been a fly-by-the-seat-of-his-pants kind of guy, not thinking or planning too much, just doing. And that formula had always worked. Heck, so far, it seemed to be working with Rue. He had been plowing ahead with her just as he would have with any other woman. But now that he had a moment to think about it, he wondered if he had been rude, asking her so many questions and not considering anything from her perspective. She did seem rather naïve to the ways of love and also to the fact that she seemed to have a very self-contained existence, maybe even somewhat sheltered, being blind and on her own. Would that be a problem? Then, in the next instant, he thought, well, she seemed okay so far, didn't she? Why was he even giving a second thought to it? Everything was going off like gangbusters.

After the heat of the water nearly pickled him, he shifted his thoughts to work. He began ticking off his planned sales calls in his head – three downtown, one in Mountain View, and one in Santa Cruz. He would be busy. He was behind, having contact names for ten companies left over from last week's conference. He would be lucky to get through half today.

More importantly, he had an impending crisis looming over him – how to deal with the wrath of a woman scorned in the embodiment of Alyssa Greer. She had been texting him incessantly all night, wondering why he wasn't responding. He got out of the shower and noted that he had three more texts from her this morning, plus a missed call. He sighed. Like a dog with a bone, that one.

Sure, he liked Alyssa – they had been having their hot, steamy time together for months, but she was a flash in the pan. He had let it go on too long already. Josh's waning feelings for Alyssa amounted to this: *she was fucking crazy.* She was all on, all in, and all intensity, all the time. Hey, he was a young, healthy man, so most of the time he took it for what it was – an easy lay. But lately it had started to get old. He wanted to break free. And shit, she was married! God help her husband. Didn't he know? Fool. She wasn't the most discreet person. Maybe he looked the other way – heck, might be some type of relief valve for the poor sucker. Maybe he was out every night himself. Who knew? Josh had never asked nor cared.

But things were changing. Right when he suspected she wanted more from him, he decidedly wanted *out.* And *now.* Couldn't she just go back to her husband? He didn't want a huge "row," as Harsha would call it. He wanted a quick and easy break. He had tried (rather weakly) to break it off before by letting it slip that he'd had several one-night stands. To Josh's amazement and horror, she had brushed them off, saying what did she care – go have fun with those other whores (her words) – just make sure he was done right quick and get back with her. WTF! Who thinks that way?

Josh needed a plan B. This was different. Rue was different. This was not a one-night stand. Josh found himself thinking about her – her peculiar periwinkle eyes with those long dark lashes, the smell of her skin, the taste of her lips, her perfectly formed little body. The fact that she was blind and that, to his amazement, he wasn't intimidated by it and even found it rather interesting. She was simply different from anyone he had ever known. And best of all, she didn't know her own worth! She was beautiful, deep, intense, and open, and yet here she was, ripe for the taking. How lucky he was to have found her! He liked her modesty, her quiet stillness, her calming presence. He smiled to himself, thinking about their time together, those few short hours. He got out of the shower, dried off, and texted her: "Good morning, beautiful. Miss you already. Can't wait to see you tonight."

She wrote back, "Okay."

That was the other thing about Rue that he liked – she didn't talk his head off. She was choice with her words. Josh knew he was the exact opposite – always rattling on and on. It was what made him a great salesman: he could strike up a conversation with a complete stranger and be totally at ease. He had the knack. And when it came to dating, he gravitated toward outgoing, extroverted types like himself. Alyssa was a perfect case in point. She was bold, brassy, and in your face. Josh now felt a sense of intrigue and wonder at the thought of someone introverted and quiet. How does one get to know someone like Rue? Would she reveal her thoughts to him easily, or would he have to wrestle them out of her? What a prospect to find out!

Josh got dressed, went out to the kitchen, said morning to Harsha, filled his mug with coffee, and ate a few pieces of toast. He asked Harsha what he thought of Rue.

"Oh, she seems great, but isn't – well, isn't your plate rather full right now, mate?" Harsha raised his eyebrows at Josh across the kitchen.

"Yes," Josh agreed, but shrugged. "Well, I'm about to shrink my dance card significantly."

"Great, I heartily support it, but how on earth are you going to manage *that?*"

"Not sure yet," replied Josh, looking down into his coffee.

Harsha chuckled at Josh and raised his coffee mug at him, "Good luck."

"Thanks," Josh said weakly, not lifting his mug in return, watching Harsha walk off to the bathroom.

Josh stood there, thinking back to when Alyssa had started working with him. She had walked right into his office, hot as hell, and had immediately demanded a raise, a bonus, and an upgraded work phone. He wasn't even her boss! She was a piece of work! Then over the past few years, there had been the requests for every possible perk she could connive, beg, borrow, and steal. He had laughed at her chutzpah – and her sense of entitlement and creative assertiveness. She knew what she wanted – the perfect opportunist. When she set her sights on something, she got it. Was that so bad? After all, it had led to their torrid affair.

But now, he thought, OMG, I am so fucked!

How was he going to "manage" her, as Harsha said? She wasn't the type to go quietly into that dark night. Josh envisioned something closer to an atomic bomb in broad daylight in the middle of a city square. She would want blood, torture, revenge, a pound of flesh. What if she blurted everything out to the team? God, what if she told Human Resources! Josh groaned.

It was Friday and she was probably already in the office. He tried to think. What to say? What to do? Maybe he could just…stall. He would be in his car most of the day anyway. He decided to ignore her. He drove downtown to his first sales call. A little over an hour later, he was feeling pretty confident that the client would buy; he just needed to run some numbers for him. He sat in his car on his computer, calculating, when he saw Harsha's number come up on his phone.

"Hey Harsha, what's up?" Josh asked.

"Um…hey…you talk to Alyssa today?"

"What?" Josh asked, annoyed. "No, why?"

"Well, dude, she just came down to my office to ask about you."

"Fuck! Okay. What did she say?"

"Just asked where you were, if I'd seen you…why you weren't returning her calls…"

"What did you say?"

"I told her the truth – why, was I supposed to lie?"

"That depends. What do you mean 'the truth'?!" Josh asked in alarm.

"No, not *that*, you putz. I told her you were on a sales call. But hey, listen, you need to call her." Harsha lowered his voice and said, "You know how she is. She's pissed and on a *tear*. You need to call her and calm her down before she does something rash. Nip that in the bud, mate. Stop being a pussy and *nip it!*"

"Yes, yes, okay, alright, I will," Josh answered reluctantly, irritated, then said goodbye and hung up.

Josh rolled his eyes and tightened his jaw. He dialed Alyssa, a sense of dread filling him.

She picked up on the first ring and yelled into the phone, "Fucker! Where have you been? Why haven't you been returning my texts or calls?"

"I've been busy," said Josh evasively. Then casually, "Why? What's up?"

"Hang on," she replied, anger still in her voice. "Let me find a place to talk." Josh could hear her moving away from some muffled voices in the background. God, had his whole team just heard her yelling at him? Then before he could process that, she was raging in his ear, "What the hell, Josh? I've been trying to get a hold of you!"

"I told you, I've been busy. I've been driving to my calls. What do you need?" He knew his voice had an edge to it and that she'd detect that and pounce on it.

"Do you think I'm an idiot? Don't give me that bullshit. Come on – where were you last night?!" Her voice had hit defcon 1.

"Alright, alright. Calm down. Okay? Listen, I'm sorry I'm not at your beck and call every goddamn moment. You're not my mother," Josh hissed back. Then, more softly, trying to temper the situation, "Would you calm down, please? Everyone's going to hear you."

"I don't give a shit if everyone hears me!" she screamed, and Josh thought, she's really lost it, the fucking psychopath. She continued, "Were you on a date?"

"Maybe…," Josh said, growing impatient, trying to devise the best escape plan. Was honesty the best policy?

"I knew it! You asshole!" she screamed, and he thought, no, definitely not honesty.

Instead, he said, "Listen, if you're going to freak out, I'm just going to hang up."

"Uh-huh," she said sarcastically. He could hear her breathing over the phone, but then suddenly, without warning, her voice grew soft and slow. She asked, "How was it?"

"How was what?" replied Josh, caught off guard. What was she up to now? Alyssa's voice was like butter now, smooth and calculating. "The date."

"The date?" he was trying to adjust to her quick change. "Um…does it matter?"

"No…well…no…I'm just curious, that's all. How was it?" she repeated.

"Um…fine."

"Good…good," said Alyssa in a strange, thoughtful voice. "Where'd you meet her?"

"What? Seriously, Alyssa? Why?"

"I'd like to know."

"A bar, not that it's any of your business."

"So, where'd you go?"

What kind of sick trap was this? He answered, "Dinner. Now, that's it, okay? You don't need to know anything else. Can I call you later?" Josh asked, trying to get her off the phone.

Alyssa replied, still all lightness and solicitude, "Okay, okay, no worries, I was just curious. So…let me see…I should be able to get out of here today at around four. You don't need to call – I'll just come by your place when I'm done. That sound good?"

Josh wasn't sure how to respond. He had promised Rue he would come see her, but he hadn't given a specific time. Maybe if he tried to reason with Alyssa in person – break it off with her – it might just work, and he could still make it to the Big 4 by seven or eight.

"Er, um, okay, yes, sure, that should work. I'm not sure I'll be home right at four, though…"

"Oh, don't worry about that…I'll just let myself in," said Alyssa smoothly. Josh thought, damn it, I forgot – I gave her our keycode. He would have to remember to change that after tonight. She ended with, "See you later then?"

"Yep, sure, bye."

"Bye Josh. Oh, and Josh?"

"Uh-huh?"

"Can't wait to see you," all sultry with equal parts venom.

"Okay, bye," Josh said, hanging up. He thought for a minute, then called Harsha back.

"Hey, listen, Alyssa's coming over to our place after work."

Harsha snorted in response.

Josh continued, "And I'm going to try to break it off with her. I don't know how she'll react…you know how she is…"

Harsha murmured, "Yes, I'm familiar. Oh what a tangled web we weave, my friend."

"Yeah, I know. I'm in shit up to my eyeballs. Anyway, listen, what do you have on tap for tonight?"

"What? Why? Do you want me to join in on the breakup? Because I'm going to need a discount on the rent…and some type of defensive weapon."

"Very funny. Would you just listen?" asked Josh, exasperated. This was serious – he wasn't sure how serious, but knowing Alyssa, he figured his life might be at stake.

"Okay, so I was thinking," continued Josh. "If you show up, let's say around six, which would give me plenty of time to break it off, you could come in and make sure there's no bloodshed and sort of scoot her out of there. Take her for a drink or something. Or make something up…tell her the apartment's getting fumigated and we all need to get out...I don't care, but she needs to *vacate*..."

"Right. Okay. Sure, piece of cake." Harsha replied dryly.

"Listen, I'll help. I'll think of something...I'm not sure what...but just be there, okay? I need reinforcements."

"I don't know how you rope me into your dreadful schemes...bloody hell...okay, I'll be there. Cheers," Harsha said, hanging up before Josh could say another word.

Good. That was worked out. Now all Josh had to do was brace for impact.

Josh spent the rest of the day driving around to his calls. By four o'clock, he was beginning to feel anxiety creeping down into the pit of his stomach. He knew Alyssa would never let him off the hook. She would tackle it head-on – like the master negotiator that she was – taking him like a high hurdle ready to be straddled handily. How to convince her that this time it was really over? And why had he diddled with a writhing python? Foolish, horny, stupid idiot!

He took a deep breath as he walked through his apartment door. Was she there already? He called her name tentatively at first, clearing his throat. Then louder, but still no response. Phew! He had beat her. He grabbed a beer out of the fridge and chugged it down to calm his nerves. After a tedious hour watching a ball game, on the edge of his seat and starting in on his third beer, the door opened and Alyssa walked in with an alluring smile on her face and a brisk, "Hi, sweetie." He looked up at her skeptically. What was she all about? Fucking actress. He checked the clock quickly – five ten. Okay, he had exactly fifty minutes before Harsha got there. He should be able to wrap it up in that time, right? He guzzled down the beer in his hand, took a deep breath, and stood up to greet her. Game on.

As he came toward her, she reached up for a kiss, which he laid on her cheek instead of her mouth. Her eyes instantly sent daggers, but then her face swiftly changed into a mask of indifference.

"Hey, how's it going?" she asked casually, walking into the kitchen. She took a beer out of the fridge and looked back at him for a response. "Want one?"

"Sure," said Josh tentatively. "I'm good, fine, cool. How are you?" He suddenly felt as though they were talking like complete strangers. He shivered. What exactly did she have in store for him?

She came and sat down on the arm of his chair, carefree, flippant. "Great.

What a day! Quite busy, you know, the testing and all. Had some blips with that throughput relay, but we'll get it worked out."

"Oh really? How so?" Josh said, stalling, feeling the sweat break out on his forehead. She was so close to him, like a hawk, her eyes boring into his.

"Somehow the code sent the relay out on a loop – you know, the ERP module. It took half the day to figure out where it was getting stuck. We found it finally, but now Pankaj has to work through the fix tomorrow. I'm not worried. More of a nuisance than anything. It'll set us back a day, but we can probably make up the time during beta. We'll see…," she said, shrugging her shoulders. She was so calm, so precise, so direct, so unaffected. What was her game?

Josh continued, still hedging, "Well, okay, glad you've got it figured out. So, what else is new?" Really, Josh, you are complete chickenshit.

Her eyes narrowed at him, then quickly cleared as she said with meaning, "Nothing with me, Josh. And you?"

"Well…now that you bring it up…," Josh began, clearing his throat. "I was thinking, you know, about…well, about us…and…and…and," he stuttered and stopped.

"Yes?" Alyssa said, not giving an inch.

"Well, I was thinking…maybe we should give it…give it…I mean, take a…take a…" God, his mouth was dry!

Alyssa waited, not moving.

"Um, maybe, well, I've been thinking lately—"

"Lately?!" Alyssa cut him off with scorn. Finally, the real Alyssa snapped out of her shell – a viper striking! "Lately? Josh, you were just *fucking* me into the wee hours of the night less than seventy-two hours ago, and now you're starting this sentence with 'lately'? Please don't insult my intelligence! I know what you want, and I know why I'm here, but let me just set the record straight: you *can't*. Period." She stood up, her blue eyes piercing him to the bone.

Josh regarded her, astounded. You can't? What did she mean? As if he was without free will! Who did she think she was? He set his jaw and tried to continue calmly, "Alyssa, you haven't even let me finish—"

Alyssa interrupted again, "I already know what you're going to say, and I'm just telling you right now, there is NO need to say it." Her face was a block of ice, her voice shredded the air like cracked steel.

"What? Why? Would you just let me speak for a minute!" His patience was running thin.

Her eyes narrowed and froze on him. "Sure, go ahead," she replied finally, folding her arms tightly across her chest.

"Okay, I'll just say it: I don't think we should see each other anymore. I mean, you're married. And we work together. And I think people are beginning to suspect. Not to mention, the timing's all off. And we always knew it couldn't last…" He paused. God, her stony blue eyes were like death, weren't they? He began again, lighter now, "We've had a great time, though, haven't we? It's been a fun ride. I know I've enjoyed it…and I think you have too…" No reaction. Hmmm. He plodded on aimlessly, "I mean, you're great – awesome, so amazing – and it's nothing personal or anything – it's just that… just that well, you know, I need to move on…and you…well, you need to get back to your marriage…or whatever you need to do…and…well…" Josh stuttered, his train running slowly out of steam.

Alyssa waited, then said flatly, "Are you done?"

"What? Yes, I guess so," said Josh, deflated and withered.

"Okay, I'm glad you got that off your chest," began Alyssa, suddenly warm and cozy. Alyssa knelt down in front of Josh's chair, causing him to recoil. What was she up to?

She smiled, her teeth white and gleaming, her lips a cherry red, her eyes suddenly soft and glowing. She placed her hand on his upper thigh, ignoring his reaction. She said, smooth and clear, "I get it. You think it's over between us. You want to end it. And you want to date someone else. I'm not stupid, Josh. I get it. I totally get it! And guess what, I'm fine with it. What is *that* look? Ha! You're shocked? But seriously, I mean it. Really. I don't mind at all. Like you said, I'm married and you're single. You go do what you have to do. I never said we were exclusive or anything, did I? That would be ridiculous anyway, given the circumstances. Essentially, I have urges and needs, and so do you – I'm not asking for anything more than to have those needs met once in a while."

She paused and Josh felt relief wash over him. This was not exactly the outcome he had envisioned, but still, maybe he was overreacting. Maybe she was going to let him off the hook. Well, essentially that was what she was saying, right? Or something hinting at that. Hmmm, he wasn't sure; is that what she was saying?

Alyssa, noticing his slow smile, continued, "Like right now, for instance." She wormed her body in between Josh's legs, pushing her chest into his groin, looking up at him with perfect innocence and giving eyes. She pulled back slightly to unbutton the top of her blouse, revealing an inviting valley of flesh.

Josh attempted to keep a handle on his thoughts, his resolve, but then he was finding himself warmed by her touch. His vision became blurred and then morphed into something new. Was it so wrong to keep things floating along as they had been? It was certainly easier – that was for sure. And after all, if everyone was being satisfied, having their needs met, what harm would come from it? Wasn't this the more logical and safe way to handle things? Stay the course. Status quo. I mean, maybe he could have his cake and eat it too, right? Would that be so bad? Sure, he'd had his flings in the past, but he'd never tried to date two women at once. However, he'd also never been given a free pass like this before…how bad could it be? Sure, he'd have to finagle a few things with Rue – make sure she never found out, make sure to keep her away from Alyssa, but it could be managed, right?

As Alyssa took Josh's hand and placed it on her breast, helping him squeeze the tight, taut nipple there, his earlier resolve quickly vanished. He groaned. Her mouth was on his, probing and urgent. Pressing against each other, she abruptly stopped, pulling him up and leading him to the bedroom, slamming the door behind them. They were suctioned together in an instant, without a second to reflect, without a second to wonder, without a second to regret.

Sometime later, there was a loud knock on Josh's door. Shit. Harsha. Josh hollered through the door, "Sorry, change of plans. Go ahead without me. I'll catch you later."

Harsha coughed and said, "Are you sure?"

"Yep, I'm good. See ya later." Josh stifled Alyssa's giggle with his hand.

"Bloody hell," Harsha swore as he walked off.

❧ Chapter XIV ❧

Rue was lost in thought when Hank rammed his head into her hand. She stroked him absently, thinking how happy she was to be back in her apartment where she could obsess about the night before without distraction. Every. Single. Detail. She had made it through the workday, and her reward was to sit quietly for forty-five minutes in sweet, blissful abandon. Good god, she could absorb it like the sun! She was in a complete lover's haze – surrounded by it, reveling in it – those kisses, those hands, those muscles, those haunches, those memories – imprinted like a stamping machine onto the very essence of her being. So different from what she had expected! She pressed her hands to her face, trying to push down the perma-grin staked there between the cherry cheeks. It was no use.

Lord help me, she thought, how did I manage to get through the day? It was a blur. She remembered struggling to perform her daily duties and waiting patiently for Vy to come into the office, at which point (just based on Rue's face) Vy ushered her into a conference room.

When the door closed behind them, Rue paused – should she flat-out tell her everything? Rue began shakily, with a laugh, "Vy, we…um…we…um…" Rue blushed to the roots of her hair and put her head down on the table.

Without another word, Vy guessed and screamed, "What?! No way!" Vy couldn't have been more astounded. She exhaled and said, "Spill."

Rue took her time lifting her head and then, like a child confessing her part in a cookie caper, she rattled off the following in short order: "We went to dinner and, well, I had some wine, and you know what a lightweight I am. Then there was the valet stand, and he was so tall and strong – oh my god, I think I… I think…I called him a redwood!" Her hands went reflexively to her cheeks and she continued, "But then I had this revelation right about the time the car was pulling up, that I should, well, you know, I should *live* a little, right? So, a few minutes later, we were in his apartment talking to his roommate, and I was sipping another glass of wine, and we ended up in his bedroom kissing and I was…well, we were…it was…it…it was like a lightning bolt, you know? It just happened!"

"Wow!" For Vy to have only a one-word response was a testament to her utter amazement.

Rue sat there breathing hard. Finally she asked Vy, "Well? What do I do?"

"What do you do?" Vy laughed. "Enjoy it! You simply have a sex hang-over."

"A what?"

"A sex hangover! A wonderful, dreamy, fantastical bubble – ain't nothing better! You should have called in sick today so you could stay home and lie in bed thinking about it."

"Vy!" Rue cried.

"Well, good gracious, Rue, when was the last time you called in sick?"

"That's beside the point…"

After a few minutes, Vy stopped laughing long enough to take Rue's hands in hers. She said, "So, you slept with him on the first date. Big whoop. Happens all the time. How was he?"

"I'm no expert, obviously, but I think he was good. Actually, I think he was really good. Like off-the-charts good. Let's just say I've never felt that way before."

"Extra-large and in charge?"

Rue shook her head. Jeesh. She had to laugh. She said, "Would you stop that! Help me!"

"Oh please, nothing to help. You're fine. First, answer me this: how did you get home?"

"To my place? He drove me, why?"

"Good. That's good. If it was a one-night stand, he would have just kicked you out the door afterward. Did he set up another date?"

"Yes, he said he'd come by the lounge tonight."

"Okay, well, if he comes, then you're golden. Easy-peasy."

"Yes, but how do I…how do I…get through the day?"

"Rue! Seriously? Focus! My friend, focus! I know it won't be easy. Be thankful that no one can read your mind."

Rue nodded to that. After a few minutes, she asked, "Vy, how long did you date Anthony before you had sex?"

"Honey, we had sex *before* we started dating!"

Rue laughed, not exactly knowing how that was possible but not going so far as to ask. She confessed quietly, "Vy, I really like him. I mean, I know I don't know him very well, but I really like him."

"Of course you do, sweetie. He's your hot tamale. But if I could give you one piece of advice, it would be this: don't put your blinders on, my friend. And I'm not talking about your handi-capableness. What I mean is, don't fall head over heels and then find out he's married or psycho or a dick – heck, he could be one of those con artists, for all we know, or a serial killer, or a player, or a used car dealer, or who knows what? He could be abusive or controlling or stupid or poor. Oh god, I hope not poor. Take it slow, that's all I'm saying, okay?"

Just then Josh texted Rue, and Vy stole her phone away, reading out loud, "Morning, beautiful. Can't stop thinking about last night. I'm counting the minutes until I see you again tonight."

Vy said, "Good god! Barf. Golly, he's got it for you too! So maybe not a dick. But the jury's still out on him being a player. Or any of the other options. No blinders! Do you hear me?"

"Yes," Rue confirmed, reluctantly, thinking, what blinders? Eyes wide open! Maybe for the first time in her life!

Back on her couch with Hank, Rue realized with her eyes wide open that her forty-five minutes were up, so she got ready, shot out the door, and headed up the hill to the lounge. She wondered when Josh would come in. It's funny, she remembered telling him less than a week before that she didn't want him coming to the lounge because it distracted her (which was true!), but here she was wanting him there. Would she be able to function? He hadn't texted or called again, so she wasn't sure what time he'd be there or if he'd bring anyone (Harsha?). Walking in the door of the Scarlet Huntington, even Hayes noticed her pink haze and asked her something cryptic about swallowing a canary. She laughed mysteriously, knowing she couldn't keep it off her face – the look. It was written in every line. She ate a little at the bar as she talked to Bob. After the lounge filled up, she began her set with "Milord" by Edith Piaf. She felt she could conquer the world that night – even French! It was her best rendition, and the patrons' applause seemed to ruminate in Rue's chest. She felt so good!

Slowly, though, things shifted. She played for one hour and then two. She put off taking her break, thinking Josh would show up at any moment. Her spirits began to waver and then to wane. Where was he? Should she text him? Maybe he was just waiting to come for the "late shift"? What did Rue know? A lot of people didn't go out until nine or later. Should she worry? She finally took a break at nine forty-five, feeling the slightest doubt creep into her heart. He wouldn't stand her up, would he? She hadn't misinterpreted his text this morning, had she? She listened to it again as Bob gave her a hot tea at the bar. Bob asked if anything was wrong, but she shook her head and planted a replica of the smile from earlier on her face. She was being ridiculous after all, wasn't she? Maybe something came up...or he was simply late...or he had forgotten all about her...or...or— Suddenly someone was wrapping a set of muscled arms around her waist and squeezing. She jumped, her tea toppling over on the bar.

"Oh! Sorry about that!" cried Josh, laughing, breezy, helping clean up. "Didn't mean to startle you." Rue choked and wiped the tea off the cuff of her shirt. "Sorry we're late. How's it going, beautiful? Did we miss anything?"

Her entire being was instantly washed with relief. He was here! Who cared about the spilled tea! He was here!

Harsha spoke up, saying hello and asking how she was doing. The barstools around her were full, but Josh pushed in beside her and planted a kiss on her mouth – right in front of Bob and Harsha! She blushed and stuttered, "Jo-Jo-Josh!"

"What? I can't kiss my girl?" Then he whispered in her ear, "I've been thinking about that all day!"

Rue's eyes widened, thinking, god – so have I! She said, "Okay, you're forgiven."

Josh kissed her again as Bob brought her another tea.

Harsha asked, "Did we miss your singing?"

Rue said, "Just my first set. I'm on break. Good timing, actually." It was as if all her doubts had melted away. "I can talk for a few minutes first, though. Have you eaten?"

"Nope," answered Josh, turning to Bob to get a couple of menus. A few stools opened up at the end of the bar, and Rue heard Josh sweet-talking the people beside her to shuffle around. Finally, all was right with the world again as Josh and Harsha placed themselves next to her and ordered their drinks and food. Why had she been so paranoid? Silly girl!

Josh said, "I'm starving."

"So, where have you guys been?" asked Rue.

"Work ran over, you know…," Josh answered vaguely. "How about you? How was work for you?" he asked politely, grabbing her free hand and pointing their intertwined fingers at her chest as he said the word "you."

"Oh fine, nothing exciting, just the usual." She sipped her tea. Bob brought their beers, and they did a cheers, clinking their glasses against her tea mug.

They chatted for a while. Harsha wanted to know where Rue worked, so she talked about the law firm and Vy and Mayumi a bit. She asked Harsha what it was like working with Josh (to which he said, "a real nightmare") and then, "What was it like growing up in England?"

Rue tried to remain focused on Harsha's sonorous British voice, which wasn't as easy as it seemed because it was loud in the bar and more so because Josh was rubbing her fingers with his hand.

"…then I lived in London for a time, but I wanted to come west and try out the States for a while, so anyway, here I am. What about you? Are you a native of San Francisco?"

"Yep, born and bred."

"Nice," Harsha said politely.

For the next twenty minutes or so, the three of them chatted, and Rue felt relaxed and happy. She thought it was so interesting how Josh and Harsha played off each other – like brothers – half contentious, half silly. Their shenanigans made Rue smile. Bob brought their food, and eventually Rue stood up. She asked if they had any requests.

Josh kissed her and whispered in her ear, "How about your favorite song?" She smiled.

She sat at the piano, tinkering on the keys a moment, then as a ruse played the chorus to Amy Winehouse's "Rehab." They both thought this was hysterical, and she distinctly heard Harsha say to Josh, "I like this girl!" Then a few chords of The Ramones' "I Wanna Be Sedated." That really got them! Finally, ending the joke, she began Norah Jones's "Come Away With Me."

An hour later, most of the tables had emptied, so she asked Josh to grab her things from Bob. Josh came over and asked if she wanted to go home with them or go out for another drink somewhere. She said no to both. He said, "Pretty please" several times, bringing his face down to hers, but she was tired, and she wasn't sure if she could handle a repeat of the night before. Plus, would he expect her to sleep over? Somehow the thought of sleeping with him felt even more intimate than sex. Was she ready for that? He asked if he could see her tomorrow instead. He was so persistent! She was due at her brother's house at noon. He asked if they could do something together in the morning or later in the day. She thought the morning would be fine since she would have had a full night's sleep by then. They offered to walk her home, but she said there was no need. Josh insisted on walking her to the corner, so that's where they headed. He put his arm around her shoulders, and it felt so reassuring. In what seemed like an instant, Josh was kissing her goodnight, and she was waving goodbye, pulling her cane out of her purse, and walking the rest of the way to her apartment building.

Was this how first love felt? Or first lust anyway. Those kisses – she still felt them on her mouth! And she was astounded by the fact that time with him seemed to either fly by or stand still. She almost had the sense of residing on a different planet with him, apart from the rest of the world. She had nothing to compare it to, but she knew beyond a shadow of a doubt that this was something magical. Back at her place, she snuggled with Hank in bed and contemplated the wonder of love.

Chapter XV

Kevin wasn't sure how to tackle Alyssa. The strange calls to this unknown number made him curious. Was it a dead end? He wasn't sure what to make of it. He knew Alyssa wasn't a lesbian, so that wasn't it. Maybe that woman was someone from work or a new friend. No idea. Kevin watched Alyssa warily as she got up Thursday morning and headed off to work as usual, barely noticing or acknowledging him. Later that night, she was checking her phone multiple times over dinner and texting incessantly, which wasn't necessarily unusual but was still annoying and rude. He had made chicken piccata with wild rice and broccoli, one of her favorites, but she just picked at it, sullen and preoccupied.

Finally, he asked, "Alyssa, how are you? You seem a bit distracted tonight. Do you like the chicken?"

"What? Oh sure, it's great, thanks. I'm really busy with work, that's all." She forced a weak smile.

"Do you want me to run you a bath after dinner? Here, have some wine." He filled her glass.

Her eyes were unfocused, looking through him as she said, "Thanks. Um, no, I need to get back online in a few minutes and answer a few more emails. I'll probably just take my computer into the bedroom and finish up. I'll close the door so I don't disturb you."

"Don't worry about that...I mean, that's fine, but hey, Alyssa?" asked Kevin, forcing her to look him in the eyes, those piercing husband eyes that he knew she now feared and dreaded.

"Yes?" said Alyssa, cagey and cautious.

"Do you think you'll ever want to spend time with me?" He paused after this sentence, letting it sink in. She stared blankly. He elaborated, "I rarely see you as it is with your travel schedule. And when you're here...you're not really *here.*" He took her hand in his, but it lay like a dead leaf. "I can't re-member the last time we made love, can you? I don't want you to feel stress or pressure from me, but at some point I think we need to sit down and talk. What do you think?"

He read the quick flash of panic in her eyes before they turned stony and false. She removed her hand. "I know, I know, I'm really sorry…about ev-erything. I know I've been…distant. It's work. I'm just…well, there's just…a big project, you know, the Chicago project…been running into some snags. So…I've been thinking about that…and I guess I'm too tired for anything else."

He could sense something behind her guarded eyes, the falsehood there, but he could also see he wasn't going to get it out of her tonight. Kevin said, "Okay, I'm sorry work is so busy. I can see how that would be tough. But maybe we could set aside time to be together this weekend. Maybe tomorrow night – go out on a date. What do you think?"

"No!" Alyssa cried, too quickly and too vocally. Kevin's eyes narrowed at her. She tried to recover and faltered, "I..I..I have to work late tomorrow night. I don't think I'll even be home until at least nine or maybe even later. We're…we're…testing something, an error that came up this week, might take a while to get it worked out. We have to get it fixed before Monday, so better off working late tomorrow than having to go in this weekend."

As she stumbled through her story, Kevin let her go, then responded, "Okay, then Saturday. Are you busy Saturday too? We could go for a walk or bike ride. What do you think?"

"Um…maybe…sure…well, it depends, actually. On how the testing goes tomorrow night. I'll let you know. Okay, thanks for dinner. I better get logged in." She stood up abruptly and hastily headed to the bedroom with her computer in tow. Kevin watched her, frowning.

Kevin sat at the table and sighed. What was he going to do? He knew something was off. Actually, more than off at this point. It had been months since he had felt a connection with Alyssa, months since they'd had an inti-mate moment – physically, emotionally, or otherwise. He was beginning to wonder why they had married at all.

He knew his wife. He knew her inside and out. He knew she was ambi-tious beyond all rational thought, beyond logical reason. He knew she could completely blind herself to every extraneous thing in order to get what she wanted. Kevin also knew that this was how she had conquered him, not that it had been that difficult, not that he had put up a fight. Kevin fell to her like a lamb to the slaughter. Sure, before Alyssa, there had been other girls, but they had never pursued him. And when she put the full force of her charms and sexual prowess into action, Kevin was sunk. He had been, and still was, simply dead gone on her. He had said those vows to her because he had meant them.

Now, just shy of five years later, here they were – like strangers living in the same house. Roommates. And disconnected roommates at that. It wasn't as if they argued or had knock-down-drag-out fights. Kevin might have welcomed that at this point. It was all just nothing, void, quiet, and inexorably unreachable. He was extraneous to her now. Like an old, dirty sock lost behind the washing machine, never to be found (or even considered) again.

He put his dish down on the floor so the dog could lick it off; her dog, that annoying little piece of shit, Dixie – the other thing in the apartment that Alyssa never noticed anymore. Kevin said to the furball in commiseration, "Looks like we're in this together. What should we do?"

He began to think through the options. He had tried the direct route so many times, similar to his pathetic attempt tonight – just ask her what's going on. Failure number one. Now, he wondered if he planned an elaborate, romantic endeavor, if that would fly. Would that draw her in or make her run away? It was worth a try, wasn't it? If another man (or other men, plural – gulp!) were the issue, then Kevin had to find a way to lure her back to him – force her to see what she was missing. He knew he wasn't an "all-star" in the romantic department, but he wasn't a lackey either. He could hold his own – or her own, as the case may be – he knew the right buttons to make her happy there. Or at least, he used to. Would she allow him to show her again?

He logged onto his computer and started to look at weekend getaways. Sausalito was a bike ride away – that would be fun, although they had been there many times before, but never to stay overnight. He could book a hotel for Saturday night. Or maybe they could take the ferry over to Vallejo and catch an Uber to Napa, visit the wineries. She might like that. What about Monterey? They could go to the aquarium and then stay in a bed-and-breakfast. They could rent a car and drive the Pacific Coast Highway, stop at a park or two. Would she like that?

He wasn't sure. He wasn't sure what she would like anymore. Who was he kidding? She probably wouldn't want to do anything with him, especially not an entire weekend. She had already embellished her fake work story to make herself unavailable. Kevin put his computer down on the coffee table and laid back on the couch, looking up at the ceiling with a sigh. He began to think about the trajectory of his life. He had loved his life up until recently. His parents and brothers were kind and supportive throughout his childhood. He still talked to them, back in Indiana, at least once a week. He had met a beautiful, dynamic, smart woman in college and married her. He had done well at Purdue University and now here he was, working at an amazing dream job as an engineer at a big architectural firm in downtown San Francisco. Who could ask for anything more?

But he did want more! He wanted a happy marriage. He wanted to wake up in the morning looking into his wife's face that was a mirror of his own – love, care, concern, support. He wanted a true partner – a best friend, a confidante, a sharer of mutual passions, a lover. As he stared at the ceiling, he let himself give into the wave of overwhelming depression that he had been keeping at bay for months. He started to cry. Before he knew it, his body was shaking with sobs. He sat up and put his face in his hands. What was he going to do?

He couldn't remember the last time he had cried – maybe his grandfather's funeral seven years ago. He realized he had been walking around in a fog these past few months – focusing on work and daily life and trying his best not to think about the elephant in the room. Trying not to imagine a life without Alyssa. Was that possible? Had they reached that point? He knew that if something didn't change, and soon, there was no hope. And then, how was he to face the world without her – without Alyssa, who had become part of him, who was his wife, the holder of his heart and future dreams.

God, he was so mixed up! He let the tears fall, his head sinking like a rock.

What seemed like hours later, he got up and grabbed a tissue, blowing his nose and reflecting. He said to himself, come on, you're an engineer! You were made to solve problems, to rethink an issue, to gain inroads where none existed before, to redesign, to remodel, to renew. That's the way you're wired. You can fix this! There must be a way! Think!

What would he do if this were a work project? Hmmmm, let's see...the first thing would be to understand and assess the existing process and variables. Okay. Who was Alyssa Greer? Well, she was smart, ambitious, and athletic. She was the middle child, stuck between two sisters who were just as beautiful and talented as she. She did everything she could to stand out, to grab attention, to conquer. The three sisters were raised by a strong father who had been robbed of his dream of a house full of sons. He had settled for raising his girls as if they were boys. He enrolled them in every sport, taught them to compete with vicious malice, and sunk every ounce of energy into making sure they knew how to be independent and ruthless winners.

To her credit, Kevin noted, Alyssa had taken her father's tutelage like a duck to water, making honor roll every semester, becoming homecoming queen, dating the quarterback of the football team, and becoming captain of the soccer, basketball, and track teams. Girls wanted to be her, guys wanted to be with her. She could kick your ass or hold you in the palm of her hand. And she knew it.

Kevin remembered the first day he saw her. She was hard to miss – it wasn't every day you saw a hot girl walk into an advanced engineering class at Purdue. To be clear, it wasn't every day you saw *any* girl walk into *any* class at Purdue. This sleepy Midwest town didn't know what hit it. But there she was, like a bright ray of sunshine, coming through the door on a summer breeze. Kevin couldn't keep his eyes off her, well, that is until, after weeks of staring, she finally turned around in her seat and said with derision, "What are you gawking at?"

Imagine the stuttering that ensued. What an idiot!

Then, out of the blue, several months later, to Kevin's utter amazement, Alyssa started talking to him. He thought she might need tutoring or to borrow money. It seemed completely implausible that she actually wanted to talk to him. He had his guard up – formidable and intact – behind the wave of eager, overwhelming admiration and obsession he was trying rather tenuously to obscure from his face every time he saw her.

He couldn't believe it. But there it was. Every day in class. Her bright blue eyes gazing into his, asking inane, innocuous questions. All he could think was, oh god, those eyes! Those lips! That smile! And no matter what she droned on about, he found it fascinating. "Did you finish the formula on page nine? When were we supposed to turn in the insert exercise? Who's working with you on the group project? Did Professor Stott say 'actuator' for this loop sequence? How do you work that? Can you help me with design forty-three this weekend? How did you handle the cutter case study?"

Then she started to ask more personal questions, which completely flustered and flummoxed him. "What dorm are you in?" "Who's your roommate?" "Where did you grow up?" "Do you have any brothers or sisters?" "How old are they?" "Do you play any sports?" "Do you have any pets?" "Why did you come to Purdue?" "What do you want to do after your graduate?"

Then one Wednesday, she asked, "Are you going to Alpha Chi Rho's party on Friday night?"

Kevin froze. He was assessing her face: was she asking for a reason? He couldn't do it – he couldn't assume she meant anything by it – even if her face and those forceful, beautiful blue eyes were saying so. He answered slowly, as if a question, "No...?"

"Oh," she said, her perfect cherry lips turning down into a frown. "That's too bad. I really want to go, but I don't have anyone to take me. My friend Brian hooked me up with two invites. So anyway, it's too bad..." her voice trailed off.

Was she implying...?! Kevin said hesitantly, "Well, I mean, if you have two invites...are you...do you...?"

"Great!" she exclaimed, a strike from a boa. "Pick me up at eight."

Kevin nodded and managed to squeak out, "Right. Okay. Will do."

His head was reeling. Had she just asked him out? It was as though he was having an out-of-body experience. Alyssa Greer had asked *him* out?! Him. Geeky Kevin Warren. This could not be!

When he got back to his dorm room, still on cloud nine (or maybe cloud ten – was that the cloud of disbelief?), he asked his roommate (who was much cooler than Kevin), "Pete, you know Alyssa Greer?"

"Yeah, why?"

"What's her deal?"

"What do you mean?"

"Well...I guess...is she dating anyone?"

Pete laughed at that. "Why? You gonna make a play?" Nothing could be further from Pete's realm of possibility.

Kevin was a little insulted. Granted, he couldn't be more astonished himself, so could he blame Pete? Still, Kevin thought for a split second, I'm not that much of a dog, am I? Naw...more like a charming pet lizard. Ugh.

He answered Pete vaguely, "I don't know. Maybe. Would that be so ridiculous?"

Pete looked at Kevin's serious face and dropped his wry grin. "No, I guess not. Hell, what do I know? She just seems to be outside your...well, out of your league, man, if you know what I mean. No offense."

"Uh-huh," Kevin answered, acknowledging it. "I know. Of course, you're right. But I guess I just wanted to know more about her." For some reason, he didn't want to tell Pete that he was going to the party with her. What if it didn't pan out? Then what would he say? Pete would think he had made the whole thing up. Kevin thought, it'll be a miracle if it happens. There are two days between now and then – she could come up with a lot of excuses in that time.

Pete regarded Kevin again and chuckled, saying, "It's your funeral, dude – why not? I don't know much...she's from New York, she's obviously hot as hell, okay, so I don't need to tell you that! I think she was dating Tyler Hactor, you know, the point guard from the basketball team, but remember when he tore his ACL a few months ago – the Michigan game? I heard she dumped him after that. Yeah, right, she's *that* kind of girl. Come to think of it, maybe you should steer clear."

"Yeah, maybe...," Kevin answered, thinking, what kind of game was she playing? From the point guard to him?! Didn't make a stitch of sense. And she had dumped him! Whoa.

By the time Friday arrived, Kevin gave up all hope of understanding and plowed ahead heedlessly. He wore his best green Henley (which his mom had bought him and told him, "It shows off your forest green eyes."), light brown barn jacket, and faded blue jeans. She looked spectacular in a light blue sweater and skinny jeans that accentuated every curve of her fabulous body. Her blond hair was in a high ponytail, and he couldn't believe how beautifully her rosy cheeks made her face glow and soften.

They went to the party. It was November. He was a junior, she was a sophomore. That was when she told him (out back by the bonfire, two Solo cups in gloved hands), that she had devised a ten-point life plan when she was eleven years old: (1) Get a scholarship to a top-ranked university; (2) make captain of the women's basketball team; (3) keep a 3.5 GPA or higher; (4) pick an engineering concentration based on job placement and salary predictions; (5) meet Mr. Right; (6) graduate early; (7) start the perfect job; (8) get married; (9) have two kids, a boy and girl, sometime after five years of marriage; and (10) live happily ever after.

Then she informed him she had already completed points one through five.

Kevin thought about that for a moment. He gulped and asked, "So... number five...?"

She grinned and leaned over to kiss him. Kevin felt himself slipping...how could a woman so strong-willed and determined have such soft, inviting lips?

There was no defense, no caution, no pausing, no reticence, no reflection; it was full steam ahead as Kevin began the bullet train ride that was Alyssa Greer – willingly, eagerly, inexorably, inevitably.

And here he was, now, drying his tears, sitting on the couch they had picked out together – brick red color because it matched the tiny roses in the antique wallpaper. Why did that day seem like a lifetime ago? Why did menial things they had done together back then seem like staring into a faraway dream world now? What had gone wrong? Hadn't he been sufficiently awed by Alyssa's beauty, brains, and brawn? She told him once, early on, that she liked the fact that he was steady, stable, and smart, and then she added, it didn't hurt that he idolized her.

But did it?

He had tried to take care of her. In a way, he had wanted to shield her from herself. He knew she was a fatal amalgam of spoiled entitlement, clever cunning, and ruthless ambition. She was used to getting her way, and she would crush anyone and anything that was a barrier. A very admirable quality, really, unless of course you were on the receiving end. He had tried to protect her from her own exacting nature. He had coached her through job interviews, explaining how to soften her delivery while still showing her skills. He had talked to her about her friendships – how she was too demanding, expecting too much of people, and became irate and irrational when they weren't up to snuff in her mind. He had trained her in deep breathing exercises – how to stop in the moment to pause and breathe – when something or someone was falling short or not her version of perfect. But all this was for naught. She lived like a lit fuse, always on the edge of incinerating, always wanting more, always thinking the grass was greener. After a while, he gave up – after all, it appeared as though she was the mistress of her universe, and everything did gravitate toward her like a moth to a flame. Who was he to temper her? She was winning! And what was he doing?

As he sat up on the couch, he thought to himself, what's next on this project plan? Now that he knew the existing process – inside and out, Lord help him – the next step was to understand the gaps in the process. What was broken? The communication, the intimacy, the connection, the sex, the time, the support, the caring, and blasted, the love! That was broken too, wasn't it? Shit! There was more broken than working! Was there more broken than could be fixed? At his job, this would have been called a "complete teardown."

He shook his head and got up, thinking, NO. It can't be. I just need to think. There has to be a way! He scooped up Dixie.

"You can use the living room – I'm going to bed," he said flatly to Alyssa when he opened the bedroom door. She looked up absently from her computer and, without a word or a second glance, went into the other room. He watched her go, wiping another stubborn tear from the corner of his eye.

Friday came and went quickly. Friday night Alyssa came home at nine fifteen, said she was tired from the testing, and went right to bed. When Kevin got into bed a few hours later, he noted that they slept like strangers now, back-to-back, making sure not to touch any of their body parts in the middle. Once, a few weeks ago, he had rolled over and put his arm around her stomach. She had awakened and stiffened in response, as hard as a stone, then slowly slipped out from under him and gone to the bathroom.

Saturday morning, he was sitting at the kitchen table, eating a bowl of cereal and drinking his coffee when she came out of the bedroom and said good morning.

"Morning," began Kevin tentatively, as cheerful as he could muster. "Any plans for today?"

She looked up and through him, evasive and tense. She said, "Um, not sure yet. I might meet some friends later. Why?"

"Well, I thought we could do something…together…maybe even go somewhere. Napa or Monterey or Sausalito. What do you think?" He tried to remove the pleading cry from his face and voice. He wasn't sure if he succeeded, though, because she looked at him, finally focused on his eyes, with a look just shy of pity.

"What? No, no," she replied incredulously, as if he had asked to style her hair or make her a balloon animal. Then she quickly removed that look from her face and replaced it with one of indifference as she poured herself a cup of coffee. "I don't want to do anything like that. Like I said, I'm meeting some friends later and besides, I need to go back into the office at some point this weekend to finish up a few things. I'm not sure for how long yet. I fly to Tulsa on Monday morning. We have an install there. I'll be back Thursday. I just can't afford to take a break right now. Sorry."

As she turned to go into the living room with her coffee, Kevin grabbed her free hand and said, "Alyssa." She stopped and looked down at him, her face still blank, patiently waiting for him to speak, but clearly with no mind to hear him. "Alyssa," repeated Kevin, trying to force his way through that wall. "I think we should get away. Reconnect. Do something. I…I miss you! I miss us. I feel like…like…we're not even married lately! Don't you want to talk about it? To try to fix…whatever…this is?"

She said, "Listen, I'm really busy right now…don't take it so personally!" Her tone was short and snippy. Kevin dropped her hand like a hot rock. She continued, "I need you to give me some space right now—"

He cut her off, angry. "Space! Space! Alyssa, you've got to be kidding me—"

She interrupted, "No, I am not kidding you, Kevin! Listen, I'm already stressed out enough from my job, and here you are, giving me more shit?! This is exactly what I don't need right now! Can't you see that? Can't you just be supportive? That's all I ask, and you can't even do that for me!" She was fuming, breathing hard.

Kevin found himself raging – seriously, was the Earth flat?! He felt helpless, small, dark. "Alyssa, I am supportive of you! How can you not see that?! But for once, can we have a conversation about us instead of about your stupid job?! I wanted to—" Before he could finish his thought, she tried to cut him off again. He stopped her with, "Hear me out!" He took a breath and started again, calmer now. Her blue eyes were blazing at him. He continued, trying to blast through that concrete wall. "I know…I know you're busy with work, but at a certain point, our relationship must come first. I'm beginning to feel like I'm living alone. Don't you feel it too? Don't you want to have a healthy, happy marriage? I'm scared that you won't even acknowledge that something is wrong between us. I mean, if it truly is just work, then that's fine…I can wait for you…I will wait for you to…figure out…whatever it is that you're going through. But if it's more than that, I need to know! You need you to tell me…if this…whatever this is…is bigger than just work!"

Her mouth was tied up in a tight button. She paused and said, "Can I speak now?"

Kevin assented with a sad nod, crestfallen as he slowly recognized the dark, cavernous well of indigo blue in her eyes had turned an even darker shade of night and receded into a remote pool of nothingness.

She simply said, "It's just work. That's all. Now, can I go drink my coffee?"

He nodded, lost in the abyss, as she turned away.

꧁ CHAPTER XVI ꧂

RUE WOKE UP EARLY, hearing her phone ding. It was Josh asking what time he could come get her. She couldn't believe it – it was seven fifteen! Maybe he had fallen asleep thinking about her too. She texted back and said eight. She jumped in the shower, fed Hank, put on some makeup, and assessed her closet. She listened to Vy's descriptions of several outfits, finally settling on: "Black yoga pants with a white hoodie. Pair with black-and-white checkered Vans. This is for downward-facing dawwwwwg in the house." Whatever that meant. Rue threw it on and met Josh at the entrance to her building.

He came up to her and kissed her. He smelled so fresh and clean, like a mountain spring. She liked the way his mouth tasted so early in the morning – minty with a splash of cologne.

"Mmm, yum," said Josh, his voice in her ear, warm and smooth. "You are perfectly delicious, you know that?" Rue smiled, thinking how odd and wonderful that they were thinking the same thought at the same time.

"Where should we go?" he asked.

"I was thinking about this place…it's a walking trail, and there's a café nearby. Maybe we could eat and then walk. What do you think?"

"Your wish is my command."

"Okay, great, it's on Marine. The café's right by the walking trail."

He laughed and said, "Are you talking about Crissy Field?"

She faltered and said, "Oh! You know it? Sorry, I thought it might be a surprise."

He replied with a chuckle, "I realize I'm only a lowly Flagstaffian to you, but yes, I've lived in this mighty city by the bay for years now."

Rue felt foolish. "Of course. I'm sorry."

He squeezed her hand, laughed, and said, "No, I'm just kidding. There's so much about each other we don't know."

As they drove along, he stroked the back of her hand with his thumb. She felt him maneuvering swiftly through the city streets. She turned toward the window, feeling the morning sun flicker on and off her face.

After a few minutes, he said, "So, tell me more about yourself. What do you like to do?"

"Well, I don't know…the usual…work, read, TV, eat, sleep, repeat. Nothing too exciting. And I do a little painting on the side."

"Wait. You paint?" asked Josh, incredulous.

"Yes, a little," she answered self-consciously. "As far I can tell, I'm no Monet or anything. It's just a hobby."

"Very cool," he replied. After a few moments, he said tentatively, "I've been curious since we met…"

"Yes?"

"Well, maybe I'm being intrusive or just plain stupid, but how do you do things, like paint or get to work or cook or put on makeup or well, anything?"

Rue chuckled – Josh wasn't the first person to assume she lived in a dark cave somewhere, trying to decipher the mechanics of a thimble.

"Well, as far as the painting goes, I cut out stencils first, then paint over the top of them. I'll show you sometime if you're interested."

"Let me stop you right there," he jumped in.

She paused and then asked, "Yes?"

"Don't ever say, 'if you're interested,' okay? Just assume I always am."

He said this so flatly and sincerely that Rue was dumbstruck. There had been so few people who had ever really shown an interest in anything she did or said. She blushed and stopped speaking for a few minutes.

He squeezed her hand and urged, "Go on. How is it that you came to know Crissy Field? Or the Cliff House? Or anywhere in the city? How does a blind person get around – I mean, aren't you sort of at the mercy of others for transportation and food and other necessities?"

"No. That's a common misconception, though," she answered definitively. "I mean, when I was younger, there were certain things I had to learn differently from the average child, like how to count steps, how to walk with a cane, how to read braille, how to cook – without burning myself, that is. What a fun process that was…"

He looked quizzically over at the scars she pointed out on her knuckles, wrists, and hands, and said, "Ouch."

"Yup. You should see the ones on my legs. Furniture was my frenemy back then. A couch is a great thing to grab on the way to the chair, but something entirely different when it attacks you full force on the shin. Anyway, I eventually figured things out. I went to a sighted boarding school, so I was forced to adjust quickly. The fact that it wasn't the most accommodating place for blind students ended up being less of a nightmare than the fact that it was an all-girls school." Rue grimaced at the memory.

"Were you teased?"

She scoffed. "More like tortured. Girls are just horrible at that age, especially if you are in any way different. But now that I look back on it, as much as I hated it, I have to admit it made me stronger and forced me to become resilient. I'm not saying it was worth it or justified, but I survived, so that's something."

"Yeah, that's something, for sure. I can't even imagine what that must have been like…"

Rue continued, "They used to say to me, 'Weebles wobble, but they do fall down.' You remember those little toys…nice, right? Anyway, it wasn't all bad. In fact, I had a few teachers who were great to me and also a few friends, but the few girls who were bad, well, they were really bad. This one girl, Julie, she would steal my cane and purposely run into me. She was the worst…"

"God!"

"Yeah, not fun." Rue shifted to a lighter tone, "And later on, it didn't matter anyway – I outshone them all when I became the first person in my class to get a driver's license – boy, were they jealous!"

"Wait, what?! How—? What—? Do you mean you—"

Rue burst out laughing at Josh's confused stuttering, and he stopped and shouted, "Hell – oh! You! You little liar! I'm going to make you pay for that."

He grabbed her chin in a soft pinch, and Rue put on her most innocent baby-doll face. He could only laugh between his feigned anger.

At the café, they ordered their food and coffee at the counter and then carried it to a table. Rue continued, "Actually, what's amazing today is how many new tools are available for people who are visually impaired. A couple of years ago, they came out with this huge audio-tactile map for the entire BART and Muni lines. It's spectacular – I took a weekend or two to memorize it, and now I can pretty much go anywhere by myself. Before that, I stayed home a lot of the time or counted steps or had Vy (or complete strangers sometimes!) help me."

"So how does that map thing work – does it just tell you the street names in braille, or are the dots in the shape of the streets or what?"

"No, well, I mean, not exactly. First, the braille describes instructional steps for the important places at each stop. So maybe, for a specific stop, I need to know how far the train exit door is from the concourse stairs, or maybe I need to know which Muni stop gets me how many steps away from a certain cross street. And another thing that's nice to have is one of those Echo Livescribe pens – it has a small camera inside the tip that can read braille dots and also other details on the page that I might miss – smaller ingrained dots that even sighted people wouldn't be able to see. Anyway, I'll show you sometime – it's pretty cool."

"Sounds like it. Heck, I work with technology every day, but your world sounds way more techie-awesome than mine."

"Jealous? Yup, all the new apps really help too. I'm not saying it's always a walk in the park, literally or figuratively, but it's a lot more convenient than it used to be."

"I bet. Speaking of walks in the park...?" Josh asked.

"Yes, sir?"

"Crissy Field – will it be too rough for you?"

"Not if I hold on to you."

"Deal. Okay, another question."

"Shoot."

"Why wouldn't you stay over with me last night?"

Rue thought about that for a minute. "I guess because I basically stayed over with you Thursday night—"

"Is that what you call what we did?" he interrupted with a joke in his voice.

"Um...I don't know what I would call it, but the point is, we should maybe just...hang out for a while and see what happens. Maybe not rush things...you know?"

"Hmmm, I may be getting mixed signals," he answered with a laugh, and she blushed to her tips. He tempered it with, "Listen, no rush here. Just smooth and slow and easy. Okay?"

"Okay," Rue said with a soft smile.

They finished their food and coffee, then drove over to the Marina and parked the car. They decided to head over to the Palace of Fine Arts before Crissy Field. The weather was fine with the sun shining, and Rue had a heady sense of guileless freedom and cheerfulness – she was out walking with a man! She heard two people with dogs in tow and several kids on bikes racing by.

Josh weaved Rue's hand through the crook of his arm and held it there. She loved the feeling of his arm, so strong and safe. She asked him to describe their surroundings.

He said, "Big stone buildings. Very big."

Rue asked, "Bigger than the skyscrapers downtown?"

"No, not that big, but still…quite big."

"Bigger than a house?"

"Oh yes, bigger than that."

"Bigger than an airplane?"

"Hmmm, maybe about the same size if you stood an airplane on its nose."

Rue laughed. "You remind me of how my nieces describe things."

"Hey!" he replied, insulted but with laughter in his voice.

"Well, it is rather curious, isn't it? The way in which we learn words. I'm always asking my nieces to tell me what they see, but their vocabulary is so limited. They use the most basic words – some of which are descriptive, but most of which are not. I'll ask, 'What are you playing?' and they'll say, 'A game.' I'll ask to hold it, and they'll usually put their tablet in my hand, which always cracks me up. The first time they did this, I asked, 'Is this an Etch-A-Sketch?' I remember kids playing with those when I was younger. I still don't really understand what that is, but I'm guessing it's some type of art you make on a screen. My one niece, the older one, thought my response was hysterical. She said, 'What's an Etch-A-Sketch?' Then she said, 'Aunt Rue, it's my tablet! Don't you know what a tablet is?' I shook my head. 'It's like Daddy's phone, but bigger,' and then I understood what I was holding, but that still didn't help me understand 'the game.' Oh well, Aunt Rue's in the dark again…"

"That must be frustrating," Josh empathized.

"Yes, it is. Sometimes they give me a break and hand me a ball or a block or a paintbrush. Then I'm golden. Or we'll go for a walk. I love our walks. I get a little more of their vocabulary, like 'house, street, dog, step, flower.'"

After a while he said, "So are you telling me I need to use my big-boy words with you?"

She laughed and replied, "Something like that."

Josh pressed, "Are you saying if I don't, you won't play with me?"

She shrugged with a grin, leaning into his side. "Well, that remains to be seen."

"Or heard, as the case may be. Let me try now. Let's sit here on this bench."

She complied as he sat her down beside him. He started, struggling in the most charming way to grasp for words, deconstructing something that had always been second nature to him, "Okay…so, there's a pond in front of us…the water's green, well, I mean, like the color of money, oh, wait, that won't work, it's the color of frogs…ha, that won't work either, will it?"

She said, "Don't worry about the colors. Like I mentioned before, they're mostly irrelevant."

"Okay, hmmm, let's see…the water in the pond is rather flat, and there's a sort of fountain thing shooting up in the middle of it. I see a bunch of birds – in the pond and up in the trees around the pond."

"What kind of birds?"

"Oh, I don't know…some little ones flying around in the branches of the trees and then a couple of bigger ones down by the water."

"Do you see one that's tall and grayish-blue in color with a yellow beak?"

"Hmmm," he paused, then exclaimed in shock, "Yes, I think I do! How did you know? What is it?"

"A great blue heron."

"Yes, but…but…but," he stammered as Rue giggled.

She said humorously, reluctant to alleviate his confusion, "Right over by the trees," she said, pointing. Josh gave his astounded confirmation of the fact.

Then she added cheerily, "Surprised?"

Josh laughed and said, "I think at this point it's safe to say that nothing you say or do will surprise me…at least not anymore. But seriously, though, how did you know?"

"Oh, that's easy, I heard him squawk a minute ago. There are also a few seagulls and a belted kingfisher…should I go on?"

In answer, he kissed her smiling face.

Awhile later, he said, "I bet you didn't know about the swans, though, did you?"

"Are there swans? No, they're so silent, I never know they're there."

"Yep, two, just gliding around and about. Even I know what they are."

"What do they look like?"

"White. Fat. Orange beaks. Long necks."

Rue commented, "Hmmm. Did you know that swans mate for life?"

"No, I didn't know that," answered Josh. Then reflectively, "But that sounds like a nice plan, doesn't it?"

She nodded and leaned her head on his shoulder. They sat in silence for a while, and Rue wondered, was this some type of dream? Things like this didn't happen to her.

Eventually, Rue inquired, "Hey, can I ask you a question?"

"Sure, anything."

"Well, your phone seems to make noises a lot. Like incessantly. Doesn't that drive you crazy?"

"Oh, that," he said, casually. "No, but I'll turn it off if it bothers you."

"Well, no, it's not that…it's just…well, what is it all about? It is work or what…?"

"Yes, mostly work…and some notification settings I have turned on."

"But it's Saturday."

He explained, "No rest for the weary…"

There was a hint of something in his voice. What was it? A reticence, an uncomfortableness, but why? Rue pressed – direct, but light, "So, none of those noises are…from a girl…or from several girls?"

He laughed, but it wasn't as casual as he intended it to be. He said, "Nah. Why? Jealous?"

"No," Rue answered honestly. She wasn't even sure what jealousy felt like, but she knew this wasn't it. She clarified, "Just trying to see what I'm in for, that's all."

"Ah, I see," he said slowly. Then abruptly changing the subject, he said, "You ready for our walk? Come on. Let's go."

"Okay," Rue assented, trying not to read too much into the shift.

They got up from the bench and headed to Crissy Field. As they walked the boardwalk, Josh used his "big-boy" words to describe the scene – the Golden Gate Bridge in the background, the surf, the people and pups walking and jogging along beside them, the fog off in the distance. It was rather entertaining, listening to him struggle for words.

At a certain point, he described an older couple walking directly ahead of them, holding hands and speaking softly to each other.

Rue asked, "That's so sweet. Are your parents like that?"

He scoffed and said, "No, definitely not. Don't get me wrong – they love each other and all, but they're both so busy, I don't think I've ever seen them taking a leisurely stroll together. I remember once when we were growing up, someone at church asked Dad how he and Mom found any time alone together with all of 'those kids,' and Dad's response was, 'We manage – how do you think we ended up with seven?!' pointing at us. I remember my mom scolded him and turned red, and I didn't understand why. Of course, now I understand, and I have to hand it to the guy – when they do find the time, he still chases after Mom like they're teenagers." He paused and Rue smiled. "I hope to be just like him someday." He squeezed her hand in the crook of his arm, and Rue's face beamed. Once again, a dream?

It was a beautiful day, and Rue enjoyed the sounds of the surf washing up on the beach, the dogs barking, the people talking. The air tasted like seawater, and she wondered what it would be like to swim in the ocean. She never had. She wasn't the best swimmer. When she told Josh this, he said he'd take her out someday, which made her laugh. He was so enthusiastic! And boundless, like those dogs she could hear running headlong into the water.

As they finished their walk and drove over to Daniel's house, Josh chatted about his childhood, his siblings, his favorite foods, his job, and his friends. Rue could tell he was also trying to be disciplined – forcing himself to pause and ask her about her life instead of monopolizing the conversation. She replied as best she could. It was hard for her to talk about herself so much. And yet, he drew her out so readily, so unselfconsciously, despite their differences. On the way to Daniel's house, she explained that Daniel and his wife and kids were the only family she had left. He couldn't believe it, couldn't imagine a family unit so small.

As they got closer, he said, "I can drop you off, but if you like, I can come in and meet them. What do you think?"

She was taken aback by his direct request, not wanting to be rude but also not wanting to invite him in. She still felt rather reserved with him, especially about her complicated childhood. She hadn't told him much and didn't intend to anytime soon. It was like a fragile egg she was keeping close to her vest. Plus, she knew Daniel and Cathy would be completely shocked that she had a boyfriend – if, in fact, that was what Josh was. She wasn't even sure of the whole thing herself, let alone ready to open Pandora's box by sharing it with them. But then she also felt such gratitude that Josh was initiating the conversation. She wasn't sure if this was natural – for a guy to ask this after only a few dates. Regardless, though, she knew her response.

"No, not today. It's too soon," she hedged. "Maybe in a few weeks, okay?"

"Sure, sure, no worries. Maybe some other time." He seemed a little hurt, though.

She explained, "It's just, well, it's just, this is all new for me. Dating. You see, I don't date. My brother and sister-in-law will be surprised. They might also be worried for me. They might go into anaphylactic shock. Or have a coronary." Rue stopped to chuckle. He had no idea how uncommon this entire situation was – how could she make him see? "It would be like snow in San Francisco! They'll need time to process. They've always seen me as a sort of...child. Daniel still babies me, and it drives me crazy! But also, really, especially when it comes to men...or the lack thereof. They won't know how to react. I'll need to ease them into it. I don't want them to give you the third degree before I've had the chance to talk to them. Do you mind?"

"No, that's fine. I get it...so, you're gonna hide the big, bad wolf from your family for a while." He growled and squeezed her hand.

"Right. Exactly."

As Josh pulled into the driveway, he exclaimed, "Wow, nice house! Your brother must be doing all right."

"Yes," she replied simply.

"What does he do?"

"He's an entrepreneur. Owns his own business, something financial or techie, I'm not really sure. He's had several start-ups over the years. That's kind of his thing – he starts a company, then he sells it, and then he starts another."

"Wow, very cool. Tell him if he ever needs a sales rep, you know a guy."

"Will do," Rue said.

Josh put the car in park and leaned over to kiss Rue on the mouth. His kisses were always so sudden and impulsive, they took Rue's breath away. She would have to get used to that. It was such an amazing thing to feel that strong mouth on hers in all its vigor and vitality.

He said, "Let me come around and help you out."

Thinking of the probing eyes perched at the window, which may have already seen too much, she said quickly, "No, no, I've got it. Thanks for the fun morning. I'll text you later."

He balked at her snub with a laugh and said, "Okay, until then." She waved as he drove away.

Chapter XVII

Alyssa woke up early and left the house. She'd had just about enough of Kevin's inquiries. So annoying, like a fly that won't stop buzzing around your head. Didn't he get it? Leave her be, for Christ's sake. She texted Josh about fifty times, then called him another twenty, but no response. He was probably still sleeping. Or avoiding her. Whatever. She went into the office for a while and finally, at eleven, when she still hadn't heard from him, she went over to his apartment. Harsha was home, but no Josh. Harsha said he had left early that morning. What the fuck? On a Saturday morning? Harsha said he didn't know where Josh was, but Alyssa didn't believe him.

Alyssa sat down on a chair to wait. Harsha was still in his bathrobe, watching TV. She asked, "So, what'd you do last night?"

"Not much," Harsha answered, looking away evasively. "I went for some sushi and then out for drinks."

"With who?" she challenged.

Harsha raised an eyebrow and said, "Myself. Well, Josh met me for drinks after a while."

"Uh-huh," she said suspiciously. "Where?"

"Oh, some place up on Nob Hill."

What place was he talking about? And why wasn't he just saying the name flat out? Alyssa was running a list of bars on Nob Hill through her head. There weren't many. Alyssa narrowed her eyes at him, and he stood up and excused himself, saying he had to get ready. Whatever, run away, you coward. Based on his answers and body language, they had clearly been out with the new whore. Fucking hell. Alyssa needed to figure out who she was and why the fascination so she could work on a plan to crush her.

Alyssa waited impatiently, clicking through the channels, finally settling on some off-the-grid home-building show. She wondered absently how these people could live without all the amenities. How does one pick up a box of emergency tampons when you live fifty miles from anywhere? Does Amazon deliver there? What about the pill? Does Express Scripts deliver to East Bumfuck, Alaska? About the time they were setting up a solar-powered hot-water pipe system on the roof, Josh came in. Her guard was up immediately upon seeing his flash of dread at her presence, quickly masked with a cheery "Hey."

"Hello, lover," Alyssa greeted him with sugary venom.

No response.

"Any particular reason you can't answer your phone?"

He shrugged and said nonchalantly, "Oh, did you call?"

"Seriously? Where've you been?" Not laughing.

"Listen, Alyssa, I thought we had an agreement. Remember our chat yesterday?"

"Oh, yes, I remember our chat. Is that what the kids are calling it nowadays? How sweet."

He rolled his eyes and said, "You know what I mean. You said you'd give me some space, and I said that would be fine."

"Hmm, I don't remember those exact words, but yes, I agree, it was something about letting you go fuck around for a while, but I guess I didn't think you'd take me quite so literally or do it quite so quickly."

They stared at each other in fuming silence. Finally, she smiled and said, "Anyway, what's the plan?"

"For what?" he asked as a brush-off.

"Well, I have the whole day free, and I thought we could do something. Lunch?"

He regarded her for a moment, and she imagined an old grandfather clock as the mechanism inside spun in abstracted turns. Finally, he said soberly, "Okay, let's go."

In the car, he asked where she wanted to go, and she told him Donnie's Subs on the off chance that the location would make him feel guilty. After all, it was one of their favorites, and they had spent many intimate hours in the back booth, testing their secretive relationship by seeing what dirty things they could get away with in public.

After they ordered, though, the plan didn't seem to be working. He was unusually quiet, fiddling with his napkin and looking around the place, completely ignoring her. Probably trying to devise new lies to tell her. As if she couldn't see through his bullshit.

Their food came, and just as he was about to take his first bite, she blurted out, "So, what does she do?"

"Who?" asked Josh, not skipping a beat, chomping down.

"This new wh—woman of yours."

He furrowed his brow in irritation. "None of your goddamn business. And how's your hubby?"

"Fine," Alyssa answered rather brightly. Why not? Maybe he wasn't going to spill, but why shouldn't she? "In fact, he wanted to take me on a romantic getaway this weekend. Doesn't that beat all?"

Josh grunted a laugh. A small piece of roast beef came out of the side of his mouth, and as he pushed it back in, he said, "Well, why didn't you go?"

"Very funny," she answered with a scowl. She munched on a forkful of salad and tried not to show her annoyance. Must he always bring up her marriage? It was his one card, and he always managed to play it. No imagination.

"What'd you tell him?"

She swallowed and replied, "That I had to work. As a matter of fact, since your ass was busy this morning – literally and figuratively – I did go into work for a while."

She could see relief wash over his face – she wasn't sure why at first, but when he started asking her detailed questions about the progress of the testing, she realized he was happy to have something else to talk about. Chickenshit.

For a while, they ate and she gave him a break, chatting innocuously about work, but about twenty minutes in, she stopped abruptly and said, "You know, our earlier conversation isn't over."

He smiled coyly, grabbing her knee under the table, and said, "Let's not spoil this." His hand started drifting up her leg as he asked, "You ready to go?"

She regarded him and finally said, "Don't ignore my texts next time. Understand?"

"Sure, whatever you want," he said, sweet as pie. He paid their bill and they left.

Back at his place, they banged, ate, and watched a game. He kicked her out around five, and she went home to an empty apartment. Good. Kevin was out. Didn't have to fabricate another scenario, emotion, or thought for the day. Scot-free. She sat down on the couch and read a magazine, thinking in the back of her mind, *I wonder what it would be like to date a Scott.* She never had. Such a definitive, strong-sounding name. Is that why people said scot-free? Or was it something to do with being from Scotland? She'd never dated a Scot either, for that matter. She needed to look for a Scot named Scott. She laughed out loud at herself right as Dixie crawled up in her lap, joining in on the fun.

Just then, Kevin walked in and said, "Well, you're in a good mood."

Fuck. Caught in the act. Of being happy. Now what. Think of a distraction. She said quickly, "I'm taking Dixie for a walk."

"Great, let me put down my things and I'll join you."

"No," Alyssa replied too forcefully, and then nicer, "Um, no thanks, I'm… I'm gonna stop by Janet's place and visit with her for a while. I'll be back later."

Kevin's hurt face was enough to make her want to vomit. She quickly grabbed her purse and the dog's leash and nearly ran out the door.

She got outside and thought, shit, now I have to kill some time. Oh, what a tangled web. She called her friend Janet, who didn't answer. She tried a few more friends, but with no success. She wished she had brought her computer with her – then she could have gone into a coffee shop for a few hours. Finally, she sat outside a café, sipping a latte and reading her phone. She tweeted a few things and then posted a pic of Dixie on Instagram, laughing at the comments she got back. She especially liked it when her friend Dustin wrote, "Is that a dog or a chipmunk?" Poor Dixie. She called one of the guys from work to see if anything was going on later. He seemed rather surprised that she didn't already know. He said Josh had texted everyone, saying they were meeting at the Big 4 at eight thirty. Ding! The bell went off. Nob Hill. The Big 4. The Scarlet Huntington! Of course! She said nonchalantly, "Okay, great, see you there." Her heart was thumping.

Alyssa called her friend Sandra, who was always game for anything on a Saturday night, and they agreed to go together. Alyssa said, "I've gotta ditch my dog and get ready, but I'll be at your place around eight. That sound good?"

"Perfect. We can Uber."

"Cool. Later."

She let Dixie off her leash the moment she got home and ran into the bathroom to get ready, telling Kevin she was going out with some friends and wouldn't be home until late. She didn't hear a reply and didn't bother to see if she'd missed any. As she applied a dark layer of lashes, she thought about meeting the new whore. Wondered what she'd be like. Probably sweet and stupid. Oh well, it didn't matter. It was temporary at best. She was glad she was going with Sandra. She was hot and brassy. The brunette version of Alyssa. When they went out together, there was no stopping them. They thought of themselves as the modern-day Jackie and Marilyn, though Sandra always said she didn't want to be Jackie – she thought Jackie was too stuffy and asexual. She said she wanted to be Jane Russell. Splitting hairs, Alyssa told her, splitting hairs. So, Jane and Marilyn took an Uber to the Scarlet Huntington, dolled up like two walking felonies. Before they got through the door, Alyssa took a deep breath of glee. She remembered back to the conversation a half-hour ago in Sandra's apartment.

"Listen, this place we're going tonight, I need to ask you a favor."

"Sure, what?"

"The guys from work will be there and, well, do you remember that guy Josh I introduced you to a few months ago?"

"The tall, dark, hot one? Yes, that's not the type of guy I would forget. Why, what about him?"

"Well, I'm sort of…seeing him."

"Um…okay…," Sandra responded, thankfully without judgment, just with curiosity. "And…?"

"And…I think he's kind of interested in someone else now, but I'm not one hundred percent sure. Anyway, I think she might be there tonight, so help me stalk her. I'll try to get at her myself, but I figure Josh might have warned her about me. But he wouldn't have warned her about you. You see?"

She laughed and said, "Sure, I see. No problem. I'm on it."

"Great, thanks."

They breezed into the place like a tsunami. They were fashionably late and straight-up fashionable. The place was crowded, and all eyes were on them. Alyssa glanced at Sandra and winked. This was going to be easy. Josh and the guys were at the bar, talking animatedly with the bartender. No sign of a woman in the group yet. Good. They would have a head start on her then. All the better to assess and corner you, my pretty.

They bellied up to the bar and ordered drinks. Josh tried to act casual, but she noticed he scowled at her before turning away toward Harsha. The other guys were like stink on shit when Sandra got near them. She was a natural flirt, and the techie nerds from her team didn't know what hit them. Alyssa stood back to observe and get the lay of the land before gearing up for the conquest. One of the guys got up and offered his barstool. She sat down, drank a martini, and watched the door.

Chapter XVIII

RUE SPENT A HOMEY AFTERNOON with Daniel, Cathy, and the girls. Cathy bundled the girls up, placing them in a double stroller, and Rue, using the stroller like a walker, took them for a walk. As she slowly coursed through the neighborhood, Raquel helped, pointing out her friends' houses and letting Rue know when to turn left or right. Raquel's accuracy with directions wasn't exactly stellar. Once they ended up near the marina, and Rue had to call Daniel to come get them.

As they strolled along, Rue felt happy and smiled, thinking about how sweet the girls were and about her last kiss with Josh. Raquel continued her toddler chatter, now about her Barbie's latest caper in the Barbie cave. Apparently, Raquel had constructed this cave (a hidden doll oasis inside her bedroom closet) to ward off any monsters that might decide to take up residence there. Jordan, for her part, sat in the stroller, straining over her belt to point out the neighbors' dogs with an "Augggg." Raquel somehow knew all of the dogs' names ("Aun'rue, thad's Jack! Thad's Thor! Thad's Bella! Thad's Woger!"). Rue waved at the neighbors as best she could, although Raquel once said, "No, Aun'rue, thad's a bush!" Some neighbors came up to say hi to the girls and chat uncomfortably with Rue. One elderly gentleman yelled into Rue's ear, apparently thinking she was deaf. This was disconcerting, to say the least, but Rue smiled and talked about the weather. Raquel was a share-all kind of gal, just like the expression "Strangers are only friends we haven't met yet." She would say, "Thid id Aun'rue" and "This id 'Ordun." So polite! And Rue loved the fact that Raquel found no need to explain Rue's blindness. To her, she was Aun'rue – nothing more, nothing less. Or rather, "nuddin" more or less.

When they returned to the house, Daniel and Cathy had lunch ready for them. As they ate, Cathy asked if Rue had gone through Great Aunt Louise's jewelry box. Rue said yes, part of it, but not all. She wondered if Daniel had seen the diamond ring.

"A real diamond ring?" he asked, incredulous.

"Yes, it used to be Mom's. I remember the feel of it. She used to let me play with it when I was little. I thought I might wear it now…but I wasn't sure… I wanted to ask you first."

Daniel shrugged and said, "Sure, have at it."

Cathy asked, "That's so strange. I wonder why it was in Great Aunt Louise's jewelry box."

Rue and Daniel grunted in unison at that question.

Raquel asked Cathy, "Mommy, why is Daddy wearing the monster face?"

Daniel's tone changed as he picked up Raquel and said, "Daddy's imitating Shrek. Do you want to imitate Fiona? Let's go find your Fiona outfit, okay?"

Once they were out of the room, Cathy asked, "Did I say something wrong?"

Rue sighed. "No, of course not. Has he told you about Great Aunt Louise?"

"Not much. Just that she was your guardian after your parents died."

Rue answered flatly, "Yes, and our fleecer."

"Hmpf. Hang on, I'll be right back," Cathy said, and Rue heard her carry Jordan away.

When Cathy came back, she was with Daniel. The girls were napping.

Rue asked Daniel, "You haven't told her?"

"Why bother? Water under the bridge."

"Kind of a big bridge," Rue said.

Cathy said, "Would one of you just tell me?"

Rue replied, "Yes, I'll tell you. When Mom and Dad died, they placed us with Great Aunt Louise, whom we barely knew and who was a crotchety old spinster. She had the Victorian notion that children should be seen and not heard." Rue added with a sneer, "She was quite annoyed by the fact that I could hear but not see. Ha! Anyway, you get the picture…"

Cathy breathed out a funny little chuckle as Daniel took up the story, "So, the bitch promptly sent us to boarding school. Separate boarding schools. She didn't believe in those 'co-educational institutions' – they were 'dens of debauchery.' Anyway, it was hell. For both of us. We'd just lost our parents, and then we were separated in a scary new place. One day during my senior year, the principal pulls me in his office and tells me Great Aunt Louise has had a stroke and died. I was like, good riddance, but then the principal goes on to explain (with some fake-ass apology) that she failed to pay the bills the past few semesters, and he wanted to know if everything was going to be settled up. What the fuck? What was he talking about? Of course, I had no idea how she had been handling the bills. She was our legal guardian! Everything had been handed over to her – the life insurance, the house on Arguello, the vacation cabin in Aspen, the cars, the furniture, the bank accounts, the savings, everything! We had foolishly assumed she was managing it for our benefit. But what we didn't know was that the old battle-ax had spent all of our money – every last cent and then some. She timed her death perfectly, leaving us with absolutely nothing and saddling us with a boatload of debts to boot."

Cathy said sadly, "That's awful! I didn't know! Daniel, why didn't you tell me? So...so, your parents didn't have a will?"

"Apparently not," Daniel answered. "Then again, who knows? Great Aunt Louise was very efficient."

Cathy was silent for a few minutes and finally said, "What did you do? I mean, when I met you, Daniel, you were doing fine."

"Yes, on my own! One hundred percent self-made, my darling. Self-made and tenacious as hell – which I guess I should thank Great Aunt Louise for," he grunted, "but I won't."

Rue sighed and chimed in, "Luckily, Daniel had a friend at school, Michael, whose parents helped out – they gave Daniel enough to graduate from the academy."

"Yeah, and I paid them back!"

"And you, Rue?" Cathy asked.

"I dropped out and started working."

"No! I didn't know that...so you never graduated high school?"

"No, I went back and got my GED instead."

"Oh, good for you. My goodness, I had no idea. The whole thing is so awful. I'm so sorry."

Rue shrugged, and Daniel simply repeated, "Water under the bridge..."

Toward the end of the afternoon, Rue mentioned casually that she had met "a boy," which caused both Daniel and Cathy to become completely mute. She assured them it was true but that it was still "very new" and she wasn't sure "where it was going." They instantly suggested that she bring him around so they could meet him, but she declined, saying she wasn't ready. They knew Rue well enough not to press.

On the drive home, Daniel mentioned to Rue that they would be out on the boat next weekend and would therefore miss their Saturday afternoon ritual. Rue wondered with a Mona Lisa smile if she would spend the day with Josh instead.

Walking into her apartment building, Rue stopped in the hallway to talk to Chen. He called out to her directly, saying he was playing checkers with his friend Xie. Chen asked her who the man was.

"My brother, Daniel," Rue answered.

"But a different guy picked you up," he said curiously.

"Yes, that's true. Are you spying on me, Chen?" she asked with a grin.

"Just wondering. Usually, I only see a black girl with you."

"You mean Miss Vy?"

"Yes, Miss Vy. I like her. She's got style!" Rue chuckled at that. Then he continued, "Now, out of the blue, you have two guys with nice cars."

"Maybe I'm getting popular. What do you think of that?"

"Hmm, that depends. Will I meet them?"

"For an inspection?"

"Yes, I'll check them out for you, Miss Rue."

"You think I need protection from my brother?"

"No, I suppose not. But the other guy, he was big. You might need some help with him."

Rue laughed and said, "Like a defibrillator?"

"Huh?" Chen responded, bewildered.

Rue redirected, "Just kidding. Listen, I'll bring him around next time, okay?"

"Okay."

"Bye, Chen."

"Bye, Miss Rue."

She went up the stairs, laughing to herself. Chen, her little superhero. So sweet. Up in her apartment, she cuddled with Hank, who had been missing her. Loosely, in the back of her mind, Rue wondered if she and her "big guy" would spend next weekend together. That would be fun and different. A seed planted, she spent some time imagining them together, maybe driving up to Muir Woods (she could commiserate with Chen!) or over to Napa or walking around town. Or he could come to her place and see her paintings and play with Hank. They could just *stay in*. How those words enchanted her! To have him in her arms again – the touch of the man – those sensations were like nothing else. The thought of them now set her skin on fire. For a whole weekend!

She awoke from her musing with a text from Josh: "I'll swing by the lounge tonight, if that's okay."

She might have to keep him at bay in order to perform, but she figured Bob would entertain him, so she wrote back: "Okay."

She showered, dressed, and headed up the hill to the lounge. She wondered if it would be busy that night. Probably. Saturday nights usually were. When she got there, Bob asked if she would be having any "visitors" tonight (with an impudent tone, the teaser!), and she answered mysteriously, "Maybe...," and to "mind his own beeswax." As he chuckled and walked away, Rue wondered what time Josh would arrive. She wasn't going to sit on pins and needles this time, waiting to see when he would arrive. If he came, he came; if he didn't, he didn't.

Rue therefore felt foolish during a rendition of Nat King Cole's "I Don't Know Why" when Josh interrupted her with a kiss on the lips, causing her to choke and then laugh with a blush. Did the patrons see that? She was sure Bob saw it. Ugh. She heard Harsha say hi, and Josh mentioned he had brought some friends. Rue smiled and nodded toward where she thought they were standing, but she wasn't sure and felt awkward. She decided to continue playing as they drifted away to the bar.

At the end of the song, she felt her watch – it was only seven fifty and too early for her break, so she pressed on, trying to ignore the sound of the ever-expanding group loitering at the bar. She heard Josh's deep voice and hearty laugh in the mix. He was so popular! So many friends! There was no Vy or Anthony to buoy her tonight. She was a woman on an island with a piano. She wondered if it might not be easier to continue playing and not have a break at all. Then she wondered self-consciously if they were talking about her. She must be a novelty: a blind lounge singer girlfriend. What would his friends think? How would he explain her?

Around nine fifteen, her throat was dry, and she was thirsty for her hot tea, so she stopped and went over to the group, trying her best not to run into anything or anybody. Bob said her tea would be ready in a minute. He seemed to hover a few minutes, maybe to provide cover, which Rue thought was curious. Josh put his arm around her and said to the group, "Hey everyone, this is my gal, Rue. Rue, this is everyone!" They said hello in unison. Then, strangely out of place with that hearty hello, she heard one woman say derisively, "Oh! This is Rue, Josh?" and then another woman said with a bite, "Seriously, Josh? You have *got* to be kidding!"

Josh fairly hissed at them, "Shut it!" to which they both laughed outright, whispering something dismissive and corrosive. Rue was confused, hurt, mortified. She had several thoughts all at once – the first being, who were these women?! Why were they being so rude? She was blind, not deaf, for goodness' sake. Then she thought, so this was how his friends viewed her? It was worse than she could have ever expected! Was she really that bad? How did she look? Since she hadn't spoken a word, this opinion must be based solely on the way she looked. She pulled down on her dress self-consciously and tucked a lock of hair behind her ear. She thought back to Vy's hanger recording of her outfit: "The quintessential little black dress, but with a twist – it's made with jersey – no, not the cow, the fabric! Comfy, casual, daytime or night. V-neck must be worn with the silver pendant necklace, which falls discreetly down into the bosom of love." Rue grabbed her hand around the pendant and held it fast. What was it that warranted their censure? Or did she have something on her face? Did she have something in her teeth? She ran her fingers across her cheeks quickly and ran her tongue over her teeth. Oh, the dreaded lack of mirror capabilities at a time like this!

Thank goodness for Bob. He jumped in and said to the two women, "Ladies, need a refill?" and then to Rue, "Here's your tea," and under his breath, "You look like a million bucks. Don't pay any attention to the dog pound."

Rue smiled gratefully. Okay, so they *were* bitches. Phew! Nothing to be done with that. Rue had encountered the same sort her whole life. She knew the method of recourse – complete lack of acknowledgment. Josh, either oblivious or not knowing how to navigate the situation, turned to the guys and said a little too loudly, like the salesman he was, "Isn't she an amazing singer? She memorizes all those songs too." Rue nodded uncomfortably and sipped her tea.

After a few seconds, Josh turned his attention back to the guys, trash-talking over sports and techie jargon. Rue, sitting quietly by his side, felt oddly alone in the loud sea of people. She heard Bob at the other end of the bar, taking orders and serving drinks. Then, out of the blue, like a breath of fresh air in a stifling smog, Harsha came up to her and said with his friendly

English accent, "You sound great tonight. How are you?"

Rue breathed a sigh of relief and smiled gratefully before answering, "I'm okay, thanks. I didn't realize…I'm feeling a little…stupid because, well, because I didn't realize Josh was coming with quite so many people tonight…"

"Yeah, sorry about that. You know Josh – he texted two guys, and twelve people showed up. Anyway, don't worry about them. Did you have a nice afternoon? Josh mentioned something about your brother?"

"Yep, visited with family. Went for a walk with my nieces. Played Barbies and dress-up – you know, everything was very hands-on," she said with a laugh. "What did you do?"

Before he could answer, Josh was there at her side, asking them, "Hey, what are you two talking about?" Then, before either could answer, he said, "This place is packed tonight, isn't it? You ought to do very well, Rue. How much do you make in a night anyway?"

What had gotten into him? He was acting so strangely, so different from their walk earlier. He seemed nervous or uncomfortable or just plain *off*. She couldn't place it.

Rue and Harsha were both silent, thinking their separate thoughts.

Thankfully, Bob came over right then and asked Rue if she wanted anything to eat. She said, "No, I'm fine, thanks."

"You sure?" he asked, hovering. It was as if he wanted to stay and protect her, but from what? She was suspicious and on edge.

She replied slowly, "Sure, on second thought, some fries, please."

Before he could place her order, Josh hollered, "A round of shots," which got the entire group riled up. After Bob brought them, Josh tried to get Rue to take one, but she insisted she couldn't – she was working. She wondered if his behavior was related to the alcohol, but she sensed something more lingering under the false display. She finished up her tea, took a few nibbles of the fries, and went to the ladies' room. She stayed awhile, breathing and thinking. What was the deal with Josh acting like the big man on campus? Why? Nervous about introducing Rue? She tried to picture the glass half full – maybe he wanted to show her off to his friends. Maybe he wanted to be near her. Maybe he wanted to show his support. Then she thought, maybe he wasn't ready for this. Maybe he realized that dating someone like Rue was more than he could handle. Maybe he wasn't ready for the inevitable ridicule that would come his way. People have a funny way of reacting to things that are different, and usually not in a warm and inviting way. If Rue knew anything about life, she knew this. Could Josh's simple, easy, popular personality take this hit? Had he even thought about it? Was he just realizing it tonight and having second thoughts?

As she ran her hands under the sink, trying to wash away her pondering, she heard the door open and the voices of two women come in. If Rue was not mistaken, they were the two women who had mocked her earlier. Of course! They had come to ambush her. Rue braced herself, quickly grabbing a paper towel to dry her hands and escape, but before she'd made a clean getaway, they were beside her, one touching her arm.

"Oh, don't rush away on our account. Stay. Rue, right? Isn't that your name?"

Rue nodded, thinking: don't engage, stay calm, flee.

The other woman said, "Such an unusual name." Then, related to nothing, "I remember my dad used to say, 'I rue the day I started smoking!' And you know what? He died of lung cancer. I've always hated that word ever since."

Rue couldn't help herself. She asked flatly, "Cancer?"

The woman sputtered, in shocked anger, "No, you idio—"

The first woman interrupted, cinching her grip on Rue's arm, "Now, now, Sandra, don't scare the girl away. Haha, sorry about that, Rue." She cleared her throat and said with false sweetness, "We just wanted to chat with you for a few minutes. You don't mind, do you?"

"Well, actually," Rue hedged, thinking, get your freakin' hand off my arm, woman! "I have to get back..." She tried to break free but to no avail.

"I'm sorry – we're being rude, aren't we? Let me introduce myself. I'm Alyssa Greer and this is Sandra Thompson."

Rue said begrudgingly, "Hi, nice to meet you." She supposed they were friends of Josh's, after all, so she should attempt to be civil, even if they weren't.

"And you are Rue...what was the full name?" Alyssa purred.

Rue raised an eyebrow but answered, "Cavendish." Really? Was this a meeting with the queen – she needed my full name?

"So, you're...what...like, dating Josh?"

"Um, yes...I'm sorry, I really need to get back..."

"Oh, we won't keep you but a moment. So how did you two lovebirds meet?"

"Take a guess," Rue replied with a pinched smile, waving her hand toward the door.

Alyssa said, "Oh...! Here, then, eh? Interesting..."

Sandra spit out, "But…but…you're…you're blind!"

Seriously? Alright. These chicks were pissing her off. Rue said quickly, with a wrench of her arm and a dodge toward the door, "Yep, as a bat. Gotta go…"

"Wait, we have a few more questions…I was curious…" Alyssa said, but Rue grabbed the handle of the door, effectively barricading herself from the reach of the vultures.

As Rue scooted out the door, she said breezily, "It's been a pleasure."

The two women were like, "Huh?"

Rue cried back through the doorway, "To leave. Later!"

In the lounge again, Rue breathed a sigh of relief – she felt as if she had escaped a coroner's inquest. Jesus, what the hell was *that* all about? So shady! Clearly one or both of them wanted Josh and were trying to get the skinny on Rue, but Rue didn't play those mean-girl games. This wasn't her first rodeo.

She sat down at the piano and began Dinah Shore's "Buttons and Bows." She closed her eyes and tried to wrap herself in a musical cocoon, switching next to Tracy Chapman's "Give Me One Reason." In between this and her third song, she heard Josh greeting a new group that had just entered the bar. More friends? Was it like this everywhere he went? Always so popular! As she listened to the commotion and began singing, she was startled when she felt that oh-so-lovely grip on her arm again. Alyssa!

"Hi Rue! I'm putting a big bill in your bowl. Can you play 'Don't Stop Believing' for me?"

Ugh. Rue hated that song with a passion. She said, "Sorry, don't do it."

"Oh, come on, sure you do," Alyssa insisted, singing a few pitchy bars of the chorus.

Rue redirected, "Sorry, it's not one I play." Where was Josh? He must have been distracted by his visitors.

Ignoring Alyssa, Rue quickly began another song. Alyssa added a little twist to Rue's arm before letting go (who does that?!) and walked away with a loud, "What the fuck! She wouldn't play it! I'm taking my twenty bucks back." A second later, Rue heard her rifling around in the fishbowl and wondered absently if she took more than her twenty, the bitch.

The next hour and a half went slowly. Rue tried to tune out the sound of laughter and loud, raucous voices up at the bar. She heard Josh, deep in the mix – joking, laughing, drinking – doing just about everything to make it seem as though nothing was out of the ordinary. And maybe for him, it wasn't. But for Rue, she felt alienated in a way she hadn't before. Of course, she was used to being teased and prodded by unfeeling, prejudiced, moronic idiots, but this was different. Was Josh endorsing their behavior? Maybe only ignoring it, but still, did that absolve him? Was he even aware of Rue's presence anymore? Her mind was spinning as she pounded away on the keys, willing her feelings and the night away quickly.

CHAPTER XIX

IT WAS LATE AND THE LOUNGE was quieting down, so Rue finished her set with Lionel Richie's "Lady" and slowly headed over to the bar, where she could hear Josh's gang still partying. They were rather lubricated, and Rue tried to figure out how to put Josh off and get out of there. No such luck. She asked Bob for her things, and there was Josh, like a magnet, his arm around her, slurring words into her ear, his lips on hers. She tensed up, stayed inert, and waited.

He said to the gang, "Let's go to Bogie's next. You guys down?"

As they responded in the affirmative, Rue stood there, mute. All she wanted was to get to her bed and Hank and the things that made her feel safe. As the gang settled up their bills, put on their coats, and headed out the door, Josh was still oblivious to Rue's demeanor as she kept a firm grip on the bar.

He grabbed her hand and tried to lead her out the door, but she stopped him, saying, "Josh, I'm kind of tired. I think I'll just go home."

She felt him lean over her and say, "What? What do you mean? You don't want to go out with us? Why not? Come on! It'll be fun!"

"I told you, I'm tired," she emphasized and tried to release herself from his grip. "You go ahead, have a good time."

"But...but...I just assumed you'd go out with us after your set was over... we all waited around for you to finish...you don't want to go?"

Putting this on her! Seriously? Like she'd held him up! She hadn't asked for them to come in the first place! She took a deep breath. "Josh, listen, it was great meeting your friends, and I'm glad you brought them in to see me, but right now, all I want to do is go home and crash. I'm sorry."

"Well, okay...so...so...do you need me to take you home...do you want me to come with you...?"

Just then Rue heard Alyssa's voice say loudly, "Josh, come on! We're waiting!"

Josh answered his own question, "You're alright then…you sure? Yeah? Okay? Okay. I'll call you tomorrow."

Rue stood quietly. He gave her a quick peck on the lips and was off, saying to Alyssa, "I'm coming. I've got first round!"

She went home to a cold bed and a confused heart.

The next morning, Rue woke up feeling better. Mornings always put things in perspective. As she fed Hank and drank her coffee, she reminded herself that she was just along for the ride with Josh, right? Who cares if he has more friends and a fuller life (by society's standards anyway) and that his friends seem skeptical, if not hateful, toward her. Maybe that's how it goes when you first start dating someone. What did she know? Besides, that Alyssa chick was obviously after Josh – why else would she act that way? Despite that, Rue hadn't seen Josh reciprocating, so why get bothered by her? Clearly, Josh still wanted to be with Rue and give *her* his time, as was apparent by his five early-morning texts, all proclaiming how sorry he was about last night, that he drank too much and wish he had taken her home instead of going to Bogie's. He said he was paying for it with a "monster-sized hangover" and that he'd "learned his lesson." Rue wondered about that. Then he asked when he could see her again.

She tried to think of him in a fresh, objective light. She did enjoy him. He was fun, if not deep. Sure, he had been drunk and mostly oblivious to the dark undertones of the night, but then she couldn't very well hold him accountable for something that happened in the ladies' restroom. And so what if he hadn't come to her rescue last night? Had she ever needed rescuing before? Hadn't she always taken care of herself? Hadn't she always sealed herself against the haters? Hadn't there always been haters – her whole life – no matter the circumstances? Why give them credence? Why give them the power? Wasn't it better to simply ignore them and rise above?

And this was just a fling, right? It didn't matter. Nothing really mattered when it was all for fun anyway, right? So what if Rue had been thinking about Josh nearly constantly since the moment they met and about that night in his bedroom where she had gone to a distant planet filled with new, spectacular sensations. So what if she couldn't get the taste of him out of her head. So what if his laugh and teasing sent a shiver down her spine. So what if he was a little boy who needed to be coaxed and coddled just like Raquel and Jordan.

Did that mean she was in over her head? Did that mean she should walk away when she was barely out of the gates? Did that mean she should be bothered by Alyssa?

Rue contemplated, scratching Hank's neck. She didn't initially respond to Josh's texts, but then he sent this: "Can I come over? I need to talk to you."

She thought about that. She wrote back: "Sorry, not today, I have to do my laundry."

"Are you sexting me?"

Despite her cautious mood, she laughed. "Very funny. Seriously, though, I'm headed to the laundromat in a few minutes. I'll catch up with you later."

"I can't even interest you in lunch?"

"Sorry, I really am busy. Rain check?"

"Um, no rain check, whatever that means. Listen, the thought of you putting quarters in a grimy, rusted-out laundromat is making me want to slit my wrists. Why don't you come over here and use our washer and dryer?"

"I don't know…"

"Why not? Harsha won't mind. We have detergent and dryer sheets. More importantly, NO quarters required!"

Rue smiled. Well, it would be easier…and it would save money. Just a fling, right? "Okay, pick me up downstairs in fifteen minutes."

"You're on!"

"Btw, they no longer use quarters."

"No quarters? What? Mind BLOWN!"

"Cards with credit."

"You learn something new every day. Okay, see you in fifteen."

"Okay."

She smiled as she grabbed her laundry basket and purse. She gave Hank one last scratch, locked up, and headed downstairs. When Josh pulled up, he parked and came out to help her, leaning down to kiss her and take the basket. The spark she felt set her mind at ease about last night. After all, who cared what his friends thought of her? He didn't seem to notice or mind, so why should she? And his kiss! Still with the shiver and the fire.

Awhile later, up in his apartment, they got the first load started and sat down in the living room. Eventually Harsha came in and talked briefly about the night before. Rue sensed he somehow knew or understood about the unwelcome exchanges with the two girls, but he didn't bring it up and neither did she. Instead, they both focused on Josh as he said to Rue, "We missed you at Bogie's last night. You should have come." Then to Harsha, "Oh my god, that place was packed."

Harsha replied, "Yes, and it smelled like a reefer den."

Josh laughed and replied, "Yeah, I was a mile high just from breathing it. Of course, the two tequila shots didn't hurt."

Harsha said, "Well, I decided – quite wisely, I think – to forego the shots, and I would suspect I'm feeling a damn sight better than you are this morning."

"The important thing, though, is that I'm still *looking* better."

"Bloody hell you are!" Harsha countered, tossing a pillow at Josh's arm, which brushed against Rue's leg. Harsha excused himself to get ready. He was meeting friends who were in town from London. He groaned, saying they wanted a full tour of Fisherman's Wharf.

Once he stepped away, Rue said to Josh, "Glad you had fun last night."

"Outside of missing you, yeah, it was fun. Next time, you should come."

"Hmmm, I'm afraid I'm not much of a drinker. And besides, I'm not so sure all of your friends would have wanted me there."

"Don't be ridiculous – they loved you."

"Oh, I don't know about that…"

"What do you mean?" His tone was curious and slightly defensive.

She sighed and said, "Who were the mean girls, Josh?"

"Oh! Those two," he scoffed. Suddenly intent, "Why, did they bother you?"

"Yes, a little. They were…rude."

"What did they say?" he asked sharply.

Rue paused and finally said, "Enough. It was as if they already…hated me. I can't imagine why…can you?" Her inflection didn't leave much of a question.

He chuckled uncomfortably. "Just ignore them."

She said quietly, "So…you're not…*with* either of those girls?"

"What?! Hell no! Come on! Seriously?" he protested too much. "I don't even know the one woman, and the other is just some woman from the office."

"You mean Alyssa?" Rue asked, trying to keep the tremor out of her voice.

Before he could answer, Harsha came back in the room and said, "Bye, wish me luck."

Josh spoke quickly, with a fake laugh, "Bring us back some trinkets."

As the door closed behind him, a deafening silence filled the room. Josh came over and pulled Rue up from the couch and wrapped his arms around her. He whispered in her ear, "I'm sorry. They mean nothing. She means nothing. Okay? I'm sorry about last night. I should have been there for you. I didn't realize."

Rue's face was pressed against his chest, but she pulled away and asked again, "Alyssa?"

He stepped back and groaned. Ah-ha, there *was* something! Rue's stomach instantly filled with knots. He sat her down on the couch next to him and said slowly, "Okay, yeah, I mean, she's had a crush on me for a while. I've told her (many times!) I'm not interested, but well, some girls, they can't take a hint, you know? But I can assure you, it doesn't mean a thing! For Christ's sake, she's married!"

Rue listened, trying to decipher his words and the meaning behind them. He seemed sincere, and she felt vindicated. She wasn't dreaming. The fact that he wasn't denying it was reassuring. But when he said it didn't mean a thing, did that also mean nothing had ever happened between them?

Taking her hands in his, he continued, "I'm really sorry if she bothered you. To be honest, she can be a real pain in the ass. She's just plain pushy sometimes. If I didn't have to get along with her for work reasons, I'd want nothing to do with her. I always feel like I'm navigating a minefield with her because she's rather volatile. The guys get annoyed with her too. Sometimes you have to be a team player. I'm sure you get it – you work in an office too, and things can be dicey, but you figure out a way to get along with everyone, even the people who drive you crazy."

Rue nodded slowly. After a minute or two, she said, "Um, okay, I guess. Not to beat a dead horse or anything, but you're saying you two never hooked up, right?"

He exhaled and kissed her cheek before saying, "Right. Nothing like that." He suddenly stood up and said airily, "So what should we do today? Do you want to stay here or do you want to go out? I could pick up some takeout and bring it back. We could watch a movie or something on TV. Or listen to some tunes and dance around. I'll tell you my favorite XM Satellite Radio channels, and you can tell me yours. Or we could go for a drive. I'm open to anything. Your choice. You pick. Today is going to be called Rue's Choice Day! We can do whatever you want, whenever you want, and I'll be a slave to your selections. Go ahead – gimme, gimme!"

She sighed. She found herself smiling. All right. She wasn't an idiot. He was changing the subject and doing it in his oh-so-Josh charming way. Should she let him get away with it? What was the alternative? Did she really want to waste her Sunday talking about this woman at his office, even if there had been something between them? Did it matter? Like he said to her that first night, he was twenty-eight years old. Sure, he had a past, but he was focused on her right here, right now, wasn't he? Or at least he certainly seemed to be as he lifted her off the couch in a warm embrace.

He slowly kissed down the length of her neck, and she felt herself melting. Just then, they both jumped as the washer buzzer sounded. He laughed and led her over, helping her with the lid and the dryer sheets. As she moved the clothes from the washer to the dryer, Josh grabbed her around the waist. He asked, "Well? What'll it be? I'm on pins and needles. What's Rue's Choice?"

She said, "Hmmmm, let me see, what were the options again? Movie, TV, music, drive? What about basket weaving? Macramé? Photography? Quilting? Skydiving? Skeet shooting? Bungee jumping? Water aerobics?"

"Whatever you want. Your wish is my command," he purred into her hair.

She laughed and finished with her clothes, slowly turning around to face him. He kissed her and she sank into it, letting her body relax against him. Finally, they broke apart and she said, "What do you think about just…staying in and hanging out?"

His answer was a kiss with a murmur, "Mmm-hmmm, sounds perfect."

They spent the next few hours washing, drying, folding (he ended up doing his laundry too), kissing, listening to the TV, laughing, eating, talking, and generally getting to know each other better. It was easy and relaxed and fun. She marveled at the fact that they got along so well after having only known each other for less than two weeks. It was new and fresh and exciting.

At some point halfway through a Jack Ryan movie, they were making out on the couch and he asked if she minded moving to the bedroom. Her lips and body were on fire and she nodded.

He wrapped his arms around her, lifting and carrying her to the bedroom. As he gently placed her on the bed, his lips found hers again, and they lay together in a warm embrace for several minutes until he broke from her and asked, "Want to get under the blankets?"

She said, "Sure," and stood up beside the bed. He pulled back the covers and then, kissing her, placed her lightly down against the pillows. His hand began to reach cautiously toward the bottom of her sweatshirt and inched underneath it. His fingers were so soft, they caused her to jump. Confused, he yanked his hand away. She chuckled and said, "Sorry, ticklish." He exhaled and replied, "Oh, okay, phew." His next touch to her skin was less cautious and more purposeful – a seeking from her navel to her breast. Her body reached toward the touch this time. It felt like the heat of the sun on a cold winter's day. She wanted more and he responded by lifting her top over her head and cupping her breasts to his face. He quickly un-clasped her bra and ran his tongue over her nipples. She closed her eyes and felt every single inch of her chest and groin on fire. It was like a miracle, she thought randomly, how her body could be so alive in a way it had never been before. How did this man do it? He was a master mechanic who knew how to operate a vehicle that had been out of commission. He had brought it back to life! She let out a sigh of pleasure and he moved his mouth lower, kissing her stomach, and then investigating her lower regions in a studied mastery of her most untouched inner parts. She let herself succumb to every touch, every feeling, every raging nerve ending, every warm flow.

At some point, he took his clothes off and she used her hand to explore him. He lay back and groaned under her touch. Finally, when both were in a state of near-climax, he placed himself inside her and moved forward until she cried out for him to stop, clutching his haunches to her in a rush to orgasm, a tight pleasure-filled clench. He whispered something in her ear, but she put her finger to his lips, "Josh, shhhhhh." She felt his smile as he moved his mouth mutely away. She reveled in the intense spasms of the orgasm, which reached into the white-hot space of her inner island. The minutes ticked by unacknowledged until she was back with him and feeling his tightened jawline with her hand, nodding for him to go, to which he waited not a moment too long, plunging into action, swift and complete.

They lay back on the pillows for a while, and then he went to the bathroom and came back. While he was away, she pulled the covers over her and lay on her side, snuggling up to the smell of him in the bedsheets. All thoughts of the night before were gone. She was in a cocoon of bliss. He came back and, without another word, lay down beside her and wrapped his arms around her. They slept.

Rue dreamed she was walking a tiger on a leash by the beach. The tiger led her in and out of the water. The tiger kept splashing her, and she tried to lead him away from the surf, but he wanted to play and she couldn't restrain him. Finally, her arms got tired, and he led her into the water until she was in above her knees and then above her waist and then above her chin. She started to panic and tried to release him, but the leash was suddenly around her neck and still attached to the tiger as he swam deeper and deeper into the water. She woke with a start, breathing hard and raising her fingers lightly to her neck. Josh woke up and asked, "You okay?"

She shook it off and said with a shiver, "Um, yeah, bad dream."

He took her in his arms, pressing her face against his chest. A half hour went by. Then Rue mentioned her laundry, so he helped her to the bathroom and handed her a warm, wet washcloth. She smiled up at him as he kissed her and closed the door behind him.

Back in his room, he helped her dress and then grabbed her in a bear hug, lifting her off the ground and saying with feeling, "God, I think I love you!"

Rue pulled away in shock. *What* did he just say?

"What? What did you say?" she choked out.

He put her down and said again, more soberly this time, "I said I think I love you."

The strangest thought occurred to Rue at that very moment. It was this: What a farce! Then a split second later, this: He wants me! He loves me! This gorgeous hunk of a man picked *me*!

She gulped – mute, flat, inert.

"You have nothing to say?" asked Josh, now with a cautious hedging in his voice. "Have I freaked you out?" He formed his hand into a fist, placing her hand on top, and moved it to his heart like an arrow stabbing there. Rue remained quiet and thoughtful. Josh continued, "Listen, it's cool. I'm not asking for anything...in return...for you to feel the same way...at least not yet." He laughed self-consciously. "I know it's...well, it's fast...I get that. I couldn't stop myself from saying it. I wanted you to know how I feel and that this isn't just a fling for me. This isn't just sex. Although, if it was...well...," he squeezed their conjoined hands.

Rue was processing, processing, processing. He was so impulsive! Finally, she said with reserve, "Josh...," she paused, "I like you...I really like you... and I am so amazed by...this thing we're doing. I have to pinch myself! I can't possibly understand it all, you know? It's as if I've landed on another planet!"

She stopped as she felt him breathing in and out against her hand. She continued softly, "But you don't know me yet, and I don't know you...not really...and frankly, I'm not sure how I feel. I know I like spending time with you, and I like the way you make me feel, but—"

"No buts!" Josh cut in. "No buts for now, okay? Like I said, I get it…it's fast and I'm crazy and you need time. No worries, let's just forget I ever said anything, okay?" He let her hand go.

Rue's heart went out to him. "Josh, it's not that I don't want to feel that way about you. I do. But I need time. Okay?"

She stood on her toes to pull his face down to hers. She placed her lips on his, and he kissed her back with some reluctance. Then he slowly bent into the kiss with care and raised her back up into his arms.

He said with a chuckle, "You know I'm like putty in your hands."

She replied, "Yes, you're my Play-Doh. Now, let's finish the laundry."

He smacked her butt and set her down. "All right," he relented.

They went back to the living room and tried to forget the "love" conversation. As they finished the laundry and listened to music, the brief darkness that had swept over the mood was gone. They were happy in their time together and in the newness of it all (whatever "it all" was).

Harsha showed up after a while and told them about his "full tourism immersion experience," saying his friends were amused by Fisherman Wharf's famous "bush-man" who was on the "warpath" and had scared the "living daylights" out of so many tourists that he had trouble getting his friends to come away. Josh burst out laughing, but Rue was perplexed and asked what they were talking about. Harsha explained that it was some homeless guy who dressed up like a bush and crouched down on the sidewalk until "some poor sucker" walked by and was startled by this inanimate leafy thing jumping up and screaming at them. Apparently it was hysterical, but to Rue it sounded a little cruel. She didn't get it. Regardless, Rue had to admit that Harsha's storytelling ability was entertaining. She laughed as she sat on Josh's lap, reveling in the thought that no matter what happened last night with those two witches, she was here with Josh now. She was his and he was hers, and nothing could take that away.

When Josh drove her home, she kissed him goodnight and asked about next weekend, telling him how Daniel and Cathy were going to be gone. He said, "Hey, we should go away somewhere!" She said that sounded great, thinking, wow, in for a penny, in for a pound! He explained that he would be out of town during the week – to Idaho on Monday, and then to Oklahoma Tuesday through Friday, but would call her every night and would plan a getaway for them for Saturday and Sunday. She said she would have to see if she could get out of her shift at the Big 4 on Saturday, but since she rarely asked for time off, it shouldn't be a problem.

Back in her apartment, she gave Hank extra cuddles; he had been lonesome without her and showed an uncharacteristic need for attention. As she petted and scratched him, she contemplated Josh's earlier proclamation. Love really was like a drug, wasn't it? Her whole life, she had prided herself on being practical, methodical, and reasonable. And yet, against her better nature, against everything that felt stable and normal and steady within her, she wanted to say "I love you" back. She wanted to jump – no, dive – off that cliff! Not because she was head over heels, not because her heart was one hundred percent full. Because in reality, her head was still leading, and her heart still came second. She wasn't sure how to turn that hierarchy around, but boy, how close she had come! The way he touched her! The way he whispered in her ear and kissed her on the mouth and held her in his arms. There was something otherworldly about it – as if the veritable air they breathed together was hot and sultry and intoxicating. As if they were the only two inhabitants on earth and were perfectly in sync, intertwined, symbiotic. How could she not love that?

As she got ready for bed, she wondered, *did* she love him? Or did she love the feeling of love? It was so new to her – could it just be the novelty? It was hard, though, not to connect this newness with the sense of him. After all, there was no one else to compare him to. There was the rub. How could she be certain? She had no idea! It was funny – sometimes she wondered if she even *liked* him. He was so different from her – impetuous, bold, uninhibited. In his enthusiasm and eagerness for life, he seemed to exhibit a sporadic thoughtlessness, a need for reassurance and placating, a lack of regard for others. She had to admit this bothered her.

But then, she contemplated this thing called love. How was she to judge? It was like trying to describe the meaning of life to a salamander. She was at such a disadvantage! A thirty-two-year-old with no prior experience at love, with no way to temper the physical and emotional pull of it. Even the amazing biological aspects of it – she was a baby against its powers – endorphins, serotonin, pheromones. Lions and tigers and bears, oh my.

And there he was – a man with big shoulders to grasp and strong arms in which to sink. It really was like falling, wasn't it? Just like they said. Whoever *they* were. It was as if someone had dropped her from a twenty-story building, and instead of falling to the hard cement below, she had fallen into a fluffy, white cloud of warmth and serenity. She fell asleep thinking about the cloud and the feeling of Josh's arms around her.

Later that week, while rifling through Great Aunt Louise's jewelry box, Rue found a few items she couldn't decipher. She brought them to Vy. The first, Vy told her, was an old postcard that said, "Hello from Grant Rapids, Michigan" on one side and on the other, "Louise, wish you were here! We saw some spectacular sculptures and flowers at the gardens today and artwork at the museum. Weather good – 74 and sunny. Hope to see you in a week. Love, Bunny." Who was Bunny? It was hard to imagine militant Great Aunt Louise with a friend named Bunny. Rue shrugged and handed Vy the next item.

It was made of hard card-stock paper, folded over once, with embossed writing on the inside. She felt a raised photo on the front. Vy said it was a photo of two people framed in an oval shape. Above the photo, it said, "Welcome. Thank you for joining us as we celebrate our special day: The Wedding of David Cavendish and Sophie Reasoner."

Rue cried, "My parents' wedding program!" Her hand flew to her mouth as Vy continued reading.

Vy opened it and said it listed the date, the sermons and songs, and the wedding party. Rue didn't know any of the names except Great Aunt Louise, who was listed as "Aunt of the Bride." They had been married in Grace Cathedral. Crazy – that was just a few yards from the Scarlet Huntington!

Vy read the only other words on the program:

Sonnet 116
Let me not to the marriage of true minds
Admit impediments. Love is not love
Which alters when it alteration finds,
Or bends with the remover to remove.
O no! it is an ever-fixed mark
That looks on tempests and is never shaken;
It is the star to every wand'ring bark,
Whose worth's unknown, although his height be taken.
Love's not Time's fool, though rosy lips and cheeks
Within his bending sickle's compass come;

Love alters not with his brief hours and weeks,
But bears it out even to the edge of doom.
If this be error and upon me prov'd,
I never writ, nor no man ever lov'd.
          ~ William Shakespeare

Rue made Vy read it a few times until she had it memorized. Love. Never bending, ever-fixed, does not alter, never shaken…her parents' love was like this! She suddenly remembered back to the times when her dad would get home from work, come racing up the stairs, and sweep up her mom into his arms and kiss her. Her mom would laugh and kiss him back, eventually pulling away, saying, "David! The kids!" Rue also remembered how he would bring her mom flowers. She would put them in a vase by the kitchen sink and would let Rue smell and touch them several times a day. Even when her parents' friends were over, Rue remembered that her parents were always so close to each other, whispering in each other's ear, laughing at some inside joke. Although Rue was young and blind, she felt their love for each other – she sensed it in their very movements and in their energy and in her own being, knowing she was a reflection and result of that love.

Rue asked Vy to describe the photo of them. "Hmmm, let's see, it's a pretty little lady with dark hair and blue eyes – she looks a lot like you, especially around the eyes and mouth. Your dad, let me see, he's got feathered brown hair, sort of '80s-ish, and he's tall, or a lot taller than her anyway."

"What are they doing in the photo?"

"They're standing in front of some trees. She's smiling at the camera, but he's looking down at her, with oh-so-much love, girl – I wish you could see! His arm is around her waist, and they look like they're having a grand ol' time, you know?"

Rue nodded. "Do they look…happy?"

"I'll say!" Vy replied. "And then some."

Rue sighed and smiled. She said to Vy, "Thanks."

"Sure, honey – that's some legacy you have there."

"Yeah…yeah…," Rue replied distractedly.

Later that night, Rue wondered, was she meant to have a love like that? Was Josh meant to be that love?

Chapter XX

Kevin was beginning to fray around the edges. He couldn't help it. He was not the guy to wear a chipper facade when he was feeling black as death inside. One of the women at his office asked if he was ill. Another coworker thought he'd been burning the midnight oil. Kevin laughed mirthlessly. Yes, that was it, if the midnight oil was the lovelorn crud that got mucked up in your veins slowly over the course of months, dragging you down, down, down into a puddle of gritty onyx sludge.

Kevin had given Alyssa her space, dutifully, as she had requested. If it was her job that was the issue, he would let her work. He would be there for her when the work was done. And in the meantime, he would make her meals – when she was home (less and less often) – and she would eat them like a phantom guest visiting a haunted graveyard. He would make sure the laundry was done, the bed was made, the groceries were bought, the place was cozy and inviting. He would feed and walk Dixie. He would make sure everything was *just so* for when she returned to him.

Foolishly, yes, irrationally, Kevin held out hope. He tried to block out the warning signs. The signs that might as well have been written in neon and displayed across his city block. The signs that screamed, "She's having an affair!" "She doesn't want you anymore!" "She's just using you!" "She's over you!" And they might as well have been sealed with "You idiot! You naïve, hapless, helpless, hopeless, stupid imbecile!"

One day in early spring, he stood in his living room staring at the photo of the banyan tree. He remembered all those months ago – it seemed like ages ago – when he had stood on this same spot and thought how he was just like the tree – a mixed-up, tumbled-up mass of roots, spreading out in all directions, with no set course or strong base on which to settle. No foundation, no roots! And now, as he stood mesmerized again, he realized the thing he had missed before: the roots were strangling the tree! They were an insidious thing, weren't they? Wrapping their fingers around the neck, the arms, the body, and tightening, squeezing, pinching their claws deeper and deeper into the core of it, into the pulpy, multilayered, vulnerable insides. Soon the strangulation would be complete, and the tree would sag down into a crumpled pile of death and degradation.

In a morass of abject depression, Kevin lay down on the couch and called his dad. "Hey, Dad. How's it going?"

"Oh, good, good. Your mother and I are headed down to the car show in Louisville today."

"That sounds nice. Classic cars or souped-up jalopies?"

"Classic cars. Wish you were here. Remember the time you and Matthew came with us and that old guy let you ride in his Aston Martin?"

"How could I forget? He went so fast, I thought Matthew would throw up."

He laughed. "Yup, I think Matthew's had an aversion to fast cars ever since."

"No doubt," Kevin agreed. Then he paused before he said softly, "Hey, Dad, different topic: I was thinking about coming home."

"Oh yeah? That would be great! It's been so long! Wait, let me tell your mother. Vivian! Vivian! Come here – Kevin and Alyssa are coming home! Won't that be great?"

Kevin gritted his teeth as his mom grabbed the phone and launched into orbit. "Really? When? Oh my gosh! I was just saying to your father how we hadn't seen you two in forever! Now, let's see…I'll need to get your old bedroom ready…I've been working on a quilt there for a few months, but I can clear it out before you get here. When are you coming? Do we need to pick you up at the airport? Don't forget to bring your boots – we'll go out for a long ride. Let me hang up and call Matthew; maybe he and Stacy and the girls can come too. Of course, then I'll need to make sure the basement's ready. Dean, have you moved those crates out? I'll need to get in there to clean things up and make up the bunk beds. Oh, I just can't believe it – the whole family together again! Oh! I can make that mac 'n' cheese recipe you boys love. Wait, how long can you stay?"

Kevin sighed, laughing, and said, "Slow down, Mom. Listen, it's just me coming, by myself. Alyssa…um, Alyssa can't come." He cleared his throat and continued, "She has to work. But I was thinking…maybe I'll come for

Easter – how does that sound? Maybe stay the whole week…?"

"Yes! That's perfect! Wait, why not Alyssa? She has to work? That's too bad; is she sure? It would be so nice to see her again."

"Yeah, um, she's been pretty busy lately."

"Oh, well, okay, we'll certainly miss her. So, hmmm, I better get the Easter baskets out of the attic. The girls will be wanting to do a hunt by the barns. Dean, let's stop at Walmart on the way back from the car show – I need to get some eggs and candy and that fake grass. Oh, this is going to be so much fun!"

She prattled on with the details for what seemed like several more hours. Finally, Kevin said goodbye and hung up, finding his face in an unnatural posture – a smile. He got on the computer and booked his flight.

Later that night when he mentioned the trip to Alyssa, her only response was, "How long will you be gone?"

"A week."

"Good," she had answered. Nice. Then she tried to backpedal slightly, saying, "Well, because I won't be around much anyway."

Kevin just nodded.

When Kevin saw his dad waiting for him at the airport, it took every fiber of his being not to burst out crying. His dad gave him a bear hug, and Kevin said gruffly, "Hey, Dad."

On the drive to the house, his dad talked about the farm and the family and the news of the town. Kevin sat listening with his window cracked, breathing in the fresh country air. God, it was good to be home!

As they were pulling in the long, hilly driveway, he saw his brother's truck by the barn and asked, "Matt and Stacy already here with the girls?"

"Yup, just arrived this morning. Your mother sent Matthew out to play with the girls in the barn so she and Stacy could make the Easter eggs for the hunt tomorrow. Erica kept sneaking back in the house because she was 'thirsty,' but your mother wasn't having that. She went right up to the child and said, 'Git back out there and take a swig from the hose if you're thirsty!' That little spitfire stuck her tongue out and ran off like a wild banshee, but not before Grandma snuck a quick pat on her bottom."

Kevin laughed. He said, "Sheriff Nana's in town and on duty!"

"You're darn tootin'! Come on, let's get inside. I think your mom is holding dinner for us."

Kevin stepped inside the familiar farmhouse to a whirlwind of smells and
sights and sounds and, even more precious, hugs and kisses and girl's screech-
es of "Uncle Kevin! Uncle Kevin!" He laughed and tried to hold two wiggly,
climbing bodies in one big embrace, failing miserably as one girl sunk to the
floor in a heap of giggles and the other went up one side of him and down
the other. His brother shook his hand (and took control of the girls), and his
sister-in-law waved from the other side of the kitchen as she stirred a pot.

His mother grabbed his face and kissed his cheek as she said, "You look
thin." Kevin just smiled and shook his head. Of course, those were the first
words out of her mouth – she would be the one who noticed immediately
that something was off. They sat down and ate and drank and caught up on
each other's lives. Kevin felt he had stepped back in time to a safe sanctuary
of heart and hearth and home. He realized at some point during the meal,
probably around the third shot of jalapeno wine (his dad's homemade spe-
cialty, said to put hair on your chest, but really just burned your insides out),
that he, Kevin Michael Warren, had been missing life. God, he had been
so depressed! Probably clinically. Probably for close to a year. This moment
made him realize, for the first time in a long time, what open, honest laughter felt like. This moment made him realize that there was a way to live that
wasn't shrouded in mystery, defiance, anger, hurt, confusion, and pain. This
moment made him realize that he hadn't been living at all. For a long time.
For what seemed like forever. And it wasn't right. It just wasn't *right*. Now he
needed to figure out what to do about it.

As he went to bed that night (in his childhood bed!), he thought back to
his carefree childhood on the farm. He remembered how he had been raised
to use his brain and his back – study, compassion, hard work, reliability,
stability, kindness. How his parents had taught him to love and care for himself and for others. Struggles – yes! But knowing how to power through the
struggles, to get back up again when you get pushed down.

Kevin had a hazy memory from the day his baby brother came home from
the hospital. Kevin was only three, but he remembered that he didn't feel the
expected jealousy – oh no, his first thought was to protect this little innocent
kicking, whimpering, crying person. He had a thought: it is my job to keep
this person safe. I am his big brother, and I am his guardian. Kevin had put
his hand gently on his brother's soft head and said simply, "Help." Kevin

remembered that his mom praised him and told him, "That's right, Kevin – you will be Mommy's little helper with baby Matthew, won't you?"

Kevin and Matthew shared all the scraped knees, bruised shins, and cut eyebrows, always with Kevin picking up the pieces when Matthew cried or fussed or needed consoling. And Kevin was there for his mother too – he would follow her around the house, pushing the vacuum, folding the laundry, doing the dishes, cleaning off the table, taking care of the baby.

As he lay in bed all these years later, contemplating his early life, Kevin realized he had always been the caretaker, the helper, the protector. And he still was – for Alyssa. But she didn't want it. She didn't want him. Not anymore. He had to face it. She wanted something else. Maybe she didn't even realize what that something else was. Or maybe she did. But regardless, Kevin wasn't it. Kevin couldn't protect her anymore – from her ambition, from her recklessness, from herself. But maybe it was time to protect himself – to seal the gaping wound in his heart. God, to throw in the towel was such a cop-out! But what other choice did he have? He fell into a fitful sleep, wondering what it felt like to write a concession speech when you lost an election.

Later that week, after the girls had eaten the ears and tails off their chocolate Easter bunnies and their baskets were relinquished to green, grassy tornado piles on the floor of the living room, Kevin spent every waking moment soaking up every aspect of being home. Playing hide-and-seek with the girls out in the barn, taking long horseback rides in the morning, running errands with his mom, sitting out on the back porch to watch the sunset with his dad, going out to the local pub with his brother, meeting up with high school friends, and simply getting back to the basics. It felt good.

Suddenly it was Friday afternoon, and he was leaving the next morning. He went out to the barn to shovel away his sadness. His dad came in after a while and sat on a stool, watching him.

"Hey, Dad, what's up?" Kevin asked, noticing his dad stick a piece of straw in his mouth and munch on it thoughtfully.

"Well, actually, I do have something on my mind, son. Your mother and I were just talking, and we wondered…well, we wondered if something's wrong. You don't seem to be quite yourself."

Kevin sighed and said, "Is it that obvious?"

"Well, you're out here shoveling horseshit instead of enjoying your last day in town, and a fine day at that, I might add." His dad stared meaningfully, his green eyes a mirror of Kevin's.

Kevin didn't say anything for a few minutes, trying to think and not think, holding tight to the handle of the shovel. Finally, he sat down on a stool next to his dad and confessed slowly, "Yeah…I'm not sure how to begin…"

"Come out with it…," his Dad said softly.

"Let's see," Kevin wavered, "remember when you were in the Army National Guard and you taught me and Matt that one expression – and then you told us never to use it in front of Mom?"

His dad laughed and said, "Ha! Can you narrow it down?"

Kevin looked at him significantly and said with a pathetic smile, "SNAFU."

His dad nodded and replied, "Ahhh, I see. That bad, eh?"

Kevin shrugged and answered straight out, "My marriage is over."

His dad pulled the straw out of his mouth and said sincerely, "I'm sorry, Kev."

They regarded each other silently.

His dad asked slowly, "What happened?"

Kevin shook his head – as if he could sum it up in a few words! "I don't know. I honestly don't know. The only thing I'm sure of is that she doesn't love me anymore. She's simply done with me."

"Have you talked to her, fought for her?"

"I've tried. Really. But I think…I mean, I don't have any proof or anything, but I sense…I'm pretty sure…she's having an affair."

His dad nodded, saying, "Oh."

"She's never around. She's blames it on work, but well, it's obvious that's not it." Kevin stopped and then choked out, "What do I do, Dad? What do I do?"

"Have you confronted her? What does she say?"

"No, I mean, she denies everything. Doesn't even acknowledge anything's wrong. How do I tackle that?"

"Hmmm, difficult. I guess the question to you is – do you *want* to save it? Is there enough left to save?"

Kevin looked up at the beams of the barn, trying to explore his emotions, trying to contemplate the desired trajectory of his life. Was it worth it? Was *she* worth it? Were *they* worth it? He answered cautiously, "Yes, yes, I think so. If we could somehow get back to the place where we were a couple, like a few years ago, then yes."

"Son," his Dad said quietly, "there is no going back…you must only try to salvage what's left in order to move forward. Can you do that, knowing it'll be an uphill battle? You'll have to forgive her – and forgive yourself – that's the only way."

Kevin nodded slowly, resolutely. "Yes, yes, I think so. I mean, I want to try."

His dad stood up, putting his hand on his son's shoulder, and said, "Good. Then that's your answer."

✥ CHAPTER XXI ✥

WEEKS WENT BY, AND BEFORE SHE KNEW IT Rue was swept off her feet. Josh was true to his word. Yes, that word! Rue's earlier reserve was slowly dissolving. He called her or texted her constantly, telling her he missed her and loved her. He was very affectionate with her, holding her hand, walking with his arm around her, kissing her. He paid for everything, everywhere they went. He gave her little gifts: a bracelet, flowers, new paintbrushes, even a toy for Hank. He started spending the night at her place and she at his. To Rue, it was surreal: odd and new and amazing, flattering and sweet. He coaxed her to do things she had never done before. They went on trips together, they went on double dates with Vy and Anthony, he came to her office to take her to lunch, they hiked Muir Woods and spent a weekend at Yosemite, and they went boating with Daniel and Cathy and the girls. One Saturday, he spent the entire afternoon holed away in Rue's closet with Vy, reorganizing Rue's clothes and recording a new snippet description for each hanger. These new recordings were even more hysterical than Vy's earlier versions, and Rue spent many mornings replaying them and laughing as Hank's collar bell ran off into the other room, wondering why Mommy was acting crazy.

Josh and Rue: they were a thing.

Somewhere along the line, several months in, Rue realized she had let her guard down – well, more than that! Actually, it was shattered into oblivion. Rue had opened herself up to Josh in a way she had never opened herself up to anyone before. In every possible physical and emotional way. Like a thunderbolt!

One Sunday morning, Rue woke up with Josh wrapped around her, realizing it had been five months since that fateful day in February when Josh had dropped a hundred-dollar bill into Rue's fishbowl. And now she was living in a dream state – one in which the hours on the clock ticked in sync with the beating of her heart. She found her happy place in the crook of his arm.

Josh commented with a laugh that Hank was scowling at them from the chair next to the bed. As Rue stirred, she heard Hank stand up and stretch, arching his back with a mew and licking his paws. At first, Hank had been protective of Rue, hissing and swiping at Josh, but eventually he warmed up to him with a fine, indifferent loathing. Rue laughed at them both. Now when Rue tried to get up and reach for Hank, Josh swatted her hand away and grab her in a bear hug so she couldn't get to him. Hank trotted away in disdain until Rue managed to squirm out of Josh's grasp, got up, and whispered in Hank's ear, "Don't worry, Hank, you'll always be my first love."

Josh didn't like that, and as he laughed, he grabbed her back into bed. She turned around to face him and they kissed. Within a few moments, her laughter turned to groans as he began a slow exploration with his hands and mouth along her naked body, stopping at times to wait for her reaction to certain sensitive pulse points. He loved this game – the waiting, the reaction, the readjusting, the reasserting. She opened herself up to him, as wide as a cracked oyster, exposed and raw, closing her mind to all else except the sensations as they happened. Sounds drifted out of her throat – sounds that were part and parcel of their lovemaking, sounds that were involuntary and carnal. Finally, she felt herself tightening for him in a strong, steady, rhythmic beat and then releasing. He wasn't done with her, though. As she lay back in a trance, he lightly placed her on top of him, sliding himself inside her, lifting her from the waist like a doll. He urged her on with his movement and his hands holding her breasts up to his face and mouth like two soft globes. She moved her pelvis so she could feel all the angles of him inside her. She sought the wave again and found it swiftly and exultantly. Shortly after, he grabbed her behind to clench their two bodies together, flipped them both over in unison, and finished with a satisfied groan.

They broke apart and lay breathing hard. It was an eternity.

She never wanted to leave this space. It was perfect.

Slowly, in the soft morning light, Rue went into the bathroom. When she came out, she heard Josh in the kitchen.

He said, "Morning, sunshine. That was some wake-up call."

"Hmmm," she agreed with a smile.

"Coffee?"

"Sure."

"Hey, I was just looking at this latest painting of yours."

"Yes?"

"Didn't you tell me once that swans mate for life?"

"Uh-huh," said Rue, taking her mug from him and sitting on the couch.

He came and sat beside her. He asked, "Then why are there three swans? Shouldn't there be two?"

She said, "Bring it here. I want to feel it."

He obliged and she felt the thick, crusty edges of her design raised up on the canvas. She said thoughtfully, "I don't know...I used to do four of everything, but lately I've been painting three...I'm not sure why." She thought of Josh, Hank, herself. She sat silently for a minute. Then she said teasingly, "Hmmm...maybe one of these is a male rival seeking to break up the love union."

"Oh no he didn't!" cried Josh, taking the painting from her hands and flinging it across the floor.

Rue screamed, "Hey!"

Josh laughed and retrieved her painting, placing it safely back in her hands. "I thought you only did flowers."

"No, not always just flowers. Also, well, Jordan has a new tactile children's book I've been fingering. It reminded me of a book I used to have as a child. You know, furry kitty, hard-shelled turtle, scaly fish, plastic dolphin, and feathered swan. Anyway, I thought I'd try my hand at something new."

He said, "It looks pretty good. But no more threes. You're my swan, babe. No one gets between us."

She nodded, wondering with awe at the truth of this. Had she really gone from total solitary exclusion, containment, isolation to this? *Were they to mate for life?* It seemed insane, impossible, ludicrous! And yet, here she was, putting her painting down and holding this handsome man's face in her hands, kissing his delicious lips, as he drank coffee with her in her third-floor walk-up in Chinatown. Astonishing!

After a few minutes, she said, "I have to go downstairs and pay Mrs. Wai Hing my rent today. Do you want to meet her?"

"The landlady? Chen's mom? Sure. That ought to be fun."

"Now, now, don't be hating on Chen. It's not his fault that he likes to screen my visitors."

"Visitors plural? How many rivals do I have?"

Rue kissed him and said, "Oodles. Anyway, Chen and I have been buddies for a long time, so it makes sense that he interrogates you every time we meet. He just wants to make sure you're not a poser come to take away his Miss Rue."

"Yeah, yeah, I get it. He's your little superhero."

"And hey, he also comes in handy when something breaks around here and I need his translation skills with his mom."

"Okay, I won't pick a fight then. With him or his mom."

"Good."

Josh asked, "Let's see, what time is it? Ten twenty. Hmmm, do you have any plans? Some of the guys at the gym were talking about a pickup game of volleyball down at Ocean Beach. You want to come?"

"Sure, that sounds fun. As long as I don't have to play!" Rue said with a grin.

"Funny. You know, I could teach you."

"Right, nothing like a bloody nose for lunch."

Josh's wheels were spinning. "Seriously, though, they make balls with these little whizzy noisemakers inside them."

"Shut up," Rue said skeptically.

"I swear! I'll buy you one and we can play around with it."

Rue laughed and shook her head.

"I will!" Josh pressed.

Rue simply said, "Okay, okay, slugger. Sounds good. Go get ready."

"Only if you help," he purred into her ear. She smiled, putting her hand on his chest to push him away, but he grabbed her in a tight hold and kissed her neck. She ignored the distant rumble of Hank's growl as she sank into Josh's arms. Then she laughed and shoved Josh away from her, saying, "Get ready."

Josh responded with a pout. "Party pooper. Okay, okay."

Later, Rue introduced Josh to her monthly ritual wherein she knocked on Mrs. Wai Hing's door and said, "Rent" and Mrs. Wai Hing said, "Okay" and Rue said, "Syeh, syeh" which was her butchered version of thank-you. But this fine Sunday morning, Mrs. Wai Hing said, "Tall!" with some type of hand motion that Rue only sensed like a flutter in the air as Mrs. Wai Hing marveled at the size of Rue's man. Josh shook her hand, and Rue heard something more foreign than Mrs. Wai Hing's accent – a young girl's giggle. Mrs. Wai Hing was *taken*. A handshake was all it took. Rue shook her head and grinned. Figured! Only Josh…! Seriously!

Then she heard Chen as he came up and grabbed Rue's hand.

"Hello, Chen. What are you up to this fine day?" Rue asked.

His mother whispered a reprimand to him in Mandarin, but Chen ignored her and said to Rue, "Dom and I are skateboarding," then to Josh, "What are you doing?"

Josh laughed and said with mock anger, "None of your beeswax. And give me back my woman's hand."

Josh grabbed Rue's other hand as Chen, the cutie, simply laughed and said, "She was my girl before she was yours."

"You calling dibs? You little…" Josh scuffled against Chen, and Rue interrupted with, "Alright, alright, nobody's calling dibs. I'm my own dibs. You two, buzz off." Rue took her hands away from both of them and said to Mrs. Wai Hing, "Thank you. Have a nice day," and then to Josh, "Come on, Tarzan."

Chen ran off, laughing and screaming, "She will always be mine!"

On the way to Josh's car, he said, "I think I like that kid."

"Yes, he's quite entertaining."

They drove out to the beach where Josh's buddies were playing volleyball. Josh propped up a bag chair for Rue and sat her down with a bottled water. Rue counted ten distinct voices on the sand and two voices sitting next to her on the beach who introduced themselves as Amanda and Jennie. They were nice – apparently the wives of Tyler and Dylan. They chatted about their jobs and their men and their lives. Rue found, as usual, that she need not contribute much to the conversation and could stay contentedly in her silence, smiling and nodding when required.

The weather was fine – warm and sunny. The crashing of the waves made Rue remember back to that fateful morning when she ran into Josh at the Cliff House in between her audiobook of Zane Grey and the photos of Sonja Henie and Tyrone Power. She felt a slight nostalgia at the thought. She wondered what Roy was up to right now – pouring someone's coffee and talking about the dolphins swimming by the big rocks. Did he ever think of Rue? She hadn't been back since that day. Her life had gone off on a whole new trajectory. In fact, it was almost as if her life was no longer her own. Or at least it was a combined sort of existence. Was it strange to think that? Maybe she hadn't realized it until just this second. She heard Josh spike the ball with proficiency and laughed as he came over to softly touch her arm. She smiled up at him and received a kiss in turn.

Could it be possible that her life was now filled with the likes of this sweet hunk of a man? Oh yes, he was handsome, there was no doubt about that since Vy pointed it out every time she met him, but it was more than that. Josh was kind, supportive, thoughtful, affectionate, warm, and funny, and more importantly, Rue realized with swift clarity: he had been the catalyst for the release of her soul. It was as if he had opened up a door she didn't know existed before, and she had walked through it to find herself.

It was more than the sexual enlightenment (although that was extraordinary!) – it was also her understanding that she could bring more to her life – she could fill it with new people and experiences, thoughts, sensations, and feelings, and actually be enriched by them. She had been so afraid of new things before. She hadn't realized it at the time – she had always thought of herself as independent, strong, organized, and self-sufficient. But she had also been reticent, shy, reserved, and fearful. Of course, all of those qualities (good and bad!) were still true of her, but when she met Josh, the solitary, insular loneliness was annihilated. Slowly but surely, her reserve was washed away like the waves she was hearing in the distance, rolling off into a sea of memories from the past, now happily replaced by a revival of sorts, an awakening and quickening of her soul, an enhanced version of Rue – new and improved! And she had to admit, she found the new Rue wonderful!

Then Rue's phone rang.

On a Sunday afternoon? That was unusual. Must be Vy. Or maybe Cathy with some news about the girls. But it wasn't. As her screen reader said the number, it wasn't one of her contacts. Vy always said unknown numbers were robocalls and told Rue not to answer them, but for some reason, Rue did.

"Hello?"

"Ah, hi, um, yes, hello. Is this Rue Cavendish?" said a male voice.

"Yes, this is she," replied Rue cautiously.

The background noise from the volleyball players, grunting in their effort, was distracting and made it difficult to hear, so Rue stood up and walked a few cautious paces back behind her chair and put a finger in the other ear.

"Yes, I'm Rue," she reaffirmed, waiting.

After a moment of hesitation, the male voice said, "Hi. My name is Kevin Warren. You don't know me, but I know quite a bit about you."

"What? Who is this? How do you know me?!" Rue exclaimed, a shot of fear racing in her veins.

"My name is Kevin Warren," repeated the voice, more firmly now, but with calm. "I know your boyfriend, Josh. Well, I know something about him anyway. And I'd like to talk to you – in person, if possible – for a few minutes, about Josh. There's something you need to know."

"I need to...! What do you know about Josh? How do you know him? How did you get this number?!" Rue cried with as much muster of menace as she could elicit. "I'm with Josh right now. Should I go ask him?"

"No, no, please don't do that. I'm certain that he would just deny everything, but that's only because it's in his best interests to feign no knowledge of me. I'm actually thinking about *your* best interests right now, Rue, not Josh's. I got your number inadvertently through him. Will you agree to meet me? You can pick the time and place. I live on Russian Hill. But I can come to any location, anytime. Some place public, a park or café..."

"But...but...," stammered Rue, trying to process what she was hearing, absently noting Josh grunt in the distance as he spiked the ball. "I'm not sure I want to meet you. What could this possibly be about? I can't imagine there would be anything you could tell me that I don't already know."

"Sadly, I don't think you know this," said the voice with a quick catch.

How strange! Who was this person, and what did he want with her? And why did he sound as if he had the weight of the world on his shoulders? What could it be?

"You can't just tell me now?" Rue challenged.

He replied reluctantly, "No, it would be better in person."

"Okay, I'll meet you," said Rue slowly, thoughtfully. "Brioche at five. Do you know where that is?"

"Near Chinatown? Yes, that's fine. Thank you."

Rue hung up and gripped her phone, no longer hearing the crashing waves or Josh's voice or anything. Her stomach hurt. What could it be? What could it be? *What could it be?* She wracked her brain. Was Josh ill? Surely not that! Was Josh in some type of trouble? Gambling? Stealing? Driving too fast? Fighting in a bar? What? No, none of those; the man sounded sad, not mad. Had Josh worked with this guy? Maybe Josh had fired him? Maybe he was jealous of Josh and wanted to slander him in some way? Rue tried to think of the people Josh had introduced her to in the past several months – were any of them named Kevin? She didn't think so, but there had been so many...it was possible, she supposed. Maybe it wasn't anything bad. Maybe it was some surprise for Josh. Maybe it was a party for his friends or his family. Or maybe it was some deranged shooter or rapist or who knew what?! Good God!

Rue slowly walked back to her chair and sat down. Josh came over after a few minutes and leaned in to kiss her neck.

"What's wrong, sweetie?" he asked. "I don't like that serious look."

"Oh, nothing, nothing," said Rue absently, trying with all her might not to burst out with the news or to burst out crying or to burst out screaming. She was on the brink of all three. She said slowly, "I guess I'm not feeling very well."

"No? Sorry to hear that. You wanna go back?"

"No, no, I think I'll be okay. How long will we be out here, do you think?"

"Maybe another hour or two…why?" he asked. He grabbed her hand and crouched down beside her.

She squeezed his hand, gaining strength from his strong, safe warmth, and said, "That's fine. I'll be okay."

"Okay, you let me know. We can go at any time."

He went back to playing. Rue felt her watch – it was one twenty. She was trying to think of what to do. She could just ignore the whole thing and not show up. She could confess the whole thing to Josh and see how he reacted. Somehow, her instincts told her not to do that. She wasn't sure why. She could call Vy and ask her advice.

Or she could go meet the guy.

She sat for the next two hours weighing each option. Finally, resolutely and maddeningly, she decided on the latter. It couldn't be anything else, after all, could it? She had to know! And besides, she knew Josh – she had held the man in her arms for months now. There couldn't be anything to hide. She trusted him. She knew him. Inside and out. What did she have to fear? Whatever it was, she would face it.

Around three thirty, Josh said goodbye to his friends, and they started to drive back. A few blocks away, Rue told Josh she wasn't feeling well and wanted a "freebie" night. This was their code for alone time. He laughed and said he didn't like "freebie" time, but he gave in, knowing it was Rue's polite way of saying she needed some space. He gave her a long kiss at the entrance to her building. She knew he sensed that something was wrong, but she hoped he chalked it up to her being sick and nothing more. He mentioned he'd be out of town for a few days for work and how much he'd miss her. She gave him extra kisses for that. He said goodbye and texted her his love a moment later.

She trudged up the stairs to her apartment, went inside, and shut the door, leaning her forehead against the wooden frame, thinking and dreading. Hank came up to rub his side against her calves. She picked him up and squeezed him fiercely. Oh, Hank! What to do?! He pushed off her chest and growled. She sighed and released him.

She sat at her kitchen table and typed into her computer, "If I don't return, I'm meeting a man named Kevin Warren at Brioche at 5:00 p.m. He said he has something to tell me about Josh." She left her screen up and paced her apartment, feeling her fingertips along her paintings, thinking back to the moment when she learned her parents had died and reflecting on how everything can change in an instant. Shivering slightly, she put a can of mace in the outside pocket of her purse so it was easily accessible and left her apartment, holding her phone in her left hand and her cane in her right.

In retrospect, if only she could have armed her heart.

As she walked down the street to the café, she remembered the time, not so long ago, when she had met Josh at this very place. She remembered finding him obnoxious and cocky. It was hard to believe she ever felt that way about him. He was like a baby in her hands now. And here she was, with butterflies in her stomach just like that other time, meeting a stranger in a café. But these butterflies were anxious, erratic moths bumping into the walls of her stomach with angry jabs. When she opened the door of the café, she stepped in tentatively, a toe in the deep end, letting the door close softly on her back. She suddenly panicked – she could still turn around. Should she?! She broke out in a sweat and began to reach around for the door handle, but before she could, she heard a quiet, nervous voice say her name just a foot away.

The voice faltered. "Rue? May I...I take your arm?"

There was a momentary lapse in her ability to use her voice. She nodded and felt a warm hand placed lightly on her elbow. He smelled like soap, and his voice hovered about six inches above her – he was tall, but not as tall as Josh. She followed, trying helplessly to breathe.

He said, "Hi, I'm Kevin. I'm sorry, I...I didn't...I didn't know...you were..."

"Blind?" Her voice came back. "Yes, what gave it away?" she said with a nervous laugh, folding up her cane. There was some comfort (crazy as that sounded) in the fact that she had caught *him* off guard. After all, she had plenty of experience dealing with that. He placed her lightly in a chair and she said, "Since birth."

"Ah," he responded with confusion and awkwardness. "Wow, okay, I didn't realize. I also didn't realize you would...would...be...be...so...so—," he stuttered, and Rue wondered whether the stuttering was ingrained or just nerves. What was he trying to say? She thought through potential adjectives – sticky, clumsy, ugly, tiny, drab, smelly? What? Then to her utter amazement, he said thickly, "beautiful."

She started. Unexpected, shocking, uncalled for! Yet, she couldn't help herself – she smiled.

He began again, "So…can I…can I get you something? Cof-cof-coffee, wa-wa-water, tea?"

She shook her head. He sat across from her. She waited. Silence.

After a few moments, he said, "Well, then…then I guess…I guess I'll just get to it." He cleared his throat several times. With each passing moment, Rue felt her stomach flip-flop. He continued, "Rue…I have to tell you something. Something I don't…I don't want to and that I've debated about telling you for months." Rue looked up – months! She let out a small breath of shock. His voice stopped and she sensed him holding back, shrinking below the weight of the words and his…his…what was it? His *concern* for her! There it was – a stranger's empathy!

That thought sent her into a frenzy, and she said abruptly, "What is it? Please just tell me."

"Okay," said Kevin, and then rather quickly, as if he wanted to rip the bandage off, "My wife is having an affair with your boyfriend."

Rue felt her face drain of color. She slowly shook her head. She sat there mutely for a pregnant, unholy minute. Then she said simply and quietly, "No."

"Yes…yes, yes. I'm afraid it's true…I'm sorry, I'm so sorry." His voice dropped an octave and caught on the word *sorry*. He swallowed and said, "Believe me when I say I wish it weren't true. But I *know* it's true."

Rue's mind was a tornado – disbelief, confusion, doubt, horror. She couldn't process it. It couldn't be – it just couldn't be! No, no, no, no, no, NO.

She said the word again out loud, as if to make it be so. "No."

He repeated softly, "I'm sorry."

"Who…who…?" Rue could not seem to formulate a sentence.

Without waiting, Kevin answered, this time his voice steadier, "My wife's name is Alyssa. She works with Josh. They've been having an affair for quite a while – I believe for months before Josh started dating you – and my wife is under the misguided impression that…well, that they're a couple."

Rue's memory lit up under the weight of that name – Alyssa! That night, so many months ago, that wretched restroom encounter…something dreadful clicked into place. Rue's mouth was suddenly dry. There had been no interaction with her since. None!

He cleared his throat again, and as if wrenching the words from his heart, he said, "She left me this week. Moved into an apartment with a friend. She's searching for a bigger place, one where she can live with…with him, with Josh. They're leaving together on a trip tomorrow…I'm not sure where…"

Rue flashed to Josh's last words to her…he would be out of town for work…he would miss her…he loved her…

Finally, after the longest moment in history wherein Rue relived the last five months of her life in an instant of retrospective agony, she said out loud with a croak, "How do you know? How are you sure?"

He sighed and started slowly, reluctantly, "I'll spare you the details, but let's just say that I have irrefutable proof that they're together. They travel together nearly every week. And I suspected something many month ago – I think around the time you started dating him. Do you remember getting a call that was from a wrong number that same week? That was me. I got your number off her phone. I dialed it thinking it would help me solve the mystery of her behavior, but it was just you, which confused me even more. Eventually, though…well, I'm here now, so…unfortunately. My life has…been… rather a nightmare ever since."

He paused, trying to gather himself. Then he said, "I hate to admit it because it's not what I'm normally about – it's not what *marriage* is normally about – but I investigated my wife. I read her texts and emails and posts, and I found she was communicating with Josh all the time, at all hours of the day and night. She was trying to hide it, but it was all there. She deleted texts to him immediately after writing them, but sometimes she left them in her deleted file. I found a few. It was awful, there were words I…I still can't… can't unsee. I waited to confront her because I wanted her to give him up on her own and come back to me. I hoped for that. I would have taken her back and not asked questions. If only she had! But by the time I did confront her, she was already too far gone, working on her plan to leave me and get him. She didn't even bother to deny it and simply said she'd already seen a lawyer and that I would be served divorce papers soon. You see, she's a very determined girl.

"The only thing in her way right now, frankly, is you. Which is why I'm here, warning you. I know, from firsthand experience, that this information is like torture...I know! And I am so sorry! But I wanted you to have the truth before...another day passed...before you and Josh...went any further...before they went any further without you knowing. Believe me, as awful as this seems, I've tried to spare you...certain things, salacious things, horrid things that are emblazoned on my brain forever. I only wish I could remove them! Now that you have enough of the facts, though, I hope you'll protect yourself. I'm honestly not sure how it will all work out, even now. Alyssa won't seek to hurt you – not physically anyway. I'm not worried for your personal safety or anything; she's not dangerous in that way. But she *will* seek – and will probably succeed in getting – Josh. She's a woman who gets what she wants. Of course, I still hope and pray that she fails, but I'm realistic and preparing for the worst. I obviously know nothing about your relationship. Maybe Josh will reject Alyssa's plan, although, again – I'm sorry – as far as I can tell, he hasn't resisted her so far. But what do I know? Maybe he's different from...from how this...appears. Anyway, I can't say it enough – I'm sorry."

He stopped, breathing hard and waiting.

Rue was also breathing hard as she listened, and a large, hard lump formed in her throat. Despite every effort to hold it together, several frustrated, angry, hopeless tears squeezed out and ran down her cheeks that she wiped away quickly with the back of her hand. With every fiber of her being, with all the resolve in the world, with every synapse in her brain fighting against it, holding it back, wanting to deny it – she couldn't help it – she knew, with the dread of a thousand locusts, she was hearing the truth.

Flashes of memories popped into her head – Alyssa's (seemingly arbitrary) scathing treatment of her at the Big 4 and the fact that Rue hadn't seen or heard a word about her since the day after that, when Josh had explained it as an unreciprocated "crush" – the blight of the lack and absence since then! Josh's strange behavior that night, the times when he turned the sound off his phone, the voices Rue heard in the background of his calls, the times when he was mysteriously unavailable for hours at a time (and then called or texted Rue ten times an hour afterward), his vacillating feelings toward her – utter, over-the-top, speedy love followed by immature, surface-level, evasive ramblings of superficial unconnected words and actions. She had rationalized it away – oh, he's young, he's working too hard, he's more experienced than me, he's popular, he's busy, he's friendly, he's got a lot going on. And what did

Rue know anyway? This was her first relationship; who was she to question anything he did or said?

Rue cringed from it. From the heavy knowing. From the dreadful, caustic, corrosive truth staring at her with its poisonous barbs pointed at her soul. And from her own naiveté, gullibility, stupidity. From her part in the crime that was their relationship, from day one. She had fallen hard, with no net, no brakes, no deep thought of the consequences or the future. She remembered with sickening conviction her carefree "Come what may, Rue – come what may!" She had opened her heart like a child – innocent and replete with eager longing. She hadn't even put a protective cushion around it – there it was, wide open for the taking. And the crushing.

She had always lived in a world without the sun and the moon and the stars – these were foreign, obscure, nebulous objects with no meaning to her – but now, she knew what it was like to have the sun sucked out of your soul. It was as if the very earth turned black and a darkness permeated her insides.

She didn't say a word. After a quiet eternity, she stood up abruptly and stumbled out of the café. She heard the man say something, but it was in a far-off place where he could no longer reach her. She didn't turn back.

Instead, she walked. And walked and walked, not going home, not going anywhere. She walked the streets, for hours, until she couldn't anymore.

Until she just couldn't.

And then she went home, opened the door of her apartment, nearly collapsing on top of Hank, who was there with his reassuring bell, and cried and cried and cried into her furry sanctuary until there were no more tears left in the world.

PART III

✥ Chapter XXII ✥

One Year Later

Kevin Warren was standing in his apartment on a Friday evening in July, looking at his photo of the banyan tree. What a tangled mass! He chuckled. Much like his life this past year. Roots popping up in all directions, straining to find steady ground. Here he was, still straining and still standing. Barely. Would that ground ever be found?

Alyssa had been true to her word. She had left, and for good. But was it? For good? Divorce and a severing of love seemed less good and more like a rotten, festering, evil, poisoned wound. Was it enough to know that he had tried every possible means to keep her? Pulled out every arrow from his quiver and pointed them at her heart, her mind, her conscience, her body? Rationalized, pleaded, agonized, prostrated?

He had come back from his parents' house a year and many months ago (what seemed like a hundred years ago), written up a project plan, and attacked their doomed marriage with reckless abandon. He tried to shower her with love, flowers, attention, gifts, texts, letters, phone calls. That approach sent her into a rage. Then he gave her space, only to find that her definition of space meant goodbye. Next he tried to catch her by surprise at places she frequented. He became enemy number one. She stopped frequenting and started screaming, threatening a restraining order. Finally, open begging and crying. She laughed.

Nope. Nada. Blip. She was gone. And that was that.

Here he was, looking back at his futile little project plan, and he realized with a jolt that he didn't care. He had gone through all the stages of grief – denial, anger, bargaining, hurt. Maybe now he was in the acceptance phase, or what he liked to call the "fuck-it" phase. He laughed out loud. Wasn't it grand? He could do what he wanted, when he wanted, with whom he wanted, and nothing and nobody would stop him. Of course, nothing and nobody would care either.

Ho hum. God, that smacked of pity, didn't it? There was the rub – to walk through life with a voice whispering in your ear, "What's the point? No one cares." He railed and rallied against it, saying he wasn't being fair. It wasn't even true! His parents cared. His brother cared. His nieces cared. His coworkers cared. His friends cared. Right?

Right. Okay. So, he wasn't exactly on the ledge, but still…it was a strange thing to go from being married to being alone. Even when Alyssa was distant, he still had a "someone" in his life. Someone to care for, someone to look out for, someone to think about, to sleep with, to talk to, to cook for, to go to movies with, to *be* with. And now, his daily life was filled with meaningless things to keep his mind and body occupied, but it still felt *empty*.

Staring at the photo, he pondered. At some point during the year, he had Wiki'ed "banyan tree" – he wasn't sure why – and had learned about the "great" banyan tree in India. Two hundred fifty years old and over four and a half acres. It had survived two cyclones and was still growing new roots every day. The "great" banyan tree. He sighed, thinking he was a lot like the great banyan – a survivor. Sure, from an outsider's perspective, the tree looked like a tangled mass of disorder, irregularity, and discombobulation. He had to admit that his confidence and self-worth had taken a hit with the divorce. It was only natural, right? Several months of "Woe is me," followed by "Now what do I do?" ending in "Fuck it." Hindsight was twenty-twenty, and when he reflected on his relationship with Alyssa, he thought maybe they'd been doomed from the start. She was, after all, a complete nut job. And mean to boot.

The grass was always greener with her. He knew it when he met her, with that over-the-top ten-point plan for her life, but back then he had chalked it up to her being ambitious, and what was wrong with that? So, he had stayed by her side, even when she was thoughtless and cruel, even when her cruelty was unwarranted, even when his faithfulness and care were unacknowledged and often scorned, because he thought they would eventually achieve their dreams together – equal partners on life's journey. He thought he was being noble, taking her neglect and derision on the chin because he was going to stay with her no matter what she did to him or to herself. He thought he was protecting her from her own rash behaviors and decisions. Now he saw their relationship for what it really was: a one-way fleecing. He couldn't remember a time when she had been voluntarily giving or unselfish with him. Wasn't there always an ulterior motive? Had she ever put him before herself? Had she ever thought about anything for purely altruistic reasons or heck, thought about anything for more than five seconds for *any* reason before plowing ahead, no matter the outcome, no matter the consequences? What was amazing was, despite this, or maybe because of it – who knew? – she seemed to get her way and seemed to be unstoppable. And Kevin was beginning to take a page from her playbook.

All the thoughts and feelings rolled into the years of experience with a single person intimate to you – was that all that counted for "worth"? Was it based solely on another person's opinion, time with you, thoughts about you? Lord help the poor sucker who thought a woman and her actions defined a man. Kevin now knew better.

Case in point, here was this crazy-looking "great" tree. It was perfectly formed to the specifications of the "great" maker. Yes, Kevin had to admit it, during the long, lonely nights, he thought about God. He thought, what went through God's mind when forming that massive, ugly, insidious tree? God's great plan, God's great creation. Wonderfully and marvelously made – every last branch, every last leaf, every last root. Was Kevin part of His great plan? Had God brought his parents together all those years ago, and planted a seed, and Kevin was the tree that sprung from that seed? Was Kevin a tree seemingly as irregular, unwieldy, and directionless as the banyan? Where were his roots now? Yes, he had survived the storm, but now he sometimes felt as though he was that seed again, this time floating aimlessly in the wind. He needed to get his footing again, to be grounded, to be centered, to be planted.

Finally, resolutely, Kevin walked away from the photo and went into his bedroom to change. The good news was that he had already started to rebuild his life a few months back and was feeling more positive and hopeful about the future. He was going to "plow" ahead himself. No, not exactly like Alyssa's playbook – he didn't have the heart to destroy people along the way, leaving collateral damage as if it were an ant stomped underfoot. Instead, he was going to forge ahead on his own – fill his life with the things and people and activities he liked, and with a confidence in who he was and his take on the world. Why not? His seed wasn't dangling in the wind anymore – it was planted here in this big, marvelous city, with the world opened up at his feet, just waiting to be snatched up and examined and explored.

He had started a new routine – a call to action, as it were – part of his "Project Kevin Michael Warren, version 2.0." Abandon marriage recovery plan – check. Begin new self-enlightenment, self-discovery, self-improvement plan – check. He signed up at a gym and was exercising four times a week. He was eating better, getting out with friends, taking in a play or a museum, walking around the city, putting himself out there. Some days he spent hours simply sitting in a park or on a bench by the bay with his drafting paper, drawing and thinking about how life was actually spectacularly beautiful, with its twists and turns and its many-splendored settings and people and diversity. You could never get bored with so much scope for the imagination. He thought back to that photography class – how the teacher had talked about snapping the macro and the micro. He started training his eye at the smallest flower peeking up from a crack in the sidewalk and at the distant mound of Alcatraz rising from the bay's surface. And everything in between – the girl walking along the pier eating an ice cream cone, the cormorants ducking and diving for fish while the seagulls squawked and hovered over-head, the smell of sourdough bread baking near the Wharf, the paintings of workers toiling on the walls of Coit Tower, the sound of a fly buzzing against his screen window. And the slowing of his heartbeat as it thump-thumped happily, marveling at the world.

Before long, he found his life full again, with rarely a thought of what had transpired with Alyssa other than to make him grateful for the way things were now. He even thought once or twice about dating someone new. He was amused and slightly scared (he had to admit!) when he was approached by women. Having been married for so many years, he wasn't exactly experienced, and he wasn't sure how to react when they did approach. Usually he smiled and turned them down politely. Sometimes he went so far as to explain that he had just gotten divorced, but he usually just did what he could to avoid being approached in the first place, sticking close to his buddies and married friends. Sometimes he was rather shocked at the assertiveness of women who were attracted to him. He reasoned that his new self-confidence must have been evident to others. Plus, he had slimmed down and was styling his hair in a different way. He had started wearing contacts instead of glasses, and he had shaved his beard. He had more money now that the divorce was final, so he updated his wardrobe and bought himself a Vespa to get around town easier. Regardless of his accoutrements, he was feeling much better about himself and was thinking it was time to start dating again – take a risk and get back out there.

Kevin found himself looking in the mirror more often now. It wasn't vanity – sure, he looked better, but it wasn't as if he had changed into a narcissist.

Honestly, in the beginning, it was him trying to do the thing that hurt the most – examining himself. Really looking. Into his eyes. Into his soul. And then forcing himself to see what others saw there. It felt like a prison sentence – to regard a face of despair and brokenness. Wasn't it pitiful, woeful, ugly? Didn't he deserve what he got? But slowly, over time, when he saw the bigger picture and was thinking more rationally, and as he enacted his 2.0 plan, he began to see something new. A man of resolve. A man of action. A man with a desire to experience life. A man with a mission to be better. To be more. To live and to become and to be. And really, hadn't God created a man of value from the beginning? Kevin wasn't chopped liver, was he? There was something there already, wasn't there? And now it was refined, polished, and ready to *go beyond*.

At work, when there was a new version of engineering specs, they said the old version had been superseded. Kevin's goal was to supersede his life. Throw that catastrophe in the archives, never to be seen or heard from again. Or so he imagined anyway. Technically, he was still trying to devise the new specs – would they be spicy, cocky, self-assured (ugh) or peppy, bouncy, chatty (doubtful) or thoughtful, kind, soft (wah-wah) or smart, sassy, witty (maybe) or calm, cool, collected (Bond, James Bond) or some combination thereof with a hint of the Kevin of days gone by (hmmm, yes, getting warmer)? He supposed the point was: he didn't know. The design specs were still being drafted, analyzed, piloted, tested, reiterated, finalized, implemented.

As he pulled on his shorts and T-shirt, he laughed because no matter what the status of the specs at this moment in time, he was absolutely astonished to find that the man he regarded in the mirror was a man he wanted to see and a man he wanted to be! He was fit and healthy and strong, and his green eyes had a sparkle – like a magician with a new card trick. He was loving life and taking it all in. He didn't know what was around the corner, but wasn't it exciting to think of the possibilities?

He drove his Vespa over to the gym and walked in the door with a new swagger. He actually glanced at his reflection in the window as he walked by – who was that guy? Oh yeah, that's me! Then Kevin laughed, thinking, that's about enough of that, sparky.

Sometime later, on his third set of bench presses, Jessica walked up and offered to spot him. She was tall and lanky, dark, with a hard-core toned body.

"Pecs today?" she asked with a smile.

"Mmm-hmm, and legs," Kevin answered between grunts.

"Didn't see you here last night," she stated with a bit of disappointment.

"Yeah, I had to work late. We're about to start a new project, and I've been up to my elbows in structural assessments."

"Well, I missed you," she purred.

"Thanks," Kevin answered, wondering how else to respond. Here's where his lack of experience was a slight detriment. She had been pursuing him for weeks, but he was a man whose legs were poured in concrete.

"Big plans this weekend?" she asked hopefully.

"Um, no, not really," he faltered. Was he ready to take the bait? That was the big question.

"That's a coincidence," she said, smiling down on him. He stopped his reps and waited. She said, "Let me slip in for a set."

"Sure." He jumped up. He helped her slide two of the weights off the bar and went around to her head to spot.

"You see, I'm free too, and I was thinking," she started, with a rep in between the words, "maybe we should go out," a grunt and a grin, "we've been talking for weeks," groan, "and we seem to both be...available, right?"

Kevin stood looking down at her dark eyes with consternation. He said, "Well...yes, but..."

"No buts, Kevin, no buts," she pushed out of her mouth on the press-up, so that the last word sounded like a hiss: butttsssss.

Kevin's mind was racing. Her expression reminded him of something. Or was it someone? Good god – Alyssa! He looked away quickly, his hands sweaty. Yes, he knew he should get back in the game (so to speak), but did he want to with this woman? If she was anything like Alyssa, he should run for the hills. Sprint, rather, as if a hungry, angry bear was chasing after him!

Breaking into his thoughts, she put the barbell back on its rack and said, "Jeesh, aren't you looking frightful! Did I scare you? I'm sorry, I know I can come on strong. Really, though, it's no big deal – I just thought it might be fun to go out sometime. If you're not into it...?" she let the words trail off, and Kevin stared at her, wondering if he was simply being overly dramatic. Certainly, she was attractive and seemed to be put together. He wasn't sure what she did for a living or where she lived, but she was friendly enough – talkative, easygoing, assertive. Why was he jumping to conclusions? She really wasn't anything like Alyssa, right? And wasn't this what he had just been thinking about – potentially going on a date? Why not break the ice? God, it would be nice to get laid! Yes, he thought that! And he couldn't stop himself from staring down at her breasts for a second. He looked away and wiped the sweat from his brow.

He said, "Sure, okay, why not?"

She smiled and said dryly, "Why not? Don't butter me up too soon, Kevin."

He laughed, realizing he was being ridiculous, overanalyzing, as usual. He said, "Okay, yes, let's. What do you want to do?"

She sat up, wiping her face with a towel, and said, "Hmmm, so many options...let me think about it. Tomorrow night okay?"

Kevin nodded.

"Maybe dinner or a movie or a show. I'll think about it and let you know. Hand me your phone," she said as he took it out of his pocket, unlocked it, and handed it to her. He watched as she typed her number in his contacts and then dialed it, calling herself so she had his number too. He had a momentary flash of panic – now I really have to go through with this! It had been...well...forever...since he'd been on a date, and his face reddened as he thought about his last memories of intimacy – kissing, touching, sex – these were long-dead relics that had been obliterated in his mind as of late, but they were now popping back up like the Hindenburg.

He stuttered, "Okay then, gr-great. I'll call you."

She laughed and said, "A text is fine, my dear. Perfect. Later then. Ta-ta," she said, gripping his arm and walking away toward the locker room, all the while smiling back at him with her eyebrow raised.

Holy shit!

❦ Chapter XXIII ❦

RUE GOT UP WITH A JOLT. It was Saturday and it was Vy's wedding day! Rue felt her clock – it was ten twenty-five already! She had been instructed to be at City Hall at noon on the dot. She pushed Hank off the bed and jumped in the shower. It had been so long since she had felt this happy and excited. She was going to live vicariously through Vy today. And Vy was the happiest bride she had ever known. Vy had been talking about Anthony and the wedding plans incessantly for months. Mayumi and Rue were stuffed to the gills with it. Rue had to laugh – it was hard to be annoyed with someone who was positively over the moon and exultant, even when each word out of Vy's mouth cut like a knife into Rue's bruised and battered heart. Oh well, she didn't begrudge Vy her happiness – how could she? Vy had been waiting for this day for years, and she deserved her fairytale ending more than anyone.

Rue styled her hair and put on her makeup. She zipped herself into her bridesmaid's dress and felt along her waist. The subtle curves of her body were hugged into an hourglass silhouette, and she thought to herself, I think I must look rather pretty today! Not that anyone would notice. Not that anyone would care. Rue had been through so much over the past year. Her wallowing was a testament to her sorrow, as if she needed a reminder. It sat with her every day like a lost piece of unclaimed luggage.

But, she thought, shaking off that dark shadow, she was feeling better lately. Decidedly better. Things were looking up. She was pumped about this day of love, joy, and unity, and she was determined to let it envelop her and hold her in its grasp. She had been helping Vy with her wedding plans, and this was the culmination of those efforts. Why shouldn't she sit back and enjoy?

And, lo and behold, life had gotten less monotonous a few months ago when she was promoted to research assistant at the law firm, reporting to Mayumi. Gone were the days of directing visitors to the bathroom. No more memorizing each attorney's smell or cough as they walked in the door. She was Mayumi's right-hand gal! Rue now spent the days scrolling through the audio equivalent of reams of transcripts, examining the electronic law books for cases and precedents, and talking with attorneys, clients, witnesses, counselors, coworkers, defendants, you name it! Rue – yes, quiet, little, reserved Rue Cavendish – was actually quite assertive when pressed. This was an adjective never applied to her before! She reveled in it. She realized that at the bright old age of thirty-three, she was a competent, upstanding, autonomous go-getter. And the extra money didn't hurt either. Mayumi had given her a bonus check several months into the job, telling Rue her thoroughness and attention to detail had been the reason for several cases settling out of court, much to the benefit of Mayumi and the firm (and Rue!).

Rue still had her regular gig at the Big 4 on Friday and Saturday nights. Nothing had changed there other than that she was sometimes struck by a dreaded sense of déjà vu when anyone came up to her piano with a smooth, deep voice and put something in her fishbowl. She wondered sometimes when or if that feeling would ever go away.

Daniel and Cathy were ecstatic because Cathy was pregnant with baby number three, a boy this time. They had sailed the South Pacific with the girls for several months last fall and, what do you know, she came back pregnant. Raquel wasn't exactly thrilled about the idea of a boy coming into their cotton-candy pink princess world, but Jordan was enthused enough for both of them, thinking she was finally getting her own bona fide baby doll – one with real-life spit-up, drool, potty action, and animatronic voice box! Cathy laughed and said wait until Jordan realizes the baby doesn't stop crying when you punch it as hard as you can on the chest to turn off the box. Rue told Cathy she hoped Jordan would never have cause to realize that.

Rue ordered an Uber (today was surely a day for an Uber and not the Muni) and sat in the back, trying not to wrinkle her dress (which Vy had described on the hanger as "Ding-dong, it's my wedding day! It's my wedding day! I'm going to the chapel and I'm gonna get maaaaarried. Put this dress on and get your ass over to City Hall STAT!"). Rue smiled, trying not to let any other thoughts break her good mood, including the memory of the day when Vy came over to re-record all of her hangers so there wouldn't be any vestiges of Josh's voice remaining. Big sigh. Shake it off.

Wow, a wedding! She couldn't remember the last one she had been to. Maybe Daniel and Cathy's, and that was, like, ten or twelve years ago. She began to think about marriage. She wondered how much she believed in it. In many ways, it seemed completely abstract to her, like believing in God or ghosts or the lost ark. How did it even work? How did people find each other, get together, and then live every single day together…for years and years. Just the two of them. Knowing everything about each other and still staying for more. How? She grunted. She hadn't even been able to make dating work. But then, she had been a novice then, hadn't she? She didn't know then how people lied, how people betrayed, how no one was as they seemed. It was the duplicity of people, just as she had noted in February at the lounge, listening to that young couple. No one was really as they seemed at first, were they?

Now she knew.

It crept back in. Damn it. She had to admit that she wondered – on days like today, when she least wanted to – what ever happened to Josh. Was he married to Alyssa now? To someone else?

That phone call. The one that still stuck in her craw like a sour cherry filled with lead.

Josh's happy-go-lucky voice. "Hey, sweetie pants, what's shakin' and I don't mean your hot-taffy love cheeks either."

Silence.

"Rue? Hello? Earth to Rue. What's up? Are you feeling better now? Want to revoke your 'freebie'? Consider it canned. I'll be there in ten shakes. Put on your dancing shoes."

She let out a despair-filled croak and said, "Josh, how could you?"

Inaudible mutter of shock. Then the wheels spinning. She could feel them moving through the phone. The stuttering guilty reply, "Wha-wha-what? What's up?"

"You know," Rue said, accusing, distinct, no-buts-about-it.

He let that sink in.

Then he whispered, "What's the matter? You sound so…so different."

"You know!" Rue repeated, screaming into the phone.

His desperate reply: "What do you mean?"

"Stop. Just stop, Josh! I know everything. I know all about your…your… *affair*."

"What?! What are you talking about? Who have you been talking to, Rue? Tell me!"

Rue took a moment to cry, to sob, to wail into her hand. Not answering his asinine questions – she wasn't going to play along with his little game of pretend – bracing herself, she nearly howled, "How could you? You knew, you KNEW I was vulnerable…a naïve child when it came to this…you knew I wasn't experienced…and yet—you deceived me, lied to me…from day one! You cowed me – that's what you did! Like a lamb to the slaughter! Remember, Josh? I was a lamb!"

"Rue, Rue, listen to me. Let me explain," he began, suddenly smooth and quickly thinking out loud. She felt his mind turn over, clever and swift, in desperation, realizing what he was about to lose and trying with all his might to hold on. "It didn't mean a thing. I love you, Rue, you have to believe me. She was just a passing thing. I wanted it to be done long ago, you have no idea how much! But…but she wouldn't let me go. She refused to release me. She was like a dog with a bone. I couldn't get away from her, and I tried, believe me, I tried! And she doesn't matter anyway, it's over, it's done, and all I want is you, Rue, I swear. You just have to believe me. I'll never hurt you again, Rue. I'll be here for you always. Please, Rue, please. Give me another chance. I love you."

"I have to go," Rue squeezed the words out and hung up, only to wither in a heap on the floor, bereft of strength. True to his word, he was pounding on her door ten minutes later. She got up and let him in. She felt his arms around her, his tears on her cheek, his lost-soul mournful spirit begging her. The physical aspect of him still felt so good, so reassuring, while at the same time her heart wished there was a way to use her physical side to pummel his head, thrash his chest, kick his knees – to make up for her weak, tortured emotional insides. Instead, she simply stood there, inert, without will.

After a while, he tried to lead her to the couch, but she stayed standing, placing herself apart from him and waiting. He sat down anyway and apologized again with as many pretty words and intricate phrases as he could muster. She wondered absently if his face during these speeches matched his words. Of course, this is something she could not know, had never known, but now she thought, is this how sighted people guess at dishonesty in a person, even before they've spoken a word? Maybe Josh's pathological lying throughout their relationship was based on the premise that his words never matched his face or his actions. For not the first time (or the last), she thought about how she was at such a disadvantage with those who wished to deceive. If it was written on someone's face, how would she know? But still, with Josh, how was it she hadn't noticed through other means? He could win an Oscar. That was undeniable, but still, she was so drawn in, so swept up, would she have noticed? Maybe she had looked the other way, put her head in the sand, been blind. Yes, truly blind!

Until this fateful day of reckoning. He stayed a while, but she never spoke a word and kept herself carefully wrapped in a tight cocoon that refused to be touched outside of that first desperate hug of his, so he left. Oh, but he wasn't done. Not by a long shot. After weeks of his persistent rationalizing, proselytizing, cajoling, enticing, she finally gave in, mostly out of sheer exhaustion. Later she would look back and think, foolish, foolish girl! But for a while, it worked. A few weeks, a month, who can remember? It was like a dream, to be back in his arms and under his protection, thinking all was well again. He had really repented, that woman was out of his life, he was there for Rue again, and they could start anew. Right?

Then Alyssa came, in all her glory. Rue had foolishly believed Josh when he said they were over, that he never took trips with her anymore, that he never thought of her anymore, that she was dead to him. Then why did Alyssa casually walk in the locked door of his apartment (alive and well, with an overt sense of entitlement that could not be denied) one fine Sunday (smoothly typing in the keycode, even!) and shove her hot, angry, hateful breath in Rue's face while Josh yanked her daggerlike fingernails off Rue's arm? Was Rue living in an alternate universe? How could someone lie so thoroughly and effectively? He was, after all, a spectacular salesman. So clever, so conniving, so convincing, so ruthless. And who knew, maybe it was Alyssa's doing. Did it matter? She was there, in their space, screaming in Rue's face about how she was still "fucking" Josh and "nothing" with them was "over" and "never would be." The drama of it all, the absolute quickening of the blood in her veins as her heart and mind raced for escape, for release, for exodus! She stumbled out of the building and out of Josh's life. This time for good. Or for bad. It took her a long time to realize, to absorb, to convince herself which.

That was the thing – the understanding. It came slowly, brutally. He wasn't stupid. He knew she had been a universe in and of herself before he met her. She had been fine! She had her routine, her jobs, her friends, her family. He broke her. Shattered her walls. Left her open and raw and exposed in every possible way. She had jumped in all the way. And maybe, she recognized, just maybe his intentions (in the beginning anyway) had been good. Sure, he was impulsive, erratic, spontaneous, and he had loosened and lightened her. They had fallen in love – yes, real love – both of them. But he had a conundrum

– he had an *Alyssa*. He couldn't talk or rationalize her away, no matter how much he tried. When Rue found out, he said it was only physical. Nothing more. As if that mattered. As if that made it better. To think of his hands on Alyssa, his lips on her, skin to skin with her. How was that better? Those hands, those lips, that skin that had been Rue's oasis for so many months, her awakening, her ripening. Now her oasis was like a dirty penny at the bottom of a grimy street drain.

She tried to believe him – maybe she did believe a little that he still loved her – but it didn't matter; it didn't take it all away, did it? The betrayal, the horror, the waste. It remained. Like an anvil tied around her neck, weighing down her body at the bottom of a deep, dark sea. No matter how she tried to remove it, forget it, block it out of her mind. Rue thought back through things as logically as she could and realized she was partly to blame – she had let him in so easily, so quickly, so unthinkingly. She had been lonely and hadn't even realized it. She had been in a barren desert, and he had brought her water. Of course, she drank it! Oh so much amazing, crystal clear, fruitful, potable, portable, delicious, tasty water!

And Rue had overlooked many things – the obvious lies and deception, but also the fact that they weren't compatible. Not really. They say opposites attract, and certainly in the bedroom, that was true – okay, she would give him that. But what they don't say is opposites are also sometimes terribly, horribly wrong for each other. Rue was lost in the shadow of Josh. He said he liked her little routine: her singing and playing, her painting, her reading, her birding, her walks about town. But in reality he was an observer, not a partaker. He didn't actually want to do any of those things with her. He wanted her to do his things with him. And for the most part, she complied. They went out – drinking, socializing, sports, partying. She lived in the crook of his arm for months, compliantly, happily, and sometimes inertly, like a baby in a bassinette.

Looking back now with a relatively objective mind, she knew he was a surface-level kind of guy. He wanted the cheap thrill, the quick fix, the visceral reaction, the physical stimulation, the superficial input and output. Nothing too heavy, nothing too deep, nothing too caring, nothing too…anything! How could Rue reconcile this? She knew she wanted more – a stronger connection, a deeper understanding, a lifetime kind of love. But it had all been so easy – to be swayed by him, to feel his strength, to let him lead. Rue could see it clear as day now: he had gotten his way his whole life! And she fell right into his hands and his lap.

When the breakup happened and she finally stuck to her guns (the hardest thing she had ever done!), she nearly felt sorry for him – he was ill-equipped to deal with it, having never lost a sale before. Right on the brink, though, she always remembered that hateful woman in her face. But oh, the pleas, remorse, manipulation, rationalizing, sadness, and anger from the man! Rue had to steel herself against his iron will. Finally, months later, he gave up. The texts and calls stopped, the visits to her office, the flowers, the gifts, the emails, the letters.

Then Rue found there was something worse than too much attention, which was absolute, fathomless, solitary despair. The breakup brought up her old abandonment issues from childhood. After her parents died, she remembered the sense of desolation, hopelessness, dread, and fear of the world. Now it was back with a vengeance – the blackness carrying her down into a deep, dark hole. Rue went through the motions of life, mechanically, in a fog, but essentially shunned everything and everybody. The pain was unbearable – the loss of love, the humiliation, the shame of opening herself up only to be stomped, stabbed through the innermost, vulnerable part of her being. She had always been so careful in the past. This time she had been irresponsible, foolhardy, headlong. Why? For a man!

Sometimes a dreaded, ponderous thought seeped into her brain: Why was God punishing her? What had she ever done to *Him*? It wasn't fair! Born blind, losing her parents, teased by those horrible schoolgirls at boarding school, forced to make a way for herself in this cold, unforgiving world, and now this! Heartbreak. It was *enough*! She couldn't take anymore. Selfish, wallowing, lonesome pity. She was in it and of it and all about it. A quagmire. She had never been to church except for weddings and funerals. But lately, at night, she began to pray: God, please give me a break. I'm done. Can't you let me be? I don't know what I've done to deserve this pain, but can't you take it away, can't you make it stop, can't you give me absolution, abatement, a panacea, a cure?

She was nearly sick to death of herself. Was this what it had come to? She had always been so strong! Now, degraded to self-pity and blaming God?! It was enough to make her want to scream.

One day midway through her recovery, a man on the street touched her arm and said a tiny "hi" with an English accent. Harsha. She stopped in shock.

Then he said, "How…how are you, Rue?"

"Um, okay…," she answered breathlessly, hesitantly. Of course, he knew everything – and probably much more. She frowned. Had he been complicit? If Alyssa worked with them every day and had the keycode to their place, what other conclusion could she draw?

He must have read her face. He said swiftly, "Rue, I want you to know…I am so sorry! I really am. I wish I could have…I don't know…done something. I feel awful."

Rue stood stock-still, spiteful, not wanting to give an inch. She said blackly, "So you knew the whole time?"

He stumbled, "Well, I mean, yes…and no…I wasn't aware of everything, but well, yes…I knew…but I didn't know what to do…you know Josh – he has his own way of dealing with things…I am *so* sorry."

She wanted to punch him.

Deflecting never solved anything.

But sometimes it sure felt good.

She dug in, "You feel awful? You and your cronies, you all just looked the other way, didn't you? Sat across from me at meals, talked directly to my face, let's see, about a thousand times, and you couldn't mention, even once, that my boyfriend was cheating? I can imagine it now – off having your side conversations about the poor, stupid blind girl caught up in a web of lies that she doesn't even know about. You're all a bunch of cowards!"

He began to speak, "Rue, no, it wasn't like that—"

She cut him off, "I'm sure!" She was fuming, nearly panting. Through clenched teeth, she said curtly, "I have to go."

Before she could walk away, he grabbed her arm and said softly, "You know, he still misses you. He really did love you."

She stopped and stood fuming. Then with a wild, ragged breath, she deflated like a spent balloon. God! That word! Right to her core. After a moment, she said thoughtfully, "I…I know. I wish it had ended differently…I *do*, but you know, it didn't, and I can't change that. I just *can't*. Do you see?"

He squeezed her arm and replied, "Of course."

She waited a few seconds and then asked quietly, "Is he…okay?"

He chuckled mirthlessly before answering, "Well…he's Josh, so yeah, he's okay."

She nodded.

Then, mustering all the magnanimous feeling she could, she said with restraint, "Good."

Finally, they said goodbye. Rue maneuvered around him, feeling her heart race and her chest heave as she walked away, knowing Harsha was still standing there watching her go. That was the most venom and depleted generosity she had ever spewed before. It felt…right. She went home that day and wallowed in a sort of gleeful malice combined with willful resolution. She imagined Harsha going back to their apartment and telling Josh all about it.

In the following weeks, whenever she thought of the encounter, she realized it was a sort of catharsis for her. As spring dawned, Rue knew she had moved on. She was done thinking (or actively trying not to think) of Josh. She realized that as much as the breakup had caused her pain and heartache, she had also learned a thing or two. Number one being what kind of man was not right for her and to listen to her inner monologue when warning bells were going off. Women's intuition was nothing to sneeze at. Why had she doubted it? Never again!

And she slowly began to think that God had heard her plea. Things were getting (dare she say it?) *manageable* again. At first, she hadn't expected more – her threshold was lower than the lowest bar. Rue willed herself forward toward a small, fractured shaft of light. In the beginning, it was just muscle memory, forcing herself to smile at people again – Willie at the market, Chen and Mrs. Wai Hing, Roy at the Cliff House, Bob and Hayes at the Scarlet Huntington. Visiting some of her old haunts. She even found herself grinning involuntarily when she plopped a coin in the slot for Laughing Sal at the Musée Mécanique. For months prior to this, Rue cringed with ire that Sal was laughing *at* her and not *with* her, but now she realized that Sal was actually offering a buoyant chortle of commiseration.

Rue started to go to lunch again with Vy and Mayumi. She could tell they did everything they could to avoid the subject of Josh, which was fine with Rue. She stopped crying into Hank's fur every night and instead started a new hobby – string art – which involved hammering nails into a wood board and looping a thin string from one nail to another in a pattern. The hammering was therapeutic. Bam! Bam! Bam! She gave her first completed board, a boat anchor, to Daniel and Cathy for their anniversary. Rue thought it was quite good, and Daniel and Cathy confirmed it by tacking it onto the wall of their sailboat's sleeping berth.

She was back in her routine, with her well-ordered life, but now she had something more to show for it – a newfound sense of the wide-open opportunities of life and how one has to grasp at those chances, even if they are scary and unknown and risky. How else does one learn? You can't get to the rainbow without the rain. Rue's former cocoon was shattered into a million pieces, and she now knew she was all the better for it – despite the pain, despite the risks she took, despite the heartache. She now knew how to peel off those nuanced layers – every new encounter and experience – and to take each layer in with the good, the bad, and the ugly. And still live to see another day. Another day with all of its glory and wonder and life.

Now, on this day, Vy's day, Rue smiled from ear to ear and said cheerily to the Uber driver as he dropped her off at City Hall, "Thank you, sir. You have a wonderful day!" He laughed and said, "You too, miss!" She felt like a new peach that had just turned ripe in the orchard. Rue clicked her cane toward the entrance of the building with a smile. Vy and Anthony were getting married! And Anthony had filed the paperwork to adopt Kaylen – the icing on the cake! In Rue's fog over the past year, she hadn't investigated or understood exactly what had occurred to change their minds about getting married, but apparently something had, and here was Rue taking an Uber to their wedding. Would nothing cease to amaze?!

Rue took a deep breath. The air was fresh and clean, and the sun was shining on her face. It's going to be a great day. She heard several tourists taking photos. She touched her watch. It was eleven thirty-nine. She used her cane to walk up the steps with a catch in her throat and noticed immediately upon entering the building the acoustic perfection of the cathedral-like open atrium. She gasped and felt someone touch her arm. Mayumi. Rustling in her bridesmaid's dress, she uttered a soft word in Rue's ear: "Come." Mayumi brought her into a side room, where Rue heard the quaint, quick chatter of the women getting ready. Vy called to her from across the room, "Rue! Get over here, girl! I need your help."

Mayumi led her over, laughing. Vy leaned forward from her chair, where someone was arranging her hair, and kissed Rue on the cheek. Rue smiled and said, "Yes, your highness, what can I do for you?"

"First of all, you look beee-uuu-tiful!"

"Thank you, Vy. You look beautiful too."

That got a laugh out of her. "You blind, lying fool. You don't know what I look like."

"I can tell by your voice," Rue stated flatly with a grin.

"Uh-huh. Well, listen, I really do need something from you. I need you to tell me, and don't you lie. Be honest – I need to know if I have too much perfume on. What do you think?"

Rue leaned in and sniffed. She said, "No, my dear, you smell as light as a buttercup and as fruity as a stick of fruit stripes."

"Oh! I like that! Yes, that sounds about right. Not at all like a whore in church. Okay, phew! I was worried. Anthony doesn't like it when I stink it up. Good. Okay, okay, okay…," she stuttered a bit in her excitement. "Let me see, what…well…then what else?" This last question was directed to the person working on her hair, her mother. "Momma, what am I forgetting? What time is it? Where's Anthony's boutonniere? Did someone pick up the programs? What time did we arrange the limousine for? Oh my god, I can't remember a thing! I'm starting to sweat! Momma, I'm going to stain my dress!"

Rue heard Kaylen rustle up to her mom and say, "Momma, don't worry. You're fine, everything's fine."

"I don't know, I don't know…I can't think…"

Rue groped for Vy's hand and squeezed it, saying, "Everything's going to be perfect."

Vy took a deep, shaky breath, and something about her vulnerability at that moment (a quality Rue had never detected in Vy before) made Rue tear up.

Vy said severely, "Oh no, oh no, oh no…stop that! Don't you look at me that way, don't you…start!"

Rue laughed through her tears as they streamed down her face. Vy was getting married! Vy leaned forward, and Rue felt the heave of Vy's chest against hers. Then Vy pulled away abruptly, saying, "That's about enough of that, my dear. I don't want my dress to wrinkle. And I certainly can't afford to start crying now. You'll mess with my makeup. You hear me? You get those tears away right now!"

Rue wiped her face and said, "Yes, sergeant!"

Mayumi led Rue away to other side of the room so Vy's mom and Kaylen could finish her wardrobe and accoutrements.

Rue asked Mayumi quietly and a little self-consciously, "Do I look alright?"

"Yes, you look perfect. Pink is your color."

"Thanks," she said gratefully. "So, how will the ceremony work?"

"I'm not exactly sure, but I think the groomsmen come in to get us and walk us up the stairs."

"Oh, are there stairs?"

"Yes, I think so, because we're supposed to end up upstairs near a sort of upper lobby area. I think Anthony will already be up there, waiting with the preacher. Then Vy will be escorted up by her mom and Kaylen."

A moment later, Vy's mother came over to them and said, "Go!" Rue felt a large, reassuring man weave her hand through his elbow and say, "Hello Rue, my name's Travis, you're with me."

Rue smiled and said quietly, "Hi, okay."

Rue paused and grinned back toward Vy, who promptly said, "Rue, get a move on, girl – don't hold up the nuptials!"

Rue giggled on the way out the door. Vy sounded ecstatic. As Rue ascended the stairs with her groomsman, she thought about the many years she had known Vy. Had it been ten? Twenty? She couldn't remember. All she knew was that Vy was her best friend. And in all of those years, Vy had never treated Rue any differently from anyone else. Rue had never felt as though she was Vy's "blind friend." She was simply Vy's friend. Rue couldn't have asked for a better friend. Vy was steady, kind, sassy, practical, and warm. She was helpful without being intrusive. Rue admired how Vy had arranged this chaperoning of the bridesmaids as an easy way to get Rue up the stairs without making it uncomfortable. Vy was always so considerate that way, and she never let on that Rue's blindness figured into any situation. How did she do that? Rue smiled. She was happy. Really happy. For the first time in a year. For Vy, for her little family, for this beautiful, sunny day (even in July, even in San Francisco!), and for the transformation that had taken place in her own heart so that not one ounce of envy or sadness could inch its way into her.

The ceremony proceeded without a hitch. Anthony and Vy spoke to each other clearly and succinctly, with love and devotion and only a slight tremble in Anthony's voice when he said, "I thee wed" while placing the ring on Vy's finger. Kaylen cried and asked Mayumi for a tissue at some point, which Mayumi readily provided – to her and to the other bridesmaids, including Rue, who let a tear or two slip out. Vy's mother only put her oar in about four times during the ceremony – to fix Vy's dress and to adjust her hair, pluck her flowers, and ensure that the rings were set properly. Finally, Vy said under her breath, "Momma, shut it!" and that was the end of Momma's interruptions before a thankful continuation of the final, smooth rendering of the preacher's words of matrimony.

After the ceremony was over, the photographer asked the bridal party to pose on the grand staircase inside and then on the front steps outside. The photographer was arranging Vy's dress and Anthony's stance while the other members of the wedding party chattered quietly, awaiting instruction. Rue was asking Mayumi how they were riding to the reception when Mayumi abruptly cut her off, saying in a whisper, "Rue, there's a man off to the left staring at you."

Rue scoffed at this. "What? Who?"

"I don't know, some guy…"

"Well, you know, people stare at me all the time, or so I'm told. I guess the novelty of it…I wouldn't worry about it." Rue tried to feel as confident as she sounded. But with a sense of dread, she wondered, was it Josh? Would Mayumi recognize him? Rue tried to remember back, had Mayumi ever met him? Surely Vy would say something, although she was distracted right now… maybe it was one of Josh's friends? Please let it be one of the attorneys at the office! Of course, then Mayumi would certainly know him. Who was it?!

Mayumi was saying, "I don't know…he's definitely staring directly at you…he's about our age, sandy hair, medium height, green eyes, good looking…"

"Mayumi!" Rue exclaimed. Although she was relieved, this was not a description of Josh – that much she knew.

"Oh! That won't do…he's definitely interested or mesmerized or something…let's see…should I go talk to him? Ask who he is?"

"What?! No, of course not. Who cares if some stranger is looking at me. Let's ignore him and he'll go away."

"Okay, good plan," Mayumi said reassuringly. Then, "By the way, he's coming over here. Right now. To talk to you."

Rue felt her face flush and her stomach drop.

"Hi, Rue," he said simply, with a warm, kind, sweet voice that Rue recognized in an instant because it reverberated in her mind like a coin dropping in a steel pan. How could she ever forget the voice that had told her with regret and empathy, "My wife is having an affair with your boyfriend."

She shook her head and replied unwillingly and inevitably, "Hi, Kevin."

He took her left hand in his and held it a moment saying, "It's good to see you."

Mayumi walked away discreetly, saying, "I'm going to check on Vy." Rue nodded.

There was a moment of silence.

He asked, "A wedding?"

"Yes, my friend Vy," she answered lamely, pointing her bouquet in the direction of the voices.

"You look…you look…lovely," he said sincerely, and Rue smiled, touching the soft inner texture of the flowers in her bouquet reassuringly.

"Um…what are you doing here?" Rue asked.

"Oh…well, it's a sunny day," he replied, and she could still feel the imprint of him on her left hand. "I…um…I'm sort of working…we have a client… she told us she loves City Hall, so I thought I'd come down and take some photos. Get inspiration…"

Rue suddenly remembered the feeling of the ornate scrollwork along the inside stairwell and the atrium's spectacular bowl-like sound. It was a remarkable old building, wasn't it? But then, they were standing outside now. She asked, "Are you a landscaper?"

He laughed. "No, no, I'm an engineer. I work at an architectural firm."

She nodded, still processing and studying, and said blankly, "Oh, that sounds interesting."

"Yes, it is." He paused and Rue stood quietly waiting.

"So…so…how have you been…Rue?" he faltered on her name, like a word he had been saying in his head for a long time, but not out loud until now. He was gauging her reaction to him. He was timid.

"Actually…okay," Rue began, with a small smile. "Decidedly…better… lately. You?"

She heard him breathe out with a small "hmpf." He said, "Good. Me too." He paused and Rue sensed he was on the point of taking his leave, but instead he said, "Hey…I know this goes without saying, but I wanted you to know…how sorry I am…was…about everything."

She could hear the emotion behind his voice. She reassured him, "No. Please. You did the right thing. It was…hard…awful…dreadful, really, wasn't it?" Rue continued with a mirthless laugh. "But in the end, it was…needed." She felt along the ribbon that held her flowers, blinking her blind, dry eyes down at the bouquet.

"Well, I guess I should be—" he began.

Suddenly Rue didn't want him to leave. She cut him off, "Do you… do you ever hear from her?"

He exhaled and said, "Naw, well, in the beginning, yes, to get the rest of her stuff and her dog. But after that, not really, only through the lawyers."

He paused and she felt him shrug it off as water under the bridge. "Do you? Hear from him?"

"Oh no," stated Rue. "He finally gave up. Thank goodness. It was painful. Agonizing, really. I couldn't take it anymore."

He thought about that for a minute and said, "Hmmm, I bet."

She heard Vy calling her name. Rue said softly, "I have to go."

Kevin lightly touched her arm and said, "Rue, wait. Before you go…can I…can I call you sometime?"

A pregnant pause followed. Finally, she said, "Okay."

"Okay?" he answered as a question with some surprise, and then as a statement, "Okay. I will. Hope you have a nice time, um, at the wedding."

"Thanks," she said and grinned.

Mayumi was suddenly back at her side, leading her away, and she heard Kevin say, "Bye, Rue."

"Bye," she shined back at him as Mayumi whispered in her ear, "He's still watching you. Who is he?"

"Kevin Warren!"

"Kevin War—oh! The husband?!"

"Yes! Well, not anymore…"

"Wow!"

"Yes."

Mayumi paused and Rue felt her cheeks flush. Mayumi said, "He's really good-looking."

"He is?"

"Yes."

Rue grinned at her and said thoughtfully, "And nice, too."

"Good," Mayumi replied, squeezing her arm. "Will you see him again?"

"I think so," Rue answered, still smiling.

Later, somewhat surprisingly, Rue enjoyed herself at the reception, even dancing with several of the groomsmen, then with Mayumi, then with Kaylen, then with Vy, until she couldn't dance anymore and sat down to enjoy a piece of cake in peace.

Vy was radiant, filled with exuberance and joy. Anthony was relaxed. Kaylen was skipping around. Even Vy's mother had graciously given the happy couple a toast: "I have always dreamed of this day, a day when my precious baby would find her happily-ever-after with a strong, faithful, hardworking man. Don't let me down, Anthony! I'm counting on you, and I'll be watching..." Rue heard Vy's laugh and had to smile.

Rue had been worried that this love bomb would set her heart ablaze, and not in a good way. But to her own surprise – dare she say it? – she felt quite content and filled with hope. She had Kevin Warren to thank for that. So strange – why had he been here on this day, at this location, at this exact time? After a year?! Crazy!

When the sun was sinking in the sky, those who were left from the wedding crowd stood outside and lit sparklers in a halo over the bridal couple as they slipped into a decked-out Cadillac headed to the Palace Hotel. As Vy called goodbye out the car window, her dress sounded like crumpled newspapers. Rue and Mayumi listened and waved and cried with joy. Shortly after, the quiet of the night ascended over the murmuring crowd. Rue wiped her eyes as Mayumi ordered them an Uber, saying, "Wow, what a day!"

Rue nodded and thought about Kevin Warren.

Chapter XXIV

RUE CAVENDISH! HOW MANY TIMES had Kevin thought of her over the past year? Hundreds? Thousands? Wondering where the pretty blind woman was at that very moment. She would pop into his head while he was out walking in the city or eating at a restaurant or getting ready in the morning. He had always found it so strange – why? A woman he had met only once, under horrible circumstances, was there, like a foggy angel apparition haunting his daily life. And yet, he had never run into her. Never seen her since, not even from afar, not even at the local coffee shop or at his favorite sushi place or downtown on the street.

Until today.

She had looked so…so endearing, like a beacon in the night. Standing on those regal stairs, in front of the ominous and ornate front door of City Hall. Owning that body-hugging pink dress, her shoulders kissed by the sun, her hair longer and darker than he remembered. And those lips – like a pink ribbon tied in a perfect bow. Very kissable lips.

Was God playing a trick on him? The day before, after over a year of abstinence, he had planned a date. With Jessica. Which was scheduled for that very night! Yes, damn it, he was a man of his word. And by golly, he would go. He looked at the clock. It was already six. They were going out for dinner. And who knew what else afterward. Gulp. He was supposed to meet her in an hour. He sat in his apartment, cursing the banyan tree – screw the tangled mass; he was seeing black. He needed to sort through his confused, anxious thoughts. What to do? What to do? He chuckled wryly. He had been with the same woman for nearly a decade, and now, in the course of twenty-four hours, he was struck (as if by lightning!) with two new options. Talk about a fish out of water! Flop, flop, flop went his pathetic, scaly, unseasoned, inexperienced heart.

He looked in the mirror and said out loud, "Pull it together, man!" Seriously. At this juncture, he needed to purge Rue Cavendish from his mind. It was too far-fetched anyway. How could he possibly date the ex-girlfriend of his ex-wife's boyfriend? Even thinking this was ridiculous – what, like, dating his friend's second cousin twice removed. Ludicrous! Unthinkable! And yet, he thought. Of Rue. Again. And often. It was more than just her beauty; it was her quiet, thoughtful repose and her way of stopping and thinking before she talked. He liked the kind, sweet intensity of her. He simply wanted to be in her presence, like a magnet pulling him to her.

Focus! He dressed in a dark gray polo with a pair of khakis and brown loafers, thinking he looked more like his dad than he ever had. What an idiot. He had no idea how to dress for a date. He glanced in the mirror and cursed. Oh well, good enough. Jessica had essentially asked him out, after all, so she probably wouldn't care what he was wearing. When he arrived at the restaurant, she was already at a table, shimmering in dark red plunging top with tight jeans and high-heeled short boots. She was certainly showing *all* her assets. He had to admit she was attractive, with a supremely fit body. She stood up and kissed him on the cheek. Her perfume was poured on, so he smiled, trying to hide the fact that he didn't like it. For an instant he recalled that Rue smelled light and fresh, like a small flower in the springtime.

"Sorry, was I late?" he asked, sitting across from her. Fake it till you make it, brother!

"Nope, I was early. You're fine," she smiled back.

"Good. So, you been here before?" he began.

"Sure, a few times. They have great pork chops, but pretty much everything on the menu is good."

They ordered beer and sat talking for a while. She said she was a freelance writer and blogger. Apparently she wrote about fashion, using herself as a model. She sometimes solicited her friends on shopping trips, videoing them and posting "who wore it best" or "how to dress for less." As she chatted, Kevin felt as though he had been dropped in a foreign country and was attempting to immerse himself in the local culture. At some point, she paused in a long soliloquy on the current plague of sequins in fashion today to inquire, "You have no idea what I'm talking about, do you?"

He laughed and admitted, "Not at all."

"Oh," she said, with a slight frown. "I guess I should have known."

He wondered what she meant by that. After a second, he inquired,

"My outfit clue you in?"

She tried not to show it, but her quick look at his shirt gave it away. She said, "Oh no, that's not what I mean. I just figured you weren't too interested in fashion. I get it – it's not everyone's bag."

Kevin felt slightly bad – he really hadn't been paying attention. Not in the way he should have. For a date that he actually cared about. Was his mind still—? Stop it! He recovered with a quick chuckle. "Sorry, it does sound interesting. I wish I knew more about it. I guess I'm hopeless on that front. I tend to wake up every morning and throw on whatever's clean and fits."

She frowned slightly, "So, does your size change a lot then?"

"Well, no…well, yes, lately it has, a little," he stuttered, beginning to think how to drop the bomb without making a crater, "because well, because, I was recently divorced."

"Oh, sorry to hear that," she said while conveying something entirely different with her eager eyes.

He cleared his throat. "Um, ahem, yeah, thanks, it's fine, I'm fine. It's been a year – actually, over a year now. And it's just that I've lost some weight recently. You know, it was…it's been kind of…hard…and I guess I wasn't eating enough or something…and plus, I started working out, and well, anyway, my pants were falling off, so yeah, I needed some new clothes." He was starting to ramble and wasn't sure why. It might have been nerves, or it might have been the fact that he had just confessed the divorce thing and wondered how that would land. He plunged ahead, "When I was home a few months ago, in Indiana – that's where I'm from – my mom insisted on taking me shopping. She said I looked like I had 'droopy drawers' and needed suspenders. I bet you can't imagine that in the fashion world – anyone under the age of eighty wearing suspenders?! Just kidding, I mean, I would never…really… just kidding, don't look at me that way, I swear." Oh my god, Kevin, get it together! "Anyway, so we went shopping…it was really nice, I got some new things and had quality time with my mom…but…but, haha, clearly, she may have influenced what I bought. Since I started working out, you know, it's hard to know what to buy that will fit…I'm bigger in certain spots and smaller in others…my body's changed quite a bit and it's all rather new to me…"

"Yes, I see that," she purred and raised her eyebrows. Ah, there it was again – she wasn't leaving anything to chance, was she? Clearly, she wasn't frightened of the divorce thing. In fact, she seemed oddly enticed by it. He understood why when she admitted, "I'm divorced too. Twice." Shit, she only looked to be about thirty to him. Wow, quick work. "Yeah, they were both assholes. The first one beat the shit out of me, which is why I joined the army. Oh yeah, I forgot to mention that, didn't I? I was in the army for seven years. I mostly joined to get away from him. He was my high school sweetheart – very controlling, a total dick. I signed up right after I graduated. He insisted we get married before I went to boot camp. I think he thought it would keep me from cheating, which it didn't, by the way, but at that point it was easier to just do what he said than to fight with him. For the first few years, I was stationed at Fort Drum in New York, and he moved up there to be with me. But he couldn't keep a job – always pissed people off and got fired. I was supporting him financially, and he was still beating the crap out of me every night. It was awful. I was totally pumped when my division got deployed. Finally I could get away from him. I did two tours in Afghanistan. It was the best time of my life. Crazy, right? When I came back, the dick had found some local whore waitress to fuck while I was gone, but I was like, good riddance!"

"Wow, that sounds horrible," Kevin said, thinking man, I'm in over my head…a lot of information to digest on the first date. And then there was more…

"Yeah, it was pretty bad. Of course, by the time we divorced, I was no longer afraid of him – I could have snapped his neck in two with one swift kick. The asshole. He's lucky I never did."

"Hmpf," Kevin nodded lamely, with a slight tingle in his neck.

"Yeah, so that was hubby number one. Hubby number two I met in Montana after I was discharged from the army. He was on the rodeo circuit, you know, traveling all over the west. I thought he was the hottest guy I'd ever met. I went on the road with him for a while, but it was hard doing that nearly three hundred days a year. I finally bought us a house in Idaho, thinking he'd come home and settle down, but after two years he never did. He just kept going. He's probably still out there, wrestling steers instead of rolling in the hay."

At this last statement, she grinned at Kevin, and he looked down at his hands, thinking he would never look at hay the same way again.

The food came and they were eating when she asked abruptly, "So, what's your story?"

He choked for a second, then said, "Oh, well, not too much to tell. Grew up in Indiana, moved here right out of college, got a job—"

She cut him off. "Ert – no, not that…I mean, what's your story with your ex? She fuck you over?"

"Um, well, no, not exactly, I mean a little, but not really…," he stumbled.

"That means yes."

He shook his head unconvincingly. "We'd been together since college, and yeah, we went through some bumps, but ultimately it just didn't work out."

"She still around…?"

"Nope, well, not around me anyway. I haven't seen her in a long time."

"Well, you know the cure for a broken heart, don't you?" she asked with a grin.

He shook his head.

"Right back in the saddle you go!"

He felt her eyes devouring him. He shifted uncomfortably in his chair and stared back mutely. He was so not prepared to handle this kind of attention. He laughed self-consciously and changed the subject, "How did you end up in San Francisco then?"

"Oh, that's easy. Another guy." He was beginning to see a pattern. His throat seemed to constrict on his pork chop. She continued, "First, I was writing my blog from Idaho, you know, mostly fashion for female hunters. Hey, don't laugh, I'm serious! You'd be surprised. I had quite a following. It's like a total niche market. Anyway, some rich guy down here DM'ed me about his hauling trailer company – I swear, you can't make this shit up! He thought I would make a good spokesmodel, so I moved and became "Trailer Hitch Trish. You know, he dolls me up with hot outfits and poses me next to his trailers, then I blog about it and post ads online."

"No!" Kevin laughed.

"It's true. You wouldn't believe the groupies. Insane! I still get spotted on the street – complete strangers walk up to me and grab my ass. Seriously."

"You're still working for the guy?" Kevin asked, now wondering if she always unintentionally (or intentionally) planted things in men's minds like that ass comment.

"Oh yeah, on occasion I still do an ad or two for him. What can I say? It pays the bills."

"But, so, were you *with* the guy?"

"Tony? Hell no. Well, of course we used to hook up all the time, but not really anymore. Well, only once in a while. He's up in Bayside. We were never a couple or anything – it was all just fun, you know?"

"Uh-huh, okay, so, then you, um, do the fashion blogging still?" He was starting to sweat. Just the talk of sex was sending him down a tunnel somewhere between tantalizing intrigue and abject fear. He took a big gulp of beer.

"Yeah, I decided to shift my focus. I wanted the hunter girls and trucker girls to know they could wear girlie clothes too. It's been a bit of a transition, trying to figure out how to look sexy and still wear practical outfits that are durable and comfortable. I've had some hits and misses." She paused for a minute and then asked him (did she have any other setting than blunt?), "You got money?"

"Money?" he asked with an uncomfortable laugh. "Not really. Well, some, I mean, I get by."

"She sucked you dry, didn't she? Not just money either. I know the type. I'm glad you got rid of her. You need something new. I'm looking for a different kind of man now myself, so I get it. Maybe this will be good for both of us."

"Uh-huh," he responded evasively. And what was *this*? She was eyeing him again and he looked down into his beer. He could relate – he certainly wanted a different kind of woman. But wasn't Jessica seeming more and more like Alyssa – bold, brassy, no filter? What the hell was he doing? Still, how to proceed? He was no doormat, but he also wasn't experienced in rejecting women, and especially not outspoken, aggressive women like Jessica. He needed to think of a plan, and quick. In the meantime, after many additional beers (more than he could count), she declared, "Time to bounce, my friend. Where d'ya live?"

Damn the alcohol! He wasn't thinking clearly. He stalled and finally said, "Um, not too far. We can walk."

"Let's go."

He paid, and in what seemed like a half-second later, he was putting the key in the door of his apartment as she leaned her body against him and slammed the door behind them as they tumbled in. Before he could say a word, she put her tongue down his throat, pushing his back against the wall. He tried to break free and laughed uncomfortably, but she was having none of that. Her mouth was on his as she launched him down on the couch. How did she do that so quickly? It was instinctive with her, apparently, to map out the place where fornication must happen in an unfamiliar place. In his drunken brain, he marveled absurdly at this fact while she placed her body full bore on top of his, grinding her groin against his. After a few minutes, he tried to summon the willpower to stop. On the one hand, his body was being sucked in as she groped him in ways that left nothing to the imagination. On the other hand, literally, in the sense that his other hand was reaching for the coffee table for leverage, he was attempting to escape and run for his life. She didn't like that. She grabbed his hand and placed it directly on her breast, helping him squeeze it. Then she sat up quickly and pulled her shirt off, taking his hand again and repositioning it on top of her lacy black bra. She lifted his shirt over his head and pushed her nakedness against his. He tried to focus, to think clearly, but his mind was a blur of body parts and automatic responses. Finally, in the midst of her reaching for his zipper, he managed to jump up, nearly throwing her off, as he teetered beside the couch and said breathlessly, "Hold it!"

She was stunned and breathing hard and cried, "That's what I'm trying to do!"

He shook his head with an exasperated laugh and tried to be clearer, "No...no, I mean, let's hang on...let's stop. Sorry, can we stop for a second?"

"What? Are you fucking kidding me?" she nearly shouted at him. Her face was awash in incredulity and rage. She reached for his hand, but he pulled it away.

He was a little afraid of her and took time to calm his voice before responding. He said simply and quietly, "I'm sorry. I...I...I can't. You're... you're, well, you're great and all but...but...this, this is too much. I'm not ready for this."

She scoffed in utter disbelief. Kevin himself was half doubting – had he really just said that?! She stared at him, scowling, her breasts heaving up and down. She paused and finally said, "Seriously, dude?"

What could he do? He held his ground, and said lamely, "I'm afraid so."

She responded angrily, "Fine! Fuck this! I'm outta here!"

Out she went as Kevin called "sorry" after her retreating form, but she didn't look back. He stood by the door for five minutes, wondering if she would return to plow through it, but she didn't. He locked the door and went and sat on the couch, holding his head in his hands. His mind went: That went well. Great job, Kevin! Could you have messed that up any worse? Why on earth did you bring her back here? What were you thinking? You knew within the first five minutes of that date that she was not the woman for you, yet you sat there like a worthless dolt, letting her take over, knowing you shouldn't – couldn't – go through with it. You couldn't have offered to take her somewhere else? A movie? Drinks? A walk? Anything! You bring her back here – what did you think would happen?

He lay down on the couch and stared at the ceiling.

Epic fail.

Maybe he shouldn't date.

Maybe he should become a monk.

Maybe he learned his lesson: don't date anyone who reminds you of Alyssa.

Maybe he was stronger than he realized.

Maybe he finally did the right thing and said no to a pushy woman.

Maybe he was ready for someone better than that.

Maybe he should call Rue.

Maybe he shouldn't.

Maybe he should.

✲ CHAPTER XXV ✲

RUE DIDN'T HEAR FROM KEVIN right away. She didn't think she would. And she was glad. She had just started to feel normal again. She didn't want to rock the boat. She was back to liking her life again – back in her easy, predictable, no-fuss-no-muss routine. And being open to new things, if and when they came up. Granted, she didn't know what Kevin's intentions were. She didn't want to assume, but then…something about his voice at City Hall gave her the idea that she probably *could* assume. The spark. It was there. Palpable. Undeniable. But still…better to play it safe, better not to think along those lines…

A few weeks later, on a Sunday afternoon, she was at her drafting table, painting one blue dahlia. Even though she loved the string art, lately she had gone back to her stencil painting. All of the fours and threes and twos were put away in a corner, stacked up beside the string art boards. Now it was one. Yes! One! Cozy, quaint, self-contained. One. Singular.

When her phone rang, she jumped and heard Hank pop off the couch. The phone was a few feet away, and she walked swiftly to get it, trying not to run into the coffee table. She heard the phone say "Kevin Warren," which set her heart racing. Should she answer?

Finally, she did. "Hello?"

"Hi, Rue?"

"Yes, yes, hi."

"Oh good, I caught you. Hi, this is Kevin. Kevin Warren. How are you?"

"Hi! I'm…I'm fine," he said, a little too excitedly. Chill out, Rue! "You?"

"Good," he said in a laughing, nervous voice and then repeated, "Good, good. So, it was great to see you a few weeks ago. I'm sorry I haven't called…"

"Oh, it's okay, no worries, I kind of thought…you might not…ever," Rue said, matter of fact.

He laughed, and a tension seemed to release from him. He said, "Ha, me either. How was the wedding?"

"It was great. They're back from the honeymoon. They…they," Rue was thinking how inane small talk was, but she plowed ahead anyway, "they encountered a shark while snorkeling, so we've heard a lot about that…"

"Wow, really?"

"Yeah, it was just a reef shark, and it swam past them, but to hear Vy tell it, you'd think it was *Jaws*."

Kevin chuckled and asked, "Funny. So, how do you know Vy?"

Rue said with a realization, "I guess I forgot for a second that we don't know each other at all, do we?"

"Nope. Not a thing. Well, except the obvious: that we're both rejects."

"Ha! Yep, pretty much," she said with a grunt.

"Hmmm, on the other hand, I'd like to think we're both warriors."

"Warriors?"

"Fighting off the bonds of evil betrayers, aren't we?"

Rue thought about that for a second. It was so medieval. She liked it. "Yes, I suppose we are. I'm wearing a helmet next time."

"Me too. And carrying a sword."

"Perfect. We have a plan!" Rue stated, and they both laughed. After a moment, she said reflectively, "Maybe the best defense is no defense."

"Maybe. What about the old adage 'Fool me once, shame—'"

"Um," Rue interrupted. "Let's just agree right now that we're both a couple of fools."

She could feel his smile through the phone. He said slowly, "A ship of them!"

"Yes, let's try not to sink. What do you think?"

"Okay, let's not," he answered quietly. "Rushing in…"

After a pause, Rue said mysteriously, "Maybe" and then, answering the original question, "Vy's my best friend, and we work together."

"Ah. Where do you work?"

"A law firm downtown. That's job number one."

"Wait, job number one? You have more?"

"I'm also a lounge singer."

"What? Wow!"

"Yup, researcher by day, lounge singer by night. And you? An architectural firm by day?"

"Yup, engineer."

"Nice."

"Yeah, you too."

There was a pause. She could hear him breathing. He finally said, "I just wondered, well, I wondered if you wanted to meet for...lunch...or something...sometime."

"Lunch?" Rue asked with surprise. Maybe she had misjudged.

He shot in quickly, "Or dinner. Whichever works for you. Sorry, I wasn't sure..."

She chuckled. Okay, he didn't know what he was about. That was good. For a second, she flashed back to her life over a year ago, where someone *did* know exactly what he was about. Look where that went. She said, "No, no, lunch is fine."

"Noon on Tuesday?"

"Great."

"Let's see, where can we meet? What about the Greenery? Would that work?"

"Yes, yes, that's perfect. I go there all the time; they have the—"

He cut her off, "Five-dollar soup and bread on the side!"

She laughed in happy surprise. "Yes!"

"Well, okay then." He sounded relieved.

"Okay, see you then. Bye, Kevin."

"Bye, Rue."

And thus, a friendship began, or something...

For many weeks, they simply met. For breakfast, lunch, coffee, drinks, the occasional dinner. At the park, museum, wharf, ferry building, theater, stores, restaurants, bars. Rue thought it was rather funny. It was almost like a joke in her mind – how do two shy, quiet, reticent people get to know each other? The answer: Slowly. To be clear: Not just shy; gun-shy – the worst kind of shy! They had extended periods together when they sat in silence. Rue didn't mind. Even with the hit to her standard routine, it stemmed the tide of loneliness and felt peaceful and comforting – like a warm blanket on a cold day.

In the beginning, they talked about impersonal things – work, hobbies, the latest television show or story on the news. Sometimes he talked about his family back in Evansville, about the farm and his nieces. But when he asked about her family, she was brief, talking only about Daniel and Cathy and the girls, and leaving the rest close to her vest. Once she let it slip that her parents were dead, and she noticed the tone of his voice dropped an octave – he had questions, but he didn't want her to open up if it hurt her. That was when she had a revelation about this man – he was unfailingly kind. Such an impossibly rare quality! She nearly spilled her guts right then and there but held back, fear gripping her – was her revelation real? Was she just reading something into his character because that was what she wanted more than anything – a kind man to be her friend and confidant? She must brace herself. She must not fall, as the saying went. She must stay strong. She remembered how giving her whole self ended the last time.

After several weeks, he told her (in not so many words) about his failed date with the infamous Jessica.

"Wow," Rue commented, "You probably think I'm a tiny, flimsy sort of weakling after that, don't you?"

He laughed and said, "Yes, praise be to the Lord!"

"Did you ever see her again?"

"No," he said. Then, laughing, "Be afraid, be very afraid."

Rue smiled.

"Kind of sucks. I gave up my gym membership – for a pretty penny, I might add. I bought some free weights instead…use them at home. Not quite the same, but still, better than facing the wrath of Jessica in the flesh."

"You should bill her."

"If only I could," he said with chagrin. Then he asked, "So, what about you? Lots of men chasing after you?"

"Ha! That's a good one. Naw, I really haven't ventured out…"

"Nothing ventured, nothing gained…," he said philosophically.

"I don't know…," Rue replied cryptically. She thought, was that true? She was inclined to believe, nothing ventured, nothing *pained*.

Sensing her ironic tone, Kevin joked, "So, you haven't been swiping right? Or is it swiping left? I can never remember."

Rue chuckled and said, "No, I'm afraid I haven't been swiping at all."

"Me either," he admitted. Well, that was good. She wasn't sure why she thought it was good. What did it matter if he was dating? Did she care? Did she mind?

Later that evening, tucked under the covers of her bed with Hank weighing down the blankets at her feet, she forced herself to examine these questions. Did she have feelings for Kevin? She loved being around him and talking to him and listening to him. She knew that much. She loved the way he smelled too. Like a man, but not too made up, not too much cologne; more like a rich body scent, natural and organic. She loved the way he made her feel – like she was the only person on earth, like he was hanging on her every word. And he always remembered to hold her elbow or her arm or her shoulder to guide her – gently, thoughtfully, properly. On the few occasions when she took his arm, she felt a tingle light up her insides – he was so strong! She sometimes wrapped her fingers around his arm to touch the muscle there and to feel the warmth of his chest against the outside of her hand.

But were her feelings for him romantic? Thinking back to Josh, she could only remember a hot, burning flame stoked into an inferno that was a force beyond control. And yet, it was so quickly snuffed out! Was that the legitimate way of romance – to be set on fire only to be burnt and left for dust? Why couldn't it be a pot left to boil slowly over a bed of warm, simmering coals? Why couldn't it be deep and methodical and authentic? Was it authentic with Kevin? That was the real question: whether it was *real*. Her love for Josh had been authentic, and she felt his for her as well. But his brand of love was forked down the middle, as if he had many versions of himself and could spread them across all the valleys of sharing and intimacy. This was not Rue's brand of love. She wanted one steady, constant, all-encompassing kind of love. Was Kevin the man to bring this into her life? What was *his* brand of love? She was reminded of the fact that he had never strayed from Alyssa (as far as Rue knew), even after her negligence, even after her lack of commitment, even after her betrayal.

She still wasn't sure of her own mind or her own heart on the subject. On the one hand, it would be so easy to simply give herself to Kevin (she sensed he was waiting for her to do exactly that), but on the other hand, she might just be stepping right back into a roller-coaster ride. She knew her constitution couldn't endure another round. It wasn't worth that pain again, ever. In the absence of a definitive answer, Rue went to sleep, thinking, it must come to me when I'm ready to know the answer. What good is forcing these things? I'll wait.

A couple of weeks later, Kevin and Rue were sitting on a bench outside the Ferry Building, listening to the seagulls squawk. Kevin asked her quietly, "Rue, what happened to your parents?" She wondered when he might ask. It was one of the striking things she noticed right away about Kevin – unlike Josh, he wanted to *know* her. Not just on the surface, not just her superficial thoughts about the latest TV show or political discussion or news story (although Kevin wanted to know those things too), but he also wanted to know who she was, her fears and ambitions and loves, how she got about in the world (emotionally as well as physically). He wanted to know her. It was flattering. And scary. Thus far, she had held pieces of herself back, despite his best efforts.

She took a deep breath and sighed. She hadn't told anyone the full story, not even Vy, and certainly not Josh. Oddly enough, Josh had never asked. Daniel refused to talk about it. He was still bitter. Rue had tucked the whole thing away like an unopened suitcase stashed in the attic. Kevin took her hand. It was the first time he had done that. It felt warm and soft and firm. Yes, he had been leading her around the city by her elbow for weeks, but this was his first intentional touch. It was like the first touch of sunlight on her face when she went out of her building in the morning. She gathered courage from it.

She started, "Well, have you ever heard that song by Willie Nelson 'Blue Eyes Crying in the Rain'?"

Kevin said, "No, I don't think so."

"I'll have to sing it for you sometime. Once in a while, someone requests it at the lounge, and it always makes me think of my mom. It's very…difficult…for me to play," she said slowly and continued, "You see, when I was little, people always said that I had my mother's eyes. Apparently hers were large and blue, with dark lashes, like mine."

He squeezed her hand, and she went on, "It was raining the night the police came. I remember the rain pounding on the roof. Nanny Alex hadn't let us go outside and play that day because of the rain, and I was mad at her. I was in bed reading. It was late, maybe ten or eleven, on a Friday night. My parents had left that morning on a private plane for a weekend ski trip to Squaw Valley. It was their wedding anniversary, so they hadn't taken us with them. Usually we would all go together."

Rue paused and Kevin asked, incredulous, "Wait. Skiing?"

She nodded and said with a grin, "Yes, I ski. Tethered to Daniel. He hated it, but I loved it. It was like being in an icy wind tunnel. Racing down the mountain as fast as I could, the snow on my face and in my mouth. Daniel would get mad because I went too fast and he couldn't steer me properly, but I didn't care. When we fell, it was like a big snowball of body parts rolling down the mountain. I liked that even more. Daniel would curse. Poor

Daniel. He had a lot to put up with, having me as a sister."

Kevin chuckled, thinking about that. He was still holding her hand. Rue continued, "Anyway, as far as we knew, our parents had been in Nevada skiing all day. There was a loud banging on the front door. I put my book down and opened my bedroom door an inch to listen. I heard Nanny Alex get up and go downstairs. I had a strange foreboding. It was as if the quibbling from earlier in the day had stayed with us in a dark, hovering mass. I stood in my doorway, transfixed, wondering who would knock on our door so late. I heard muffled voices downstairs talking in short, quick sentences. Suddenly I felt Daniel's hand on my arm, and I jumped. He asked, 'What is it?' I shook my head and began to cry, so he led me back to my bed and told me everything was okay and he'd be right back. After what seemed like hours, Nanny Alex and Daniel came back and stood by my bed. Finally, Nanny Alex told me that our parents had died in a plane crash on the way to the ski resort. It had taken the authorities all day to get to the crash site and identify the bodies. The pilot died, and another couple as well. It was awful. The next day, it was on the news and in the papers."

Rue paused to wipe a tear away and Kevin said softly, "Oh Rue, I'm so sorry." And then, "How old were you?"

"Ten. Daniel was twelve."

"God!"

"Yes…"

They were silent for a moment or two. He put his arm around her shoulders, and she leaned into him. He asked, "So, where did you go after that?"

Rue sighed. "That's when things got really ugly. You see, up until that point in our lives, Daniel and I thought all children grew up the way we did – surrounded by loving parents, with money, security, activity, comfort, warmth, full bellies…anything we wanted. It all came crashing down in an instant. My dad had been a successful real estate broker, and Mom was a stay-at-home-mom. We called ourselves the 'fabulous four.' We did everything together. But on that night, Nanny Alex called our one remaining relative, Great Aunt Louise, who came to take over and ruin everything. She was a cold, hard woman. She never had her own children and thought of us and the whole situation as an annoying nuisance. She went directly into business mode – making arrangements, selling our house and our belongings, and promptly shipping us off to boarding school."

"Wow," Kevin said empathetically.

"Yeah, it was pretty awful." Rue rubbed her eyes and grunted. "But it taught me a lesson very young – life ain't no walk in the park, and I must learn to rely on myself, and only myself. Even Daniel couldn't help me since he was shipped off to his own nightmare."

Kevin said, "Wasn't that hard, doing everything on your own...?"

"Yeah, it wasn't easy," she agreed, "but it made me the independent person I am today. I guess I should thank Great Aunt Louise."

They both sort of snorted at that. A few minutes later, she wiped her tears and said, "But come to think of it, I'd rather not thank her, because after she shipped us off, she piddled away all of our inheritance, promptly died, and essentially left us screwed!"

They laughed together in a bittersweet way. Then they sat in silence for another half hour, listening to the water pound against the pier.

After that day with Kevin, Rue's shell began to crack. A little more every day. She found that she couldn't keep it together – perhaps didn't *want* to keep it together. She found herself trusting Kevin.

He began to feel like home.

Chapter XXVI

"Hey," Rue said, with that sweet voice, and Kevin smiled. How did she do that? Over the phone, even! It sent his heart soaring. It was right out of a Harlequin romance. And he didn't even flinch at how cheesy that sounded. He was as soft as a pillow with her.

He sat down on his couch and said, "Hey."

"What'cha doin'?" Rue asked.

"Not much. Just got home from work," he replied. Then, "You know, I've been thinking…"

"Yes…?"

"Would you like to come over? To my place? For dinner, I mean. I'll cook. You don't have to do a thing – just come. What do you think?" He waited, his heart beating; she had never been over. They always met in public places. This felt like a big step. Was she ready? Was he ready?

"Sure, that sounds great," replied Rue with a smile in her voice. He let a gush of air leave his lips as they both laughed. She kidded, "Did you think I'd refuse?"

"Well…yes, maybe…sort of…I wasn't sure," he stammered.

She chuckled. "What's the address?"

"Oh! Should I come get you? Or meet you halfway?" he offered.

"No, no, that's fine." She typed his address into her phone. Ironically, it was only six blocks away – how did they not realize they lived so close?! They laughed. She said she'd get ready and be there in thirty or forty minutes.

He ran to the corner market, his head in the stratosphere, and picked up a few things for their meal. Back at his place, he prepped the food and began cooking it. Only a few minutes later, he heard her cane before he saw her and went to meet her at the gate.

He rose with, "Rue!"

She answered back, "Kevin!"

He took her elbow and led her into the courtyard as she folded her cane and stashed it in her purse. She asked, "Will you do me a favor?"

"Sure, anything."

"Will you describe every single thing to me in minute detail?"

He smiled. "Yes, of course. Hmmmm, where should I start?"

"Everything!"

"Okay, okay, let's see…" he said, taking her hand and intertwining his fingers with hers. "So…you just came in through the gate that leads into the apartment building's courtyard. You're standing on red stone pavers lined by a small green yard on both sides, several ornamental trees, hmmm, not sure what kind, and three benches in a U shape, each with built-in flower boxes. There's my Vespa, chained to one of the benches. And my grill. There are four apartment doors – two on each side of the courtyard."

"Your Vespa?" she marveled.

"Yep, I'll take you out on it sometime. We can drive around town or across the bridge."

"Helmets?"

"Of course. You don't trust me?"

"Well…," she teased.

He squeezed her hand and laughed. Then she asked, "Is that Elvis I hear?"

"Costello? Yes, wow, good ear. Believe it or not, I have a real record player with real records. Remember those?"

"Vaguely," she answered with a smile. "Very cool."

She sang a few bars of the song as it drifted out to them, and he said, "God, you have such a beautiful voice. Will you let me come see you at the lounge now? I've been asking for a while, and I think I've earned it."

She joked, "Oh, you have, have you? We'll see…it might be make or break at this dinner tonight, lest you forget the last girl you had over…"

"Ouch!" he cried, "Not that! I can't be held accountable. I've nearly wiped the whole encounter from my memory banks."

She laughed and said, "Okay, I'll let it slide…what smells so wonderful?"

"Our meal. You like salmon?"

"Mmm, yes, definitely…okay, more of the tour…?"

"Right. Let's see…my apartment building is, how to describe it? Well, it's old. Big surprise. This is the City, right? It has white wooden siding and black shutters with black shutter dogs holding them back. And, um, the door over here, to my place, has the number twenty-three on it."

"Can I feel the number?" she asked.

He chuckled and said, "Of course – here." He placed her fingers on the four-inch two and three. "Is that how braille feels?"

She thought that was hysterical. "No, can you imagine? The books already weigh twenty-five pounds."

He grinned. She took her hand off the numbers and felt lower on the door, landing on the iron knocker. She knocked it three times, grinning like a mischievous child.

Playing along, he inquired, "Hello? Who's there?"

"Your date. Let me in!"

He laughed and exclaimed, "Well, get yourself in here then!"

He opened the door, and suddenly she wrapped her arms around his neck and kissed him long and hard on the lips. Within a split second, he was completely lost. He stopped breathing and succumbed to the ecstasy. She pressed her frame against him. He pulled her close, his arms encircling her. After a few minutes, he stopped and exclaimed, "Wow!"

She nodded and said, "I've wanted to do that for weeks."

"Me too!" He pulled her into his apartment by the waist and by the lips. His mind and body were exploding into a million sparks, like a hot light bulb combusting. He was fervent, feverish, magnetically charged on the brink of an explosion.

They stood in the middle of the apartment and kissed like no tomorrow, for several minutes, when, with the restraint of an ox, he held himself away from her and said, "Hang on, I have to check the food. I'm sorry…you have no idea how sorry!"

She laughed and released him, standing awkwardly. After a moment, she asked, "Tell me where I am and what you're doing."

He was rifling around in a drawer. He said, "You're standing in the middle of the dining room, if you can call it that – a small space with a small table – reach your hand to your left and you'll touch the table. Yep, right there. There are two chairs – have a seat. I'm just getting a spatula out of the kitchen drawer and checking the potatoes and green beans." He pushed the veggies around as she sat down. He said, "I'm going to check on the grill. Be right back." He left the spatula on the stove and walked out toward the grill, pausing on the way to pass his hand lightly along the small space between her shoulders.

He looked back, and she was touching her cheek. He checked the salmon and tried to concentrate on the food, but his mind was screaming, those lips! Like molten lava drawn up from the depths of the earth. He put the lid of the grill down and came back inside.

He asked, "Are you okay?" She had a look of peculiar otherness on her face that he was trying to decipher.

She nodded and smiled. Then he sat down beside her and took her hand. She said slowly, "I didn't know...I didn't realize...it would be like this."

He laughed in agreement, saying, "God, neither did I! Then he took her face in his hands and said with feeling, "You are simply the loveliest human I have ever beheld."

He saw her breath leave her body, and he sensed she was about to cry out of sheer happiness. He pressed his lips to hers. At some point, he asked with a laugh, "Should we just let dinner burn?"

She grinned in response and then said, "Tempting. But no. I'm starving. And besides," she said with allure, "I want to take it slow."

He kissed her again. He was having difficulty concentrating on anything in the practical world, as if he was living in a dream state, a bubble that was Rue's lips.

Eventually, though, he retrieved the meal and set it in front of them. Then he poured two glasses of wine and asked, "So, what changed your mind?"

"What changed...what?" asked Rue, not sure what he meant.

"About me. What changed your mind?" She smiled mysteriously and didn't answer. He continued, "Rue, it's been, um, let's see, eighty-four days since I saw you at Vy's wedding." He chuckled and added, "I think you should know it's been a sort of slow torture for me."

"Oh!" she cried, "has it?" After a minute, she admitted, "Yes, for me too. I guess I had a few things to work out. In my head. In my heart."

"Ah. Okay. Totally get it. For me as well. I wish...I wish...it wasn't the case."

She spoke thoughtfully, "I wanted to be sure. For both our sakes. And ultimately, I didn't want what happened to us...in the past...to be the reason for us to be together now. Or the reason for us *not* to be together either! I wanted it to be about *us*, not about...about...anything or anyone else. On our own terms, you know? With our own rules, with no...baggage or misgivings. Just us, free and clear, just this." She squeezed his hand.

"Amen, sister!" responded Kevin.

She asked, "What time is my plate?"

Kevin frowned and said, "Huh?"

"Now that you're dating a blind girl, you need to be more helpful."

"Oh! I'm sorry, I'm such a cad. Salmon at noon, beans at four, potatoes at eight. Uh-wait, *am* I dating a blind girl now?"

"Hold onto your hat – yes you are. Definitely yes!"

"Good," he said with a kiss. "I'm glad we've finally established that fact."

"Yes, it's about time. And the silverware?"

"I'm sorry, of course, um, three and nine," he answered, feeling like a worthless slug.

She burst out laughing, and he was flummoxed. She teased, "I was just kidding about the silverware. Pretty much always on either side of the plate."

He laughed. Duh. Endearing and funny. Could he have asked for more?

He got up and changed the album to Big Star, grinning when it played "I'm in Love with a Girl." He felt his heart leap when she smiled knowingly and said, "Oh! I love this song," and began to sing along with the chorus.

"Me too...can't beat the older alternative stuff, can you?" he said.

"No doubt – so sincere, you know – straight, simple lyrics," she said, continuing to sing. And then, "By the way, you're an amazing cook. This is delicious."

"Thanks. I love to cook. Sort of de-stresses me after a long workday."

"You can de-stress for me anytime! Or, the other option, you can come over to my place next time and I'll cook. What do you think?"

He laid his hand on her arm and said seriously, "Lady, I'm yours for the taking. Whatever and wherever you want me, I'm there."

They munched away happily.

After a while, he said cautiously, "You know, I ran into her a week ago."

"Who?" Rue asked and then clarified, "Alyssa?!" Her eyes got big. "Ugh, how did that go?"

"Yes, her, *Alyssa*. It was...interesting. Damn it, I'm not going to lie – it made me want to vomit. She was with a friend. Someone I didn't know. At Old Navy. I was going to turn and run, but then I thought, what the hell, why should I run? I was there for new jeans, and by golly, I was going to get them! When she saw me, she nearly jumped out of her skin. It was rather amusing, actually. She said something saucy to her friend like, 'What the fuck, my ex-husband is standing over there, and clearly he's been fluffing himself up since we last met. He looks better than he ever did when we were together, but what the fuck do I care; been there, done that!' To which her friend replied, 'Right?! Who cares? You traded him in for a better model, plus ten.' Alyssa responded (a little too loudly, I might add), 'Ryan is that, isn't he? Definitely a keeper. He drove me out to his family's winery in Napa last weekend, we ate at that new restaurant in Yountville, it was awesome…' I walked away, not listening to the rest. I must admit, though, I felt pretty good and actually laughed out loud, thinking, got that over with!"

"I guess it was bound to happen one of these days," Rue stated wryly.

"Yup," said Kevin.

Rue said with a chuckle, "See now, I never have to worry about that."

Kevin thought about it for a second and laughed, "Ha! No, I suppose not. Lucky dog. So, you've never…"

"Nope. Thank goodness."

Near the end of the meal, she asked, "Why did seeing Alyssa make you want to vomit?"

"Oh, I don't know…I guess the initial shock of seeing her after all this time. My fight-or-flight instinct kicked in, and I was like, oh my God, where's the nearest exit? Stupid. I know…"

"Well, you stuck it out anyway – that's what matters."

He confirmed, "Certainly. It'll be easier next time. Hey, maybe it'll be like nothing next time."

"Maybe *I'll* be with you next time!"

Kevin choked on his food in response and had to get a glass of water. She waited patiently until he could talk, at which point he laughed and said, "I can't imagine. That would be great!"

"Let's not imagine," she replied definitively.

He agreed, "Let's not."

And that was the end of that.

After dinner, they sat on one of the benches in the courtyard. For a long while, they sat in silence, her hand on his knee, his arm around her shoulder. He saw her taking deep breaths and asked, "What are you thinking?"

"Just breathing in the clean, fresh air and the feel of you next to me. It's wonderful. This courtyard is lovely. I can hear the cars off in the distance and people in the next building talking and cooking with their windows open. And I think I smell gardenias, off somewhere."

"Yep, there's a gardenia bush by the gate. Great sense of smell!"

"And an even better sense of touch," she responded, moving her hand up his leg. He kissed her for a long time, wrapping her into the alcove of his chest. She felt soft and sweet and giving. At some point, she pulled her mouth away from his and lay her head in the space between his neck and shoulder, snuggling under his chin. He kissed the top of her head and sat still, admiring the feel of her in his arms.

A half hour later, she asked to "see" the rest of his place (using air quotes for "see," which made him chuckle). "Sure, come on," he began, leading her. "It's not a big place, so this should take a hot minute." Big Star was over, so he put on a Beatles album and she did a little shimmy in his arms.

As he led her around, she said, "Wait until you see mine – a postage stamp! And you'll have to become friends with Hank. That's a must."

"Oh, is that the monstrous beast I've been hearing so much about?"

"Yes, Hank is a roving, plundering pirate, but still a necessary appendage to my life, so you two must get along."

"I'll bring presents. Does he like catnip?"

"Couldn't hurt," she said and then, "Can you describe everything for me? I want to get to know you this way."

"Through my stuff, you mean?"

"Yes. What makes you tick? I'm sure it'll all be clear by the number of shoes in your closet. Or by the number of skincare products in your medicine cabinet."

"I'm afraid you'll be sorely disappointed on that front. What about the number of books? Or magazines?"

"Sure, I know how you are – you'll hand me a *Playboy* and tell me it's an *Architectural Digest*, won't you?"

"Ha!" he laughed. "I actually do subscribe…! To *Architectural Digest*, I mean. The most lurid thing in there is naked houses on the beach. Sorry to disappoint." He kissed her again and she giggled in his arms. "Honestly, though, I'm not much of a magazine reader; I'm more of a book reader. What about you?"

She said simply, "Same."

"Okay, so let the tour begin. Come on. Let's see…you've already been in the kitchen/dining room. There's not much else to speak of."

"Wait, what do you have on your counter?"

"Oh, okay, we're going old school, eh? Everything. So, I have a couple of plants on the windowsill. You want to touch them? Here – tiny, leafy, spiky guys – I'm not sure what they're called. Then I have a Keurig – I'm mostly a one-cup kind of guy in the morning. You too? Wow, another thing in common. I have a medium-sized vase in the corner with nothing in it. You can help me pick out something for it."

"Bamboo!"

"Ha, yes, that would be perfect. We can meditate in front of it. Okay, you ready for the living room? I have a boring old brown leather couch, a coffee table with some work stuff on it, a big green plant in the corner – once again, don't know the name – I would be a horrible horticulturist – and a white sit-down chair off to the side, a couple of random coasters, the TV, a bookcase, and that's about it."

"What books are in the bookcase?"

"Come on, really? We'll be here all night..."

"Yep, that's what I'm hoping," Rue said coyly. Kevin nearly cried for joy. They kissed and kissed until she got him back on track with, "Books."

"Right. Books. Um, mostly architecture and engineering books, but some novels. I'm a big fan of Chandler, Rand, Burrows, Hemingway. I was on a Russian kick for a while, so there are a bunch of those. And believe it or not, a whole bunch of Louis L'Amour – don't judge."

"Please!" Rue exclaimed. "No judgment here. I went through a serious Zane Grey phase about a year ago. I was obsessed. So descriptive! Made me want to trek through the entire Southwest. But then I realized I would probably fall into the Grand Canyon."

"I'll take you sometime. I'll hold onto you."

"That would be wonderful," she said and laid her head on his chest. He kissed her hair and she asked, "Nothing on the walls?"

"Well, yeah, a few things. I have a large framed blueprint of Grand Central Station. Some guy in my office was from New York, and he left it when he retired, so I brought it home and put it up. I also have several artsy prints of miscellaneous flora and fauna."

"Wait until you see my art."

"Your art? You have art?"

"Yes, I paint and hammer things."

"Sounds intriguing. But...but...you can't—"

"See them?" she completed his sentence. "I know, that's true, but I can feel them. And I can react to them the same way anyone else does. They move me, in that strange way that art does. Oh, don't get me wrong, they're foolish, pathetic attempts, but I enjoy making them."

"Wow, I can't wait to see," he said. Was it normal to be fascinated by everything someone said and did? He shook his head and smiled.

She grinned, sensing his feelings, and squeezed him tighter. Then he continued, "So, finally, I have this photo I took of a banyan tree."

"What's a banyan tree?"

"It's this type of tree with roots that grow above the ground. They fall from the branches, splayed out like a spider, in all directions."

He saw her face trying to process the image. She asked, "So, it's an upside-down tree?"

"Kind of. I mean, it still has leaves at the top, and for the most part it looks like any other tree. It just has this super-intricate root system. It's almost as if the roots are intertwined with the branches and the trunk and the ground. I took the photo in Florida and printed it in black and white. Sometimes I stare at it and think it represents my life – a strangled, colossal mess." He laughed self-consciously.

She thought about that for a minute. She said, "Not anymore."

He smiled down at her beaming face and kissed her with more feeling than he could express in words. He said, "No, not anymore. I'm growing new roots now."

"Yes, new roots. New R-U-E-T-S!" she exclaimed.

He laughed at her silly pun but then said seriously, "Yes, let's both start growing new R-U-E-T-S together."

"Let's," she replied as he swept her up in his arms.

The End

Acknowledgments

I would like to thank Katie Stambaugh and Jennie Ruggles for their time reading early versions of *Rue* and for encouraging me to continue. I owe a huge debt of gratitude to Mark Dresen for answering hundreds of questions about being visually impaired. I'm also grateful for my editor extraordinaire, Kira Freed.

Finally, I would like to thank my husband, Scott, for his love and support, and for his faith in me.

About the Author

Amy Q. Barker holds a BA from Syracuse University and an MBA from Rensselaer Polytechnic Institute. She enjoys exploring used bookstores, hiking national parks, and binge-watching anything British on the latest streaming service. She lives in Indiana with her husband. *Rue* is her first novel.

CPSIA information can be obtained
at www.ICGtesting.com
Printed in the USA
BVHW061321230920
589478BV00013B/1145